THIS is HOW we FLY

Also by Anna Meriano

Love Sugar Magic: A Dash of Trouble

Love Sugar Magic: A Sprinkle of Spirits

Love Sugar Magic: A Mixture of Mischief

PHILOMEL BOOKS

PHILOMEL BOOKS
An imprint of Penguin Random House LLC, New York

First published in the United States of America by Philomel,
an imprint of Penguin Random House LLC, 2020.

Visit us online at penguinrandomhouse.com.

Library of Congress Cataloging-in-Publication Data is available.

Printed in the United States of America

ISBN 9780593116876

1 3 5 7 9 10 8 6 4 2

Edited by Kelsey Murphy.

Design by Monique Sterling.

Text set in Breughel.

For Sophie Bonifaz Pérez, Brandi Cannon,
Mollie Lensing, and all the quidkids

1

Xiumiao takes one look at me standing in her door-way in my graduation dress that I hate, jaw clenched to hold back tears, and says, "What if we just don't go?"

Connie's car has already disappeared around the corner, so it's safe to wipe my watering eyes. "Won't your parents be disappointed?"

"Oh, they definitely weren't coming." Xiumiao rolls her eyes. "I told them it was next week, after we leave town. I didn't want all the fuss."

And without another word she spins me 180 degrees and tows me toward the strip mall at the end of her block. I guess we're officially skipping graduation.

Xiumiao strips off her hoodie and offers it to me to cover up the dress before we enter Tea Corner, which marks maybe the fourth time I've seen her without it all semester (the other three being choir performances). The hoodie is a mark of her true dedication to the street urchin aesthetic even in ninety-degree heat.

Our wardrobe swap leaves her in a tight tank top and me in a short swishy skirt under my hoodie, and the unusually feminine looks don't escape Counter Guy. We don't know his name, but we've watched him grow from the confused first-ever white employee at the boba shop to a competent Counter Guy.

"Hey, y'all look nice today," Counter Guy says. Not in a creepy way, but my face turns red—this is why I normally dress like I just rolled out of bed and also might be a troll.

"Thanks, but we're miserable," Xiumiao says. "One taro and one jasmine green tea, no milk. Both with tapioca, please."

She pays, and we sit on cute but uncomfortable armchairs in the back. Nubby canvas scratches the backs of my knees as I try to settle without flashing the world. Xiumiao hands me my cup, not even teasing me for my nondairy preference like she usually does. I slurp until the lump in my throat gets a little smaller.

"So . . ." Xiumiao's not exactly asking anything. She didn't ask questions when I texted twenty minutes before graduation looking for a ride, either. She just told me to come over.

"They completely bailed," I tell her. "Dad got tied up at work last minute, as usual, and Connie thought it would be boring." I knew my stepmom didn't want to go to my graduation, but I guess I didn't think she'd really blow it off.

"It *is* going to be boring," Xiumiao says. "It's the school's last-ditch attempt to bore us to death before we escape their clutches."

"I know," I sigh. "But I wanted to go."

"We still can," Xiumiao offers.

I shake my head. It's not like I care so much about sitting on folding chairs in the gym for two hours. "I don't know, maybe I just wanted to go because Connie didn't."

"You need to learn to fly under the radar." Xiumiao shakes her head. "Just do whatever your parents want, and then let the resentment eat you up until you're dead inside. It's a perfect system."

I snort. "Yep, you've got it all figured out."

Xiumiao's parents are nice, and they love her and all. It's just that they have strong opinions about her singing in the church choir and getting good grades, and they would probably prefer if she grew up to be straight and got married to a dude and had straight babies, which is probably not the way things are going to play out.

Not that Xiumiao's talked about it with them, so they're really just Schrödinger's homophobes. But she doesn't want to open that box, which is valid.

"We can tell Melissa to record it so you don't miss the boredom," Xiumiao says.

I sip my tea. "Nah, that's okay. Besides, she abandoned us. Best friend status revoked."

"That's not at all what happened, Ellen. You just have abandonment issues."

"Wow, sounds like you're abandoning me to side with Melissa. Best friend status revoked."

Xiumiao snorts. "Well, if you don't want to watch the valedictorian speech on a two-inch screen, do you want to go back to my house and watch *Rent*? You can borrow shorts."

There is something to be said for a friend who's known you so long that they understand what you need even when you don't. I follow Xiumiao into the morning heat. Maybe this was the perfect way to end high school after all.

OF COURSE, MRS. LI WANTS AN EXPLANATION, AND SHE kind of wants to feed me.

"I didn't know you were coming," she exclaims, "and don't tell me you're drinking all that sugar for breakfast! And you look so pretty! What's the occasion?"

I think the law of the suburbs says that your friends' parents have to love you, but Xiumiao's parents have always gone above and beyond ever since Mrs. Li met Dad crying outside the pre-K classroom door and decided to take the struggling single parent under her wing. I used to carpool with them to and from kiddie sports and choir events and occasionally to their Chinese Baptist church in one of their not-so-subtle gambits to save me from my heathen Catholicism.

Xiumiao is quick to cut the conversation off. "No, Ma, she ate before." Untrue. "She just came from a funeral." Super untrue, and also out of nowhere even if my dress is black. Then Xiumiao invents an (untrue) scholarship essay contest we have to work on, and we retreat to the library, which is the kind of room you have when you're an only child in a five-bedroom house.

"We're using your Netflix," Xiumiao warns, handing me her dad's tablet with the login screen open.

"Really? You watch every other musical movie on their account. At this point it's probably more suspicious that you *haven't* watched the gay one."

Xiumiao glares.

"Sorry. You can always use my Netflix to watch gay things."

She raises a very worrisome eyebrow.

We settle onto the couch, sipping tea and scrolling

our phones and humming along to the movie we have mostly memorized, until Xiumiao says, "You know it's just a ceremony. Your diploma comes in the mail either way."

"No, I know. It was more about Connie and Dad showing up for me." Xiumiao nods. "And, like, closure."

"Wow, no, super can't relate. Case closed. Burn it all down."

My phone dings in my hand, notifying me that Xiumiao is also on Tumblr and liking my posts while we talk, which is either tragic or extreme best friend goals.

"You don't want to celebrate before Melissa and I leave town?" I ask. "Soon you'll be stuck here missing our faces."

Xiumiao is making her parents' dreams come true by staying in Houston for college, while Melissa goes off to the rural wasteland (by which I mean medium-sized college town) where Texas A&M is located, and I'll be in Austin at the University of Texas. Xiumiao and I have been in the same classes since pre-K, and with Melissa since sixth grade—it's weird that soon we'll be in totally different cities/rural wastelands.

"I think I'll remember what your face looks like." Xiumiao gulps tapioca, totally unconcerned. "And anyway, I've been thinking . . . as far as *she's* concerned . . ."

I put my phone down, because whenever Xiumiao stops

using Melissa's name it means we're entering the secret romance zone, where Melissa is not our best friend that we speak to and about normally, but instead the object of Xiumiao's long and painful crush on a straight girl.

"Yeah?"

Xiumiao loses some of her nonchalance, stabbing her straw up and down in her cup. "I've been thinking that I need to get a little space."

"Oh? That might be good." Especially since Melissa's been dating her current boyfriend for a while now. "You've got that vacation coming up, right?"

"That's, like, a week. I'm talking about actual physical, mental, emotional space. A total disconnect. High school is over, and it's time to move on."

"But," I stammer, surprised by the sharp edge in Xiumiao's voice. "You're not going to stop hanging out with us?"

Xiumiao's face falls, but I can't figure out why. She hides it quickly with an eye roll. "That's kind of exactly what I'm trying to say."

"But . . . she'll notice." Xiumiao's biggest fear in life, after her parents learning anything about her, is Melissa learning about her crush. And it's probably not cool of me to use that against her, but I feel a tiny bit panicked. We're about to be forced to get space. Why does she want to speed it along?

Xiumiao shrugs. "I'll be really busy this summer," she says. "Shadowing at the hospital, church stuff, camp. And we're all going to be getting ready for college anyway."

If by "getting ready for college" she means "desperately clinging to friends who are basically family before circumstances beyond our control separate us," then yes, totally, we're on the same page here.

But we're not. Is she really ready to just move on?

"So am I supposed to lie about hanging out with you, or what?"

Xiumiao frowns and opens her mouth like she's going to respond, but instead she just sips her tea. The silence stretches a little too long. "Like I said, I'm going to be busy."

Wow. So maybe it's not just Melissa who Xiumiao wants to move on from. She goes back to her phone while angry New Yorkers sing about capitalism. Usually comfortable silence is our jam, but right now it feels ominous.

I suck up the last of my tea, leaving a lonely pile of gloopy tapioca. My summer plan was to spend all my time at Xiumiao's and Melissa's houses, avoiding Connie to avoid fighting. Is Melissa thinking the same thing Xiumiao is? Does everyone expect us to stop being friends now that high school is over?

While I pick at the hem of my borrowed T-shirt and watch a found family grow closer through adversity onscreen, my phone buzzes. Melissa is tagging me in photos of empty graduation seats with sad-face emojis. Where are my friends? the caption reads.

I text her, My family is the worst, so Xiumiao and I ditched. Have fun.

Ugh, sorry, tell me about it later? And thanks, it's actually really boring, Melissa responds.

I smile, about to tell Xiumiao that she was right. But maybe she doesn't want to hear anything about Melissa, or graduation.

Anyway, happy official start of summer! Melissa texts. You're definitely coming to quidditch practice with me and Chris this week, right?

I text back ellipses, which seems nicer than "I thought you were joking about that" or "Seriously?"

Melissa's boyfriend Chris plays quidditch. Yeah, that quidditch. Melissa really wants to check out the real-life version of the Harry Potter game, but she's already in marching band, so joining a nerdy outdoor activity isn't as much of a stretch for her. It's been a long time since I've willingly participated in any team sports.

You have to! Melissa texts. Quickly followed by, It's our bonding activity for the summer! She sends an assortment of sports-ball emojis, plus a wizard in a pointy hat, making my phone ding with each text. I snort.

"What?" Xiumiao leans to see my screen, probably expecting a meme.

I tilt the screen. "Nothing," I say. "It's just from . . . Nothing."

Xiumiao nods. "Thanks," she says. "You can tell Nothing to enjoy graduation. But, uh, actually don't say it from me." Then she turns back to her phone with a determined nod.

She's really going through with this. The tapioca rolls like marbles in my stomach.

I'm not one hundred percent sure how I feel about going to the park to pretend to cast spells, but I know that I don't want to disconnect from everything this summer, and Melissa must not want to, either.

Fine. I'll try it.

It's not a solution to my fears about life after summer, but at least it's something to do with my friend.

But, I mean, how are we supposed to fly?

WHEN THE MOVIE ENDS, CONNIE STARTS TEXTING. HER texts come rapid-fire, always too impatient to wait for a response.

Where are you? she asks first. Your father wants to have a celebration dinner. This perks me up momentarily, until the next ding: We need to clean and decorate the kitchen. And finally, The ceremony should be over by now.

I tell her that I went to Xiumiao's.

Well, you should head back soon. Ding. I can pick you up

on my way back from the mall. **Ding.** You don't want to overstay your welcome.

I pause the credits. "I have to go. Connie."

"Boo." Xiumiao nods. "Good luck. See you . . . whenever."

I change out of the borrowed clothes and drop them in Xiumiao's lap as Connie texts me that she's pulling up.

"Uh, bye," I say. It feels wrong—we usually have a relationship that supersedes small talk and greetings in favor of just walking in and out and ignoring each other—but the way she hesitated, I'm not sure if Xiumiao intends this to be the last time we ever hang out or what. "Have a good vacation, I guess." Have a good summer? Have a good life?

"Sure, yeah."

I've never been broken up with, but I feel like maybe this is a taste of that when I put my (annoying) heels on and walk out the door, a weird pit in my stomach. I climb into Connie's car, relieved when she starts talking about the new curtains she's considering without asking anything about graduation.

That's it for high school. And other than a summer of trying to fly under the radar with Connie, and I guess playing quidditch with Melissa, I have no idea what comes next.

2

"Thanks," I say, holding back my building eye roll, "but I'm not even that hungry."

It's six o'clock and Dad still hasn't made it home from work, so we're starting graduation dinner without him.

Connie draws a deep breath in her trademarked reverse sigh, pulling Styrofoam out of the brown paper bag from Tortillas a Go-Go. "Try a fish taco."

"Vegan," I remind my stepmom for the twelve thousandth time since last semester.

"That's why I got fish." Connie grabs my empty plate and heaps it (aggressively) with piles of rice and beans and guacamole. Mexican food—sorry, Tex-Mex, which is nothing like real Mexican according to Connie—was one of the hardest things to give up, and watching the glazed blue ceramic plate disappear under globs of sour cream makes my traitorous mouth water. Theoretically there are plenty of vegan tacos I could be eating, but the problem is that most of them are in the cool parts of Houston and none of them are my family's favorite takeout choice. Being Mexican American and vegan (well, Mexican American on my dead mom's side and white Irish American on my dad's side, which is basically the Tex-Mex of heritage) is not easy.

"Fish isn't vegan." My stepsister Yasmín plunks into the seat across the table. She must've been messing around in the mirror again, because her normally neat ponytail has been attacked by a swarm of sparkly plastic butterfly clips. "It's pescatarian. You're not a pescatarian again, are you?"

Connie and I share a surprised expression. Why does a ten-year-old understand my diet better than the adult who does most of the grocery shopping in the house?

"Nope," I say, "I've decided that ethically and environmentally I can't justify—"

"Hungry, mija?" Connie cuts me off and gives me her *Not in front of my baby!* look. I don't know how she imagines that hearing about a vegan diet is going to cause a ten-year-old emotional distress, but I stop talking.

My stomach won't stop growling, so I grab a tortilla while Connie removes Yasmín's butterfly clips ("What did you do to your hair?") and wrestles her curls into their normal slicked-back ponytail. Because God forbid the kid eats dinner while looking slightly goofy instead of picture-perfect.

For someone who isn't into social media, Connie's big on keeping things picture-perfect. She's like that with the house, always making improvements, always clicking around on Pinterest, changing the curtains or the accent pillows. Her latest ambition is to turn my room into a studio after I move out so she can dedicate more time and storage space to her decorating.

"How was math camp, Yasmín?" Whenever possible, I try to talk to my little sister about something other than physical appearance.

Yasmín unrolls her taco and picks at the insides with her fork. "Mrs. Sorgalla hates me."

"What? Why?" Teachers love Yasmín. Thanks to Connie's helicopter parenting, my little sister is a total goody-two-shoes.

"She doesn't hate you," Connie scolds. "I'm sure she doesn't hate you."

"She made me check my answers three times before I could turn my paper in, even though I told her I already checked." Yasmín scowls at her plate.

"Sounds like she's teaching you a good lesson." Connie pats Yasmín's smoothed hair.

Yasmín shrugs. "She was mad because I finished too early. She doesn't believe that I already learned adding fractions."

"Do you want me to beat her up for you?"

"Don't be ridiculous, Ellen." Connie either misses or dismisses the fact that I was obviously joking. "You have to respect your teachers, mija." Which is an expected reaction from a former kindergarten teacher, I guess. I'm sure she deserved lots of respect or whatever, but that doesn't mean every teacher does.

"Well . . ." I stretch out the word as I try to soften my knee-jerk reaction to authoritarianism. "Sometimes people in power can abuse their power, and at that point you don't really owe them—"

Connie's lips press together. *Not in front of my baby.*

I turn to Yasmín. "What did she say when you tried to turn your paper in?"

Connie sighs loudly. Yasmín shrugs. "Nothing. Never mind."

"If the teacher is being unfair or singling you out—"

"The teacher isn't singling anyone out," Connie hisses. "She's doing her job. You don't need to put any of your dramatics into my daughter's head." She stalks back to her side of the table, glaring at me.

"I'm not—" Connie's glare intensifies as I try to protest. "I'm just saying—"

Deciding it's not worth it, I stuff my mouth with a

second tortilla, determined to let Connie's face defrost before I speak again.

Plain tortillas are not dinner. I wonder if there's any possibility that the beans are vegetarian, until I spot the chunk of bacon floating in the sauce.

"Ew." Yasmín reaches into her dissected taco with two fingers and pulls out one, then two, then three thin white bones. "What are they?"

Connie—who only sat down two seconds ago—jumps up so fast her fork flies off the table. "Fish bones! Mija, don't eat it—you could have choked!" Her eyes flick to me just for a second. "Here, have mine. It's chicken." She switches her plate with Yasmín's, then starts sorting through the pile of tacos, pulling out all the ones with a sharpie-scrawled "F" on their foil wrappers.

"Dad will eat them," I tell her. *Assuming he ever gets here*, I don't say out loud.

But Connie is shaking her head, her bangs swishing across her eyes. "No, no, definitely not. Greg eats so fast; I'm not risking it."

"You're not just going to throw them away, are you?"

"Yes, I am." Connie gathers the tacos in her arms and makes for the trash can next to the stove. "I shouldn't have bought them."

"That's wasteful."

Yasmín pushes her plate away.

"You didn't want to eat them," Connie shoots back.

"Actually I do, I just choose not to because I care about the future of this planet."

"I care about the future of my family." Connie's voice is entering Danger Zone, so I don't say anything about what planet she thinks her family is going to live on when we ruin the environment beyond repair, but I don't really have to. It's not the first (or second, or fifth) time we've had this fight.

"Fine." Connie walks very slowly back to the table and lets the tacos roll out of her hands and onto the table. Her lips are pressed together, and her breath huffs and whistles through her nose. "I got these tacos for you. You can do whatever you want with them. But frankly, if this is how you're going to be acting all summer, I don't look forward to it."

"Yeah, well, me neither," I say under my breath so she can pretend not to hear it.

"Yasmín, have you practiced your flute?" Connie asks. Yasmín shakes her head.

It's completely unfair that the poor kid has to spend her whole summer on scheduled extracurriculars. But I don't say that. There are a lot of things I don't say to Connie since Christmas break.

"Then you'd better get started." She pulls Yasmín toward the living room. Halfway out the door, Connie stops and looks over her shoulder, sucking in her breath like it pains her. "This kitchen is a mess," she says.

I offer nothing. This was supposed to be my graduation dinner.

"Come on," she says, turning on her heel and ushering Yasmín ahead of her.

My head throbs. You can't just throw food away. It's irresponsible. As irresponsible as ruining your daughter's childhood, or teaching her that her appearance is top priority, or squelching her complaints without hearing them.

I know I spend a lot of time on certain social-justice-obsessed corners of the internet, but I don't understand why my stepmom can't see the harm she's causing.

I don't understand why she won't listen.

I could talk back and start a real fight. I could storm to my room and slam the door and spend the rest of the night scrolling through environmental feminist blogs. But that would be Christmas break all over again.

Instead, I cover all the open Styrofoam containers and arrange them in the refrigerator. I stack the dishes next to the sink and start filling it with hot water and soap and a capful of bleach—Connie's secret recipe for dish water. I wash the dishes; I even dry them and put them away. Then I pick up all the tacos, put them back in the cactus-emblazoned bag, and pull out my phone.

Xiumiao normally receives the brunt of my family complaints (she has more sympathy and similar complaints to share), but I'm not sure where texts fall in terms of "getting space." Besides, I don't just want to text about whose parents are more frustrating. I need to get out of the house fast. So instead, I text Melissa, Best friend emergency. Please send help.

By the time Melissa pulls into the driveway, I've distracted myself with YouTube and desperation-snacks. I have to scramble to pocket my wallet, keys, and phone and then grab a thin purple sweater (to protect me from the frigid Houston air-conditioning). Melissa sends an impatient text as I rush for the door.

"Ellen?" Connie's voice stops me with one foot outside. "What are you up to?"

She stands behind me with a clear view of Melissa's car, so it's less of a question and more of a test.

"I was just going to give the food to Melissa, and we were going to hang out for a bit," I say.

"Hang out where?"

"At Melissa's house?" I hold back a sigh. "Like always?" Connie sucks air past her teeth. "I mean . . . if that's okay."

"It's getting late," she says. "Are there going to be a lot of people there? Are you sure Mr. and Mrs. Larsen don't mind?"

"Just me. I'm sure." The pained expression stays stuck on her face until I add, "Will it make you feel better if I send a picture of their smiling faces when I get there?"

Connie nods slowly. "Okay. But don't stay out too long, because Greg called to say that he's just going to be another hour, and I know he wants to celebrate with you."

Sure, I can tell how badly Dad wants to celebrate. But it isn't his absence making me roll my eyes as I stomp through the front yard and slump into Melissa's car. It's Connie.

It's that she doesn't trust me or consider me responsible enough to make plans on my own. It's that I still have to ask her permission to leave the house. Obviously that kind of control made sense when I was twelve, but now it's just annoying. And I have to play along, because we're all trying to keep Connie happy. Dad with his promises of coming home at a decent hour. Me gritting my teeth against our usual arguments. Even Yasmín, unless she just really loves the idea of math summer camp. We've all been walking on eggshells since Christmas break, trying not to cause tension. Hoping Connie won't leave again.

"Vegan struggles?" Melissa asks when I slam her passenger door way too hard.

I nod and shove the taco bag into Melissa's lap. "And stepmom struggles. And taco struggles."

"Ew. Keep your taco struggles to yourself," Melissa teases, jerking away from the curb as she digs through the bag. "So that was a couple hours at home before you needed rescuing? I think that's a record, even for this semester."

"What can I say? Connie's being record levels of crappy."

Melissa tuts around a mouthful of taco. Unlike Xiumiao, she cannot always be trusted to take my side against parents on principle. "Are you sure you're not just mad about the whole graduation thing?"

I mean, she's not wrong. But she's not right, either, thinking that my fight with Connie has a simple cause and a linear solution. Dad's been trying that sort of counseling with me for at least a year now. *Be honest about your feelings. Count to ten before you speak.*

I've known Connie since I was eight. She showed up at Dad's single-parent support group freshly divorced and new in town with nine-month-old Yasmín on her hip, and the rest is history. She's been my family for so long that I only vaguely remember life before the wedding. We made it work, with a few bumpy moments. But it's like the older I get, the less we fit together, my personality clashing with Connie's vision like a mismatched area rug. It's not a matter of any single fight anymore. It's a war.

"It's fine." I breathe and take in the weird crayon smell of Melissa's car and the late-evening sun seeping through the windshield. "Thanks for getting me. Sorry I need rescuing."

"Don't be ridiculous."

I relax into the worn seat with another deep breath. That's the thing about Melissa. She has this ability to make me feel totally welcome, like I'm not just joining her life, but improving it. She's like the anti-Connie.

By the time we get to her house, I'm almost smiling.

"Oh, hello, Ellen!" Mrs. Larsen waves from the treadmill in the front room and shows off her gums in a huge smile. "We missed you at graduation. What's all this?"

Mrs. Larsen looks just like Melissa—blonde and tall and curvy, with a pointy chin and invisibly light eyelashes that (they think) require daily mascara use. She's wearing layers of neon workout gear, the same kind of bright tight-fitting clothes she fills Melissa's closet with.

"Fish tacos." Melissa holds up the bag. "From the Lopez-Rourke-Treviño household."

"Oh, how nice," Mrs. Larsen chirps. "I was going to ask if you two wanted to finish up the macaroni and cheese."

"She's vegan, Mom." Melissa rolls her eyes. I smile and shake my head, because it bothers me less than zero when people I don't live with forget my dietary restrictions.

"Oh, of course. There's fruit salad left, I think."

"Thanks," I say, "maybe later."

"I'll put these in the fridge," Melissa says. I trail her into the kitchen, and Mrs. Larsen follows us.

"It was nice of you to bring them, Ellen. Did your stepmother make them? I'm sure she's an amazing cook."

"Mom!" Melissa slams the bag onto the gray marble countertop. "They're obviously from a restaurant. But please, continue being racist in front of my friends."

"That was not racist!" Mrs. Larsen protests. "Was that racist?" She turns to me. "Melissa thinks everything is racist these days."

Melissa groans and I shrug, holding back an uncomfortable laugh. I can practically hear the curt response Xiumiao would give ("Maybe that's because we live in a racist society where most things are racist, *Sharon*"), but I'm not as quick (or as fearless) as she is.

I snap a picture to send Connie, and we make our way to Melissa's room. I stop at the sight of the calendar taped to her door. "Oh, wow, you flipped it."

The last time I was here, the calendar still showed May. Now June stares back at me, blank and beautiful and missing any of the bright red dots that mark tests and major projects, or yellow stars for exciting, stressful events like prom or Melissa's spring band concerts (Xiumiao's and my choir performances are noted with smaller gray stars).

For as long as I've been coming over, Melissa, her parents, and her older brother have all kept meticulously updated monthly calendars taped to their doors. The year I got my own color (ninth grade) marked my unofficial adoption into the household.

Xiumiao always tried to argue that her events should be marked in Melissa's color. Instead she got lumped in with me, which is probably the only time someone has been romantically rebuffed by organizational color coding.

I flip to July, which is just as empty, and then locate the first giant yellow star in mid-August—MOVE IN—and the second star a week later—CLASSES START: TEXAS A&M UNIVERSITY.

"We've got time to kill," I say, flipping back to June, but the words don't feel true.

"But that's what's great about this summer." Melissa smiles and runs her finger down the line of empty weeks. "I'm only going to do maybe ten hours a week of babysitting, so as long as you don't find a job—you're never going to find a job, right?"

"I hate you." The past month of job searching has been an exciting game of "give this crappy résumé to a bored employee and watch it disappear forever." Aside from a few hundred bucks of birthday savings, I'm going to go to college utterly broke. Dad says as long as my grades stay up, he's happy to support me. Connie seems less excited about that plan.

"Right. So we have the whole summer for bonding and movies and quidditch!" Melissa grins, gums gleaming like her mom's. "We'll have so many summer adventures!"

I match Melissa's smile, irritation evaporating. Whatever Xiumiao says, at least the two of us are on the same page.

3

Two days later, I'm digging through my closet trying to locate a decent pair of running shoes I can wear to quidditch practice. It's a little ridiculous that I don't remember the last time I wore anything but flip-flops or Converse (which, Melissa claims, are not acceptable for sports played on grass). When did tennis shoes stop being part of my everyday uniform?

I find one of the nice ballet flats Connie's sisters sent me a few Christmases ago, buried unused. It's thoughtful of them to send gifts—shoes and makeup kits and low-cut leopard-print blouses. But I never really grew into the girly look, or the girly hobbies, or the whole idea of being a girl.

I mean, obviously I'm not saying fashion interest (or lack thereof) is the same as gender identity. And the whole "not like other girls" trope makes it hard to tell if the voice in my head is just internalized misogyny or actual gender feels. I don't know. Gender stuff is weird and nuanced and I can contemplate it after I fix the rest of my life, starting with my footwear.

When did Dad and I stop shopping for tennis shoes? It used to be our tradition at the beginning of each school year, back when it was just the two of us. He'd put me on his shoulders and carry me into the store barefoot so I could wear the new shoes straight home, because when I was five I cried about hurting the old shoes' feelings. That was the year after my mom died, and everything was still a little out of whack.

It's possible that Dad stopped taking me shoe shopping because I'm a freak.

My phone buzzes in my pocket, and I read the text message even though I know what it will say.

Every. Single. Time.

Melissa is waiting (impatiently) for me. What else is new? I toss aside a cluster of dirty socks.

Maybe Dad stopped taking me to buy new shoes when my feet stopped growing, which was when I was approximately twelve years old.

No, wait, I do remember when it was—the year he

married Connie. He asked if I minded if Connie and baby Yasmín came with us on our shoe trip, to all go together as a family. Of course I didn't mind, because minding wasn't an option. But I decided that I didn't really need new shoes that year after all. The special shopping trips disappeared along with my cat Dorito, Christmas trips with Grandma and Grandpa Lopez, Friday night TV marathons, and the only two dinners Dad ever cooked (enchiladas and fried rice).

We made it work.

Melissa texts me a clock emoji, then several angry faces. I give up. Converse are still basically athletic wear, right? I slip mine on and dash out of my room, down the stairs, and toward the front door.

I stand in the entryway for a second, debating with myself. What I want to do is slip out the door without keeping Melissa waiting any longer. What I'm supposed to do is "respectfully communicate" if I want to leave the house. I've been doing an impressive job of avoiding Connie conversation since the graduation party that wasn't—tricky since I live with her, but easier when I spend all my time on my phone—and I don't really feel the need to break that streak.

Nobody ever said respectful communication had to be lengthy.

"I'm going out with Melissa," I call. "See you later!"

Connie scrambles out of the kitchen, still holding a dish towel.

"Where are you going?" she asks, a frown lurking behind her pleasant tone. "I thought we said you would help me start cleaning out the garage today."

"Huh?" My bag buzzes three times in a row, presumably because Melissa is angry-texting me. "Melissa and I have plans." I guess Connie mentioned the garage over dinner sometime this week, but I don't remember—an unexpected downside to being glued to my phone. A new pet project for her? I vaguely remember her asking me questions about her "creative vision," but I answered as noncommittally as possible.

This tension, the feeling in the air as Connie and I stare at each other, is exactly what I was trying to avoid. I know that if I play my cards exactly right—smile and grovel—there's a good chance Connie will let me go. But if I ask permission, I give her a chance to put her foot down.

I'm not going to bail on Melissa. I inch the door open.

Connie purses her lips. "I really think—"

I don't wait to hear the end of her sentence. "Thanks! I'll text if I'm going to be out past dinner," I call as the door slams behind me. I'll have no choice but to make it up to Connie later, but right now it feels good to make a decision without her—in spite of her.

Melissa's car is in the driveway, puffing exhaust grumpily. I slide into the passenger seat, already sweating because it's the kind of muggy Houston hot that makes your clothes stick to you the instant you step foot outside. Good thing I'm about to go run around the park for two hours.

"Every time," Melissa sighs. Unlike me in my END BREAST CANCER! T-shirt (free from one of the many fundraising events and charity marathons Dad's patronized since my mom was diagnosed) and knee-length middle school gym shorts, Melissa makes a believable athlete with a neon sports bra peeking out of her V-neck and a casual messy bun.

"Yeah, yeah," I say, twisting the A/C vents to blow on my armpits. The air in the car feels like too-hot bathwater. "I'm late to everything. You knew this. Why is your air so crappy?"

"It would have been better if you were on time." Melissa shrugs. "My car doesn't like to run things while it's idle."

I would point out that Melissa's ancient Toyota doesn't like to run things ever, but I take too many free rides to mock the car.

"Are we picking Chris up?"

"Yep," Melissa answers, accidentally grating her back tire against our curb. "How else am I going to find the place?"

I sigh at Melissa's terrible sense of direction. "Okay, but first you have to tell me how last night went."

Melissa had a special date with Chris last night for their four-month-iversary. "Special" included several hours alone at Chris's house while his parents drove his younger sister to San Antonio for sleepaway camp. And from what Melissa told me before leaving for her date, she was at least considering the possibility of making the date *all the way* special.

We're big dorks, but we're also sex-positive feminist dorks who read a lot of fanfiction.

Melissa bites her lip. She is the worst at spilling exciting news, especially boyfriend news. It's not even that she's embarrassed—she's just stubborn, and I think she loves to draw out the interrogation process. "I don't know. It was fine. How was your night?"

I sigh. "We have maybe eight minutes until your easily mortified boyfriend gets into this car, and I imagine you both want this conversation to be over before that happens, but by all means, keep stalling."

"You know," Melissa teases, "maybe I don't want our conversation to revolve around my relationship with a man, did you ever think about that?"

"Oh my goodness, we can pass the Bechdel test later—just tell me what base you got to already."

I really don't think that Melissa actually had sex, because she's only ever kissed any of her other boyfriends. But then, she never dated any of them for more than a month, either, so who knows?

Melissa makes me wait through three tooth-rattling speed bumps before she brakes at the stoplight outside my neighborhood and turns to face me.

"Second-ish base. It wasn't a huge deal, but, like, kind

of, because I have the whole shirt thing. And it's the Bechdel-Wallace test."

Second-ish base. Impressive, Chris Jones. Melissa hates her freckly shoulders with a (weird and unnecessary) passion, so she is very particular about who gets to see her in a tank top, much less a bra.

"Wait, bra or no bra?"

"Bra. Sort of. Bra definitely on. Hands not definitely outside of bra."

I giggle, because I am immature and have never had hands other than my own anywhere near my bra.

"Shut up!" Melissa buries her head in her hands and completely misses the light change, getting us very honked at.

"Chill y'all's pants," Melissa mutters to the rearview mirror. Her Texas shows most when she's road raging.

My phone buzzes. Connie. I let it go to voicemail, then wait a few seconds and text her: Hey, what's up? The ultimate level of sneaky teenage bullshit.

"Okay, sorry. So second-ish base. How are you feeling about that?"

Melissa considers.

"Five minutes," I remind her.

"Oh my God, Ellen! It's a complicated question!"

"Is it?"

"Yes! It's . . . I don't know. I like him! A lot! Really!"

Melissa's tone tells me that there's a "but" coming, so

I wait. For one full block, at least, and then I am forced to press her further.

"But . . . ?"

"But . . . So we were eating pizza and watching season three of *Avatar*, which is when Katara wears her Fire Nation gear and—by the way, when are you going to watch that show already?"

"Yes, it's on my list. Go on."

"Okay, so she's, like, super hot in these episodes, right? Like, wow."

"Mhm." I raise my eyebrows and circle my hands to keep Melissa going, because she can get distracted and talk about *Avatar* for hours.

"So these are basically dream conditions for romance, right?" she continues.

I know better than to disagree, though the conditions are debatably romantic at best.

"And I look over at Chris—and I'm having a really good time at this point. Really. But I look over at him and he's, like, obviously staring at me. Like, this kid absolutely wants to kiss me right now."

Sometimes I marvel at Melissa's casual attitude toward all the boys who are completely into her. I mean, I'm not jealous of her hopelessly devoted junior boyfriend (well, technically he's a senior now, I guess), but . . . damn, I wouldn't mind having just one boy absolutely want to kiss me.

"And," Melissa continues, turning into Chris's subdivision, "I realize that I just . . . don't."

"Don't want to kiss him?" I shouldn't be surprised that Melissa's getting bored of another boyfriend. But I'm a little surprised; I've been thinking that their relationship was the exact balance of gross and adorable that could withstand the test of time and Melissa's pattern of breaking hearts. Plus I like Chris.

"Not specifically. I mean, don't get me wrong, I love a good make-out session as much as the next hormonal teenager, but . . . I wasn't dying to kiss *Chris*, you know?"

I'm not sure I know, but I nod anyway. Melissa slams on the brakes before we turn onto Chris's street.

"Anyway, then we did start making out, and I obviously got more excited about things," Melissa says all in one breath, "so probably everything is fine. And I really want to try out this quidditch thing so badly, and it's his team, so . . ." She lurches the car forward and takes the turn too quickly, shoving me against my seat belt so hard it locks. "Sorry. Also I'm just kidding. I'm not dating him to play quidditch. Probably."

We pull up in front of Chris's house and watch a brown hand wave from the upstairs window and vanish.

"It was nice," Melissa says in a rush. "He's nice. I like him. And I like make-outs. And stuff." She giggles and buries her head in her hands.

I take my role as best friend and sounding board very seriously, and right now I'm not sure whether I should be calming Melissa's doubts or encouraging them. I've supported her through plenty of breakups, and I'll support her through another if I have to. But I take my cue from her and decide to pretend everything's fine.

"Well, I'm glad you had fun." I unbuckle my seat belt and open the door. "I'm going to give up the front seat, but this is a one-time deal, okay? Next time, shotgun is all mine."

"As it should be." Melissa grins and waves as Chris dashes out the door.

I have to do a double take because I didn't know Chris owned shorts that weren't khaki. I've seen him in polo shirts and sneakers for marching band, but at school it's always button-downs and vests and loafers and sometimes even ties. Before he asked Melissa out we were thinking he might be gay, but it turned out that dressing better than everybody was just part of his parents' defense mechanism for being Black in the suburbs. Which is a shame for a lot of serious reasons, and also because he looks like much less of a dweeb in a T-shirt.

As usual, I can see the total puppy-dog love in Chris's eyes when he leans against the window and says, "Hey, you," to Melissa. He was always the Ginny Weasley of the relationship, trying to get Melissa to notice him with goofy antics in band, and I think he's as bemused as everyone else that it actually worked. He ducks his lanky frame into the front seat while I climb in the back.

"Hey yourself." Melissa smiles her own goofy smile, no matter what confusion she has bouncing around in her head. "It's not my fault, I promise. Ellen made me wait. She is—"

"'Late to everything ever,'" Chris says, quoting Melissa's most common description of me as he buckles his seat belt. "Yeah, I figured." He snort-laughs, and I kick the back of his seat in reply. Some people (who are tall, blonde, freckled, and give me rides constantly) have earned the right to mock my constant lateness. Some people (who are tall, bespectacled, and don't even have their driver's license despite technically being seniors now) have not.

"To be fair, Melissa was driving slowly to give us plenty of time to discuss important *current events*," I say to torment him back. Just as I hoped, he hunches into his seat and groans.

Melissa clicks her tongue at me. "Be nice," she instructs. "And sorry," she says to Chris, "but I did warn you about the best friend code."

"I know y'all talk," Chris says in a strangled voice. "Just, does she have to bring it up?"

"She does not." Melissa gives me a stern look through the rearview mirror. "She is sorry."

"I am sorry." I reach around the headrest to pat Chris's

shoulder. "I will have an easier time remembering your delicate sensibilities if you keep your mouth shut about my time management."

Chris mutters about blackmail until Melissa reaches for his hand over the gearshift. Grossdorable.

"Hey, new best friend who doesn't tease me if he knows what's good for him . . ." I kick the back of the seat again. "Can you point the air back here?"

Garvey Park is a little south of us, located more definitely inside Houston city limits than our neighborhood, though the line between suburb and just-urb is flexible in a car-dependent city. The park is nothing fancy—a cute neighborhood green space where there's not too much competition for field time. There's a water fountain and a bathroom (crucial features, Chris assures us) and a few tall oak trees along with a lot more medium-sized saplings tied between metal rods. Yay for reforestation.

Melissa parks behind the tennis courts, and Chris slips his square plastic glasses into their case to complete his transformation into anti-dweeb. We walk toward the open field where maybe ten kids (and by "kids" I mean technical adults, since most of them are supposed to be in college) have gathered around one big tree. Chris starts waving way before we're within reasonable distance, so even though I don't see any bubble-wand hoops or brooms or wizard robes, I figure these must be the quidditch players.

"Yay, you brought new people," a boy says while giving Chris a much more legitimate hug than I expect two athletes to share—usually jocks are all about toxic masculinity and stunted emotions, right? The rest of the kids all gather around. Chris starts to rattle off introductions, but a voice stops us.

"Hey, quidditch! Listen up!"

A short Black girl with visible biceps sticking out of her bro tank is walking up to the tree, and it's pretty obvious that she's someone who runs things around here. Everyone turns and smiles, and if they don't exactly get quiet, at least they all seem to be talking to or about the newcomer.

"First summer practice!" the girl says with a smile. "Who's excited?" Enough people cheer that I feel obligated to clap a little, too. "Awesome! So hoops are in my car . . ." She points to the red VW bug parked at the curb behind her with a hand that is also holding a shopping bag full of something soft and colorful. "Everyone's got sunscreen?" We all nod or reach for the bottles that have been passed around. "Great. Can I get all the new people to circle up for a second while the rest of y'all unload? I want to get started as soon as we can."

Melissa and I stay in the shade with a few other people and the leader girl, dropping our bags in the pile around the tree. The chattier players head to the curb to start pulling a clown car's worth of hula hoops and PVC pipe out of the tiny car.

"So hi! I'm Karey," the girl says, running her free hand over her buzzed head. "Team captain, rising sophomore at A&M, chaser . . . um, anything I'm missing?"

"Badass," Chris says as he walks by with an armful of playground balls, earning an affectionate grimace from Karey.

"We're really happy to have y'all here for the summer," she continues. "And y'all are . . . ?"

We are me, Melissa, two white girls in tank tops whose names I immediately forget because I'm terrible, a white frat-boy type in a backward baseball cap who might be Carl or Kyle, and Jackson, a burly East Asian boy in an oversized Ninja Turtles T-shirt whose name I do catch, since he introduces himself last.

"And you two are Chris's high school friends, right?" Karey asks. "Super psyched to meet you. You have to be at least seventeen to play officially, but it's the summer, so definitely come out and learn the ropes, and then maybe in a couple of years . . ."

"I'm eighteen," Melissa bristles, and I nod along even though I'll still be seventeen for the rest of the summer. Stupid baby faces.

"Oh, got it, my bad. I guess Chris gets to stay team youngling, then." Karey raises her voice a little and grins as Chris passes again, struggling with a bunch of long white poles. He makes a face and scoffs while several poles slip out of his grasp and clatter around him.

"I prefer 'prodigy,' " he calls, making Karey snort.

"Have you all read Harry Potter?" Karey asks, turning back to the whole group. We nod, except for a dark-haired girl who "watched the movies, sort of." "Don't worry, you're not missing anything except an easy way to explain the rules. Anyone remember the speech Oliver Wood gives?"

"Quidditch is easy enough to understand," I say, and Melissa rolls her eyes at me like *I'm* the dork here. "Even if it's not too easy to play."

"Exactly." Karey grins at me. "Well, basically Wood is a stinking liar, because quidditch is confusing as hell to understand. If anything, it actually gets a bit easier once you start playing.

"So I guess you already know the positions to some degree. Six players per team on the field when the game starts—three *chasers*, who score with the quaffle, which is a volleyball; one *keeper*, who's basically a goalie who can also score if they want; two *beaters*, who knock out opponents . . . Oh, they don't use bats. That's important. The bludgers are just dodgeballs that you throw to knock people 'off broom' and send them back to their hoops. Um, and then there's a seventh player who comes in later, the *seeker*. If you know anything about the series, you know they try to catch the snitch. Which in our game is less of a ball and more a speedy, slippery, asshole-type person with a ball attached to their shorts. Oh, and all of this is done while holding a broom between your legs. So . . . how completely baffled are you?"

None of us answer, but if my expression looks anything like Jackson's, I'm betting Karey knows exactly how baffled we are. I know how the game works in the wizarding world, but in the wizarding world they fly twenty feet off the ground, so clearly some things are going to be different here. Jackson whispers, "Wait, how many balls are there?"

"So you'll pick a position for today," Karey says, "but you don't have to be married to it at first. Umm . . . let's start with you." Of course it's me she's pointing at. I stare blankly. Karey smiles. "Okay, look, do you play any sports?"

Why did I have to go all Hermione Granger on that first question? I do not handle pressure well. The answer to Karey's question is no, but I'm so desperate not to say no that I say something even worse.

"Uh, I'm in choir."

The group behind me erupts into laughter (at least that's what it feels like), and Karey definitely gives a little snort-laugh that she quickly tries to cover. She crosses her arms and looks me up and down, and I know she's seeing every undefined muscle, every ounce and inch I'm missing to be any kind of athlete.

"I mean, because we have to practice breathing and . . . uh, breath control." Why am I still talking? I wish Xiumiao were here to back me up—choir breath exercises are no joke, really!

I risk a glance backward. Melissa is chewing on her thumbnail, which is one step below face-in-hands mortification on the "How much is Ellen embarrassing me?" scale. Sorry, we can't all be delightfully nerdy *and* socially well-adjusted.

I realize that I'm projecting and catastrophizing, but that doesn't stop my face from burning.

"Okay, choir girl, do you have any games you like to play in gym or anything?" Karey is smiling, trying to help me out, but I wish she would just move on to someone competent and let me sit on the bench, like most of my gym teachers ended up doing.

"Um, I like basketball a little, maybe? I actually played when I was really tiny. At the YMCA." It feels silly to bring this up, but not as silly as admitting to this muscular, sports-bra-rocking badass what a sedentary lump I actually am.

"What are your skills? Did you like scoring? Are you a fast runner? How's your arm?"

"I don't . . ." I shoot telepathic hate beams along with a look of panic at Melissa. *This was supposed to be Harry Potter nerd bonding*, my telepathic hate beams accuse, *not boot camp*. "I, uh, I think I didn't like scoring?" I couldn't get the ball up to the basket, so . . .

"Great!" To Karey's credit, she looks more excited than I would be if I found out I had to play on a team with someone like me. She reaches into her plastic bag and hands me a black bandana with purple polka dots. "You're a beater. This is your headband. Put it on and stand over there and we'll do some more explanation and drills in a minute, okay?"

I stand over there. I struggle to turn my square of black-and-purple cloth into a headband and pull the resulting lopsided circle onto my head, where it immediately soaks up a gross layer of sweat. Even with the sun starting to dip below the tree line, Houston is *hot*.

Karey sorts the rest of the newbies. Melissa decides to be a chaser, which means she gets a white bandana and stands slightly apart, but that doesn't stop me from scrunching up my face and sticking out my tongue at her.

This had better not be awful, my telepathic mind beams warn her. *Also, it's hot.*

Whine, whine, whine, her telepathic mind beams respond, *moan, moan, moan. I'm Ellen, and I hate fun.*

I know she's saying this (telepathically) because she's making The Face, which is what she says I look like when I'm cranky, and which is definitely not true, because I don't do that dead-eyed mope.

Once we're all divided, Karey calls the rest of the team over.

"We should probably do icebreakers," she says. "But first I want to get everyone warmed up a little. Let's do three laps, with brooms. New players, you're going to need to get used to running like this, so you may as well start now."

I'm not immediately sure what "like this" means, and I have not yet seen any brooms. Luckily, Chris pulls a couple of plain PVC pipes out of a bag and bounces over, handing one to me and one to Melissa. "Your broomsticks." He grins when Melissa inspects the grimy duct-tape grip skeptically. "Trust me, you don't want to play with the kind that has actual straw on the end—that stuff scratches. Good luck."

"I think you mean 'mount up,'" Melissa corrects him, eyes twinkling.

I shrug, check to make sure that other people really are sticking the three-foot poles between their legs, and then mount my "broom."

I feel all kinds of ridiculous, but I'd be lying if I said that eleven-year-old me isn't jumping up and down and giggling, at least a little. How long has it been since I've pretended to be a witch on a broomstick?

We start running laps. Karey sets the pace, jogging at a medium speed even though Chris and a few other kids bunch behind her like they wish they could pass. I have no such issues. I can't figure out how to hold the broom so it doesn't whack against my legs, and I feel lopsided with my left hand pinned down by my waist. Honestly, though, I can't blame the broom for the way I'm struggling after two laps around the field. It's a big field; I'm an unathletic kid.

I fall into the back quarter of the group but manage to push through and finish the third lap without dying. A couple of players gather around the tree for water, but I hang back with Melissa, focusing on oxygen before I worry about hydration. So much for choir lungs.

"Are we having fun yet?" I ask between gasps.

Melissa is about to answer, but one of the players by the tree is holding up my flimsy burnt-orange drawstring backpack (free from the UT admissions office). "Hey, who has a phone in here? It's been going off for a while."

I roll my eyes and jog closer to grab the bag. Of course Connie doesn't understand the possibility that I might be too busy to answer the phone exactly when she wants me to. I dig past my wallet, water bottle, and house keys to pull out my phone. I scowl at the screen, half tempted to ignore my stepmom entirely.

But it isn't Connie calling. It's Dad.

"Hey," I answer, "I'm just—"

"Ellen, where are you? We couldn't get hold of you, and Connie didn't know where you'd gone—said you just took off."

"I didn't! I'm at the park with Melissa."

"We need you to answer your phone," Dad says. "You can't— I don't really have time for this, Ellen, for your . . ."

Dad takes the deep breath, the one that stops him from saying something bad.

I let his unfinished sentence hang without asking why it's always *my* dot-dot-dot and never Connie's.

"I need you to go home," Dad says. "Now. We'll talk when I get back from work. And . . . try not to start any more fights, please."

He hangs up quickly, like he's afraid I'm going to argue. But it's hard to argue when my throat is so tight and my lungs are squeezed inside my rib cage that suddenly feels too small. I've always hated that my body's default reaction to anger is tears. It makes me feel small and weak, which only makes me angrier and makes the tears well up faster.

I blink hard at the ground, my phone dark in my palm and my backpack still dangling off my wrist.

"Everything okay?" the kid who grabbed my backpack in the first place asks.

He's definitely trying to be nice, but at this moment it's the worst question anyone could ask me. I don't want this person to know that I'm upset, frustrated, confused and tired and *mad*. I can't look up, can't answer without giving myself away. I hate that. I hate my stupid tear ducts and my stupid anger and my stupid stepmom.

Melissa rescues me.

"Hey." She tugs at my arm, and I let her lead me away

from the tree. "What's up? Stepmom struggles? Anything terrible?"

"Just pissed," I mutter, knowing that Melissa will politely ignore the sniffle I can't hold back. "My dad called. He's— I think he might be super mad." My stomach twists in on itself as his voice echoes in my ears. Not even his words, just the way he sounded. Empty, tired, like he's dealing with an especially demanding client.

"Mad about what?" Melissa asks. "I thought he always wants you to be more active and spend time outside."

"Yeah, no, it's because I sort of left the house without permission. Connie didn't really want me to . . ." I shrug and sniff again, annoyed at my nose and everything. "And I kind of need to get home right now."

Melissa nods. She walks away, talks to Chris and then to Karey, comes back, and puts her arm around me as she leads me out of the park. "You're fine," she tells me. "I mean, it's crappy, but it's fine. They practice again on Sunday. It's fine."

"I *am* fine," I growl, caught somewhere between immense gratitude and annoyance. "It's not—I'm just frustrated. Everyone's going to think I'm a freak."

"They're not even paying attention," Melissa tries to soothe me.

"Chris?" I don't particularly want him around, but I don't want to ditch him here, either, and it's not like he would be a jerk about it if he noticed me crying.

"Getting a ride with Karey."

"Will you come over and talk to Connie for me? She loves you."

"Pretty sure that would just delay the inevitable." Melissa shakes her head. "But I'll call in an hour and make sure you're alive."

I snort at the compromise. "Think the Lis would let me live with them for the rest of the summer?"

We reach Melissa's car, and she rolls her eyes while groping in her purse for the key. "Drama queen alert."

"You didn't hear my dad on the phone. I'm almost certainly disowned."

Melissa laughs and pulls out her keys, and I slip into the front seat, smiling a little sheepishly, my eyes watery but no longer watering.

"You're fine," Melissa repeats.

"I know, I know. I just need to avoid talking to Connie until Dad gets home." I take a breath, my chest barely shaking. "It shouldn't be big trouble."

Melissa nods, but the words don't feel true. Everything is big trouble these days.

4

"Hey." Dad knocks on my door while opening it, one of those underhanded parental tricks designed to make it seem like they're respecting your privacy when in fact they're doing just the opposite. Dad knows a million of these tricks, probably from the parenting books taking up a whole bookshelf in his office. "How's it going, kiddo?"

"Come in," I say, only half sarcastically. I close the social justice Tumblr I was browsing and slide my phone in my pocket. "I'm fine." I made it upstairs without saying a word to Connie, letting her rant until she paused for breath and then slipping into my room to hide out. "How are you?"

"Doing better." Dad shrugs. His tone is casual, but he walks through the doorway and sits on the edge of my bed, which is sign number one that I'm about to get a talk.

"You're home late," I say, because I care about him and worry about him, and also because I'd like to derail this lecture if at all possible. "Is work okay?"

"You know, it was a really long day." Dad releases an enormous sigh that blows his receding hairline even farther up his forehead and deepens his wrinkles.

Showing vulnerability is one of his tricks to put me at ease, and is sign number two that I'm in trouble.

"Sorry to hear that," I say. "Is there anything I can do to help?" Can't hurt to earn some brownie points.

Then Dad just sits there, saying nothing. This is the third and final sign.

Dad and I communicate best through silence. Every serious discussion we have starts off with at least five minutes of empty air space, and this one won't be any different. We'll sit here, and he won't ask why I can't try harder to be nice, and I won't say that Connie has it out for me, and we won't have the screaming match that could have been. Instead, Dad will start with something general and innocent.

Dad's big on *I* statements. He's big on empathy. All sneaky parenting tricks to make me do what he wants. We'll talk about my behavior, and why it upset Connie, and what changes *I* can make in the future to avoid these problems.

But today, Dad doesn't follow his script.

"You probably can't wait to be off for college," he says instead, which comes totally out of the blue and is also a *you* statement.

"Huh?" I'm excited, I guess. But I would never say I couldn't wait to leave home.

"It will be better, I think," Dad says, reaching up to loosen his tie. "The space will be good for you. For everyone."

Ouch. What is it with everyone wanting space this summer? I cover my grimace by checking my phone. "Yeah, I'm basically counting down the hours, same as you."

Dad doesn't acknowledge my sarcasm or correct my assumption. "Have you put in any more job applications?"

I nod, but with enough of a scowl that he moves on.

"What were you doing at the park, anyway?"

"I was running," I say. Dad is always bugging me to get outside more, be physically active. Summer used to be full of biking and trips to the local pool, but between me being a cranky teenager, Yasmín's schedule filling up with camps, and Dad getting the new job, that's all over. "Melissa was showing me this game people play, quidditch."

"Well, that's good," he says. I open my mouth to squeeze in an explanation of why I left the house in such a hurry, but he holds up a hand. "Can we just try to get through the summer in peace, kiddo? I just want to have a nice couple of months. Can you hang in there?"

I think I nod. I think I smile and let him hug me while my brain is still processing.

"It goes so fast," he says into my hair. And then he leaves.

Not fast enough, apparently. *Can we get through the summer in peace? Hang in there*. It's perfectly obvious that Dad just wants me out of the house so I won't cause any more trouble, won't disrupt his calm family life.

Won't upset Connie again.

It's not like I've been a tragic outcast in my family since Dad got remarried. It took some adjusting, but we all smiled through the awkward moments until we settled into something comfortable, something good. Connie recommended all her favorite kids' books, helped me build a replica *Titanic* for my fifth-grade history fair project, even gave me the period talk when Texas public education failed to answer my most pressing questions. We used to be on the same team.

And then suddenly I was fourteen and full of angst and nobody appreciated my mood swings, least of all Connie. I was fifteen and lecturing everyone about the Great Pacific Garbage Patch, and Connie just wanted to throw away her empty shampoo bottles in peace. I was sixteen and wore the same pair of jeans until both knees wore out, and Connie didn't understand why I wouldn't put in a little bit of effort. Each new point of conflict blossomed into more clashes, and pretty soon Connie was sick and tired of my attitude and Dad was desperately trying to figure out why every conversation seemed to spin out into an argument.

Christmas break started as a silly argument. Dad was working late again, and Connie put up a new nativity set, and I pointed out that it totally whitewashed the three kings. Connie said it didn't matter, and I argued that representation always matters, and then things spiraled. And soon she was yelling that I wanted to ruin Christmas with political correctness, and I was yelling that she could uphold systemic oppression as much as she liked but it wouldn't keep her safe from its consequences because, as much as she might want to, she couldn't make herself white.

Which, admittedly, was a lot of baggage to dredge up over a nativity set. I had been building that accusation for a long time—it's the only way I can make sense of Connie's total disinterest in trying to improve the current messed-up system.

Connie put Yasmín in the car, and I thought they were going to get frozen yogurt without me or something. I didn't even tell Dad about our fight when he got home; I was hoping it would blow over. But then it got later and later, and finally she texted Dad that they had passed through the border.

She drove to Monterrey, stayed with her sisters for a whole week, all the way to New Year's. Dad wandered the house like the ghost of Christmas future, silent and depressed. Aunt Mal came into town, did the nice older sister version of slapping him to get him back on track, and reminded him that Connie wasn't *gone* gone, not like my mom, and that he could pick up the phone and fix things.

When she came back, Dad finally found his voice to tell me that things were going to be different.

It took me a couple more fights and a series of increasingly harsh lectures before I realized that what he really meant was that *I* was going to be different. And now, since I couldn't do that well enough, he's waiting for me to leave.

Well, fine. Dad's right. I am sick of being here. I'm sick of Connie and she's sick of me, and if it has to be one of us, Dad's made it clear who he'll pick.

I pick up my phone to text Xiumiao. I'm halfway through the message before I remember that she wants the summer to be over, too. Maybe she doesn't want to hear from me. Testing the waters, I send her a screenshot of the first pointless meme I find on Tumblr that makes me laugh. When I check back eight minutes later, the text has been "Read."

I try to go back to internet browsing, but I'm restless and angry. Besides, Connie's serving dinner downstairs, sounds of the microwave beeping and plates dropping against the table floating up from the kitchen. My stomach grumbles, matching my resentful feelings. I head downstairs.

Connie sets out food around an empty table.

"Oh," she says when she sees me.

"Yep. Me. Still here. Not going anywhere yet."

Connie frowns, then returns to arranging salmon burgers on Dad's and Yasmín's plates. "Can you tell your father—?"

"Is there anything I can eat?" I drop into my seat and stare at my empty plate.

"You can take the salad out of the fridge and start serving." Connie's frown deepens.

While Connie doles out the mashed potatoes (already made with milk and butter), I drag myself up and pull open the refrigerator. The giant plastic salad bowl takes up most of the bottom shelf.

"Is this cheese?" I ask even though I can plainly see the hunks of crumbly white feta nestling between lettuce leaves. I hold the bowl tight so my fingers don't shake against it.

"Oh," Connie says again. "You can pick it out, can't you?"

Yes, I can pick out the cheese. Not as easily as everyone

else could have added the cheese to their own individual salad, though.

I guess Connie hears my sigh, because she turns snappy. "You're seventeen, you know. At your age I was making dinner for all my sisters. If you don't want to eat what we have, you're more than welcome to make your own food. There's peanut butter in the pantry."

My hands clench around the stupid salad. She's not wrong. I am a sad excuse for a high school graduate who can barely heat soup. I never help Connie with the cooking, and it's not like anyone owes me a gourmet vegan meal every night. It's so close to what Dad said, too. Things will be easier when I leave, when I stop expecting to be part of the family.

I drop the salad bowl onto the table, making no attempt to quiet the clatter, just as Dad and Yasmín enter the kitchen.

Dad shoots me a narrow-eyed glance, but then he takes his seat by the window and smiles. "Look at this fancy home-cooked dinner! I feel spoiled."

I pull individual leaves out of the salad bowl.

Yasmín pokes her salmon patty, looking worried. "Mine's pink," she says. Dad and Connie chuckle. Dad takes a huge bite of burger and grunts his appreciation. Connie beams, standing next to Dad without taking her seat. Yasmín starts on her mashed potatoes.

And I sit in the corner, still fuming. One of these things just doesn't belong here.

"Ellen," Connie says, finally sitting, "I was so worried about you that I didn't have the energy to start with the garage. Let's plan to clean it out tomorrow, okay?"

I press my hands against my pounding temples, but I am not going to react. I stand and head to the counter to dig an apple out of the fruit bowl. I take a deep breath and examine the slightly browned edges. I take a bite.

"Ellen? Did you hear Connie?" Dad asks.

I shrug, swallowing a bite of soggy, tasteless apple. I don't fill my mouth with a second bite fast enough. "Yeah, I heard. She was concerned for my safety."

"And the garage?" Dad prompts.

"Yeah." I shrug. "I did think admitting she needed me for free labor threw her motives into question, but I wasn't going to mention anything."

There's a moment of silence.

"Running off without giving anyone your whereabouts is inconsiderate," Connie says. "We were worried."

"Well, don't worry; I'll be here all day tomorrow, ready to be bossed around."

"I'm just asking for your help with this project," Connie says between tight-pressed lips, leaving her seat to force an extra spoonful of salad onto Yasmín's plate. "I don't think it's an unreasonable request." She walks to the refrigerator and pulls out a bottle of ketchup. "That garage has so much potential. I've been trying to get you excited about it, but if you're so opposed to that, you could at least think about how renting out the space might help pay for *your* tuition."

"What are you talking about?" If Connie told me about her plans for the cleared-out garage, I definitely wasn't listening. Is she going to turn it into an Airbnb or something?

Connie tuts. "If we get the garage apartment up and ready to rent out, it could really help . . ."

Right, another reminder that I'm putting such a strain on the family by going to college.

". . . but right now it's a disaster zone."

"Oh, is that my fault, too?"

Connie spins around, a tiny frown forming between her eyebrows. "What do you mean, Ellen?"

I mean, it's your garage; clean it yourself. I'm out of here anyway.

I don't say anything. I drop the spoiled apple on the counter, and I turn around, and I walk away. Out of the kitchen, through the living room, past the stairs, and out the front door. Down the block. Out. Away.

When the door slams behind me I can think again, take stock. It's hot, and the sun's down, but our neighborhood is safe and well-lit. I have my phone and my wallet. Despite Connie's dire warnings about leaving the house, I don't need to go back yet.

Texting would require standing still, which is not an option right now. I cross the street and stomp past the end of the block to catch the bike trail that winds through the neighborhood, hidden by a thin line of trees, the only option for non-car travel in a neighborhood that doesn't believe in sidewalks.

My chest shakes, my eyes blur, and I stumble when I step onto the gravel bike path. Angry tears and frustrated tears and sad tears mix and spill on my cheeks, and I'm glad for the slight privacy the path provides.

Safe behind the trees, I finally stop. I breathe.

Dad's waiting to get rid of me. It will be better for everyone when I'm out of the house. It's actually hilarious that he and Xiumiao want the same thing. Space.

Everyone wants me out of their life.

It's no surprise that Connie doesn't really want me around. She would never say it, but I know, the way Melissa knows that she's her mom's favorite kid and her brother is her dad's, or the way Xiumiao knows that her parents didn't plan to have her. Connie puts up with me the best she can for Dad's sake and Yasmín's. She loves them both so much. They're hers. I just happened to come along as part of the set. I get that, even if I don't like it. I can understand.

I can't understand Dad.

I walk a little farther, but the urgency is gone. As

the angry adrenaline drains, I'm left empty and vaguely embarrassed.

"Ellen!" A voice calls my name, and feet slap-slap-slap against the road beyond my tree cover. "Ellen?"

Yasmín barrels around the tree line and stumbles as her toes hit gravel. "Oh," she says when she sees me. "Hi." She hops from one foot to another, wipes her cheek while sniffling quietly. Now I'm the jackass whose tantrum made my little sister cry.

"Hey, I'm right here." I copy the wipe-and-sniff move. "I just wanted to walk a little."

"Okay," Yasmín says, still hopping.

Sigh. "Here," I offer my hands and point my toes, inviting Yasmín to step up and stand on the tops of my sneakers. This move was easier when she was five, but I manage to stay upright with my toes only slightly squished. "You shouldn't run out into the street at night."

"You shouldn't," Yasmín shoots back.

"At least I wore shoes." We stand there, listening to the cicadas buzz. I don't spend much time with just Yasmín anymore. I don't get babysitting duty these days, so it's always me and Connie and Yasmín hanging around the house, or me and Yasmín and Dad going on a late-night grocery run. Or, more often, me and Yasmín in different rooms of the house, doing our own stuff. "How are things going with Mrs. Sorgalla?" I ask.

"Fine," she answers automatically.

"Oh really? So she totally loves you now? And she's stopped all the unfairness?"

"Umm . . ."

That's what I thought. "What's she doing now?"

Yasmín shrugs. "Um, she just doesn't let me turn my work in when I'm the first one finished, and she said I have to stop raising my hand all the time."

"Did she say why?" Tiny sparks of anger are already smoking in my chest.

"She said I was being a show-off." Yasmín stares at her feet but tosses her ponytail and scowls. My sparks catch fire.

"You are aware that that's complete bull crap, right?"

"Saying 'crap' is unladylike," Yasmín scolds like a miniature disapproving Connie.

I snort. "Hey, give me some credit for not saying 'shit,' at least."

Yasmín gasps.

"Sorry." My brain is teeming with worse words I'd like to unleash on Mrs. Sorgalla, along with some fucking research showing exactly how girls are systematically taught to downplay and devalue their accomplishments (in the name of avoiding "unladylike" bragging). What is it the teacher finds so unbelievable about Yasmín being a miniature math whiz, and would she think the same thing about the white kids in class? It's not like I, the mostly monolingual kid with lighter skin, have run into this problem much with teachers, but I've heard the comments people make when they read me as white, always followed by "Oh I didn't mean you, of course. You're not really Mexican" (like *that's* some kind of compliment). Shouldn't Connie be talking to Yasmín about this, instead of burying it with the assumption that all teachers deserve respect? Shouldn't I?

I could rant endlessly to Yasmín, warn her that there will always be asshats like Mrs. Sorgalla trying to make her sit down and shut up, and that she should never listen to them. An ocean of relevant internet articles swamps my brain, more outrage and information than I can possibly explain to a ten-year-old, especially without cursing. I wish I were Melissa, who can always turn her thoughts into appropriate words, or Xiumiao, who can't but lets them out anyway.

"You don't ever need to feel bad about showing off what you're awesome at," I tell Yasmín, and I just hope that if I say it with enough frustration and desperation in my voice, she'll believe it. "Promise you won't let Mrs. Sorgalla get to you?"

She nods.

"Good." We're quiet again. Hanging on to my hands for balance, Yasmín leans straight backward until her ponytail almost touches the ground. Then she stands back up and looks me straight in the eyes.

"Are you still mad at Mom?"

Furious. I expect the emotion to flare up again, but instead I just feel tired. I look over my shoulder for an excuse to break eye contact.

"Nah, I'm not mad." I guess this is why Dad wants peace. Fighting is exhausting.

"Good." Yasmín hops off my feet and tiptoes to the grass. "I hate when people are mad."

She offers her hand. I'm about to take it, and we're about to walk out of the trees and back to the house, but an earsplitting screech freezes both of us.

"Yasmín!"

Connie's cry is so shrill it sets the neighbor's dachshund puppy on an equally piercing barking spree.

"Here!" I shout back. Yasmín and I pick up our pace, but not fast enough.

"Yasmín!" Connie wears her full-panic face as she runs toward us, not even noticing that her heels are digging holes in the neighbors' lawns. "What happened? What are you doing out . . ." She blinks at me. "I thought you were upstairs."

"No, uh." I shake my head, confused. What is the point of storming dramatically out of the house if people don't even realize you've done it? "No, I went for a walk."

"I came to get her," Yasmín explains. As soon as she says it, Connie's lips press together and she yanks Yasmín's hand out of mine and pulls her away. Like I'm contagious, or explosive.

"I didn't know she would follow," I mumble. "I wasn't trying to . . ."

Connie sucks in her breath, so I shut up.

"I wasn't going to get lost, Mama," Yasmín whines. "I know how to walk around the block."

"Go inside," Connie orders, giving Yasmín a push toward the house. "Practice your flute. I'll come talk to you in a minute."

Yasmín sulks toward the front door. I try to slink in the same direction, but Connie's glare holds me in place.

"*What* were you thinking?"

"I wasn't—"

"Clearly not," Connie scoffs. "But your recklessness is not going to endanger my family, do you understand me?"

"We were within earshot the whole time!" I try to point out. "I'm sorry you got scared, but—"

"Do you understand?"

"—but, fuck, don't you think you're being a little bit *irrational*?"

The moment after I finish my sentence is cinematic. Freeze-frame. Mute. I watch in slow motion as twin atomic bombs detonate behind Connie's eyes.

Like any good blockbuster hero, I turn and walk away from the explosion, because what else am I going to do? I head for my room. Leaving didn't solve anything anyway.

It worked for Connie because people wanted her back.

5

". . . disrespectful. She's just getting more . . ."

I pile more pillows over my head, but I can't keep from hearing another round of Connie and Dad's discussion downstairs, an unfortunate side effect of my room being right above the kitchen.

Dad tries to calm things down like always, but *I* statements are no match for Connie's ire. Her angry words blend together as Dad's responses fade in and out. The same circle around and around: what I did, why I did it, and what to do about me.

". . . believe you. I just mean it doesn't sound like . . ." Giving in to temptation, I unbury my head to hear

Dad say, "She's cranky, sure, but . . . she's quiet."

Compared to Connie's rant, that shouldn't faze me, but my stomach drops. "Quiet." Almost everyone who wrote in my senior yearbook—other than Melissa and Xiumiao—mentioned how quiet I am. Lots of "sweet" and "nice" mixed in for good measure. It's not like they're wrong; I am quiet and awkward, especially with new people. But I don't feel quiet, or sweet, or even nice. Those are non-adjectives, words to describe someone with no personality.

I can live with my classmates not knowing me, but from Dad it hurts. I am quieter when I talk to him, quicker to snap at Connie, but I thought that meant we understood each other.

"Ellen," Dad calls, voice suddenly loud and actually intended to reach me. "Can you come down for a minute?"

I drag my socks across the carpet all the way downstairs. Maybe I can generate enough static to give Connie a shock.

Dad sits at the kitchen table, a glass of water in front of him and the rest of the dinner dishes cleared away. He keeps shifting the glass to make new rings of water on the wooden table. Connie paces the kitchen, clearing clean dishes from the drying rack.

I sit in the chair across from Dad. We start our pre-lecture silence.

"Greg," Connie interrupts. She nods and arches her

eyebrows and all but sticks her hand up my dad's ass to work his mouth herself.

"Right. Ellen, I—we think that your attitude needs adjusting."

"We do?"

Dad sighs.

"It sounds like some things were said in anger," Dad continues, "and that's not helpful for anyone."

"Sure, yeah." I try to match Dad's reasonable tone. "It's not helpful to tell me that I'm endangering the family."

Connie slams the cabinet closed and huffs, "*Greg.*"

"Ellen," Dad says.

"Rocky!"

My humor is not appreciated.

"Ellen." Dad repeats my name without a hint of irony. "Can you please try to be serious here? You can't be running off into the night, or sneaking out of the house, or—"

"I told you, I didn't . . ."

Dad holds up a hand, but I see his eyes flick to Connie and back to me. Maybe he still believes me, a little.

"Or whatever," he finishes. "You can't be acting like this."

He's looking at me like I've broken some kind of promise, but I never promised to keep the peace. He just expected me to.

Dad keeps staring like he's waiting for something.

Eventually he sighs. "I don't want to be the bad guy here, but you're not giving me a lot of options. Maybe you're acting out because we haven't set boundaries and limits. Maybe you need structure. Maybe this is what needs to happen."

I want to shake Dad. Actually, I want to remind him that this is not effective communication, but since I'm not part of this conversation he's having with himself, that's tricky to do.

"It's not unreasonable to expect you to pitch in around the house," Dad says. "You obviously have a lot of free time since you didn't find a job . . ."

"I tried! I'm trying!"

Connie crashes two plates into the cabinet, and I wince at the noise.

"Okay," I say. I'm done with this night, with this lecture. "I'm sorry. I won't do it again."

Dad nods and sips his water, which I hope means that my apology is accepted.

Except . . . "Greg?"

Dad sets his glass back down. "We also think . . ."

My scoff and eye roll don't go unnoticed. "Hey, now," Dad leans across the table at the same time that Connie shoves a glass bowl into the open cabinet hard enough to echo. "I feel like there's a lot of frustration being directed—"

"Toward the dishes?"

"Ellen . . ."

"Look." I try to breathe, to let go of the sarcasm. I try to be Dad to Dad, the voice of reason, the calm explanation. "I never meant to sneak out, and I don't have a problem helping around the house until I find a job, but I just get sick of Connie always making it seem like I'm—"

"Ellen," Dad stops me, shaking his head. But I saw the doubt in his eyes, and maybe he'll listen if I can just find the right way to explain what's happening.

"—like I'm trying to personally offend her all the time—"

"Enough." Dad's voice cuts through my stumbled words. "I don't want to hear it."

The back of my throat tightens. Not the kind of *I* statement I was hoping for.

"Greg," Connie says softly. Dad looks at her, nods, and lets out a sigh so huge it almost drags his face straight into the table. Connie paces to stand behind him. They make quite the picture of parental disapproval, the dreaded united front. "United front" meaning that Dad's about to do what Connie wants—like the time they gave my cat Dorito away because of Connie's allergies, or the time they "encouraged" me to spend a month of my seventh-grade summer at choir camp.

"We think that there need to be some consequences for the consistent rudeness," Dad says like he's reading off a cue card. The tone hurts. I want to see anger, or frustration, or even an attempt to reason with me. I don't want to see him handing down some already agreed-on punishment.

"We want accountability for your time around the house," he repeats. "We want things to stay in control. Nobody wants a repeat of Christmas break, right?"

I watch his eyes dart away as soon as he says it. Connie goes still and (amazingly) silent. I think this is the first time anyone's mentioned her abrupt departure out loud.

"Right," I say. I don't want Connie to abandon my dad because of me. I saw how much it crushed him. "But—"

"Right." Dad nods. "So from now until the end of the summer, there will be some rules in place. Chores, for one."

"I do chores," I mutter.

"We'll be cleaning out the garage," Connie adds, like I didn't already know about her pet project. "And I'll need help around the house, too. I'll make you a list."

"Daily chore list?" That doesn't sound so bad. That might actually help me avoid interacting with Connie in person.

"The list is less important than the accountability," Dad says. "While you're here, until you move out, you need to be available. Not running off to who-knows-where with Melissa and Xiumiao."

I start to reply, but Dad holds up his hand.

"Not looking for another excuse. This is discipline."

"You're grounding me." I don't quite believe the words as I say them, so I try again. "You're saying I'm grounded. For the whole summer. Just because of . . . an unauthorized walk and a rude comment?"

Dad narrows his eyes. "I think you know that the issue here is a pattern of behavior. You've been rude. You've worried us." I snort, which makes him sigh. "You're not in college yet, Ellen," he says. "And as long as you—"

" 'Live under my roof'?" I guess.

Dad scowls. "As long as you act like a baby," he says, "that's how we'll have to treat you."

You statement.

I've never been grounded before. Tears sting my eyes, and I drop my head to blink them away. "What about my friends? I might not see them once we start college." Dad sips his water, eyes hidden. Maybe it's not too late to change his mind. "Do you even know how to ground someone?" I ask lightly.

He frowns at me. He holds out one hand. "House keys."

"Seriously?" My mouth drops open. "What if I make a grocery run?"

"If we know you're going out, we can keep the door unlocked for you," Connie says, her voice dangerously sweet.

I reach into my pocket, wrap my hand around my key

chain. I never thought of the blue plastic seahorse as something precious, but now I search Dad's face for some sign that he won't really go through with this.

"Ellen, if you can't keep civil, it will be your phone next time."

I don't know this person delivering threats of dire consequences, but I pull the keys out of my pocket and deposit them in his outstretched palm. Connie snatches them away like she's afraid he might give them back.

She shouldn't worry. Dad was never going to choose me.

I'm grounded. For the whole summer. For my last summer.

6

I try to drown in internet.

Melissa's unopened message blinks at me, but I know that if I text she'll try to cheer me up or fix things, and I don't want that yet.

Social media is too calm, nothing but cute animals and silly gifs. Nothing with enough outrage to match my mood. Time for Tumblr.

Tumblr is the lawless internet hovel where extreme fan culture meets extreme opinions and extremely pointless junk posts, and I love it to death. I hardly ever post, I've mostly stopped creating *Agents of S.H.I.E.L.D.* gifsets (which is how I spent the majority of sophomore year), and I don't chat with my mutual followers the way Melissa does, but I lurk like a freaking pro, following blogs and reading posts without ever commenting.

I visit Environmentally Unfriendly, my main social justice/veganism blog. Eevie, the site's creator, is about as in-your-face angry as a person can be without becoming PETA. Xe makes a point to publicly respond to every anonymous troll who thinks they have exactly the right hate-filled message to change xyr mind about the whole animal rights thing. Like suddenly one day xe's going to read, "Your [sic] a fucking hypocrite if you ever swat flys [sic]" and be like, "Oh my god, my life is a lie."

I rage-read the troll posts. It's cathartic, but in the end I'm still angry. I'm still grounded.

AAAAARRRGGHHHH! is what I finally message Xiumiao. I need to rant. I need advice from someone who *has* been grounded before. I need my friend. But minutes pass with no answer, and eventually I shove my phone in my pocket and stare at the wall instead.

Hanging on the wall behind my desk is a picture of me as a baby, just after I learned to walk. For whatever reason, I'm making this horrible scrunched-up face that Dad thinks is the funniest thing ever (he's the one who blew up the picture and stuck it on the wall). Sometimes when I'm really frustrated, I make faces back at my younger self. Ridiculous, I know, but it's less violent than punching a pillow. Besides, one-year-old me doesn't know how good she has it.

My mom is in the picture, too, the top of her head half cut out of the frame as she stands over me with a "poor baby" smile, her arms reaching out to grab me.

I recognize so much of my face in hers. Arched eyebrows, wide overbite smile, olive skin. Dad shows up in my freckles and the shape of my chin, and I'm pale enough that I get the "What are you?" squint more often than the "You speak Spanish, right?" assumption. But I'm glad I got a lot of my mom's looks. It seems only fair, since I barely got anything else. My mom's name was Christina Lopez. She was born in Texas, same as my San Antonio Tejano grandparents, and that means my heritage is both a privilege and a weird liminal space. I used to love hearing Connie's stories of growing up in Mexico, the nursery rhymes and the lullabies, because it made me feel more connected and proud. But my mom sang lullabies in English, so are those connections even really mine?

My mom and dad met in college. He wanted to save the world from pollution, and she wanted to run a museum. She played soccer and roller derby and loved to watch my dad perform in the school musicals, though she couldn't carry a tune herself.

She had me when she was twenty-six. She died before she turned thirty.

I was almost four, which means that I both remember her and don't. I remember the idea of her, the feeling of her presence, the warmth. I remember her hand reaching back to pat my leg when I was in my car seat. I think I remember the smell of her floral perfume, but maybe that's a later memory, from when Dad still kept a bottle of it in his medicine cabinet, and we would take it out sometimes and smell it together.

I don't remember her in the hospital. There are hardly any pictures of those months. I remember being happy to visit Aunt Mal, who gave me Skittles and let me watch as many movies as I wanted.

I remember what it felt like to lose her. I don't think I understood it, not really, but I felt it. The universe changes when you have no mother, the way the air changes when it's going to rain.

When I was eight or nine, I went through a phase of reading fairy tales. I got a little obsessed. All the Disney princesses had dead mothers, so I felt like we were kindred spirits. And besides, I liked the story that every fairy tale tells. That the world is full of danger, which I already knew, and that happy endings exist, which I wanted to believe.

They also give stepmothers a pretty bad rap.

I make one last face at my photograph, and then I check my phone. Still nothing from Xiumiao, so I type (and delete, and then retype) a message to Melissa instead.

So apparently I'm grounded forever because my parents are assholes and everything is terrible. See you never, I guess, and have a good summer.

Melissa's not the complete night owl that I am, so she won't see the message until she wakes up anyway. I feel bad. I don't want her to have to wake up to that text, to that news. I don't want to wake up to it.

My phone dings at 7:20 a.m., startling me upright because I fell asleep with it right next to my face again. I nudge the screen away so I can read the text glowing on it.

Give me ten minutes. I'm on my way over.

FIFTEEN MINUTES LATER, I SHUFFLE GROGGILY DOWN-stairs. Melissa sits at the kitchen table, her ponytail silky and her lip gloss bubble-gum pink, letting Connie serve her iced coffee.

"I'm, like, eighty percent sure that this violates the terms of my grounding." I rub sleep out of my eyes, steal the coffee out of Melissa's hand, and collapse into the chair next to her. Connie sighs at my breast cancer shirt and penguin pajama shorts.

"Melissa wanted a chance to talk," she says, staring me down before I sip the stolen coffee. I guiltily slide it back to Melissa instead.

"Thanks, Mrs. Rourke." Melissa turns to me and winks,

sipping the coffee. *Don't worry*, her face says, *I got this*. "This is really good—it's got agave, right?"

"It does!" Connie beams. Melissa has always had a magical effect on grown-ups, but she must have an actual mind-control button she uses on Connie. "Just a few drops, but there's some cinnamon in it, too. It helps curb your appetite."

Melissa pokes me under the table, even though I already know not to roll my eyes or scoff or in any way express my (perfectly valid) opinion about fad dieting.

"Now, Melissa"—Connie hovers at the head of the table—"I'm sure you're upset, but this is not about you or your summer. It's about Ellen. I'm sorry."

"Wait," I start, "you're apologizing to—?" Melissa shoves her coffee at me to cut me off.

Damn it, the coffee is delicious.

"I totally understand," Melissa says. "I just wanted to talk with you and Mr. Rourke."

Connie glances into the hallway. "He'll be ready in a minute, but I really don't think—"

"I'm ready now," Dad's voice calls from the bedroom, "but if I have to handle a negotiation, I need time for the coffee to kick in first."

"Perfect." Melissa steals her coffee back and takes a huge gulp. "Ellen's going to get dressed, and then we'll be back down. Five minutes." She drags me out of my chair and nudges me past Dad, who walks into the kitchen with his tie crooked and his hair and shirt rumpled. Despite years of office work, he's about as much of a morning person as I am.

Connie clangs dishes downstairs as we enter my room. The temptation to crawl back into bed is strong, but Melissa shoves me toward the closet and vaults over my dirty laundry pile to land in my desk chair.

"So that went well."

"How do you always do that?" I ask as I dig through the clean laundry pile (also known as the closet floor). "Get parents to . . . you know."

"It's not that hard to get what you want if you ask for it. Besides, you're not grounded. It's the first day of punishment, and they're already softening. They don't have the ovaries to stick with this."

"It's too early for you to be this optimistic," I mutter, pulling on a clean shirt and shorts and leaving the closet to flop onto my bed.

"It's not optimism; I know what I'm talking about. They're going to back down, because we're going to give them something they want. The thing your dad is always forcing you to do when you'd rather be reading and interneting your days away."

I pull my blanket off the floor. "Oh, exercise?"

"Bingo!" Melissa taps my nose like I'm one of the preschoolers she babysits. "Your dad wants you to lead a healthy lifestyle, and he doesn't really want to ground you. It's a win-win."

"So . . . we're going to join a gym?"

"What? No." Melissa shakes her head like she's so disappointed in my deduction skills. "Quidditch."

I guess I should have known.

"Are you thinking of going pre-law next year?" Dad asks Melissa after she's laid out her vision. He makes that hiding-a-smile face that annoys the crap out of me, because I can tell that he's imagining me and Melissa twelve years old with pigtails and braces.

But I don't let the attitude leak onto my face, because Melissa has already gotten Dad to agree to let me out of the house for quidditch practices on Sunday mornings and Wednesday afternoons, workout sessions with Melissa, and "occasional social events deemed necessary for team bonding, including, but not limited to, team dinners post-practice."

(Melissa's words. She came prepared.)

"I'm not sure what I want to major in yet." Melissa smiles sweetly. "Lots of things interest me. But law is a definite possibility, especially considering how much you enjoy it, Mr. Rourke."

She's a brilliant magical unicorn of a suck-up.

It's annoying how Connie keeps filling up Melissa's coffee and Dad raises his eyebrows and nods while Melissa talks—not one of his listening tricks, but actual respect. He's impressed by her.

I'm glad my family likes Melissa, but I wish they wouldn't be so obvious about liking her more than me.

"So let's talk about my terms," Dad says, leaning across the table. He folds his hands and draws his eyebrows together, and it's nice to see his lawyer face. Lately he mostly comes home with his exhausted face on.

"We are prepared to hear you." Melissa practices a little lawyer face of her own.

"One." Dad ticks up a finger and points it at me. "We get verbal or text-message communication every time you leave the house. Where you're going and for how long."

"Done," Melissa says immediately, cutting off my indignant sigh. In what world does a high school graduate need to be constantly cyber-stalked by her stepmom?

Dad waits.

"Oh, yeah, done," I repeat when I realize he wants me to say it.

"Two: if you abuse the system, it's over. No three strikes. And the phone is a privilege that we will take away if we have to."

"We're not going to lie about having practice," I say. Melissa shoots me a warning glance. "I'm just saying. We don't need a strike system."

Connie glares at me. Dad waits. Melissa raises an eyebrow.

"Yes, okay, done."

"Great. And of course, number three," Dad says. "The chore list stays."

"Yeah, I figured—I mean, done. Is that all?" I try to ask with a smile so I don't ruin Melissa's hard work.

Dad looks at Connie. Connie shifts from one foot to the other. Dad nods.

Melissa shoots up from her seat to stretch a hand across the table. "Deal?" she asks.

"Deal," Dad says, shaking the hand. "And you've officially made me late for work. Why don't I walk you out, Melissa, since there's no quidditch practice today?"

"Of course." She smiles and finishes her coffee. It's not that hard to get what she wants.

WHEN DAD GETS HOME, I'M HIDING IN MY ROOM WITH A peanut-butter-sandwich dinner. After a morning spent cleaning out the fridge and helping Connie take furniture measurements for her future studio (also known as my room), followed by an afternoon helping Yasmín finish her Fun with Triangles! worksheet, I'm perfectly content catching up on webcomics and hearing Melissa's babysitting horror stories told through exclamation points and emojis.

Xiumiao still hasn't responded to my text. She and her parents left for their camping vacation yesterday, so it could be a phone service issue. Or, honestly, sometimes she's just not great at responding to messages. I try not to care, every time my phone buzzes, that it isn't her.

Dad fake-knocks, and I fake-smile.

"Hey, kiddo." Dad leans against the doorway, so I don't think I'm in danger of getting a talk. "I hear the day went well."

An *I* statement, but not a discussion. He's not asking me how I felt today.

"Yeah, fine."

"I wanted to say . . ." Dad hesitates, runs his hand through his hair. "Melissa put up quite the fight. That's a good friend you've got there."

"I know." I try so hard not to hear the compliment as a comparison.

Dad frowns and walks into the room to pat the top of my head. "What's worrying you, Jelly?"

"Nothing." There is no logical reason for me to be so soothed by the silly nickname, but it must be some kind of special Dad magic. "You know, I've seen you argue much tougher than you did today. It's almost like you wanted to let Melissa win."

Dad laughs. "What can I say? I've never been great at the punishment part of the dad gig."

I almost ask, *Why do it, then?* But I know the answer. Connie.

When I roll my eyes, Dad laughs. He's happy now, and I can't help noticing the shallowness of it. He just wants to come home and have everything be peaceful. My laughter turns bitter.

"Hey, I used to hate authority once, too, kiddo."

Okay, I do not "hate authority." I just hate certain authority figures who hate me.

"Yeah, yeah, you became a soulless lawyer to save the world from injustice, right?"

"When I remember why I became a soulless lawyer, I'll let you know. In the meantime, I'm going to see about some ice cream—or Rice Dream—before bed. Want to join?"

I guess I'm really Dad's daughter, because I find comfort in the shallow cheerfulness. I don't want to upset the fake peace. Plus, I've never been known to turn down my favorite rice-based vegan dessert substitute. "Sure, but enjoy it while you can. I can't go around scarfing ice cream once I'm an athlete."

Dad laughs. His favorite Mom story involves a surprise ice cream sundae date that was totally ruined by the fact that she had a soccer game in an hour.

"Quidditch player," Dad corrects me. "Let's save 'athlete' for now, until we see just how much of this sport is imaginary. I'm still not clear on how you're supposed to fly . . ."

7

"You're back!" Karey waves and smiles hugely for someone I met once for half an hour at most. I guess team captains have to act like weird friendship vacuums, sucking people into actually showing up for practice.

I smile back, more excited than I expected to be. To be fair, it's my first official post-grounding outing, and I'm excited not to be in the house.

We're late, so the hoops are already set up and everyone's in a circle stretching. Melissa, Chris, and I dump our stuff at the Practice Tree, join the circle, and bend to touch our toes. Ow.

Standing in the center of the circle, Karey counts the

odd numbers, and we count the evens. We do arm and leg stretches, shoulder and neck rolls, some weird cross-legged push-up that's supposed to stretch our calves but mostly kills my arms. Morning practice was supposed to beat the sun, but I'm not feeling any fresher just because it's ninety as opposed to one hundred degrees.

"Ellen, right?" Karey approaches me after we finish stretching and take a much-appreciated water break. "I'm sorry you had to leave early last time, but I'm really glad to see you again. You were going to try beating, I think?"

"Yeah." I shrug. "Sorry about leaving. My parents . . ." I grimace at the grass.

"Ah, parental disappointment. I know how that goes." Karey's wry grin is oddly inviting. I guess team captain friendship vacuums get their jobs because they're good at making people like them. Or maybe I just feel cool associating with someone who ripped the sleeves off her T-shirt.

"Well, like I said, super happy to have you," she tells me. "I'm sending you and the other new beaters—we have a few more today, which is awesome!—over to do some practice drills with John and Lindsay." She points out two of the players who have already started ambling toward the far set of hoops, both wearing black headbands and holding PVC pipes between their legs. "They'll give you the more complete strategy talk, but—hey, Roshni."

She gestures at a girl standing nearby. "Come listen to this, too. Basically y'all will be playing dodgeball with the opposing team. Peg any of them, and they're temporarily out. People who are out can't score. Any questions?"

About a million, starting with *Why is it so freaking hot? What am I getting myself into?* And *Am I going to look that awkward mounted on a fake broomstick?*

"No."

The dark-haired girl (Roshni) and I take final swigs of water and head for the far hoops. I hear Karey giving a similar welcome-back speech to Melissa, explaining where she should stand to do chaser drills. Then she raises her voice and calls to all the dawdling players, "Okay, break's over, people. Let's see those smiles! We're playing quidditch, y'all!"

I do smile, if squinting into the sun behind our trio of hoops counts. A few of the old players overtake me, sprinting to join a game of catch. When I reach the beaters, Lindsay, a redheaded girl with round freckled cheeks, starts handing out black headbands. There aren't enough to go around, so Lindsay pulls her black-and-pink-striped bandana over her pigtails and hands it to me with an apologetic look. It's damp and smells like mildew, but I slide it over my head anyway.

"If it makes you feel better, I don't think ours are clean, either," Roshni whispers as she pulls her bandana under her ponytail with a shrug. Except for her dark skin and not-invisible eyelashes, she reminds me of Melissa—athletic and tall and oozing a certain lack of social anxiety that I can't help but envy. I grin back at her and try to think of something funny to say.

Lindsay pulls the new players aside and gives us a lecture very similar to Karey's. (*Grab ball. Throw ball at opponents. Run after ball. Repeat.*) Then she calls the veteran beaters back over to join us. The other beater captain, John, starts breaking people into pairs to practice throwing balls at each other. I recognize him as the guy who found my ringing phone at the last practice. Like Karey, he's wearing a sleeveless workout shirt, and, like Karey, he's got arms worth showing off, even if his whole white-boy jock attractiveness is about as generic as his name.

He pairs us up by height, or maybe by perceived ability. I'm standing between two tall athletic people, but I am sized up, evaluated, and partnered with a tiny veteran beater. Her name is Elizabeth, she's Latina with a long black braid reaching straight down her back, and even though she's shorter than me with no visible muscles, she has a predatory look in her eyes that makes me pretty sure she could take me.

Or maybe that's just the sports goggles.

Elizabeth grabs me a PVC pipe to hold between my legs. As soon as she does, I realize that all of Lindsay's and Karey's explanations failed to really address the whole riding-a-broomstick thing. I mean, I ran those laps at the last practice, which was awkward but manageable. But now I'm supposed to play catch—an already daunting task for my hand-eye coordination—while keeping track of this three-foot pole?

I try squeezing it between my thighs (a phrase rife with innuendo potential, I know), but my legs can't stabilize the thin PVC unless I cross them. So I stand there with my left hand clutching the broom, feeling absolutely ridiculous, waiting for Elizabeth to throw her dusty red dodgeball at me so that I can try to dodge it.

We quickly learn two things: (1) I am very bad at dodging balls, and (2) my balls are very easy to dodge.

In about ten minutes I'm sweaty and grumpy, and I've managed to skin my knee. There's a stinging red patch on my arm from one of Elizabeth's harder hits, and I'm dying of dehydration and heatstroke. I also really wish I had thought to use sunscreen, because my face and neck are starting to feel a little crispy.

Eternal grounding might actually be preferable to this.

Karey calls a break, and we gather in the blessed shade of the tree. I gulp water, wiggle through a group of chatting veterans, and shove past Chris to stand next to Melissa.

"How's it going?" I ask, scowling over my shoulder as Chris leans an elbow on my head just to prove he's tall.

"I scored a goal!" Melissa pours water over her head and shakes her ponytail. Of course she's loving this. She's the one who has been so excited to come to practice, the one who enjoys physical activity. She's the one who likes meeting new people. She's the one who belongs here.

But I'm going to have to stick it out. "Awesome!" I offer her a high five. If this is our only chance for summer bonding, I'm going to make the best of it. Maybe Karey needs a team water boy or bench warmer or cheerleader. Maybe I can be personal assistant to Melissa, quidditch superstar.

We return to our drills, some of us (me) more reluctantly than others (Melissa). Roshni switches to practice with the chasers, citing small hands and a desire to score. Lindsay and John show us new exercises, talking strategies and techniques that go way over my head. I practice trying to wrestle the ball out of Elizabeth's hands. I practice racing her to pick up a loose ball. I practice aiming while she sprints past me. I fail consistently, and I fail hard. Elizabeth doesn't let up for a second, though, which makes me like her a lot more than if she'd started going easy on me.

"Watch out," John calls when his ball bounces off Lindsay and rolls past me. I try to kick it toward him but miss, knocking it into my other foot instead. I stumble.

"Keep trying, newbie," John calls as he snatches up the ball one-handed and hurls it at Lindsay, ten feet away. It smacks solidly against her shoulder, and he winks at me before running away.

I don't know what to do with that wink any more than I know what to do with my broom or my bludger or my feet.

The drills, especially the wrestling, bring up another problem: endurance. More specifically, my lack thereof. It's not just the red welts up and down the inside of my legs or the ripped thumbnail or the now multiply skinned knee. My arms ache from grabbing, throwing, grappling. My legs shake from running and falling and standing back up.

The next water break doesn't come soon enough. Elizabeth gives me a silent nod, and Lindsay gives me an enthusiastic thumbs-up while I lean against the tree and down half my water bottle. Melissa has to find me this time, because I'm busy sliding slowly to the ground.

"Isn't this awesome?" she whispers while Karey reminds us about team dues and what they'll help pay for. I keep my mouth full of water so I have no chance to answer.

Karey splits us up into teams. We're going to do a scrimmage, apparently—a practice game. Melissa raises her eyebrows excitedly at me. I try to contain my overwhelming enthusiasm.

Chris dons a green headband and moves to one side of the field. Green means keeper, which is like goalie. The other keeper—"Carlos," Melissa whispers—is shorter than Chris but about twice as wide. He has the look of a football player with a black buzz cut and thick eyebrows.

Karey sends more players to each side of the field. One of the beaters, a white girl with calves that bulge like they're trying to escape her body, twirls her broom like a baton and sends it flying into the air a few times, catching it perfectly and dipping and spinning around with each catch. Her platinum-blonde bangs flop under her black headband as she twirls. I saw in practice how her aim with a bludger is just as precise as her baton skills.

"Ellen." Karey's voice calls my name, which surprises me because I thought for sure this would end with me getting picked last. "And, um, Ellen's friend . . . ?"

Melissa looks as shocked as I feel that someone remembered my name and not hers. Karey's in charge of a lot of newbies, and I'm sure it was just luck and possibly my awkwardness that made my name stick in her head. Still, I feel oddly encouraged as I walk to where Karey points us, the side of the field opposite Chris. Melissa shakes off the insult quickly, reintroducing herself and then sticking her tongue out at Chris as he talks very mild trash about our team ("Your team probably didn't shower today! . . . Our team is way better at Scrabble than yours!"). But she has a glint in her eye when she picks up her broom, and I get the feeling that she's going into this game with one goal: make Karey remember her name.

With the draft finished, each side has nine players. The veterans on my team encourage us new players to take a spot as one of the six starting players, but I offer to be a substitute instead. I want to watch at least the first few minutes of the game before I'm expected to play.

The starters line up in front of each set of hoops. Karey, Lindsay, and John line up one volleyball-quaffle and three bludgers in the middle. So I guess this works like dodgeball as well, where players have to race to get to the balls. I'm suddenly very glad that I didn't volunteer.

Melissa, who did accept a starting position, grins at me as she scoots forward on the instruction of Carlos, our keeper. From the sidelines Karey calls, "Brooms down!" and the players kneel.

The game begins on "Brooms up!"

It's utter chaos.

I immediately lose track of which players belong to which team, other than Chris and Carlos in their opposing green headbands, and of course Melissa. Balls fly in every direction, and bodies follow clumsily. For the first few minutes it seems like anybody who picks up the quaffle immediately drops it, and it takes me a while to notice that it's because they're all getting hit by the dodgeball bludgers. The Ninja Turtle–shirt boy I met last week—Jackson—spends several plays doing nothing but running forward, getting beat, and jogging sadly back to his hoops. Beaters, apparently, are pretty crucial.

I track Melissa as she runs back and forth across the field, which helps make at least some sense of the game. I follow a pass from Carlos to Roshni to Melissa, who is waiting unnoticed behind the opposing team's hoops. She throws her hand forward as Chris barrels toward her, long arms pinwheeling.

He doesn't even come close. Melissa puts the ball straight through the hoop.

I make a noise I probably haven't made since I used to watch WNBA games with Xiumiao in elementary. I believe it is called a "whoop," and it springs out of my mouth completely on its own. I even pump my fist. Sports are weird.

"Ha!" Melissa screams, throwing her hands in the air and jumping up and down. "I scored! I am unstoppable!"

"Off your broom!" Chris calls over his shoulder as he chases down the volleyball. "Go back to your hoops!"

Melissa's broom is up in the air, distinctly not between her legs like it's supposed to be, but Karey (our ref for the moment) waves her hand for Melissa to keep playing. "Newbies get warnings," she says. "If you can't handle your girlfriend scoring on you, quidditch isn't really your sport."

"He's going to learn the hard way why you don't bring your partner to quidditch," the baton-twirling beater whispers next to me. "Quidditch breakups," she explains when I raise an eyebrow. "They're, like, the most common off-pitch occurrence, second only to quidditch make-outs. We're all messy nerds who love drama here."

"Sub!" a voice calls. "Hey, beater sub! Sub!"

"You want to go in?" The baton twirler flips her bangs and points at the figure barreling toward us. It's John, the beater boy of the nice arms and the strange wink. He wants me to sub in, to take his place in the game. Right.

I pick up my broom and start to run toward him. "No!" John yells. "What are you— Get back on the sideline!"

I stop where I am. John runs to me, pushes me several steps back, and then exaggeratedly tags my hand.

"You can't just run onto the pitch," he snaps. "You have to wait for me to get out of bounds."

Excuse the fuck out of me, Mr. Perfect Substitution Police. So much for the arms. So much for the wink.

John had a ball—a bludger—that he dropped on the ground before tagging me, so I pick it up and jog toward our team's hoops. For a second I stand there, not really sure what I'm supposed to do. Beat the other team, right? Especially if they're trying to score, or if they touch a ball. I can do that. Turning to face the other side of the field where all the chasers and keepers crowd, I take a deep breath. I just don't want to make a fool of myself.

The other team takes possession of the quaffle, and all hell breaks loose.

Chris sprints down the field toward our hoops while at least four different people scream, "Beat him!" I run forward and try to hold out my ball, but I can't get a grip on the damn thing one-handed. Chris slows as he gets near me, Carlos sprints to get in front of him and tackles, and I know that I need to beat Chris now so I step forward. At least three people scream but I don't hear what they say because something has latched on to my ball.

That something is Elizabeth. The other team's beater.

I curl around the ball and drop, pulling her attacking arm down with me. This was our drill—wrestle for possession of the ball. I may not be the best at this, but at least I know my goal. And, I realize, I don't want to lose.

It's probably the heat affecting my brain or the embarrassment of failing all day. There is no logical reason for me to hang on to a playground ball coated in dust and sweat like my life depends on it, and yet here I am.

Sports are weird.

I keep both arms wrapped around the ball and cross my legs to keep my broom in place. People shout behind me, and Elizabeth calls "Beater help!" in my ear while she digs her hand into my ribs, trying to poke the ball away.

My strategy is simple: don't let go. I'm not really thinking this plan through, but suddenly a red rubber ball cracks against Elizabeth's arm and she climbs off me screaming curse words in what I hope is an expression of passionate frustration rather than actual hatred. When she reaches her hoops she turns and gives me a steely nod and a thumbs-up, so I think we're cool.

"Good job." Lindsay, the owner of the ball that saved me, the other beater on my team, smiles. "I was busy taking out the quaffle, but nice work keeping bludger control."

Bludger control? I look at the other team's beaters. They only have one of the three bludgers in play. We have two. Advantage, us.

I smile back. Maybe everyone else already knew this, but doing a good thing in a sports game makes you feel good.

"Isn't this amazing?" Melissa asks again when I sub off the field and flop onto the grass beside her, nursing new welts and scrapes.

And this time I nod.

8

"Oh my gosh," Melissa sighs as we pull away from Chris's house and crank up her car's crappy A/C, "I'm dead. I'm so dead."

"I'm dead," I agree. "Every muscle in my body is dead, and now I'm a ghost with noodle arms."

"Did you see my goal?" Melissa pumps her fist in the air and slams her car to a stop halfway through an intersection. "I am the best chaser that has ever lived! I am Harry Potter!"

"Harry isn't a chaser," I remind her.

"I am Katie Bell!"

"You are the most awesome chaser," I assure her,

examining the scraped skin of my knee. “Your goal was epic.”

“I saw you rolling on the ground a lot.” Melissa smiles. “That’s good, right?”

“I’m not sure.” I noticed that Lindsay and John spent less time fighting for balls and more time hitting opponents. I think the best that can be said of my performance is that I’m still willing to come back next time.

“You are Harry Potter! I mean, um, who’s a beater? The Weasley twins. Shut up; I’m too tired to remember book trivia.”

I pull a leaf out of Melissa’s ponytail and shake my head to dislodge my own shower of dust and debris.

“Thanks, dude.” Melissa gropes one-handed for her water bottle and takes such a large gulp that she swerves out of her lane. “I told you it would be fun.”

“If you consider death fun.”

“Come on, just admit that I am always right and I’m the best.”

I don’t say anything, but I don’t really have to. Melissa knows.

The downside of morning practice is that there’s still a whole day of chores to do once I get home. Connie immediately sets me on the garage project.

"Get started while I finish here," she says, adding two capfuls of bleach to the full sink while I scarf down a granola bar. "I'll be out in a minute. I'll show you the curtains I'm considering so you can tell me what you think."

"No rush," I say, ducking out the back door. "I got it."

Connie likes to talk about the potential of the garage, but right now it's mostly a potential fire hazard. Even walking in feels dangerous. Dad is a bit of a hoarder, so each step is a minefield of precariously stacked nostalgia. I find it kind of comforting that all the pieces of our past stay tucked away here, but Connie has been bugging Dad for years to clean it out. I guess she finally won with the idea to rent the space, or he just gave in to make her happy.

Connie's plan for the week is to divide up the big pieces of furniture: one pile in the garage for "salvageable," one in the driveway for "trash."

The first thing I hit is a rocking chair with only one intact rocker, the seat covered in questionable brown stickiness and cockroach carcasses—definitely not salvageable. My arms ache as I try to shift the chair out from under the rolled-up air mattress lying across it.

Maybe I should start with something smaller.

The whole job would be a lot easier if the garage door worked. For almost a year now it's been sticking just a few feet off the ground. So instead of pushing furniture straight out, I'm supposed to maneuver it through the tiny door to the backyard, then through the gate to the driveway.

I have this theory about me and Connie. I know that it's more paranoid than logical, but I still can't shake the feeling that Connie would like me a lot more if I were a cis boy. She would expect different things of her stepson, things that feel more manageable, like opening jars and threatening Yasmín's bullies instead of wearing makeup and having emotional intelligence. I mean, realistically I would probably end up annoyed at those expectations too, because I'm not a big fan of the binary in general and I don't think I am or want to be a boy. Is it normal to want both, or neither? Would I even worry about any of this if it weren't for Connie?

Maybe it's completely unfair to blame someone else for my gender feelings. But how am I supposed to know if I'm uncomfortable with my capital-G Gender or just with the way people treat me because of it. Or is that the same thing?

Dad wouldn't expect imaginary dude-Ellen to form a tight mother-daughter bond with his stepmom, so he would never fail miserably. He would have already fixed the garage door months ago, probably. I don't know exactly what it says about me, but I want to live up to his imaginary example.

I climb back to the doorway to punch the garage door

button. The light blinks and the motor grumbles and the door rises about a foot and a half, at which point it squeaks and shudders and everything stops.

I press the button again; the door descends smoothly. Again—the same abrupt stop.

I shift all the big furniture away from the door, figuring it might be catching on something. I don't make a very graceful figure, panting and kicking and cursing at the old bookshelves, but I manage.

The door, unimpressed by my efforts, still refuses to rise. A problem with the tracks, then?

I'm balanced on a rusty folding chair stacked on top of an old coffee table when Connie pokes her head into the garage. I don't stop inspecting the left runner (which bends around a crusted rust spot), but I nod and wave.

"Hey, can you hit the button? I want to see this up close."

Connie stares at me like I'm speaking an alien tongue. "What are you doing?"

"I'm trying to see if the door stops right here, because I really think the problem is . . ."

Connie crosses her arms over her chest and sucks her breath in loudly.

"I know I haven't gotten a whole lot done yet," I say quickly, looking around at the space that somehow looks more crowded than it did when I started, "but this will go so much quicker if I can take things out through the door, right?"

"Okay," Connie says, in a tone that clearly indicates that it is not. "I just came out here to tell you that I made lunch. I thought we could go over some of the design ideas to give you a break from . . . your work."

"Um, I'll come in there in a few minutes?" I don't trust that I can eat the lunch she made anyway.

Connie presses her lips together and leaves (without pressing the button).

I consider giving up and just moving furniture like I was supposed to, but I want to prove that I can do this. I check online for tips about garage doors, watch a few YouTube tutorials, get distracted by new trailers for musical movies. Before I know it, Connie's poking her head back into the garage, looking even more exasperated.

"I'm going to pick up Yasmín from camp. I'll leave you to . . ." She waves a hand, the disappointment plain on her face.

I'm not trying to get out of work. I honestly want to make this job easier. I peer at the garage ceiling, double-checking that there are no other rust spots on either runner, then head inside to arm myself. Now I really have to fix this.

I return to attack with WD-40, a Brillo pad, and an actual hammer in an attempt to scrape, smooth, and straighten out the runner. When I take a break to test the button, the door sticks about two inches higher up than before, and with a lot more squeaking and wiggling. Progress.

I scrape harder at the rust, flakes raining down on my face and the rough edges of the Brillo pad digging into my fingertips. I climb down, jab the button, watch the door creak, shudder, rise, falter . . . slide. It squeals past the rust spot and sails shakily up to the ceiling. It works.

Take that, Connie.

I head inside, grab two granola bars and a jar of peanut butter. Yasmín sits on the living room couch, her head buried in Connie's phone, so I flop down next to her.

Yasmín puts the phone down and looks at me, which is always unnerving because she has this stare that makes you feel like she is one hundred percent focused on whatever you're doing, even if you're just sitting like a lump of old oatmeal, getting dust and sweat on the light beige upholstery. I sit up a little straighter.

"What's up, kiddo? How is math camp treating you?"

God, I sound like Dad at his most dorky. I didn't have a problem talking to Yasmín when she was a toddler who followed me around the house with a rotating bouquet of stuffed toys, or when she went through her pre-K hellion phase and came home covered in mud, but now . . .

"Are you in trouble?" Yasmín cuts straight to the point.

"I don't know," I answer honestly. "Did your mom say something?"

Yasmín shrugs. "No." She breaks eye contact as she says it (lie) and then returns to staring at me. "What's quidditch like?"

"Um, basically like it's described in Harry Potter." She's seen all the movies, read the first three books.

Yasmín tilts her head to one side. "You know you can't fly, right?"

How can I feel so intensely judged by such a small person? I nod.

Yasmín turns back to her phone. "Samantha from my camp says it's weird, but she never even read Harry Potter. It's not *weird*, right?"

I think about me and Melissa, running around with PVC pipes between our legs. I think of Karey's in-y'all's-face enthusiasm, Elizabeth's somber expression half hidden by sports goggles, Lindsay's sweaty headband. "What's wrong with weird?"

Yasmín thinks for a second before responding: "Weird is *weird*."

"Well . . ." Maybe I should leave well enough alone, but I can't pass up the perfect conversation opener. "'Weird' and 'normal' just depend on your viewpoint, right? I mean, at some point someone started throwing a ball at a basket, and everyone probably thought that was weird." Yasmín nods, but doesn't look entirely convinced. "So just because something seems weird by society's standards right now—"

I don't get to finish my (probably life-altering and ten-year-old-mind-blowing) point, because the tap-tap of Connie's heels cuts me off. She walks into the living room and winces at either the sight or the smell of me.

"What are you doing?" she asks.

I flinch, ready to defend my snack break, but Connie isn't talking to me. "You're not supposed to be playing, Yasmín, you're supposed to be using the flash card app." She glances at me. "Did you move any furniture?"

Damn. "Um, not yet, but—"

She doesn't wait for an explanation. "Well, it's too late now—I'm taking Yasmín to swim lessons, and I want the kitchen cleaned before dinner."

"I can go back out later . . ." My face burns, and I wish that I could avoid Connie's stare. I meant to get more work done. "I'm sorry."

Connie just shakes her head. "We'll try again tomorrow," she says, and her dismissal grates worse than a Brillo pad across my conscience. "Mija, are you ready to go?"

"Ellen's telling me about quidditch," Yasmín says. "And society."

If I had been telling her about homemade explosives, Connie couldn't look more nervous. "Come on, mija, go get your swimsuit and towel." She holds out her arms and ushers Yasmín away. *Run—don't walk!—away from the irresponsible teenager with an ideological agenda.*

I miss the days when I could fill in coloring books with Yasmín for hours and Connie would thank me for babysitting. I miss feeling like I knew how to exist in my family without setting off everyone's alarm bells.

The worst part is the voice in the back of my head, reminding me that I messed up my one job. Telling me that maybe Connie's not evil or unfair or mean. Maybe she's right.

With both Connie and Yasmín gone, I prop my feet back up. "I fixed the door," I whisper.

It doesn't come out sounding very victorious.

SEVERAL THINGS HAPPEN WHEN I GET OUT OF MY EVENING shower to make my shitty day a lot less shitty.

First, I find a red-and-purple bruise the size of a strawberry on my knee, and a longer green one running up my right ankle where I kept kicking myself with my left foot. Also a couple of little maroon ones scattered on all the pointy bits of my elbows.

I can't remember the last time I had a bruise. The ones I do end up with are usually what Dad and I call amnesia bruises. The "How did this happen?" blue spot on your shin that shows up two days after you've forgotten about bumping into the coffee table.

When I was little I climbed trees and chased pigeons, got into a couple of bad block-throwing fights (my post-Mom acting-out stage, we think). Dad didn't kiss the injuries; instead, he would sit down and ask me how they happened. I acted out the whole story while he listened, nodding along. He would pull me into his lap and explain how the cells in my body were already hard at work repairing the damage. He told me that I was a complex machine designed with well-tuned strategies to handle bumps and bruises, that I was strong, that I was healthy, that I would heal. Then we'd slather me with arnica, and Dad would tell stories of my mom using it after her soccer games.

I always felt good after showing Dad my bruises.

I feel good now, knowing that every black-and-blue spot is proof of strength. I dig some arnica out of my bathroom drawer and let it soothe the aches.

The second good thing is that Xiumiao finally answers my messages.

Hey, we're back. You're not still screaming, are you?

Then she sends me a link to a YouTube parody of *Les Mis*. Which doesn't mean she's changed her mind about avoiding Melissa and me, but it does mean that she isn't intentionally ignoring me. This makes me happy, but it also makes my pettiness rise to the surface. I close the window, refusing to answer the text immediately.

The third good thing is that while I'm staring at my phone deciding how to answer Xiumiao, a pop-up notification informs me that Karey has added me as a friend on Facebook.

I accept Karey's friend request and check out her profile. Facebook's pretty hit or miss for getting to know people—nobody really acts like themselves on a platform where their extended family might see—but it's usually good for basic info. I mostly have mine to see what's up with Aunt Mal and Connie's extended family, and to message people.

Karey's Facebook looks pretty active, though. In her profile picture she's dressed as Columbia from *The Rocky Horror Picture Show*. Her timeline is plastered with quidditch—links to tournament recaps posted by people whose profile pictures all seem to include brooms or hoops, photos of the A&M team posing with various trophies. It's weirdly fascinating to scroll through.

Right as I start getting the first pangs of Facebook creeper guilt, a new message pops up in the corner of the screen. Melissa's goofy selfie profile picture sticks its tongue out at me, and I read:

Melissa: Did Karey friend you, too?
Ellen: Dude, I'm stalking her *right now*!
Melissa: Obvs.
Ellen: I love you.

With Melissa's validation, I happily return to stalking.

Between all the quidditch there are Tumblr links, posts about the most recent police shootings, a comic making fun of sexism on dating websites.

Melissa: Can I pleeeease be her when I grow up?
Ellen: I know, right?

I'm about to move on with my life, confident that Karey embodies everything I want in a leader of my summer activities, when I spot the name of the group Karey keeps posting to: International Quidditch Forum.

This I've got to see.

I click the link and find myself transported to unfamiliar internet territory. Here be dragons, metaphorically and also literally depicted on the jerseys of several quidditch teams. In between photos, cascades of questions and comments about quidditch gameplay and equipment fill the group, posted by people from England, Brazil, Turkey, and China. Someone from Louisiana explains their team's new strategy, and a New Yorker argues the effectiveness. There are mentions of a rulebook, a referee committee, a snitch certification exam.

I haven't been this shocked since I discovered fanfiction.

My first ridiculous impulse is to call Yasmín up here. See? This is a real thing that real people do—apparently all over the world. I scroll past teams named after obscure Harry Potter creatures and spells, past Doctor Who references and Pokémon puns and pickup games with Disney themes. A smile spreads across my face.

Ellen: Dude, have you seen this forum? It's unbelievable. I love it.

Melissa: She dressed as McGonagall for a costume party. Who dresses as McGonagall? Only the MOST AWESOME people dress as McGonagall!

Ellen: Huh? What are you talking about?

Melissa: Karey. What are you talking about?

I send her the link to the quidditch page.

Ellen: There's a whole community of these people.
Melissa: Of *us* people.

I reserve judgment on that, but continue scrolling the forum like an anthropologist at a dig site.

Melissa: I'm sending this to Xiumiao. She can see what she's missing.

Ellen: Oh, let me. I'm already talking to her.

It's a lie, since I haven't answered her text, but a well-intentioned one. I don't think that your crush trying to coax you into joining their favorite new activity is good for the whole recovery thing. I go ahead and send the link to

Xiumiao, along with a quick explanation: Still screaming, but only internally. My parents grounded me forever, I guess, except to play quidditch. Which is a whole thing.

I thought your dad didn't believe in grounding? Xiumiao answers after several minutes, which I definitely don't spend chewing my nails and waiting for a response. Did you murder someone? Did you chew up all of Connie's shoes as a power move? Did you perform La Vie Bohème on the kitchen table?

I really wish I had done something like that (well, not the murder one). I also really wish Xiumiao had been more responsive when I desperately needed her twisted sense of humor. I start typing my paragraph-length response, but I'm interrupted by another text from her.

Hang on, FaceTiming one of my new roommates for next year. I've been chatting with her, and she seems awesome. Later.

I drop my phone into my lap and lean back against my pillows. I could still send my wall of text, for whenever Xiumiao has time to answer. But apparently she's "been chatting" with her roommate while she ignored me for her whole vacation. There wasn't a problem with phone service, just a problem of not wanting to talk to me.

Whatever. She isn't the only one who's moving on. I've got an international network of quidditch players to befriend.

Ellen: Seriously, did you see there's a team from Uganda?

Melissa: ☺ Did I tell you this was going to be great or what?

9

I work on the garage the next few days and manage to drag about half the big furniture out. It shouldn't really take that long, but I'm slow and sore and easily distracted by my phone, and Connie manages to catch all of my unauthorized breaks. Dad gives me a half-hearted lecture, but I think he's at least a tiny bit pleased with the working garage door.

I should work harder. I don't mind the chore, really. Sweating through my tank tops or dodging crawling insects or fighting creaky furniture is all bearable as long as Connie stays inside.

• • •

Wednesday evening brings another taste of freedom in the form of quidditch practice. Karey waves when we pull up and gives Chris a high five and affectionate head rub for his recruitment skills now that Melissa and I are "becoming regulars."

"Is that a good thing?" I ask under my breath.

Elizabeth, who's adjusting her sports goggles next to me, snorts softly. "For the team it is," she says. "We need fresh blood. For you, hopefully also yes. For Chris, we'll see. We tried to warn him about quidditch dating."

"Yeah, someone was telling me . . ." I search for the baton-twirling beater with the bangs and nod in her direction.

Elizabeth snorts again. "Erin was warning you about dating teammates? Ironic."

I'm not saying I am a messy nerd who loves drama, but I do perk up a little at the promise of gossip.

"Erin, okay. I still barely know anyone. And who's that guy in the hat?" The baton twirler has a beater friend, a pale skinny white boy with a baseball cap who's looking very comfortable leaning his head on her shoulder. "Are they a thing? Is that the irony?"

Elizabeth shakes her head. "Your guess is as good as anyone's. Erin and Aaron have been off and on so many times nobody can keep track."

"They have the same name?" I ask. "That must get confusing when they play together."

"Confusion is their whole thing. They thrive on it." Elizabeth sips her water. "Let's hope it works out better for your friends."

DURING SCRIMMAGE, I BEAT WITH LINDSAY. AT "BROOMS up!" she knocks out both of the opposing beaters—Erin and Aaron. She kicks me a bludger before chasing down her own, and from then on she's everywhere at once, knocking chasers out with soft sneaky shots that don't send her ball flying out of reach. When I lose my bludger to Aaron's tackle, she's already there pegging the thief and returning my ball. I learn that it's easy to hide my confusion when I'm playing with a partner who's so on top of her game.

Lindsay's still going strong when I sub out, breathless. For some stupid reason (the reason is society), I didn't expect that—I guess I thought you had to be, well, skinny to be athletic. Lindsay's muscles don't disrupt the soft lines of her arms and stomach, but they show in her speed, her endurance, and her powerful sniper shot. I watch her barrel down the field with her broom held solidly between her thighs, both hands out to grapple with Erin, and feel an unexpected wave of purpose. I need to work out.

"Having fun?" Karey asks as I chug from my water bottle.

"Yeah, I love playing with Lindsay. She's way too good!"

"Game sense," Karey explains. "Lindsay played chaser for two years before she switched, and she's done some seeking and snitching, too. She knows what every person on the pitch is thinking, and she reacts fast. She and John are my coaching and strategy masterminds—I like the organizational team captain stuff, but I don't love designing plays. Lindsay does. She's kind of a treasure."

"Yeah, the new beater needs to coordinate with her more, though." John ambles up and joins our conversation, giving me another wink that clashes with his lecturing tone. "You made Lindsay work too hard." Karey opens her mouth like she's going to tell him to stop being an ass, but he holds up one finger, points it at me, and asks, "What were you doing that didn't work?"

I'm caught off guard by the reasonableness of the question. He sounds like a teacher, or I guess like a coach. Not just an ass.

"I think I should throw my ball less?"

I regret saying it as a question instead of a statement. I don't want to sound unsure.

"Why?" John doesn't say right or wrong, which I like. Karey subs back onto the field, joining Melissa's chaser team. The two of them sprint for a fast break, but Lindsay shuts the play down by running straight at them, bludger brandished in front of her, forcing them to stop and consider their options.

"If I throw the ball, I either hit or I miss, and then I don't have the ball anymore, and I can't do anything until I get it back." It all looks so simple when Lindsay does it.

John takes a long sip of water, shaking damp curls out of his eyes. "Yeah, kind of. Obviously you don't want to be afraid to release, because if you never throw at all, the other team is going to figure out that you're not a threat. But you threw your bludger away on some pointless plays."

I bristle, even though I know he's right.

"What you really need to work on now is your trick move—your pump fake," John says. He lunges at me, one hand swinging toward my face, stopping midair only after I've flinched away. He raises his eyebrows and gives a cocky grin, which makes me realize how close he's standing. "Practice making it *look* like you're going to throw, and then you won't have to."

"Sub!" Lindsay calls, and John tips his headband at me and waits on the sideline until Lindsay is all the way off the pitch before running in to play. I roll my eyes at his perfect substitution.

"Good job," Lindsay gasps, patting me on the shoulder. "We kept control forever out there."

"Thanks to you," I say, but the compliment makes me grin.

"Still," Lindsay starts, but she interrupts herself with a click of her tongue, her eyes glued to the pitch. "No, stay on the quaffle," she whispers, and then as Melissa and Chris charge toward the goal she shouts it, "John! Quaffle!"

The advice comes too late for John, far to the right of the hoops, fighting with a tiny blonde blur that is Erin. Chris speeds through our defense and scores easily. Lindsay shakes her head and clicks her tongue again. "Oh well, chasers could've stopped him."

"You would've been there, though," I guess.

"I tend to prioritize defense." Lindsay shrugs. "There are advantages and disadvantages. John's great at making space for the chasers on offense—he used to play soccer and football, so he's trained to find those openings. He just gets tunnel vision when someone challenges him."

This game has a lot more thinking than I realized. I smile, watching Elizabeth sub in and attack John's ball, trying to pull him away from the center of the pitch again. It's strategy. Beaters are all about strategy and being in the right position. It's like chess. Or, better yet, it's like Connect Four, which Dad and I used to play all the time when I was little. He bought me a set as soon as I learned to tie tic-tac-toe consistently, promising me a game that was harder to solve.

I think I could play quidditch forever and never solve it.

• • •

We vote on the location for team dinner while I negotiate a curfew with Dad through text.

"We pretty much cycle through the same three places," Chris explains to Melissa and me, "because Carlos can't eat wheat and Aaron can't eat meat that isn't kosher, and nobody wants to drive very far. But vote for the vegan-friendly place."

I worry that the vegan-friendly Pine Café will be out of my price range (which is the twelve bucks and some quarters I have in my wallet). But when Melissa parks in front of the tiny restaurant in the tiny strip shopping center, the counter service and cheap plastic chairs put me at ease. The menu, which is all vegetarian and clearly marks vegan dishes, make me feel downright welcome.

"I can't believe I didn't know this place existed," I say as we approach the counter.

Melissa sighs loudly behind me because this restaurant does not cater to her love of consuming animal flesh (even though she agrees that the food industry is pretty messed up . . . she hasn't given up bacon).

The little old lady behind the counter looks just as excited to have us as Melissa is to be here. Fifteen or so rowdy teens probably aren't her ideal customers. Plus, and I say this with all the love and delicacy in the world, some of us really stink.

We push tables together in the back corner while the rest of the team orders, and I slide into the seat between

Jackson and Lindsay, across from Melissa, Chris, and Karey. The food comes out quickly, and as our flustered servers try to match plates to people, I catch Melissa's eye across the table and sing-whisper, "So that's five miso soup, four seaweed salad, three soy-burger dinner, two tofu-dog platter—"

"And one pasta with meatless balls!" Beside me, Lindsay joins in to complete the line from *Rent*'s best musical number. She holds her hand up for a high five, and I get that rush of excitement that comes with meeting a fellow musical nerd. "I always get that song stuck in my head when we come here."

"I mean, isn't that why we love this place?" Karey asks, her grin crooked. "Meatless balls?"

"I feel like you need that on a bro tank," Lindsay teases. "Karey Yates: No Meat, All Balls."

"Please, no more balls," Jackson sighs on my right, poking his noodles with exaggerated sorrow. "I've had enough balls for one day, thank you very much. I am completely balled out." His shirt today is Power Rangers, and it's streaked with dirt and grass. Poor kid seems to be a magnet for tackles and face-beats.

"You just need to get comfortable with the balls." Lindsay shrugs and raises one eyebrow.

Jackson sputters for a second, until John appears behind him to clap him on the shoulder. "Sounds like Lindsay's offering ball-handling lessons. If I were you, I wouldn't pass that up."

Karey groans and Lindsay sticks her tongue out at John, her freckled ears maybe the tiniest bit pink.

I'm about to apologize for beating Jackson in the throat during drills today (probably contributing to his growing fear of out-of-control balls), but before I can, John drags a chair up between us.

"Scoot down," he instructs Jackson. "Make room, dude."

I scoot my own chair, but there's nowhere to go without climbing into Lindsay's lap, so I tuck my elbows against my ribs and lean away as John settles into the too-small space, his arms and knees spreading until I can feel his heat on my skin. Good thing he doesn't smell bad.

I hope I don't smell bad.

"Don't worry," Chris says, leaning as though to whisper in Melissa's ear but talking loud enough for everyone to hear. "You grow immune to all the ball jokes after a while."

"And the stick puns," John adds, his elbow finding my ribs and his eyebrows waggling.

"And scoring, obviously," someone calls from the opposite end of the group.

"The snitch snatch . . ."

"Dudes beating each other . . ."

"Making passes . . ."

"Okay, yes, we get it!" Karey yells. "Please, let's try not to scare the new people off this early in the summer, y'all."

Melissa and I grin at each other. Karey doesn't need to worry about us running scared from a little innuendo; we're from the internet.

Jackson breaks the lull with a cough. "Speaking of the sticks between our legs . . ." He fiddles with his fork. "I wanted to ask . . . am I the only one who has, you know, trouble? With the broom?"

The table explodes with laughter. I see some sympathetic nods and a few pained expressions, along with a lot of rolling eyes. John puts one arm around Jackson and starts explaining exactly what to adjust to fix the problem posed by a PVC pipe in one's crotch. A waitress chooses that second to ask if we're doing okay here.

"And then just kind of wiggle the broom forward until you're settled and—ow."

Someone wisely kicks John under the table, and the conversation drops as we dig into our food.

At the far end of the table, Erin with the platinum bangs steals Aaron's baseball hat as they discuss the merits and problems of wizard rock bands. Carlos and the other two muscled chasers I don't know because we never run drills together race to finish their combo platters. Karey and Lindsay launch into less graphic broom advice and John keeps twisting everything into a genital joke while I bury my head in my eggplant and try not to snort-laugh.

"Is it weird that this is making me feel better?" Jackson asks. John claps him on the shoulder.

Once the scarfing slows down, Karey calls for attention.

"Thanks for coming out, everyone. I just wanted to, you know, go over the schedule a little bit now that we're officially starting the summer. I mean, most of you know it's the off-season, so our main goal is to have fun and work on our skills, but of course we also want to train hard so we're ready to beat Katy . . ." At the name, Chris scowls and Lindsay and John growl in stereo in my ears. I wonder whether "Katy" means a person or the town just outside of Houston, and why everyone hates her or it so much.

"So first off, the League City team asked about doing a joint practice next Sunday. What do y'all say? Want to scrimmage against someone besides each other for a change?"

People nod and smile and offer carpools to get down to League City, a little less than an hour south of us. I'm left confused again, because I've never known of a team that made up their own schedules or debated when and whether they were going to play. For the first time, I really notice the lack of adults in this activity. Not that college students aren't, you know, technically legal adults, but . . . there's a huge difference between Karey asking what I want to do and Mrs. Blackmon, the choir director, telling me what time rehearsals will be.

"Vote," Karey calls, and I miss raising my hand for either "aye" or "nay" because I'm not sure if I'm allowed to travel to a different town, even one that's part of the greater Houston area. But the team does vote—almost unanimously—to play League City next week.

Melissa pokes me and raises one eyebrow (which always makes me jealous, because no matter how hard I try, my eyebrows only move in sync). I shrug back and then change my shrug to an enthusiastic nod when Melissa glares. I guess it's not enough to silently accept her silent offer to drive me down to League City next Sunday; I also have to be silently excited about it.

It just seems like a long way to drive just to do the same thing we do at Garvey Park.

"Maybe we can drive down together," Chris whispers to Melissa several seconds too late. I can tell he doesn't mean for me to hear him, but I do, and I know that I'm not included in his "we." Which worries me not at all (Melissa will honor our silent agreement), but does make me feel sorry for the lovesick guy. Annoyingdorable.

"Yeah, I figured we'd all drive down." Melissa speaks loudly, her breezy wave shutting down Chris's attempt at secrecy. "I have one more spot in my car," she announces to the table at large while Chris sighs and stabs his tofu.

"Two if someone wants to squeeze in the middle seat."

As a short, skinny, and usually accommodating person, I can predict that the someone squeezing will be me, so I cast a silent vote for three passengers only.

"I'll snag a spot, actually," Karey says. "If you don't mind. I don't want to have to negotiate car usage with my brother and sister, and plus the fields can be hard to find if you haven't been there before."

Chris sulks, but Melissa nods. "Fun!"

"And don't forget," Karey adds while everyone organizes cars, "there's the University of Houston mini tournament at the end of June, which is great because it's close and always awesome, and good practice for the Austin tournament in July."

The experienced players at the table give little whoops at the mention of this last event. Melissa, Jackson, and I stare blankly at each other.

"The Midsummer Flight's Dream Tournament." Karey offers these nonsense words by way of explanation. She hushes the chattering veterans and continues, "It's this big thing every year, a two-day tournament with all the Texas summer teams and some from Louisiana, and it's a lot of fun and you should all go, and I'll definitely give you more details about it as I get them, but right now all I know is that it's coming up and that it shouldn't interfere with any of the freshman orientation weeks."

I smile and nod along with everyone else, but I'm not too worried about the details, really. I'm not at all sure if I'm up for a three-hour drive to a full weekend of quidditch, and I'm even less sure that any part of that plan will pass parental approval stage, and it's all months away anyway. Who knows if I'll even still be playing quidditch by July?

But as I listen to Lindsay and Carlos swap stories about previous years' tournaments, it does sound like it could be fun.

Karey passes around a sheet for contact info as everyone starts clearing the table and milling around the entrance. I scribble my email and pass the sheet to Elizabeth, who spins me around to use my back as a writing surface.

"Thanks," she says when she's done. "Ellen Lopez-Rourke?"

Her tone and face are neutral, but my stomach drops as I glance down at my messy handwriting on the paper. Everyone has a comment when they see my name, and whether it's "Oh I didn't realize you were Hispanic" or "Why don't you use the accent on López?" it always feels like people are trying to weigh my heritage to file me into a mental box.

"Um, yeah," I say. "I know, the hyphen is so gringo. Er, gringa, I guess. Or . . ." My brain spirals and my face heats as I realize that I don't know the word "hyphen" in Spanish and have no idea whether it's a feminine or masculine noun, and maybe it doesn't matter anyway because maybe I should use a feminine ending because I'm talking about myself, but then that opens the whole can of gender worms lurking in my brain, and besides, plenty of Latinx people in the US *do* hyphenate their names so does anything I'm saying even make any sense at all?

"Oh, I just meant cool initials." Elizabeth taps the pen next to her own name. Elizabeth Lomas Ramirez.

Right. Social anxiety is a liar. "Oh, nice."

Elizabeth pops her earbuds back in her ears. I could take that to mean she doesn't want to talk, but I try to push past the social anxiety and ask, "What are you listening to?"

Which I immediately regret because there is nothing more awkward than failing to recognize someone's favorite music and having to smile and nod through their disappointment.

Elizabeth still isn't one for smiling, but her expression opens up a little. "Snow Tha Product?"

Nope, abort, shrug.

"Chicana rapper?" Elizabeth raises an eyebrow. "I figured you'd know her from the *Hamilton* mixtape."

"Oh! Wait, yes." I'm glad my musical geek brand is strong enough that Elizabeth knew about it.

Elizabeth takes the contact sheet back from Aaron and makes a new contact in her phone. "*Hamilton* saved my APUSH grade back in the day, but I promise rap and hip-hop exist outside of Broadway. You should listen to her other stuff. Can I text you some links?"

Which I'm pretty sure is a music lover's way of saying "friendship bonding accepted."

"Definitely."

I'M IN BED TRYING NOT TO NOTICE THE ACHE OF MY shoulders and knees when I get the text from an unknown number (not Elizabeth, who I have saved as The Other ELR now). Ellen, what's up? This is Chris. Got a second to answer a question? Nothing weird.

Even setting aside the extreme weirdness of the message, the use of both of our names in a text message proves that this is weird. Chris and I are in that middle ground of friendship, bonded mostly by proximity to Melissa and mutual dorkhood, but we don't text.

What's wrong? I text back, hoping he's not about to ask me to sneakily find a new ride to the quidditch game. I *will* tell Melissa on him.

No, nothing, I just wanted to ask you . . . He sends this incomplete sentence and then types for eighty-four years while I watch the dots. Is everything okay with Melissa and me?

I'm planning a snarky answer because it's late and my body hurts, but then Chris starts typing and deleting again, and I realize he must really be nervous.

We've talked about relationship stuff before, but only jokingly, in front of Melissa, at school. It's weird to realize that I won't see him at school anymore, that the days of effortless friendship are over. There are so many casual acquaintances that I've interacted with mostly on autopilot, and now I have to decide how to hang on to them or else let them go. It's weird and scary. Maybe I should have gone to graduation after all.

But my body still hurts, and I don't want to deal with this right now. Melissa hasn't said anything since that moment of doubt in the car, and usually she's very vocal with her boyfriend complaints, so I'm assuming she's gotten over whatever that was. I think everything's fine, I say. Why?

Great, the reply comes almost immediately. Thanks. A cartoon smiley face pops up on the screen and wipes its brow. I was just starting to get worried that Melissa was acting, you know, weird or something.

If by "weird" he means not as clingy as he is, I guess. But I type up a (hopefully) more helpful message: I mean, if you're worried then maybe you should talk to her?

Not that I'm any kind of expert, but that seems like consistently solid advice for a relationship.

Nah, nah. I trust your info, Chris says. Plus I know how the best friend code works, so I'm assuming you'll tell her I asked.

I send a winky emoji because, well, he's not wrong. I'm already typing the text to Melissa.

She responds pretty quickly: What does "weird" mean? Everything's fine. You can tell HIM to stop being weird.

I text back, Or you could talk to him yourself, since he's your boyfriend.

Honestly, how did I become the relationship expert for these two, or for anyone? At this rate, Melissa and I are never going to pass the Bechdel-Wallace test.

10

Melissa texts me Friday afternoon: Dude, want to run and do some sit-ups or something after I finish babysitting the Goldblums? Karey's posts of her ridiculous abs are making me feel inadequate.

I'm caught up with the day's light chore list, so I agree. I don't know if Connie decided to give me a break from the garage because it's Friday, or because she's been at a birthday party for Yasmín's new friend Samantha all day, or because of the substantial progress I've made due to my dedication to the project (haha, just kidding, it's definitely not that).

I've made a dent by removing a lot of furniture, but I have to admit I'm a little wary of the next phase: sorting through all the cardboard and plastic boxes that were hidden between the larger objects. Some of those boxes have been stored for decades, which means I'll have to deal with the inevitable unearthing of Mom-residue, packed like emotional landmines somewhere in the chaos. So I'm not complaining about the break.

I'm also excited about having the house to myself. Now I don't have to ask permission to leave for a few minutes. I check the living room and Yasmín's bedroom for stray dirty dishes and then run upstairs to change into running shorts before Melissa gets here.

The slam of the front door surprises me, and for a second I panic thinking that Connie will catch me and accuse me of sneaking out, but then Dad calls out, "Hello? Where are my girls?"

My face spreads into a smile. I hop to the top of the stairs with one shoe on and lean down to call, "They're out, remember? You're home early!"

"I am." Dad smiles up at me. "Are you going somewhere?"

"I was going to text you," I say quickly.

"Text me what?"

"That I was going to jog around the block."

"Oh," Dad says. "Did you do your chores?"

I nod, pulling on my second shoe, and join Dad at the bottom of the staircase.

“Okay, great.” Dad drops his jacket into its usual spot over the side table by the front door. “If you give me a minute to change, I can join you. We’re on our own for another hour or so, right?”

“Umm . . .” I bend down to retie the loosening double knot on my left shoe. “Yeah, but . . .” I don’t know why I’m hesitating. Dad isn’t Connie; he won’t freak out just because I made a plan without his input. “But Melissa’s coming over, so . . .”

“Ah.” Dad exhales in what might be a laugh or a sigh.

I stand up but keep staring at the floor. “I could tell her not to come. Technically it’s a grounding gray area.” I don’t want an excuse to blow off Melissa, but I miss non-disciplinary Dad. We hardly ever get to hang out.

Dad pats me on the back. “Oh, don’t worry about it, Jelly. I’m glad you and Melissa are being active, and I can entertain myself for a little while.” He scrunches his face in an exaggerated smile. “I might even enjoy the peace and quiet.”

I hesitate. Is Dad just being polite? Should I insist that I want to bond? Or is he actually relieved to get time to himself? Should I leave and give him his peace and quiet? My brain jams with uncertainty.

“Um,” I say. My phone buzzes in my pocket. Melissa is here. “Okay, I guess that works. If you’re sure. We probably won’t be long anyway.”

Dad's already heading into the kitchen. "Have fun."

It's completely irrational to feel disappointed. If anything, I should be glad Dad isn't mad. But I stare at his retreating back for a second anyway, until my phone buzzes again and I jump and run outside, slamming the front door shut behind me.

Waiting in the driveway, Melissa taps what I assume is another Hurry up! text on her phone. "Hey," she says when she looks up from the screen. "Ready?"

I shrug. "It's hot." The sun is sinking behind the trees, but the humidity presses against my skin. Melissa's shirt already shows dark spots of dampness from the short trip here.

"Welcome to summer," she says, sticking out her tongue. I guess I don't laugh enough, because she cocks her head. "Everything all right?"

"Fine." I shrug. "Just, you know, worrying that I push everyone away and that's why nobody loves me." If I make a silly face while saying it, then it officially counts as a joke, I hope.

Melissa slings a sweaty arm over my shoulder. "That can't be true, because *I* love you."

I smile, because I am a ridiculous person in constant need of sappy reassurance. "Thanks." I wiggle away and trot down the street toward the bike path. "Come on, slowpoke."

Melissa's phone buzzes and she stops following me to

pull it out, snicker, and type a response. I guess she wasn't texting me after all.

"Want to hear something that will cheer you up?" she asks, tucking her phone away.

"What?"

"Karey just sent us both invites to the secret message board for quidditch-playing feminists."

"The . . . what?"

Melissa stretches her arms over her head, yawns hugely, then breaks into a sprint past me, down the street, into the trees. "Come on, slowpoke! My muscles aren't going to define themselves!"

FORTY-FIVE MINUTES LATER I LEAVE MELISSA AT HER house and jog back home. I have to knock until Dad lets me in, because Connie and Yasmín got home and locked the door behind them. After a post-workout banana, I head upstairs and find the invitation Melissa described.

> **Karey Yates** has invited you to join the group:
> S.P.I.F.: Society for the Promotion of Intersectional Feminism (in quidditch).
>
> 3 friends in this group: Karey Yates, Melissa Larsen, Lindsay Trouble Young.
>
> **Join** **Reject**

I click. The Facebook group pops open, topped by a picture of quidditch hoops with crosses and arrows to look like the Venus, Mars, and transgender symbols. I click Description to expand the writing under the photo:

> A place to discuss gender disparity issues in the quidditch community. We love the sport but condemn the franchise. (Fuck TERFs.) Homophobia, transphobia, misogyny, and other forms of asshat behavior will NOT be tolerated. Yes, that includes racism and ableism, which are feminist issues. This group is private and is intended to be a safe space. Trolls will be banned.

I feel myself smiling even as I message Melissa the biggest question on my mind.

> **Ellen:** Okay, but, like, why?
>
> **Melissa:** Are you looking at the site?
>
> **Ellen:** Yes, obviously, and I'm asking "Why?"
>
> **Melissa:** Because it's awesome! And because the sport is coed, which raises problems, and someone has to address those problems. Just, are you looking at the posts?

I am not, actually, so I scroll down.

Sydney Porter

Thursday at 6:25 PM

Hey, Everyone! I'm trying to run summer pickup games, and there are a couple of rugby guys who showed up the first week and keep making jokes about how they're only here to pick up nerdy (desperate) girls. I think they think they're being funny, but the comments are making me and a bunch of other folks uncomfortable. How can I tell these guys that their behavior is inappropriate without scaring them away from the team entirely?

Argent Mcmillan

Wednesday at 12:13 PM

Yes, weekend fantasy tournament team, please keep using the term "female beater" in strategy sessions. That is *totally* accurate and inclusive because being a girl (which I'm still not!) is the whole strategy. Thanks.

Mariana Sanchez

Wednesday at 3:13 AM

There's another "debate" in the Northeast group about whether girls should be allowed to snitch at "important" tournaments. Can someone curb-stomp these assholes, please?

Lyla Bee

Sunday at 4:55 PM

First time reffing a game where no one called me a bitch or questioned my abilities based on gender! Progress?

Wow. I scroll through the comments on the posts, which range from sweet messages of love and support and "hang in there" to the kind of expletive-soaked rage I expect from Eevie on Environmentally Unfriendly. I follow a couple of good feminist blogs on Tumblr, and Eevie will address gender issues on the social justice side of xyr blog sometimes, but this site is a little different. First, everything is related to sports culture and quidditch, obviously. Second, everyone seems to know everyone else personally. Third, Karey is everywhere.

I pick out maybe five main commenters, the really active participants who have something to say about every post. Karey probably isn't number one, but she's on the list.

Karey Yates

Sydney, I think you should try pulling the rugby dudes aside and just telling them how folks are feeling. If they respond poorly, then you didn't want to keep them around anyway, right?

Karey Yates

Argent, come back to Houston! Also hope your fantasy tournament jerks step on Legos. (Also, every time I hear "female chaser" used as a position like "point chaser," I throw up a little in my mouth.)

Karey Yates

Mariana, there will always be jerkfaces who want to debate pointless things. Keep arguing louder, and keep signing up to snitch! You're always welcome at my tournaments!

Karey Yates

Woooo! *Applause for Lyla!* Can't wait to see you kick ass at the Midsummer tournament!

I bring my chat with Melissa back up.

Ellen: This is . . . weird and cool!

Melissa: Right?

Ellen: But also sort of sad? Like, sad that this has to exist. Sad that even quidditch players can't just be non-misogynistic nice people.

Melissa: Well, some of them can.

I laugh, and glance at the count of group members at the top of the page. Apparently some 435 quidditch players actively try to be non-misogynistic nice people. I guess that's not too shabby.

Melissa: I'm going to introduce myself. Want me to include you, or will you make your own post?

Ellen: Oh, um . . .

I'm in no hurry to break my lurking streak. I don't understand where Melissa gets the confidence to post online, talking to strangers openly about herself and her life. I'd always rather stay anonymous and invisible, an observer but not a commenter.

Ellen: I wasn't planning on it.

Melissa: Oh, should I not mention you at all?

Normally that would be my preference. But it's quidditch people, and they seem cool, and maybe I don't want to stay anonymous forever. Maybe I'd even like to get to know people from this group.

Ellen: No, that's fine. I don't mind.

My computer dings with a notification.

Melissa Larsen has mentioned you in a post in the group "S.P.I.F.: Society for the Promotion of

Intersectional Feminism (in quidditch)." Click to view.

Melissa Larsen

Friday at 8:15 PM

Hey, y'all! I'm Melissa (she/her). I'm new to the group, and I just wanted to say that the existence of this group is *super* exciting! Hooray!

(Also my friend Ellen is new, too. She is also excited.)

Ellen: Yay! . . . Now I'm anxious.

Melissa: You're welcome ☺

For the rest of the night, Facebook dings every few seconds with comments on Melissa's post, welcome messages and smiley faces and pictures of llamas and cats. It's all a little overwhelming, but each one makes me smile.

It rains on Saturday, so Connie postpones garage work again. I sleep late and bring my granola-bar brunch to the couch, where Yasmín is watching cartoons. I pull out my phone to see if Karey has posted any updates about the League City game tomorrow. What will we do if it rains?

Instead, my newsfeed shows me a post on the quidditch feminism group.

Nico X

Saturday at 11:15 AM

As an athlete and a feminist, I hate that sports culture tends to be so full of this bullshit. Someone needs to tell these assholes to act their age, not their shoe size. I know quidditch isn't perfect, but we are so far above what goes on in other sports with the gender rule and this group, and that gives me hope when I come across crap like this:

Link: College football coach: "If you didn't want to be harassed, why become a cheerleader?"

I know I shouldn't click the link. I know that clicking the link will only lead to rage and unhappiness. I know that it is too early in the day to click the link. But I click the link.

A few seconds later I throw my phone onto the couch with an exaggerated sigh. Yasmín frowns at me before turning back to the TV, and I sheepishly retrieve my phone. When I click back to Facebook, comments appear under the post. A few sad faces, a few eye rolls, and one comment that startles me.

Merrick TheGreat

As an athlete and a feminist *ally*

Since you've indicated in previous posts that you're straight, cis, and male.

I try to hold back a sigh. Part of the reason I don't post is because I don't want to deal with this sort of thing—the random reminders that everything you say is going to annoy somebody. As internet comments go, this is a pretty polite message. But still, it makes me sigh.

I send Melissa a message with a link to the post.

Ellen: I don't really get the "dudes can't be feminists" argument. Like, I get why they shouldn't get cookies or lead the charge or be invited into all the safe spaces, but . . . it's an ideology, not an identity.

Melissa: Oh, I thought we were looking at the article itself, which is gross.

Melissa: But yeah, boo to that noise in the comments, too.

Melissa: I'm going to say something.

I consider telling her not to, but I spend too long thinking and pretty soon another comment pops up under the post.

Melissa Larsen
I will never understand the "dudes can't be feminists" argument. I totally see why straight people have to be allies to LGBTQ+ causes and white people are allies for people of color, but "feminist" doesn't describe an oppressed group. Feminism is an ideology, so anyone who shares the ideology should be a feminist.

I gulp. Melissa is so much braver than I am. Fearless. Just reading her comment makes me sweat, because even if it's Melissa's name on top of the post, those are more or less my (paraphrased) words up there for anyone to see and tear down.

Merrick TheGreat
Wow, no one asked you to rescue the poor white guy. I thought we were going to screen out the baby feminists to keep the group free of their toxic bullshit.

Welp. This is why I don't comment.

On the couch next to me, Yasmín calls my name at least twice.

"Sorry," I say, pulling myself away from the train wreck on my phone. Already comments are popping up, some in support of Melissa, some piling on the hate. "What?"

"What are you doing?" Yasmín asks.

"Nothing, I'm just . . ." My phone chimes.

Melissa: Well . . . I stepped in it.
Ellen: sadface
Melissa: Ugh. Whateverrrrrrr. I kind of see their point, but I still think they're wrong. Which is basically the internet summed into one sentence.
Melissa: Not even worth it.

Melissa: I'm officially taking a Facebook break. Gotta go babysit anyway. Later.

I send back the most sympathetic gif I can find (a kitten offering a hug) and try to follow Melissa's advice by exiting Facebook. The angry comments still rattle around in my brain. I leave Yasmín alone to watch Garnet, Amethyst, and Pearl punch monsters while I head upstairs to better concentrate on the flame war in my palm. Karey and the original poster, Nico, and a few others try to shut down the anger, but enough comments spiral into insults and curse words. Ladies, gentlemen, people of all genders, I present The Internet.

"Ellen!" Connie's voice is too loud as she shouts from the kitchen, "Laundry!"

I don't move. I'm reading the cheerleading article again, even the comments, because the righteous anger I feel is less complicated than the in-group fighting.

"Ellen!" Connie calls again. "The dryer is finished!"

"Can you just—?" I tear myself away from the comment thread, spin away from my desk, and stomp downstairs. I know, sort of, that it's not Connie I'm mad at, but when I see her standing in the kitchen pointing helplessly at the dryer, I almost explode. "Can you give me five seconds? I was doing something."

I carry the dry clothes into the living room and dump them onto the couch for sorting and folding. Yasmín, smart enough to sense a storm, shuts off her cartoons and makes a dash for her room.

Connie joins me in front of the laundry pile, tugging out a towel and cracking it like a whip before folding it with quick, combative motions. "I'm asking for a little bit of help," she says, her voice dangerously neutral.

"I know I know I know." I say it with one breath, hoping to stop this fight before it starts. "It's not— I was looking at some things that annoyed me. Don't worry about it."

I stare at the laundry—at Dad's frayed Star Trek T-shirt and Yasmín's pink-ribboned socks and all the miscellaneous-sized breast cancer shirts—and wait for Connie to fold two more towels before finally reaching into the pile.

I make a line of Yasmín's skirts, too fluffy to get folded. Connie moves behind me and rolls them into neat little tubes. "Something wrong?" she asks.

I wish she wouldn't ask. I wish I didn't give her an opening to ask. There was a time when we did conversations like this, but now I'm afraid anything I say will be used as proof that I'm not keeping peace in the house.

I start a stack of my shirts. Connie stares at me.

"It's just . . . the world is crappy," I finally say. "People are crappy."

Connie looks like she's trying to hide a smile, which in my current state of irritation might as well be a lit match to my puddle of gasoline.

"What?" I demand.

"You're seventeen," she says with a shrug. "It improves, trust me."

I don't want to talk, don't care if Connie understands, but the words spill out of my mouth anyway: "I'm not talking about"—my hands fumble over Connie's yoga pants, and I let them fall back into the pile—"about some shallow high school drama. I'm talking about . . . injustice."

Connie's infuriating smile does not shrink. "Oh," she says, "I'm sure that improves, too."

I want to wipe the smirk off her face. "No, it doesn't! I'm talking about a society that demeans women and glorifies some macho hypermasculine ideal bullshit and . . . and fosters sexual assault! The world is fucked up! It's not just going to improve by accident!"

At each curse word (three, counting "sexual"), Connie's eyes flicker to the doorways to make sure Yasmín isn't lurking in earshot. She finishes folding one of her camisoles, lays it gently on top of her pile of sleepwear, and then sits down on the couch right in the middle of the folded and unfolded laundry.

"Okay," she says. "Why don't you tell me what this is all about."

After a few seconds, I sit, too, and try not to get completely distracted by the surprise of Connie listening to me.

"It's just, like," I say (eloquently), "this thing with this article from the feminist quidditch group—it's a thing; don't ask—and basically a football coach said some sexist stuff about cheerleaders and how they deserve to get harassed."

"Well, that sounds like a terrible coach," Connie says, but there's a question mark hidden in the tilt of her head. She doesn't understand why it bothers me, and I don't know how to explain if it doesn't bother her.

"It's just that I can't believe he could just say that, you know? Like, I guess I shouldn't be surprised. I know things are bad. But still, I just feel—"

"Bad how?" Connie interrupts. "I think we're a lot better off now than we were in the past, don't you? Feminism certainly didn't lose."

"Well, no, it's not . . ." I shake my head, trying to get Connie's statement to settle into something that makes sense. "It's not really a matter of losing. Or of winning. It's kind of, you know, ongoing. There's still a lot of work to do."

"There's work to do," Connie agrees. "But you don't do it by finding every little excuse to be angry. If those cheerleaders spend less time complaining and more time studying, they can become that coach's boss someday and deal with him."

"I mean, you shouldn't need multiple graduate degrees

and a lifetime of rising through the ranks of academia just to escape rape culture."

Connie frowns, and her eyes flick side to side. "What are you talking about? 'Rape culture'? That doesn't sound like something you need to be worrying about."

"But it is!" I stand up, a pointless gesture for a pointless conversation. "That's what all of this is. It's something I have to worry about because I'm going to college and I can't drink or go out alone or wear shorts or—or be a freaking cheerleader without someone deciding that I deserve punishment and—"

"I didn't know you wanted to be a cheerleader," Connie says.

"That's not the point."

"Well, what is the point?" Connie's lips press tight together, and she sucks her breath in before continuing, "Those things you're describing are just common sense—you have to keep yourself safe. You should know that; I taught you that."

"So you just think that doing all the 'right' things will protect individuals from a systemic problem? That doesn't work! That line of thinking is just—that's how we get victim blaming and . . ." My thoughts aren't forming logical sentences, but it doesn't matter because the front door crunches and creaks as Dad unlocks it, and I realize that I'm yelling, or at least that my voice has gotten loud, and

I can't get into trouble for fighting again, so I snap my mouth shut.

Connie and I both watch Dad walk into the living room and drop his briefcase on the coffee table. Loosen his tie. Yawn. Give Connie a peck on the cheek and pat my head. Connie may as well be wearing pearls with her heels and cooking meatloaf in her state-of-the-art microwave.

"Hey, what's going on in here? How are my girls?"

I shrug, hoping to gloss over my outburst. But instead, Connie sets her face into a worried half frown. "We were just talking," she says slowly, "about some of Ellen's . . . concerns. About feminism."

"Feminism?" Dad laughs in one loud burst, a single-syllable explosion of air. "Okay, let's talk about feminism. What's the big bad patriarchy up to today?"

I feel coated in ice, carved from marble, or just deeply, deeply exhausted. I don't know how to yell at Dad.

He sits down on the couch, barely seeming to notice that his weight topples one of Connie's stacks—her folded camisoles. She jumps up and rushes to move the offending clothes out of his way, then returns to folding.

I can't sit here and listen to Dad and Connie explain how feminism is obsolete and I'm too young to be thinking about these things and I shouldn't get so worked up. I should get worked up. They should get worked up.

"No, it's nothing," I tell Dad. "It's fine." That's what

he wants to hear. That's what he's willing to handle.

I grab my pile of T-shirts and underwear. "I'll go put these away," I say. Walking up the stairs, I hear Dad and Connie laughing, trying to be quiet about it.

Teenagers, they're probably saying.

I've never been so glad to have quidditch tomorrow. I really need to tackle someone as soon as possible.

11

Shoes! **Melissa's Sunday-morning text reads.**

Can you elaborate? I text back. It's nine in the morning, we don't have to leave for League City until three, and I just want to sleep.

Do not show up to the League City game in Converse, please, Melissa elaborates. Find some real shoes!

I text back a thumbs-up but decide that I can't possibly investigate the shoe situation until after I check social media and eat breakfast.

My chore list is on the kitchen table along with a granola bar, a banana, and a glass of orange juice. *Kitchen: dishes, counters, clean out the refrigerator*. Typical daily stuff, which will take me twenty minutes, tops. *Laundry: wash, dry, and fold everything in the laundry room.* We just did a bunch of laundry yesterday, so there shouldn't be much. *Garage: all the trash furniture out, all the saved furniture to Goodwill.*

I stare at that last item.

"There you are." Connie walks briskly into the kitchen, heels on, hair straightened, makeup applied. "You haven't eaten yet? Heavy-trash pickup is tomorrow morning, so we need everything out of that garage today!"

I bite into my banana, still not really believing what I'm hearing. I've sorted a lot of the big furniture already—a good three-quarters forms a giant trash pile in the driveway. But it took me a week to get that far. I could maybe finish today, if I worked nonstop from now until midnight.

"But it's Sunday. I have quidditch. We're going to League City for a game." My throat feels tight as I watch Connie have zero reaction to this news except to check her watch.

"I told you about it a few days ago," I say, my voice small. It's a shock to realize that I want to go to the game—not just to see Melissa, not just to get out of the house. I want to hang out with all the quidditch people. I'm starting to really like those nerds. "You said I could go."

"What do you want me to say?" Connie asks. "It has to be done today. You can see your friends next time."

"The garage won't be ready to rent in two months," I point out. "Can't we just save whatever's not sorted yet for the next pickup?"

"And leave piles of broken furniture in our driveway?" Connie asks. "The neighbors will love that."

"Who cares what the neighbors think?"

"I care! I can't get clients if my own house is a dump."

Clients? Is she serious? I thought stealing my room to make a design workshop was enough for her; I didn't realize she wanted to actually charge money for it.

"I'm sorry," Connie says, snatching my still half-full glass of orange juice and dumping it down the garbage disposal, "but this is your project and your responsibility, and you—you need to grow up!" She washes the glass and shoves it into the cabinet before finally turning to face me. "I'll be outside when you're ready to start." She spins around and stomps out the back door.

I clutch my half-eaten banana hard enough to bruise it.

I try to stop fuming. I need to be Melissa, always optimistic, always confident that she can get what she wants. Always willing to assume the best of Connie. I take a deep breath and walk out the back door.

Connie stands in the driveway, scowling at the mess.

"What if I just focus on the trash for today?" My voice only squeaks a little.

"What do you mean?" Connie asks. She paces toward

the broken rocking chair, tugs it a few feet down the driveway before stopping to brush dust off her crisp black skirt.

"Well." I try to radiate Melissa vibes. "I'm supposed to do dishes, laundry, get the trash to the curb, *and* get the salvageable stuff to Goodwill. It's a lot to do, but I get that the trash needs to be finished today. So can we please compromise? If I can get all the trash to the curb by three, can I go to my game? I promise I will work twice as hard on the garage tomorrow, and I'll do all the dishes as soon as I get home . . . please?"

Sweat collects on my T-shirt, only partly related to the morning heat, while Connie reaches for the wobbly lamp that used to light Yasmín's bedroom. There's some mysterious gray goo spread all over the surface, which I know from last week does not come off of hands easily. "Fine," Connie says, pulling her hand back. "The important thing is to clear out all the trash. But if you're not going to do any housework, then I can't be out here helping you."

"Deal," I agree without hesitation. "Leave it to me."

Connie sniffs, but even her most skeptical face can't faze me. She disappears inside. After sending Melissa a quick text to thank her for waking me up so early, I grab hold of the arms of the rocking chair and start to lug it down the driveway and to the curb. I can do this.

• • •

LIKE FINISHING A PAPER AT MIDNIGHT THE NIGHT BEFORE it's due, I spend the next few hours in a frenzied but semiconscious fog. Splinters and dirt dig into my palms and hair sticks to my face, but the trash pile on the curb grows and the garage empties. Suddenly I can see how a car (maybe even two!) would fit, and I realize what Connie means when she says the space has potential. I finish with fifteen minutes to spare.

Tomorrow I'll worry about fitting the old blue couch into Connie's trunk and driving it to the Goodwill donation center. Tomorrow I'll go back to laundry and dish purgatory. Today, I have twelve minutes to relax before Melissa shows up.

"ELLEN!"

I wake up to thumping on the front door and my phone announcing two missed calls.

I sit up and blink at the living room carpet until I remember falling asleep on the couch. Then I stumble to my feet and shuffle to the front door. "I'm up, I'm ready," I mutter to Melissa's raised eyebrow.

We pass the trash piled on the curb. Melissa whistles. "You did all that?"

"Yeah." I admire the pile. "I was supposed to do more, but I negotiated."

"That's progress, right?"

I shrug, reaching for the car door.

"Ellen," Melissa grabs my wrist. "You are *not* wearing what I think you're wearing."

I blink down at myself, groggy brain registering nothing out of the ordinary. T-shirt—light-colored, not too hot. Shorts—mesh. Bra—sports (not that I have much to hold in). Socks—athletic and long, not the brightly colored ankle type that bunch down around my toes when I run. "What?"

"Shoes!" Melissa sighs. "You really don't have any athletic shoes?"

I shrug at the fraying holes in my Converse.

"Did you even try?" Melissa asks, her voice snapping a little.

"Try what exactly?" I ask, snapping a little back. "Try to use my nonexistent money from my nonexistent job to leave my house—which I'm not allowed to do because I'm grounded—to buy a pair of shoes?"

"Did you try asking Connie? Or your dad?" Melissa leans against her car, blocking my way in, rolling her eyes at me like I'm one of her stubborn babysittees.

The angry voice in my head wants to fight back, tell Melissa to shut up. She doesn't get how asking for new shoes could be complicated, doesn't get that whether the answer is yes or no, every interaction with Connie has the potential to make me feel like a puddle of slimy garage goo. She never gets it, but she's the only person in the world right now who actually wants me around, so I should probably not pick fights with her.

"Sorry."

Melissa frowns. "I mean, you're the one who won't be able to run."

"Yeah, sorry."

"No, don't. I'm sorry I snapped."

"Me too."

Melissa uncrosses her arms and opens the door for me. "You okay? You have The Face on. I wasn't trying to—I'm just nervous."

"Me too." I drop into the car, relaxing a little now that Melissa's not mad at me. "But it's going to be fun, right?"

"It's going to be awesome."

Chris is waiting for us when we reach his house, and he immediately pulls open the back door and climbs in.

"Late," he says with a smile. Melissa clicks her tongue, and I decide that I'm too nice to retaliate (when maybe I'm actually just too tired). "Are you ready for your first real game?"

"Karey said it's a little more intense than scrimmage, but that if I remember to listen to the ref, I'll do great." Melissa says the last part firmly, like an affirmation.

"Oh, you talked to her?" I ask, at the same time Chris says, "I could have told you that."

"I was messaging her about rides and everything," Melissa answers me. She glances toward the radio, frowns, and whacks the center of her dashboard, but the intermittent clock display stays stubbornly dark. "And I told her we'd pick her up at three thirty."

"Relax; you have fifteen minutes." I double-check my phone as I say it. Actually twelve minutes, but I decide not to mention that.

"Plus you're late to everything." Chris reaches over the seat to pat Melissa's shoulder. "Karey can deal."

Melissa sighs, shrugging the hand away. "But she's the captain. Good impressions and everything."

"It's just summer practices." Chris leans back into his seat.

"She's still the best player on the team," Melissa says. I wince a little, not because it's not true, but because I'm better positioned to see Chris's face fall when Melissa says it. "And she plays for A&M, where I'll be when the summer ends."

Chris shrugs and settles his face into a less pouty expression. "Whatever."

I'm guessing *some people* didn't take my advice to talk through their issues.

We pull up to Karey's house two minutes late, which isn't bad, considering.

"I brought raisins if y'all want any," she says, throwing

herself and her oversized green backpack into the back seat with Chris. "Is everyone as excited as I am to go kick some League City ass?"

Melissa whoops her approval, and Chris and I join in a beat later. It's fun, the group screaming, and it makes my nerves feel a bit less frazzled. I guess that's why jocks do it.

Melissa pulls out of the driveway, heading for the freeway, and we are off.

"Brooms up!"

I am not one of our team's six starting players sprinting toward the line of balls at the center of the League City pitch, but I watch as our six crash into the other six in a tangle of arms, legs, brooms, and cleats. Karey takes a hit from League City's (much larger) keeper and falls to the ground, but not before reaching the quaffle and kicking it back to Chris. Lindsay and John emerge from the chaos with a bludger each, and on the sidelines I cheer with the rest of the subs (nine of us—not as many as League City, with their full twenty-one-person roster) while our team sets up for our first offensive play.

The field is part of a public park in League City, with wooden tables and benches and shoot-water-out-of-the-ground fountains where families have brought their little kids to run all their energy out, shrieking as the water squirts up from under their feet. I'm jealous. I haven't even started playing yet and I'm already sweating through my T-shirt. I push my black bandana up out of my eyes.

Melissa showed me YouTube videos, but I've never seen a real-life snitch before. The guy snitching our game is tall and stocky, with shaggy blond hair and a neon-pink tank top that says SNITCHES *GIVE* STITCHES. I don't envy John and Aaron, who play seeker when they're not beating; I wouldn't want to wrestle the guy. His bright yellow shorts include a Velcroed-on tail—a ball stitched inside a tube of fabric—that dangles and swings when he walks, just begging to be snatched and ripped away to end the game. Before we started playing, the girl who's refereeing made sure the snitch introduced himself to the captains and the seekers of each team. The snitch and seekers don't enter the game until eighteen minutes of play pass, so for now he's chilling by the scorekeeper, looking awfully friendly for someone whose job is to try to keep either team from winning by slamming seekers into the ground.

I wince as Karey pops back up after another tackle. The League City team is big, most players taller and wider than our starters. They all wear green T-shirts, while we never discussed any particular uniform choices. Facing them, we look . . . the nicest way to put it would be "scrappy."

We hold our own with speed and strategy for a few minutes, but League City's stocky red-haired keeper proves to be an unstoppable force, powering through our defense to score again and again while our offense flounders. From the sidelines, I can pinpoint the moment that my teammates' faces crumple in frustration.

"Sub!" Karey screams suddenly, holding out her hand to stop Chris from moving up the pitch with the quaffle. "Everybody sub. We need fresh legs."

I take a step back to make room for the stampede of sweaty players turning their brooms over to the second string. I expect that our starting beaters, Lindsay and John, will swap out for Aaron and Erin, who usually play together, so I'm shocked when Lindsay thrusts her broom into my hands.

"Go! Beater sub!" she gasps.

I gulp, make sure my black headband is on and out of my eyes, and pick up the ball Lindsay dropped at the sideline. I run toward our hoops, looking around, trying to take stock of the field and find my place in the chaos. Carlos, Melissa, Aaron, and the rest of the subs join me, tugging their headbands and adjusting their PVC before they move up the pitch. I take a deep breath. I just want to be useful.

I start to run after the quaffle players, then remember that John taught me to hang back a bit to protect the hoops and make sure we don't lose bludger control. But I'm not just supposed to stand here while everyone else plays, am

I? The ball feels slippery in my hand, and I readjust my grip and check to see what Aaron's doing.

I don't even see the short blur of a kid whose plain black headband blends with his hair—at least, not until he hits me.

We aren't supposed to fly in quidditch, but I do.

When I hit the ground, I'm several feet behind where I started, and the beater who tackled me looms over me, asking, "Are you okay?" while his knees and elbows still pin me to the ground.

After taking a second to make sure it's true, I manage to answer, "Fine." Nothing vital cracked, and nothing hurts worse than my pride.

Only two things about that tackle make it slightly less shameful: (1) I didn't drop my broom, and (2) I didn't impale myself or my attacker with my broom. What I sacrificed for these two victories was my bludger, which popped out of my hand as soon as I fell.

I roll to a crouch and try to scoop the ball back up, but the boy who tackled me is quicker to his feet. Within seconds he's up and running back toward his hoops with my bludger.

Damn.

"Ellen, do you need a sub?"

I don't know who's calling from the sideline, but I nod and run off the field, letting Elizabeth replace me on the pitch. While I drain my water bottle and mentally inventory the soon-to-be bruises on my shoulders, shins, and tailbone, I hear the other line of subs cheer as the ref's whistle sounds. Point League City.

Without bludger control, the game goes south for us, and by the time Karey calls another group sub, we're down by seven goals (officially seventy points). Unlike Harry Potter book-quidditch, a snitch grab here is only worth thirty points (not 150), so our chances of a comeback aren't great.

I play again a few minutes later. Without a ball (or the skills to steal one back), all I can do is try to tackle the opposing beaters or put myself between them and my teammates in the hopes that the bludger will hit me instead of someone important. It's a frustrating and exhausting game to play, and I spend most of my time being ignored or getting beat. When Lindsay calls me back to the sidelines after just a few plays, I'm too relieved to be embarrassed. I finish my water bottle and steal a sip from Melissa's, out of breath and sweaty.

We lose, badly. Before the extra thirty points they get for snagging the snitch, League City is already up 140–50.

I've never been good at losing. I quit YMCA basketball when I was seven because I still couldn't make a basket (not even a granny shot). I don't like to play video games too often because they make my jaw ache with competitive stress. Some of my worst memories from middle school are the days when the gym teachers split us up boys versus girls for dodgeball or softball or kickball; we always lost and I couldn't even pretend I had helped my team out.

Losing this match feels worse than middle school dodgeball, though, because I *chose* to play quidditch, for some unfathomable reason. I decided to do it—I worked all day to be here—and I want to do it well.

Instead, I'm terrible.

The referee confirms the snitch grab, and League City mobs the field to hug their seeker. John throws his PVC pipe at the sidelines, javelin-style, and gets a sharp look from Lindsay. Karey ushers us to the center of the field, and we follow in a disheartened clump. We thin into a line in time to meet a similar line of League City players, shaking hands with each of them as they pass. The motion and the chant of "good game, good game" is familiar—I remember similar displays of sportsmanship at YMCA basketball—but it feels strange to be smiling at and clasping hands with the people who, two seconds ago, we were actively trying to slam into the ground. It's strange to look into each face and nod instead of screaming. Strange and oddly calming. When I find the beater who tackled me, he laughs and says, "Sorry again!" By the time I reach the end of the line, my smile is feeling less strained and more genuine.

"Circle up for a second, Houston." Karey waves her hands and waits for everyone to gather. I lean into Melissa, who leans right back and passes me her water bottle, panting.

"Hey, good job out there, everyone," Karey says. Next to me, John snorts, and Karey shoots him a glance of pure annoyance before she continues in her calm team captain voice. "I know the score didn't turn out the way we were hoping, but I saw good things out there, from all of you. We could definitely stand to be more aggressive, as I'm sure you noticed. Fight harder, push more, get in their faces."

"And you need to learn how to tackle," John whispers in my ear. I stiffen and scowl before he adds, "Though you proved you could take a hit like a pro."

Jackass. I smile.

"For those of you who played your first game," Karcy continues, "congratulations. It can be overwhelming compared to practices and scrimmages, but please know that the more you play the more this will all become normal. You've got so much potential, and I can't wait to see how much we can improve."

She smiles around the circle, and in spite of my aching right shoulder, I feel something like acceptance creeping up through my chest. Melissa stands up a little straighter.

"Hey, Houston!" The League City captain, a tall Black

boy with braids, waves from the middle of his team huddle and approaches us. "Are y'all hungry? We usually grab sandwiches after practice."

Karey shrugs, clapping him on the shoulder as she looks around the circle. "I could eat. Drivers? It's really your call. Is anybody rushing back to anything?"

Nobody is. I didn't know how long the game would last, so I'm not worried about Connie thinking I'm late, but I text that I'll be another couple of hours just in case. We all caravan the few blocks to the restaurant, a sandwich shop owned by two old ladies who know the League City team by name and are extremely excited to meet the rest of us even though they can't remember how to pronounce quidditch. I order an avocado sandwich, pleased that I have an option besides peanut butter. We sit to intentionally mix Houston people and League City people, so I end up at a table with Elizabeth, John, two League City chasers, and the short beater boy who tackled me.

"I'm Alex," he says, flashing a gap-toothed smile, "and you're alive, thankfully."

"Ellen."

Alex ignores my outstretched arm and reaches across the table to hug me, doing the hovering cheek kiss Connie's sisters always do when they see me. I'm not a huge fan of hugs, but I do like this type. I might stumble over Spanish, and I don't know any of the singers Elizabeth's been showing me, and I chose the diet favored by self-righteous white hipsters, but I can return Alex's cheek kiss and feel, for a second, that I'm not failing any identity tests.

"Sorry," he says, "I'm Colombian, Filipino, and gay; my people don't do handshakes. Good to meet y'all." He hugs John, too, but lets Elizabeth stop him when he reaches for her ("Not into physical contact off-pitch") and offers a high five instead.

The restaurant settles into a brief silence as hungry quidditch players stuff sandwiches into their mouths. My sandwich has spicy mustard and peppers and some kind of spiky green lettuce, and it is delicious. At the table next to us, Melissa chomps down on a BLT and grins at me from between Karey and the League City keeper. Across the restaurant, Chris seems to be moping again. If he's not careful, his face is going to stick like that.

When our hunger dwindles, talk turns to the game and, inevitably, to my tackle.

"You're just so tiny!" Alex exclaims between the final bites of his tuna melt. "Are you sure you're all right? You went down hard."

I grimace and rub my shoulder. I can't wait to play "find the bruises" in the shower tonight.

"She's fine," John pipes up. "This kid is tough."

This kid didn't need you to speak for her, I think, but I just shrug.

"How long have you been playing, though?" Alex asks me. "You're going to be, like, super dangerous with a little practice, I can tell. You were basically growling at me on the pitch."

I don't remember growling, but I laugh and apologize anyway. I guess I might have growled, a little. I felt like growling. "She definitely growled at me during practice last week," Elizabeth says, face impassive but eyes twinkling behind her (much-less-intimidating-than-the-sports-goggles) normal glasses. "When you're our size, attitude is all you have, and Ellen's definitely got it. I was afraid she was going to bite."

"That's also how she handles boys," Melissa, apparently eavesdropping, calls out.

"By biting them?" John asks, raising an eyebrow at me. I bury my face in my Dr Pepper until my blush fades while the whole table has a good laugh at what an (apparently) uncontrollable beast I am. I don't mind the teasing. If anything, I'm proud that Elizabeth thinks I'm capable of violence. It feels like a sign of our growing friendship.

"Well"—John shrugs—"growling and yelling don't really mean anything if you can't back it up with plays. We need people who can get physical and hold on to a bludger. No offense, but the last thing any team needs is another mediocre beater girl."

"Wow, be more of a dick, please." Elizabeth glowers.

One of the League City chasers, who hasn't said more than two words since we sat down, glances at the ceiling and tucks a strand of hair behind her ear with her middle finger. John shrugs, huffs, and then gathers all the dirty napkins from the table and piles them on his tray before retreating to the trash can.

"Don't worry about him," Alex says, reaching to pat my arm. "Every team has one overcompetitive asshole beater who hits too hard and prefers victory to friends."

I smile. Sounds like an accurate description. "Who's your team's asshole beater, then?"

"Oh, it's me, obviously. Why do you think I tackled you in the first place? You looked like the weak link, and I play to win."

Alex's smile shows off all his teeth, and I have to remind myself that I am dangerous, too, damn it, and stop myself from leaning away.

"But"—his smile turns genuine—"off-pitch and all, I'm super glad you're okay! Just work on being a little less squishy." He pokes my (sore) shoulder, gathers his tray, and follows John to the trash can, joining the group of finished players lingering around the exit.

Melissa lets me have shotgun on the ride home, even though Chris whines about it being his turn. Karey talks about all the great potential she saw and how she wants us new players to know just how important we are to the team.

I don't fall for it. The team doesn't need mediocre players, and right now I'm the weak link. Fine. Then I'll learn not to be mediocre.

"You're good, right?" Karey asks when we all get out of the car to hug in front of her house. Quidditch players (or quidkids, a term I learned today) really like to hug. "You had fun? It seemed like people were giving you a hard time . . . John's not getting to you, is he? That boy is a treasure when it comes to running drills, but I'll talk to him if he's being too harsh to the newbies."

"No one's getting to me," I say. "*I'm* getting to me. I want to do better than I did today."

"That's what I like to hear." Karey smiles. "That, I can help you with."

"So we're going for a run tomorrow, right?" Melissa asks as we climb back into the car.

"I have to check with Connie. I promised her a lot of work. But I'll try. I want to." It's true, I really do want to work out. If that's not proof that quidditch is magical, I don't know what is.

12

Dad sees me hobbling through the living room in the evening and claps me on the shoulder. "Sore muscles?" he asks.

"How did you know?"

"Oh, I used to date a girl who played soccer," Dad teases. "She made the same face when she had to go up and down the dorm stairs." He and my mom were college sweethearts, dorm room neighbors, joined at the hip from freshman year, according to the stories Aunt Mal tells. "You know, it's great that you're getting out there and active. College is a good time for that sort of thing. You might even want to play intramural soccer." Dad's eyes get a little misty.

"Oh, I guess so." The suggestion feels weird, but I can't put my finger on why. It's not like there's any reason I couldn't try out soccer. But . . . I like quidditch.

Dad laughs. "You don't have to," he says. "There are a million things to do in college. You're going to have the time of your life." He's blinking and staring at the ceiling now. "The whole world's ahead of you . . . I miss that sometimes."

I officially feel weird about this conversation. Am I the only person in the world who doesn't get the hype about college? It's just school, farther away, with none of my friends. But I nod and let Dad clap my shoulder again before I slip back toward my room.

"Make sure you're eating enough protein," he says. "And electrolytes!"

I hole up in my room for the rest of the evening, decidedly unathletic.

Melissa calls right in the middle of what I've sworn to myself is my last scan of the S.P.I.F. posts before I go to bed. I'm learning a lot about refereeing quidditch, actually, and it sounds terrifying.

It's just past midnight, too late for the responsible babysitter to be calling, so I know to answer with "What's wrong?"

Melissa's wordless sigh of dashed hope and frustrated

rage will be transcribed here as: "Uggggghhhhh!"

If Melissa were a different type of person (like, for example, if Melissa were me), my first thought might have been *family stuff* or even *existential angst*. But because Melissa is Melissa, and because I saw all the pouty faces Chris was shooting from the back seat on our ride home, I guess, "Boys are jerkfaces?"

"The biggest jerkfaces." Melissa sighs again. "I broke up with him."

"Whoa, what?" I expected complaints, speculations, possibilities, doubts. But then I expected Melissa to talk herself down, for now at least. I didn't expect her to scrap the whole relationship in one day.

"I know. He really didn't like that. He tried biking over here to get me to change my mind."

"Oh no . . ." Even if Melissa were the type to change her mind about a breakup (which she isn't), poor Chris apparently didn't know that making a scene would be a giant turnoff for her, not a romantic gesture. "What did you do?"

"I just told him that he wasn't being respectful. He asked some silly questions and I told him that no, I wasn't cheating on him, and no, my parents didn't make me dump him because they secretly hate him."

"Oh shit, he thought that?" Melissa's parents are huge fans of Chris because his parents raised him to have a five-year plan and a bank account and no aspirations to become a rock star. Also, Melissa doesn't cheat. She's dumped a lot of people, but her problem is always a lack, not an abundance, of interest.

"I think he was just freaking out." Another, smaller sigh.

"Okay, so what happened to 'tell him not to worry'? I could have gotten him more prepared if you'd let me know." I'm surprised by how guilty I feel. Chris asked me for a heads-up.

"Please don't start on me," Melissa whines through the phone. "Yes, it was a quick decision. Yes, I feel bad. But it's just . . . sometimes things just don't work out. Sometimes people break up with people. For lots of reasons."

"Yeah, of course." I pause. "Wait, so what's your reason??"

"Uggghhhhhh!"

"What? Did something happen?" Something must have happened. Something huge and game-changing. Something to explain why she didn't tell me.

I usually know about Melissa's breakups long before they happen, since we do preparation *Masterpiece Theater* with Melissa playing herself and me playing the tearful spurned beau (and sometimes Xiumiao reluctantly playing the tired-of-your-hetero-bullshit audience). Unless there's some surprise blowout fight—like the time she found out that Jared Pimentor was telling his Model UN friends that they'd had sex, or the time Xing made out with one of the other guys on the football team and tried to keep it a secret—I'm normally in the loop.

I don't like feeling out of the loop.

"What happened is that I didn't want to be dating him anymore," Melissa grumbles. "Can we just . . . I don't even want to think about it right now."

"But . . ." *Chill*, I have to remind myself, fighting the urge to whine and demand an explanation (what ever happened to the best friend code?). This isn't about me right now. "Okay. Are you okay?"

"I'm fine; don't worry," Melissa says. "But you should see if you can come over. I don't work tomorrow, and we could watch *Brave* or something."

If Melissa's suggesting *Brave*, she must be feeling worse than she's letting on. Disney princess sleepovers are the ultimate comfort activity. Maybe she's too distraught to explain herself right now, but the invitation to come over is a clear sign that she still needs me to be around to listen when she's ready.

"I have to check, but I'll be there if I can get an exception to the grounding."

"So . . . I'll head over to get you now?" Melissa asks.

We both laugh. "Give it five minutes," I say. "I'll text you if they say no."

• • •

THEY DO NOT SAY NO. CONNIE IS ESPECIALLY SYMPAthetic (I may have neglected to mention that Melissa was the one who did the dumping) and even lets me drive myself on the condition that I bring her van back so she can drive Yasmín in the morning.

Melissa's parents are asleep at this hour, like normal pushing-fifty-year-olds but unlike my dad, who had some big case keeping him up, and Connie, who's always too restless to sleep. Light seeps out from under her brother's door, but Matthew hasn't interacted with us since he started seventh grade, so I ignore him as usual and head to the upstairs den/TV room. Melissa is wearing her comfort pants, the pajama bottoms she made at Girl Scouts camp before eighth grade: bright yellow sunflowers on blue flannel held together with wobbly maroon seams, still too big on her five years later. She's already broken into her emergency stash of Thin Mint Girl Scout cookies, which she buys in bulk every February and then hoards for special occasions. Despite her bravado, she's not feeling entirely cavalier about this breakup.

"Is Xiumiao mad at me?" Melissa asks as soon as I poke my head through the door. "I feel like I've barely talked to her all summer."

"Oh, what, hmm, really?" This is not what I expected, and my improv skills are rusty.

"And I *thought* it was just because you got grounded and we haven't been doing hangouts, and maybe I wasn't reaching out as much as I should. But now she's not responding to my texts—not even to say *Brave* isn't as good as *Tangled*. Plus you were weird the other day when I said I was going to message her."

"I . . . wasn't weird," I say, weirdly. I'm not great at keeping secrets, but this one isn't mine to spill. Melissa raises an eyebrow. "I don't know, dude," I say, carefully choosing a half-truth since I know an outright lie isn't going to fly. "I'm kind of mad at her right now. I think she's blowing us off. She said high school was done, and I guess she's just . . . over it?"

Melissa looks me up and down suspiciously. "She told you this?"

"Kind of? She's barely responding to me, either." I'm actually relieved to let Melissa in on this part of the story. I should have told her immediately—I would have if the disconnect hadn't been wrapped up with the secret crush. "She's been chatting with her new roommate."

Melissa nods, sighs, and reaches for another cookie. "Wow," she mumbles with her mouth full. "Are we that easy to replace?"

Actually, I do not say out loud, *you're too difficult to replace. I'm the one she didn't think twice about throwing out with the bathwater.*

Then Melissa laughs. "Wait, no, you know what? That totally makes sense. She's just moving on. That's fair. People are allowed to do that."

Makes sense? Moving on? The relief evaporates.

"I mean, obviously it feels crappy." Melissa shrugs. "But that's what I just told Chris, so it would be pretty hypocritical of me not to accept it back."

"I guess," I say, joining Melissa on the pink futon couch, determined to regain my rightful place in the loop. "What happened with Chris?"

"I already told you," she says through a mouthful of chocolate crumbs. "Can you hit play?"

The DVD menu of *Brave* plays on the TV, the same twenty seconds of music repeating over and over and the same movie clips flying across the screen. The remote rests on my side of the couch, a fact that I exploit fully by grabbing it and taking it hostage.

"We can watch once you tell me why you're so upset."

"I told you everything already. And I warned you a long time ago that this was coming."

I tilt my head. "You mean when you said the thing about not wanting to kiss him 'specifically'? That was ages ago, and you said you were over that." Hadn't she? She implied it, anyway, by acting like everything was normal.

"Anyway, if you've been so over him, why are you freaking out now? Don't say you're fine, I know you're not."

For a second Melissa looks like she's going to argue, but I guess she knows better than to deny her feelings when the proof is falling out of her open mouth in chocolatey crumbs.

"It's not . . . it's not about Chris," she says, forcing me to attempt (and fail) a single eyebrow raise, which makes Melissa laugh. "I mean, yeah, it's about Chris. But I'm not, like, heartbroken about him. I'm just worried about everything, you know?"

I really don't know, so I guess. "You mean college? You're going to be great. You never wanted to start college with a boyfriend anyway."

Melissa sighs and pushes the box of cookies toward me, which is a polite but effective way of shutting me up. "Not college, you goof. Jeez, I'm not even thinking that far. I mean with quidditch. It's . . . going to be awkward, I think. I don't know if Chris will ask me not to play anymore."

"Hmm . . ." Maybe it's just the mint-chocolatey (and marvelously, astonishingly, blessedly vegan) goodness in my mouth, but I'm not particularly fazed. "I mean, he probably won't. And you wouldn't have to quit anyway. Apparently this happens all the time. And there are other quidditch teams. Like the ones in college." I grab a second cookie before Melissa can snatch the box back. Melissa is very protective of her Thin Mints.

"Never mind. Will you just turn on the movie?"

Her tone, on the other hand, fazes me. "Hey, wait, I'm sorry."

Melissa stares at the TV like that DVD menu is an Oscar winner, and she chomps straight through three cookies in a row.

"I'm sorry," I repeat. "Yes, it would be crappy if you—if we—couldn't play anymore. Because you know there's no way I would go without you."

Melissa makes a face like she might consider acknowledging my existence, so I go on.

"If Chris tries to get you to quit, we can tell him to shove it, because you're an important part of the team and you have potential—Karey said so."

Melissa responds with an "Uggghhh" and falls sideways into my lap. I take this as a mostly positive sign.

"Is that really what you were worrying about?" I ask. "Also, did you ever tell me why you actually broke up with him?"

Melissa springs up like some kind of wildcat and snatches the remote out of my hand before I can stop her. "Haha, sucker! The oldest trick in the book! *Brave* is happening now!"

She hits play, and the menu disappears, replaced with

the opening scene. I groan and laugh, but Melissa keeps dodging my questions, and now I'm really curious.

She makes me wait all the way through the opening credits before she speaks again.

"I didn't plan it out, all right? I just felt kind of annoyed with how he was acting during the drive and the dinner, and it was probably going to end next year anyway, and I just figured I may as well do it now, you know? And maybe I wasn't wracked with doubts the whole time, but . . . at the end of the day, I just wasn't as into him as he was into me."

"Sure." I knew that all along, really, which makes the Thin Mints settle uncomfortably in my stomach. I knew it, and I didn't give Chris any kind of heads-up even when he asked. There's the best friend code, and then there's not caring enough to step in when someone's setting themselves up to be sucker punched.

Melissa sighs loudly. "Just, why be tied down for two more months? Better to make a clean break. He couldn't have expected us to end up married."

"Gross, no." I snort, but I also don't miss how Melissa sounds like Xiumiao talking about clean breaks.

"So whatever. Maybe I want to keep my options open. Maybe this is for the best."

I'm nodding along, but my brain is juggling guilt and anxiety, so it takes me a minute to really register her words.

"Wait, do you like someone else?"

"God, what? No! I don't—no! Jeez, Ellen. We just broke up!"

So that's a yes, then. This conversation has gone from worrisome to intriguing. I need another cookie.

I wait patiently through three more scenes before I ask, "Is he on the quidditch team? Or someone from band?" Then, while Melissa sputters, I make a grab for the cookies tucked into her elbow.

I'm too slow. Melissa yanks the box out of reach and shakes her head. "Nice try. Watch the movie. And you're way off base, by the way."

"You're literally quoting 'I Won't Say I'm in Love,' an entire song about being in denial."

I wait through the rest of *Brave*, but Melissa never says anything else. Even in Melissa's room, when all the lights are off and I'm curled up against the wall under the extra comforter (Melissa's air-conditioning is always set to arctic temperatures), I'm still waiting for her to snap and admit everything. But she never does.

We always joke about our telepathic connection, but I don't like this feeling of words unsaid.

MELISSA WAKES ME UP AT NINE BECAUSE, LATE-NIGHT breakup or not, she's still a responsible human with a normal sleep schedule. I notice that the calendar on her door includes bright pink spots for quidditch practices now, plus stars for the tournaments Karey keeps mentioning, one coming up at the University of Houston and one farther away in Austin. We bring granola bars up to the den and watch Cartoon Network and brainstorm for the epic fanfiction we've discussed but never started writing about Finn the Human's biological parents. Everything feels normal, and I don't know how to bring up the weirdness of last night without making everything weird again, so I just . . . don't.

I wait until the show ends and the dishes are rinsed, and it's almost time for me to drive Connie's car back home, and then I say, "So . . . we're still going to quidditch on Wednesday, right? You're not . . . I don't think you need to be worried about Chris."

I balance on one leg next to the front door, tugging my shoe onto my left foot while Melissa leans against the side table where her family keeps mail and car keys and sunglasses. She flips through piles of bills and coupons and examines a flyer for free pizza. "Oh, no, I'm not worried. We're definitely going."

Huh, she seemed worried about it last night. "Things look brighter in the morning?" I ask. "Or was my pep talk just that great?"

"Did you give a pep talk?" Melissa asks (which, ouch). "No, actually Karey was telling me that it's fine. Everyone's pretty used to it."

"Oh." I shrug. "I'm pretty sure I told you the exact same thing." Melissa flips the pizza flyer without comment. "Did you tell Karey why you ended it or who you like now? Do I need to be best-friend jealous?" I laugh, but only halfway.

Melissa flings the flyer at me, and the cardstock corner catches my elbow. "Now you sound like Chris." She sighs. "And why do you think I like someone?"

"Oh, was he getting jealous?" It makes sense; if I saw his insecurity then of course Melissa would be seeing it more intensely and more often. Probably that's why she didn't want to deal with him anymore.

"Ugh," Melissa groans. "I'm sick of talking about it. Tell me what's going on with you and John."

"What?" I blink too many times. How can she be sick of talking about something we still haven't talked about? "Me and John and the rest of the quidditch team, you mean? There is no 'me and John' by ourselves."

"Oh, come on." Melissa raises one eyebrow. "You realize he's, like, always following you, right?"

"Okay, creepy."

Melissa tosses more mail at me. "You know what I mean! Like, looking at you, standing near you. He's totally into you."

"Well . . ." I'm not completely oblivious to the following. John isn't always nice to me, but he does always seem to be *around*, saying something. "It's not a big deal." I don't particularly want him to like me.

"He's cute," Melissa says, voice neutral.

"Yeah, but—"

"Aha! So you admit it!" Melissa giggles, way too pleased with herself.

"Yes," I repeat. "*But.* He kind of makes me feel . . ."

"Tingly?" Melissa enters giggling-fit territory.

I throw the pizza flyer back at her. "No. He makes me feel stupid."

"Oh." Melissa stops giggling and tilts her head. "Stupid like 'Oh, I'm awkward because you're cute,' or stupid like *stupid*?"

"I'm not sure." I shrug. "I'll keep you posted. *If* you promise to keep me posted about *your* new boy."

Melissa yawns, pointedly refusing to react to my probing. "Don't you have to be home in, like, five minutes?"

"To be continued," I mutter. Melissa can't be sick of talking. Dissecting interactions and decisions and feelings is what we do.

Melissa just rolls her eyes. "Whatever."

Since I almost always get rides, I'm not used to walking out of Melissa's house alone. The front door swings shut behind me with an ominously final thud, and some obnoxious not-early bird warbles an obnoxious morning song, and I'm suddenly annoyed at Melissa. Yes, fine, relationships end and that's normal and healthy, but she just dumped Chris with no warning and apparently no thought, and her biggest concern was how it would affect her quidditch participation. It seems selfish. You can't just excise people from your life without considering their feelings.

I mean, obviously you can. Obviously Melissa, like Xiumiao, did. And obviously I'm the only one who expected anything different.

When I get home, Connie is having a minor freak-out, and for once it isn't my fault. She stomps restlessly around the kitchen, offended when I don't accept a plate of scrambled eggs (still vegan). I don't know what's put her in such a bad mood until her cell phone goes off in the middle of the table, and it's Dad, and she stares at it for a long time and sucks in a huge breath before answering.

"Ellen, would you please drive Yasmín to camp?" she asks, and then storms into her bedroom and slams the door.

Damn. Apparently I missed something. A familiar sour feeling creeps into my stomach, but at least I know where Connie is and that she won't go anywhere without Yasmín.

Yasmín is in bed with her pink-and-green quilt wrapped over her head. For a second I panic that she hasn't dressed yet, but then she stands up and I see that she's completely ready, pink backpack on over her white cardigan and everything.

"What were you doing in bed, kiddo?"

Yasmín fiddles with the strap of her backpack. "Is Mom driving me?"

"No, I'm going to take you today." I bow and point Yasmín out into the hallway. "After you, milady Tailfeather."

That provokes a tiny smile, at least. A few years ago, Yasmín went through her big princess phase. We'd play that she was Princess Eustonia Belindaline Tailfeather, and I would take turns being either Butler, the man-servant, guardsman, and companion to the princess (Yasmín didn't know what a butler was, so Butler was a man of many hats), or Princess Leela, Princess Eustonia Belindaline Tailfeather's best friend.

I miss the days when Yasmín was an even bigger weirdo than me.

As we step out into the hall, Connie's voice rings out from behind the bedroom door, indistinct but shrill. The smile drops off Yasmín's face.

I have plenty of time during our drive to gnaw my lip and watch Yasmín's watery eyes in the rearview mirror. This should be the part of the movie where the sappy music starts playing and the big sibling unleashes some serious wisdom.

"So . . . are you ready for your test?"

Yasmín sniffs and then swipes her hand under her nose and pretends she didn't.

"Hey," I say. "What's wrong?"

Silly question. If I figured out about Connie and Dad's fight after five minutes at home, then of course Yasmín is aware.

"Are you ever going to get married?" Yasmín asks.

The question blows my mind in that my brain explodes with things to say, most of which don't actually answer the question at all. Things like "Why is a ten-year-old worried about this?" and "Marriage is just a social construct and an institution rife with problematic elements and patriarchal undertones." Things like "Jesus, what has Connie been saying to you?"

"Um . . . I don't know. I guess maybe, someday. I don't know?"

Yasmín looks unimpressed with this unimpressive answer. I don't know what else to tell her, though. Marriage occupies roughly the same space in my head as a retirement fund—I know it's a thing older people do, so probably I'll do it, but I'm not entirely clear on why or how?

From eighth grade until halfway through junior year, I had this massive unrequited crush on Hugo Ronchetti, who was a decent but ultimately average guy that I finally realized was not, in fact, hiding his deeply poetic soul from the harsh fluorescents of high school—but was, in fact, just kind of boring.

Apart from those few whiny and angst-ridden years (during which Melissa supported my obsession in the nicest way possible and Xiumiao told me to stop being so annoyingly straight), most of my crushes have been on actors (Daniel Radcliffe) and other celebrities (Lin-Manuel Miranda. No matter how old or married he is. Lin-Manuel Miranda forever), or unattainable (usually gay) cosplayers on Tumblr. At the end of junior year, Melissa convinced me to accept a date with Jack Reardon, a kid with freckles and Dumbo ears and super pretty blue eyes, but even though we kissed a little bit at the end of the date (three short pecks that each felt like the sample spoons you get at ice cream shops), neither of us really tried to talk after that. Melissa said he was an asshole for not calling me, but I secretly never blamed him, because it felt like we both just decided to go with the usual vanilla cone.

So yeah, I don't have as much experience as Melissa, who has dated the whole spectrum from cool to human dumpster fire. But honestly, watching her, I feel like I've saved myself a major headache.

"I'm not getting married," Yasmín announces, like she expects me to tell her she has to. "Boys are annoying and husbands are mean."

"Hey, that's my dad you're talking about," I remind her. "But, you know, that's fine. You don't have to."

Yasmín just shrugs.

"Look," I say, "don't worry. Whatever they're fighting about, I'm sure it will blow over."

I almost miss my freeway exit trying to watch Yasmín's face in the mirror to gauge whether she's buying my totally unjustified confidence. Then I almost miss her muttered comment because I'm trying to change lanes without getting us killed by any of the cars honking at me.

"They're fighting about you."

I'm surprised the hood of the car doesn't crumple against the impact of her words.

"They're what?" I croak, spinning the steering wheel sharply. Once we're on the right street and alive, I have more time to ask, "Why?"

Yasmín falls forward in her seat and buries her head between her knees.

"Yasmín, what?" I don't want to yell at my little sister, but my voice jumps several octaves and crescendos to fortissimo.

"They were yelling about money and college." Yasmín's lap muffles her voice.

Wow. All that willpower focused on not causing any more blowup arguments this summer, and I still manage to be the reason Dad and Connie fight.

"What exactly did they say?" I ask, voice turning hard and questions tumbling out fast. "Is there a problem with tuition? Do I need to not live in the dorms? Dad never told me anything . . . What did they say?"

"I don't knowwww."

Shit. "Okay, all right, it's fine. It's not a big deal. Whatever it is, I'm sure they'll get over it." Yasmín sits up to make a face at me, and I wince. "They will. Remember that time they fought about maybe getting a dog?"

"Mom won," Yasmín says with the hint of a pout.

"Yeah, that was pretty sad. But my point is that they got over it. That's what married people do. They fight and then they make up. Even if . . . even if it takes some time."

It's the closest I've gotten to mentioning the Mexico trip to Yasmín. She stares at me through the rearview mirror, and I look away first.

"I'm still not getting married," Yasmín sighs.

"More power to you, kiddo."

We turn in to her school, and I wish her good luck on her test and watch her walk into the gym where all the kids gather before camp starts. The program runs from third to eighth grade, so Yasmín's in the younger half of the camp, but she dresses and walks and rolls her eyes at the teacher who greets her like a miniature teen. It hits me, suddenly, that she's going to end up being cool and popular and socially adept when she gets older. And even though I *want* her to be strong and confident, the thought makes me anxious in a way I can't really justify. I just worry that Yasmín is going to grow up and still think I'm a weirdo, that I ruin everything. I worry that she'll grow up to be Connie.

When I get home, Connie's door is still closed, so I stop in the kitchen for some peanut butter and banana toast. I don't find a list of chores, so I head to the garage. I did promise to work on it today.

My next job is to cart not-trashed furniture to the donation center, so I start loading the trunk of Connie's van. I manage to fit the two coffee tables, mismatched dining room chairs from different eras, and Yasmín's collapsible playpen. I'm staring at the crowded back seat and debating whether I can squeeze the old patio umbrella in when Connie opens the back door to stare at me.

"What are you doing?" Her swollen eyes blink at me, frizzy curls escaping from her tight unstraightened ponytail. In her shower flip-flops, her feet look oddly small and squat.

"Just getting ready to head to Goodwill." I shrug, trying not to notice how upset she is, how she looks like she's coming unraveled. I don't want this sympathy or this guilt. "I was going to come in and ask before I left."

"Oh." She stands in the door frame, like she can't quite bring herself to step outside. "Thanks. Do you need any help?" Even as she says it, she shrinks back into the house.

"No, I'm good. Just need permission to go."

Connie nods absently. "It's looking really good," she says, staring at the half-empty garage. "We should sit down with the plans soon, see what you think of them."

"I guess." I shrug, dragging the giant umbrella toward the car.

She hovers over my shoulder, radiating nervous energy. "I won't really be able to start anything major for at least a couple of months, until we see how things are looking with your tuition." The bitter edge to her voice might be directed at her argument with Dad, but after Yasmín's comments I can't help feeling guilty. "But of course we'll have to get this in good shape before I start work on my studio . . ." Connie's fingernails tap the frame of her car. There's sleep caught in her eyelash, and lines around her eyes.

"Are you and Dad . . . Is everything okay?"

Connie stiffens a little and pulls her fuzzy pink bathrobe around her more tightly. She smooths the top of her ponytail and doesn't answer, so I slide the umbrella diagonally across the back row of seats, trying to make it fit.

Connie reaches to stabilize the end while I jostle it into

place. "Of course everything's fine," she says when we slam the door. "How is . . . your flying game going? And, oh! How is Melissa feeling?"

Her voice makes it clear which topic she finds more interesting.

"I think she'll be okay," I answer. "Melissa is very resilient."

"Good." Connie nods, and she looks like she might ask more questions, so I pull the car keys out of my pocket and hop into the driver's seat.

"I'd better get this load done," I say. "I'll be back in a bit."

"All right." Connie retreats back to the door. "And . . ." She looks down at her feet. "I'm not feeling well today, and I'm sure you don't want to be hanging around here. So you're free to make plans with Melissa. I just need the car to pick up Yasmín."

"Oh," I say quickly. "Yeah, totally." I feel guilty benefiting from a fight I might have caused, but I'm not about to miss the opportunity to escape a day of grounding. "Thanks."

It takes me most of the drive to the donation center to talk myself out of my annoyance with Melissa, but by the time I pull into a parking spot I'm convinced that I overreacted. She's been reluctant to share news before. We're fine. I pull out my phone and send a text. I know you just got rid of me, but want to grab lunch or something?

Connie's giving me time off while she has a breakdown, so let me know. I think I'm free all day.

I finish at the donation center, but Melissa still hasn't answered. I stall in the parking lot, debating my options, but I don't want to waste this opportunity.

I end up driving myself to Tea Corner, which is where I always end up because the tea isn't too expensive and tastes better than coffee. I'm sipping boba through a thick straw when someone sits down next to me on the couch, close enough in my personal space to startle me.

"Milk tea is better," Xiumiao says. Her plastic cup is nearly empty, just a hint of purple liquid surrounding a few straggling tapioca balls.

I roll my eyes automatically, but I can't help smiling. Mocking my vegan tea is such a Xiumiao staple that it basically passes for a greeting. "Hi." I can't believe we haven't been here since graduation. No wonder I was craving tapioca. No wonder I missed the teasing.

She's wearing a new dark blue hoodie with a gray owl mascot on the front, which is wild because I never took her for a school-spirit kind of person. "You just missed my new roommate," she says.

My smile freezes. I normally like that Xiumiao doesn't waste time with small talk, but there's a big difference between discarding pleasantries because you're basically attached at the hip and discarding pleasantries even after you haven't seen each other in weeks. One means you don't need to ask; the other means you don't care to.

Xiumiao doesn't catch my slight change of expression, so she continues, "We met up to plan furniture and stuff."

"Oh yeah?" I don't know who my roommate is going to be. I think I saw a name on a paper somewhere in one of my welcome packets, but all the information blurred together. Do I need to plan furniture?

"She seems pretty cool," Xiumiao says. "Painfully straight, but cool. Her cousin is in the best a cappella group at Rice, so she's going to give me tips to prepare for auditions."

"That's good." This whole interaction is weird—this whole day is weird—but despite everything I find myself smiling at Xiumiao's excitement, because part of it feels so normal. "What are your song options?"

Xiumiao slurps up a few tapioca balls. "Clarisse is going to help me figure it out. She knows what will go over well. Are you going to do choir stuff at UT?"

I chew a mouthful of boba and shrug. I'm supposed to be the one who helps Xiumiao prep for auditions, but I guess that was high school. "I don't even know my options," I admit.

"Well, you should do something," Xiumiao says. She probably means something musical, but it kind of feels like an indictment of my whole life trajectory, or lack thereof.

I drink my tea with intense focus.

"So Connie let me off of grounding for the day," I start to explain, but Xiumiao has her phone out and is laughing at something, typing quickly. I run my tongue over my teeth, scrubbing sticky tapioca out of the cracks. It's just Xiumiao being Xiumiao, glued to her phone, but everything feels different now.

"Sorry, that's . . ." She shoves her phone in her pocket. "Sorry. What did Connie do?"

"Um, I think I told you that I'm only allowed to go out to do quidditch stuff with Melissa now?"

"Yeah, which makes no sense and is probably against at least one constitutional amendment. I knew they wouldn't stick with it."

"Why are you and Mel— Why is everyone so sure that I'm not really grounded?" I sigh.

Xiumiao looks pointedly at me, sitting on the pastel couch with my tea.

"This is not a normal— Whatever," I sigh. "You don't know about any of the stuff this summer."

"Yeah, whose fault is that?" Xiumiao asks, which surprises me into a laugh.

"It's obviously yours," I say, and just saying it and seeing Xiumiao roll her eyes at me makes it sound silly. "Fine, do you want the whole rundown?"

"Make it the highlights? Church choir practice in fifteen minutes."

So I give my best recap, leaving out Melissa even though that creates gaping holes in my summer, a silent presence looming like the unanswered text I sent her.

"Wow," Xiumiao says when I finish. "This summer can't be over fast enough, right? I just want to be in college so badly."

"I guess . . ." I take another long sip of tea, and Xiumiao tilts her head, noticing my lack of enthusiasm. The bustle of conversation around us and the dip of the couch cushions under my legs and the sweating plastic under my fingers all feel so familiar. This is the first place we used to come when Mrs. Li deemed us old enough to drop off alone for an hour while she ran errands. Xiumiao came out to me on this couch, and told me about her church frustrations that turned into doubts that grew into full-blown agnosticism, another secret to keep from her parents. I spilled my guts about crushes and catalogued all the big and small ways Connie made me feel like crap. So no matter how she snubbed me, it feels safe to tell Xiumiao the truth—that my mental calendar ends at the beginning of August. That the summer's slipping away and I feel like I'm slipping closer and closer to the edge of a cliff. I'm ready to ask her, *How do you know that leaving everything behind will be a good thing?*

But when I open my mouth, Xiumiao's phone vibrates.

"Oh, my mom's here," she says, standing up and tossing her empty cup into the trash. "Later."

She's out the front door before I can swallow my boba to say goodbye.

MELISSA FINALLY TEXTS ME BACK AFTER DINNER.

Sorry, dude. Too late now. Work in the morning.

Which is fair, I guess, except that I didn't give her the benefit of the doubt just to get an hours-late Sorry, dude in response.

Where have you been all day? I text. Connie totally let me off the hook.

I wait fifteen minutes for Melissa's response. Awesome. Sorry again. Make it up with a run tomorrow? We have to get in shape for the UH mini tournament.

I say yes, and we plan to meet up after Melissa gets done babysitting tomorrow, but something feels—several things feel—off.

I find myself on Environmentally Unfriendly for the eighth time in the past twenty minutes. My fingers tap with restless energy. My bed bores me. The posters on my wall bore me. Social media bores me—nobody's posting new stuff fast enough, so I scroll through the same posts. I think about writing a text post or commenting on the latest S.P.I.F. discussion (Nico X asking for advice about how to support his little sisters when his parents don't think it's important to keep them in sports) just for something to do, but I can't think of anything to add to the discussion, so I leave it alone. I think about sending Melissa one more message, but I leave her alone.

It's long past midnight when I finally fall asleep, dreaming wordless anxiety through the night.

CONNIE IS BACK TO HER CHEERY JUDGMENTAL SELF IN the morning, scoffing at how late it is (11:15) when I drag myself downstairs for breakfast. We take more furniture to donate, and then Connie picks up Yasmín while I microwave frozen veggie taquitos (God's gift to the H-E-B freezer aisle) and fold laundry, and then all three of us push, drag, and jimmy the big blue couch into the back of the van and drive it to Goodwill.

I start to notice my phone's uncanny silence at around 4:30.

Hey, how's babysitting? What time do you think you'll be done? I text Melissa after Connie decides that we've moved enough furniture for one day. I eat apple slices and celery sticks slathered with peanut butter and scroll through Facebook, watching an awesome slam poetry video that Merrick TheGreat (the person who insulted Melissa but seems otherwise cool) posts to the quidditch feminist group. I sit with Yasmín and fail to actually help her with her homework. I eat the steamed broccoli part of the dinner Connie makes. My phone stays silent.

Eventually I call Melissa. No answer.

But five minutes later I get a text: Hey, sorry, do you mind if we run tomorrow instead? I know I'm the worst. I just had stuff going on, and I want to spend tonight getting some stuff done for college stuff.

For a second, annoyance flashes through me and I type, Please, use the word "stuff" one more time; I'm not sure you were vague enough yet.

But I delete the words without sending them. They aren't going to make me feel any better.

Tomorrow's Wednesday. You're still driving me to practice, right?

I don't get a response.

At least Xiumiao warned me before she went radio silent.

I'm spinning in circles in the chair in front of my desk, watching my *Rent* and *Wicked* posters blur, when the front door slams and Dad calls out his nightly greeting. I make it downstairs in time to intercept him on his way to the freezer and to scoop a bowl of Rice Dream for myself.

"Hey, kiddo." Dad offers his bowl, and I clink it in a vegan ice cream toast. I'm glad to see him, but a sigh slips out anyway.

Dad nods. "I'm right there with you. Long day." He

puts his face in his hands and massages his eyes.

I want to say something, but I don't really know how to ask if he's stressed out because of how expensive my tuition is without being extremely awkward.

"August isn't far off now, is it?" asks Dad, who must be thinking about college, too. "Are you getting excited?"

"Yeah, for sure!" I lie. It makes Dad smile.

"You know, I'm almost used to the taste of this now." He scrapes his bowl.

I laugh as I finish my last bite. We both glance toward the freezer.

I'm spooning out my second bowl when it hits me: I won't get to eat ice cream with Dad when I'm in college.

I know Austin isn't that far away. I know that some people move much farther for college—across the country, even across the world. I guess getting out of the house is supposed to be a good thing. But once I'm gone? Connie and Dad and Yasmín have their perfect family, and I have—what? A shared dorm room in a city I've visited a handful of times. Classes full of strangers who have no more reason to like me than anyone from high school did. I'm supposed to think starting over will erase all my problems. But what if I just end up with nothing left?

"Hey," I say. "Do you want to go for a jog? Melissa was going to come, but she's babysitting."

Yes, it's one of those white lies that I sometimes tell Dad

just to keep things simple. Lies like "I already finished my homework" or "Of course I'm happy at school." Just a little less than true. Dad doesn't need all the nitty-gritty details.

He grins. "I'm in. You really are getting more active, aren't you? Quidditch must be very transformative."

"Oh yeah," I say because it sounds less sappy than admitting I kind of want to spend time with my dad. "Didn't you know? It's a magic sport."

A MESSAGE FROM XIUMIAO WAITS FOR ME WHEN I GET out of the shower post-jog. It's just a meme, but I'm pleased to see any attempt at communication. I send back an emoji string, and then I add, Hey, are you ever going to come try out quidditch? I'm not sure what makes me ask. I miss Xiumiao, and I've been really enjoying quidditch. It's not so weird to want them to go together, is it?

Yeah, no, pass, Xiumiao texts back.

You should, though! It's really fun, and it's the only way to see me because of the grounding.

Xiumiao doesn't even dignify that last part with a response. I'm mostly over Rowling and her whole universe. Quidditch was never going to be my kind of thing.

At one point you told Melissa you'd go, I respond.

That was crush Xiumiao. I'm trying to get rid of her, if you remember, she replies.

Fine, but you're missing out. It's like a real sport with running and conditioning and everything. I have muscles now! Little ones, but they definitely exist.

Um, okay, I didn't know you were such a jock.

I decide not to respond to that. Not because I'm insulted. Weirdly, I think I'm proud.

13

I'm minutes away from asking to borrow Connie's car and just driving myself to practice when Melissa finally pulls into the driveway on Wednesday afternoon. It's a little pathetic how relieved I am, how all the mad bubbling behind my breastbone melts away the second her hunk-of-junk car scrapes the curb.

"You're on time." Melissa pretends to pinch herself on the arm. "Ouch. You're on time and it's not just a wonderful dream."

I don't want Melissa to make jokes about my tardiness right now. I want her to grovel—just a little—for blowing me off all week. I want her to explain.

Instead she hits the dashboard until the clock display lights up. "I think since we don't have to stop for Chris—no, surely that can't be right . . . But it is! We might actually be early!"

She pauses, waiting for a laugh. I don't particularly want to give her one, but I feel a smile sneaking up on me. Not because she's funny or anything, just because she's Melissa.

"How are you doing?" I ask, because she mentioned Chris, which means I'm obligated by the laws of best-friend-dom to check in (and then trash-talk him if necessary). Maybe Melissa's having a hard time with the breakup. Maybe that's why she's been weird. Has she been wallowing? "You haven't been wallowing, have you?"

Melissa's laugh is loud and sudden, the kind of laugh that makes me feel stupid for asking. "No, I have not been wallowing. Being single isn't a tragedy."

"Yeah, no, I know." But I didn't know, and that bothers me. "Now you have more time to focus on what's really important." I give my cheesiest smile and bat my eyelashes.

But Melissa's changing lanes, and she doesn't look at me. "Right! Like quidditch!"

WE ACTUALLY ARE EARLY, OR AT LEAST ON TIME. MY beater folk, Lindsay and Elizabeth, stand with Carlos the keeper under the shady tree, sipping from their water bottles and lacing up cleats. I really need to get cleats.

"Hey!" Melissa reaches the tree several seconds before I do because I refuse to run until I absolutely have to. She hugs Lindsay, and they both start doing that squeaking and giggling thing that outgoing people do in groups. I plop into the dirt next to Elizabeth and do that smiling and nodding thing that shy people do. Elizabeth returns the nod and offers me one of her earbuds.

Melissa seems so caught up with Lindsay that she doesn't see Chris hovering behind her, gazing at the back of her head like her hair's written in code. I suddenly remember his frequent end-of-semester complaints that all his friends were graduating and leaving him alone. I was too busy with finals to sympathize much, but now it feels like his fear was a prophecy and his mournful eyes are a glimpse into my future. I also realize that I could have and probably should have texted him at any point since the breakup.

I return Elizabeth's earbud and slink over to him. "Hey. How are you holding up?"

His stare could air-condition the whole park if we set him to oscillate. "I really don't want to talk about it."

Now is probably not a great time to mention that he and Melissa are two peas in a freaking pod.

"Okay, well—"

"What do you want, Ellen?"

"Just to tell you that I'm here. If you want to talk or . . ."

"You didn't want to talk before this happened." Chris kneels to strangle the laces of his cleats, not-so-sneakily concealing a sniff with a cough.

"You're mad at me? I had no idea, dude!" I try to turn my yelp into a quieter hiss halfway through the sentence, but I don't succeed very well, because suddenly heads are pivoting toward us, and John and Aaron casually meander to stand close but not too close to Chris, detached as any bodyguards. "She didn't tell me," I mutter mostly to myself. "I'm sorry."

"Look," Chris sighs. "It's good, okay? We're fine."

I nod too hard. "And if you change your mind and want to talk . . ."

"We're *fine*," he repeats. "We're not buddies."

The gut punch aches in a dull way compared to the knife wounds Xiumiao and Melissa deliver, but it still hurts.

Karey's car pulls up, and Roshni, Jackson, and those muscular chasers I never talk to show up from the opposite side of the street, just in time to offer me a safe retreat. We all shuffle over to unload hoops and brooms and the big bag of balls out of Karey's trunk. We run laps and circle up for stretching, drawing a few strange looks from other parkgoers.

Feet shoulder-width apart, I bend to touch my right

foot, the muscles down my leg straining taut. To count the stretches, Karey calls out odd numbers, and everyone else in the circle responds with the evens.

"One!"

"Two!" "Two!" "Dos!" . . . "Two!"

We are really not great at unison.

"Three!"

"Four!" "Fourrrr." "Cuatro."

My knee starts to bend as I hang upside down with beads of sweat dripping toward my forehead. Between my legs, long skinny weeds stretch above the grass, and gnats dart back and forth.

"Five!"

"Cinco! . . . Wait, crap, seis!" "Six!" "Potato!" I look up at that last one, because it's Melissa who shouts it.

Karey, who was doing such a good job ignoring our team's complete inability to count, suddenly loses it, laughing so hard she completely misses "seven." I glance up and see Melissa and Lindsay joining in the laughing fit while the rest of the team looks puzzled.

I catch Melissa's eye and arch my eyebrows, but she just laughs and shakes her head. *Don't worry about it,* her face says. *Long story.*

For a second I wonder, *When did Melissa develop intricate inside jokes with these older, cooler, Texas A&M–attending girls?* Then I remember how busy she's been this week, how she seemed to suddenly drop off the planet. I put together the two and two, and realize that I'm the fourth wheel on this cool-girl tricycle.

I catch Chris looking at Melissa, probably doing the same mental calculations I am as he realizes that she's not mourning the breakup. But as soon as he makes eye contact with me, he goes back to inspecting the grass between his feet.

"Um, where are we?" Karey asks. "Nine!"

"Ten!" Only John calls it out.

I understand Melissa's reasoning. She's going to be at A&M next year, stuck in College Station with a solid majority of conservative frat boys and peppy sorority sisters. She's going to need decent friends, friends that don't live hours away. Of course she'd rather spend time bonding with those friends over the summer. Like Xiumiao and her new roommate.

I get it. If there were UT players here, especially ones as nice as Karey, I would want to make friends with them, probably. Melissa and I aren't fighting any more than we're fighting with Xiumiao. We're all just . . . growing apart, except they're the ones doing all the growing.

I'm glad to hear that our first drill is tackling. Force and leverage. Aggression. Suits my mood.

We pair by size, meaning that Elizabeth and I are matched again. John and Karey demonstrate the drill, then circulate. I slam my chest into Elizabeth, trying to wrap around her waist while keeping my broomstick tilted safely away from both of us with my left arm. Elizabeth doesn't spin out or resist—we're just practicing the basic form for now—but I still manage to shift my weight wrong and end up off-balance. Instead of sending Elizabeth over my leg and into the ground, I sway and almost topple us both over. Not quite as satisfying as I was hoping.

"Ellen," Karey says, "can you do that one more time, slowly?" She walks over to watch. "Yeah, that's what I thought. Look, step with your other leg so you go to her side instead of getting tangled up."

I try again, getting my feet in more or less the right position this time. Elizabeth actually tilts the way I push her, and falls. It might be a little bit of a pity fall, but I grin anyway.

"Awesome," Karey says. "Now—"

"Hey," Melissa calls, waving from a few feet away with one arm encircling Roshni's waist. "Is this right?" Karey turns and readjusts Melissa's grip, leaving me and Elizabeth standing awkwardly.

"What are you waiting for?" John asks, drawn by our stillness. "Switch—let me see Ellen go down."

Um . . .

I examine John's face, trying to read through his cocky smile to see if his innuendo was intentional. Maybe it wasn't. Maybe I just have a dirty mind. Maybe people who play sports use "go down" in a totally innocent, nonsexual context all the time, like they do with butt slaps.

But also maybe not. His grin is awfully cocky.

I'm so busy not knowing how to react to John that I almost forget to brace myself for Elizabeth's attack. When the hit comes, I slam into the ground, hard. Gone are all the tips Karey gave us about how to fall properly: butt-first, slapping the ground, protecting wrists and elbows and knees and neck. I fall following my body, not my brain, and for a second, everything hurts.

"Heh, sorry." Elizabeth tugs her ponytail and grimaces. "Nice."

"Shake it off," John grunts, offering me a hand up.

I take it, and groan, and stand. Even though my butt is sore and I think I hit an acorn on the way down, I feel okay. I feel good. My brain unlocks from the panic of falling to realize, *Hey, that wasn't so bad*. Like the bruises I will undoubtedly have tomorrow, the knowledge that I can take a tackle—that I can pop back up and readjust my broom and brace for another hit—triggers a surge of pride through me. For a second, I feel powerful.

John nods, winks at me, and moves on. The drill continues. Elizabeth hits harder and faster, apologizing after every snakelike strike. We push back, trying harder to stay upright. I get grass stains on my shorts and scrapes on my elbows. By the time Karey calls a water break, my shirt sticks to my lower back and my dry throat aches with each breath, but I'm laughing anyway.

Karey joins me by the tree.

"Good job out there," she says. "I'll have to partner you with someone bigger next time so you can practice working at a size disadvantage."

My mouth still full of water, I make a face and give a half-hearted thumbs-up.

"What do you think, youngling?" Karey catches Chris as he shuffles past. "Want to let Ellen destroy you a bit next time?"

Chris startles, then shrugs, avoiding my eyes. He quickly shuffles away.

"Oh, shit," Karey whispers. "I thought that y'all were, you know, friends outside of Melissa."

I don't know what to say to that. I wonder if Chris told Karey we were, before he found out I wasn't.

Karey clears her throat. "So . . . you're going to UT next year, right?"

I gulp and answer, "Yeah."

"They have a fantastic quidditch team. Are you going to play?"

"Oh, um, I'm not sure . . ." I have given almost zero thought to my quidditch career beyond this summer. But like Dad said, college is a good time to try things out. I already know I like quidditch. I could definitely play next year.

John claps my shoulder from behind, interrupting my thoughts, and I choke on the water I was sipping. "You need to get more muscles if you want a chance to make it onto the UT team," he says.

Why does he do that? My face burns and Karey frowns at John.

Melissa walks up, water bottle dangling from her hand. "Hey, Ellen," she says, but she's smiling at Karey.

"What are you thinking of studying?" Karey asks me, shifting her whole body to face me and cut John out of the conversation. She also ends up turning her back on Melissa, who frowns and bends down to adjust the laces of her cleats. John shuffles away from the tree and joins a group of chasers talking strategy by the hoops.

"Oh, I don't know," I answer Karey's question with a shrug, still shaken. "I'm kind of undecided. Definitely some sort of social science or liberal arts thing. I want to try out anthropology and sociology and all that cool stuff they don't offer in high school." I've actually thought about pre-law, but I'm kind of embarrassed to say it out loud.

"I think she's crazy," Melissa volunteers, popping up from the ground. "I've seen my cousin's reading packets from those classes. I'm sticking with biology—good old memorization."

"Ableist language." Karey shakes her head, and Melissa winces. "And I *told* you, if you want plain and simple, engineering is where it's at. None of the stickiness of bio, but all of the linear thinking."

"Sure, but engineers have no life," Melissa retorts.

"Right, not like those party animals in the bio labs," Karey snarks. "If anything, it's the soft-science slackers who get to have fun. That's where the smart money is, right, Ellen?" She elbows me, and I know she's trying to cheer me up, so I convince myself to smile.

"Well," Melissa starts to argue, but Karey cuts her off with a loud two-fingered whistle.

"Hey, y'all! That's enough lollygagging, I think. Break up for chaser and beater drills!" She tosses her water bottle at the tree roots. "You should think about UT quidditch, Ellen. It's a lot of fun, and we'd get to play against you. Don't worry about John." She jogs away with a smile.

Melissa and I linger by the tree, and for one second she looks at me with her head tilted and I think she's about to say something, and I'm sure she's going to apologize or make a joke (probably at John's expense) and everything will be fine between us and we can sneak to her house for cookies and a Disney movie before she drives me home. But she gives me the weirdest blank look, like she's mad at me. Without a word, she tosses her water bottle to the ground and follows Karey toward the hoops.

I throw down my water bottle with maybe more force than it or the tree roots deserve and drag my feet toward the rest of the beaters.

After practice, riding home nursing my aching shoulders and still way too scrape-prone knees, I don't invite myself to Melissa's house with the excuse of "extra conditioning." I don't ask if we're going running later this week. I don't say much of anything.

"Do you talk to Karey a lot?" Melissa asks me right as we pull into my driveway. "On Facebook or whatever?"

"Huh? I don't know." Karey and I chatted a bit after the League City game, when she asked me how I felt and what I wanted to work more on at practice. Team captain stuff. "Do you?"

"I don't know," Melissa echoes. I wait for her to elaborate, but after a long silence she just sighs and says, "See you later!"

She's still lying, and maybe if I were more confident I would call her out on it, but instead I hop out of the car and drag my bruised body inside. I do the little bit of laundry and kitchen cleaning to finish my list and then use up all the hot water taking a glorious shower before curling up on my bed in a smartphone internet coma. Karey does not message me, and neither does Xiumiao, or Chris, or Melissa.

My exhaustion and self-pity run so deep, I almost scroll right past the Facebook post. Only a couple of choice curse words in the comments catch my attention, and I scroll back up to see what's causing the controversy.

It's a post in the International Quidditch Forum, some guy arguing against the decision made at a New York tournament over the weekend. I don't know what the decision was. I didn't know there was a tournament in New York this weekend. The post drops a lot of names and a lot of terms and is basically incomprehensible to me.

Most of the comments, on the other hand, are all too explicit. In between the reactionary name-calling I recognize a few people trying to have a real conversation. Merrick TheGreat and Nico X from the S.P.I.F. group (working together in this post instead of fighting like before) counter the original poster's points using paragraphs of explanation instead of angry quips, but their comments sink under the sea of bad feeling.

Before I remember that we're sort of fighting, I text Melissa.

What exactly is going on with the quidditch forum?

Her response is immediate: Give me a sec. Trying to figure that out.

Fight or no fight, it's nice to know that Melissa and I are on the same page.

So, Melissa texts a few minutes later. There was a guy

from one of the Northeast teams who wouldn't respect a certain head ref (a girl, so no surprise there). And he kept arguing with her, so she gave him a red card and kicked him out of the game, at which point he called her a f*cking c*nt in front of the whole team, so she booted him from the tournament.

Sounds reasonable, I reply. Also, what a gross guy.

I know, right? But the team's trying to make a stink, I guess, and say he wasn't treated fairly.

Which is clearly bullshit? I guess.

Clearly.

I smile at my phone. And the citation for all of this gossip?

Uh, Karey. Ellipses appear under Melissa's text as she types, stops typing, types again. She has friends who were at the tournament.

For a second, I consider staying mad, letting the conversation end and letting Melissa grow into her new friendships without me. Just for a second.

So you're going to be totally set with friends when you get to A&M now, huh? I ask. That's awesome.

Ha.

I have to wait through a lot of typing and erasing before Melissa continues, I don't know about "set." It would be cool if I can hang out with her. And Lindsay.

Cool.

Yeah. Melissa texts a smiling cat face. Also, are we on for running tomorrow? I'm sorry I bailed before, and I volunteer to do extra sprints as punishment. Besides, t-minus one week and a half until the UH tourney.

It's a peace offering, one I'm perfectly happy to accept. Being mad at Melissa gives me a headache, and running is a good break from being stuck at home. I send back several smiling cat faces and go to sleep mostly satisfied.

14

I'm elbow-deep in dishwater after lunch the next day when I get Melissa's text, so Connie picks my phone up off the counter and reads it to me.

"She says, 'Hey, is it cool if I invite Karey to run with us today?'" Connie smiles that infuriating grown-up smile at the phone. "Sounds fun. Who's Karey?"

She's been in an annoyingly good mood all day, because I guess she and Dad made up.

"Karey is the quidditch team captain," I answer. "And do you mind telling Melissa—"

"Team captain?" Connie coos. "Is he cute? I'm sending a winky face." Connie smiles. "She got over Chris fast, didn't she? Or is she inviting him for you? I always wondered why she didn't do a little more matchmaking to help you out . . ."

"Uh." I shake my hands dry and snatch my phone away. "I don't need help with matchmaking, first of all. And second, Karey is a girl. A very awesome girl, and totally worth getting to know better, but not my usual type. Although, who knows what can happen on the quidditch pitch, right?"

Connie's grin disappears and her cheeks flush. "Ellen," she huffs, "I don't know why you have to be so immature."

I shrug. "I'm just saying." Bold, calling me immature when she was the one freaking out over the mere suggestion of a boy.

Connie goes back to drying, slamming a plate into the cabinet. Her face is definitely red now. "Let's try to stay on appropriate conversation topics, can we?"

I take a long breath. "So my love life is only an appropriate topic as long as I'm dating boys? That's not fair."

"Ellen . . ."

"What?" I know I'm not being wise, but I can't just let this slide. "What, exactly?"

"I don't want to have this conversation right now." Connie picks up the colander and crosses the kitchen, heels clicking, to shelve it. "You're the one who wanted to push it too far."

"Why too far?" I demand, dropping a stack of plates into the sink with a crash. "You were joking about a potential crush, and so was I." I scrub dried marinara sauce with the rough edge of the sponge. "If anything is inappropriate right now, it's your . . ." *Don't say "bullshit." Don't say "bullshit."* "Your blatant homophobia."

I drop the plate back in the water to soak while meeting Connie's disapproving glare.

"So I'm homophobic if I don't want to laugh about you being a—a *lesbian*?"

"I don't know, but you're probably homophobic if you can't say the word 'lesbian' without whispering."

Connie stalks to the pantry and clatters more dishes. "I am not hateful or homophobic, and you know that. But I would not be . . . happy if you decided to live that way. Am I not allowed to want the best for you?"

The temptation to break dishes is real. But I don't want to blow up. I don't want Dad to think I'm not trying. I am trying. I wipe my hands on the hem of my breast cancer T-shirt. "I have to use the bathroom."

I retreat upstairs, hide with my back against my bathroom door. I breathe. I listen to Connie slam plates downstairs. So much for her good mood.

Checking my phone reveals—oh, awesome—that Connie really did text the winky face, and that Melissa's response (Uh . . . what?) is waiting for me.

Ignore that, I text back. Connie stole my phone. Have you ever met a male Karey?

One of my cousins, actually. Not the ones we hang out with, though. The ones from the weird part of TX.

I snort and text back, Whatever. Anyway, I may have gotten in a fight about her being a homophobic jerk. Because she's a homophobic jerk. So we'll see if I'm actually allowed to leave the house for jogging.

Melissa types, deletes, types some more. Sorry you got in a fight.

Not your fault. I should have known to keep my mouth shut, probably.

The typing goes on for even longer this time. I expect an essay, maybe one about the importance of challenging microaggressions in everyday situations. Instead, there's a long pause with no typing at all.

Then, Let me know.

Once my frustration settles into mild annoyance, I venture back downstairs. Connie's gone (time to pick up Yasmín), but the dishes are done and put away. The chore list magneted to the refrigerator door has been altered. *Dishes* is scratched out now, replaced with *Garage—2 hours.*

It's a punishment, but I smile. I think I'm good, I text Melissa. Just more chores.

I fish a trash bag from under the sink and head to the

garage, which feels relatively cavernous these days now that it's empty of furniture. I mean, it's still stuffed with plastic boxes, and cardboard boxes, and all the old bikes I've ever owned (that Yasmín might grow into someday), and miscellaneous tools scattered around the floor, and books and magazines piled up and slowly disintegrating in the grimy humidity. But there's room to walk now, which makes all the difference.

I sort through a cardboard box of mostly broken Christmas decorations. The HAPPY HOLIDAYS sign that doesn't light up anymore goes straight into the trash bag along with the cracked cookie jar and the nativity scene that's missing so many pieces it's basically just a model farm.

Dad joins me right at the end of my second hour. I quickly shove my phone back into my pocket and return to the box in front of me, one that has a bunch of my old Barbies and my archaeology kit.

"Hey." Dad smiles as he perches on a stack of newspapers next to me. "How's it going?"

"Oh, it's a blast. You should have been here when I was hauling trash bags."

He smiles. He's got his long-day face on, like he always does lately. "But hey, it's a good workout for quidditch, right? Build those muscles? I hear you're running tonight."

"Yeah, Melissa's trying to make it a daily thing." I wonder if we're leading up to a lecture. Dad's small talk seems too pointed to actually be casual. But his frown lines are smooth, and he doesn't stay silent.

"That's good," he says. "It's good that you're getting to be more active. I can run with you anytime you want, you know." He picks up my Little Chemist crystal-growing kit. "This looks fun."

"Do you think that would still work?" I ask. "Yasmín could have it, and we could do it together."

"You know that I—that we—Connie and I love you very much," Dad blurts, and I stop drooling over the crystals to blink at him.

"Huh?"

It's not like we're one of those families that never says we love each other, but this doesn't sound like a normal expression of affection. This is a proclamation. Are they sending me to military school? Getting a divorce? My eyes fall on Dad's T-shirt, printed, like mine, with a large pink ribbon. Is someone dying?

Before I can work myself into too much of a panic, Dad continues, "And . . . and we will always support you, and love you, no matter what—no matter who you, um, find yourself attracted to. And you can tell us . . . anything about that. You know that, don't you?"

Oh my freaking goodness. My skull is not large enough to contain my violent eye roll.

"Dad. What did Connie tell you?"

Dad lets out a big breath, a smile appearing at the corner of his mouth. "She said you all but declared you didn't want to date boys. And, uh, she mentioned how you're resistant to fashion . . ."

I tap my feet against the concrete floor and sigh. "I was just saying that if I *did* want to date a girl, it shouldn't be any different. And my gender, uh, gender presentation has nothing to do with this because orientation is different from—"

"Well, she said you got upset and defensive, and you seemed to be taking it personally . . ."

"Because it's a matter of basic respect and decency?" I clench my fists, accidentally denting the edge of the cardboard box in my lap. It *is* personal, and not just because Connie had to throw in the fashion jab. I'm thinking of Xiumiao, of course, and Alex, and probably Karey, and a whole rainbow host of internet and school acquaintances who have helped me understand all the nuances of queerness that Dad and Connie are just bulldozing. But I shouldn't have to out my friends or name gay people I care about to justify caring!

"Okay, okay." Dad holds up his hands in surrender. "Well, we thought it was better safe than sorry. What I said stands, you know."

"Yeah, sure. Thanks." I shrug. Even though I know it comes from a nice place, the whole "We'll love you even if . . ." is suspect at best. Like, do you want a cookie for not threatening to disown me? It's hard to get into that sort of thing with Dad, though. He considers himself "progressive" but then he seems so clueless about what that means and so uninterested in learning. "And you know," I add, "I would love either of you if you decided that you might be attracted to a different type of—"

"All right, Ellen, no need to be ridiculous," Dad cuts me off.

Not so progressive after all.

"Okay," Dad says after a few minutes of silence. "So we've established that your passionate defense of the LGBTQ community doesn't stem from hiding your identity?"

"Uh . . ." We haven't established that, actually, but I think Dad just wants me to say I'm not into girls, so I hold up Olympic Figure Skater Barbie, waggling the doll toward Dad. "Don't worry," I squeak, "target suitably heteronormalized."

The look Dad gives me conveys a sentiment that probably involves some ableist language.

"Well." He shrugs. "I have to admit that I'm relieved."

"Um . . ."

"I just think it would be really hard, you know? I pity the parents who have to deal with that . . ."

The Barbie drops into my lap as I shrink away from Dad's words. All that "we'll love you no matter what" doesn't carry much weight when you then actively celebrate having a supposedly straight kid.

I'm a total hypocrite, because I jumped down Connie's throat for saying more or less the same thing, but I don't want to fight with Dad.

Besides, Melissa and Karey will be here any minute to run. So I shrug and let Dad hug me and follow him back inside.

I try to ignore the nagging feeling of disappointment at my own cowardice.

I hate running. I hate running. I. Hate. Running.

It's not the most motivational chant, but it's the one I repeat as my feet scrape against the gravel of the bike path. I. Hate. This.

I keep going, though, a few steps behind Melissa, following the pace Karey sets. Sweat drips down my face and my legs drag, and *why* is this so much harder than running during a game?

The best time to run in Houston is well after dark, but at least at five the sun has taken its intensity down a notch and we can be outside without sunscreen. Following the gravel bike path through the shaded suburban forest is almost bearable, except for the running.

When we reach the tiny neighborhood park, we grab drinks from the dull silver fountain.

"You good?" Karey grins at me.

My mouth full of water I'm too breathless to swallow, I nod.

"You'll be glad when we get to the tournament," she promises. "Which reminds me"—she tugs the end of Melissa's ponytail—"remind me to post the link for registration. I need full names, numbers, and genders to give the refs, and if I don't get that link posted soon then everyone is going to forget to fill it out."

"Well, you know most of the team, right?" I ask.

"Yeah, but people change." Karey shrugs. "Erin wasn't out as nonbinary until spring semester this year. I could make assumptions, but I'd rather not."

"Oh really?" I ask too quickly, uncool in my eagerness to be cool about knowing people with nonbinary genders outside of the internet. "Have I been using the wrong pronouns?"

"Social media says she's still using 'she' and 'her.'" Karey says. "But like I said, things change."

I nod too fast, wanting to ask more questions even though it's probably not cool to grill someone about someone else's gender.

"I keep seeing posts in S.P.I.F. about the quidditch gender rule," Melissa says, "but I haven't seen it in action at all yet. How do the refs manage?"

"With varying degrees of success." Karey grimaces. "People don't have time to memorize every roster, but they can double-check with the captains before the game starts so they don't accidentally misgender people. I also know a lot of folks who just leave it up to the honesty policy. Teams are better at knowing when they have too many people of the same gender on the field. It gets tricky sometimes. I heard about a team in the UK that messed up by putting too many nonbinary players on the field at once, which is probably the only acceptable way to mess up the rule."

I'm hit with one of those sudden waves of quidditch awe. I knew S.P.I.F. was inclusive, but I've never heard of any sport where the rulebook actively encourages—requires!—gender diversity. I spend a lot of time wondering about gender things, relating to Eevie's posts on Tumblr, and generally going in circles about what I'm feeling, but I always catch myself worrying that if I didn't know my identity as an absolute fact from birth it must be fake (which I know is not true! But my brain doesn't listen!). And then here comes the International Quidditch Association (and my team captain) just announcing to the world that gender isn't always straightforward and static.

Having questions is probably okay. Having options is good for everyone. And a sport that recognizes that people can change? That's pure magic.

We take our final breaths and head back toward home.

Twenty minutes (not even an impressive run) feels like twenty miles to my whiny muscles.

I'm tempted to collapse straight into the slightly overgrown grass in my front yard, but I force myself to walk back and forth, hands laced behind my head, like I'm supposed to.

When Melissa grins and holds out a hand, I slap it with my own and smile. I hate running, but I love finishing a run.

"Do you want to come inside and grab water?" I offer. Melissa nods and starts to follow me inside, but Karey holds up a finger. She's gasping worse than I am, I realize, her chest rising in short shallow leaps. She digs in her pocket, pulls something out, and holds it up to her mouth. Sucks in a few breaths. Waits.

After her breaths start to come more easily, she catches me staring. "Asthma," she explains. "It's usually only bad in the winter, but the allergens have been bothering me this week." She kicks the ground under our oak tree, disturbing the carpet of yellow-brown pollen clusters. "Nature is truly the worst."

"I used to have an inhaler," Melissa says. "When I was way little. Swimming pools bothered me, and I felt like I couldn't breathe in the water."

"You're not supposed to be able to breathe in the water, goof." Karey laughs. "That's called drowning."

Melissa sticks out her tongue and shoves Karey. "Shut *up*; you know what I mean."

"Do I, though? You always say that, but I keep proving you wrong."

They bicker for another minute or so while I stand aside, third-wheeling harder than a wheelbarrow full of tricycles.

Karey's the one who remembers I exist. "So you've known Melissa forever," she says, and I feel a little bit better even if it might be a pity acknowledgment. "What do you think are the chances that she comes from a family of asthmatic merpeople?"

Before I can think of a clever response, Karey's laughter turns into a cough.

"Fuck the pollen," she sighs, checking her phone. "And of course, my little brother hasn't left to pick me up yet. Do you mind if I take you up on that water?"

"Of course." I gesture for her to come inside. "And I can give you a ride if it's easier. I just have to borrow my stepmom's car—"

"Wait!" Melissa grabs Karey's arm. "Don't do that. Um, I'm already driving home anyway. And I have extra water in my car. And you don't want to go in there, it's full of homophobic microaggressions. Do you want homophobic vibes in your water? *Or* do you want to go get rainbow smoothies instead?"

Her voice is jokey, but it doesn't make me laugh. Like, yeah, I told her Connie was kind of awful today, but I didn't expect her to call out my whole family in front of Karey just like that. I don't go around announcing to all our acquaintances that Melissa's mom has unexamined racist biases. Should I? Is Melissa super mad at me for not fighting harder against Connie this morning? What is happening?

"I feel like the fact that I'm still gay proves that homophobic vibes have no power here." Karey shrugs, "But you know I'm always weak for smoothies."

Melissa pulls open the passenger door of her car and tosses her a sweating bottle of water. I stay by the front door, biting my lip, until Karey looks over her shoulder.

"Ellen? Smoothies?"

"Uh, I'm grounded." And not really invited. And Melissa seems to be actively avoiding eye contact as she slides into the driver's seat.

"Oh no. Another time?"

"Sure."

The car pulls away and I stomp through the front door, face burning with embarrassment and confusion. And there's Connie, peering out the front window like a ninety-year-old busybody.

"That's Karey?" Connie asks. Her voice is unnaturally neutral, and within it hide a thousand judgments. "With the shaved head?"

I wheel to face her. "Yeah, so what? God, I can't believe you."

"What?" Connie's mouth hangs open. "I didn't say anything."

"You . . . your attitude is so . . ." There's nowhere for my sentence to go, exactly. "My friends won't even come in the house because of—ugh!" I turn to the staircase and take the first three steps in one frustrated leap.

"Ellen!"

I stop and look down at Connie, blood pounding in my head and in the tips of my fingers. If this is going to be the blowout fight that drives Connie out of the house again or gets me permanently disowned, I can think of worse hills to die on. "What?"

"Being upset doesn't give you the right to act like a brat."

She doesn't scream. She doesn't even frown. Maybe it's the angle I have from a few feet up, but she just looks small. Almost apologetic.

Her calm extinguishes all my fight.

"Yeah, fine. I guess I'm still really uncomfortable about the whole thing earlier."

Connie clears her throat. "I wouldn't say anything rude to your friend."

The annoying thing is that I know she means it, and she thinks it's enough. Like the only thing wrong with homophobia is that it happens in front of gay people. I want her to see the deeply ingrained patterns of power at work in the world, and she's stuck on personal manners.

"I don't like to hear rude comments, either," I say, because it's true and it's the easiest way I can think of to make her change her behavior.

"Okay," Connie says, but her face is so deeply confused. "I didn't know it was so important to you."

"Everything is important to me." I feel silly saying it; it seems like the kind of thing that Connie will blame on being seventeen and dramatic. But I don't get why it's radical to feel this way. "I'm not over here being a vegan because I love peanut butter!"

Connie frowns at me. "Well, that's very . . . noble. But . . . you don't have to be vegan. You don't have to get so worked up about every person—and animal—who has a hard life. You'll make yourself crazy."

Ableist language, but I let it pass. Funny that Connie thinks I'm swinging wildly at every problem in existence when eighty percent of the time I'm letting myself down by saying nothing. "I know I don't have to. I want to." *Why don't you want to?*

"You can't save the whole world."

Not if you don't bother to try.

"Well, I'm sorry *you* and your friends were uncomfortable."

"Thanks." I guess. It's not quite a real apology.

Connie sucks in her breath. "You're not . . ." She runs

her hand up and down the banister. "You're not spending too much time with . . . people like her on the quidditch team, are you?"

Nearly nice moment demolished.

"I'm going upstairs now," I say, the words coming out breathless. "I'm not talking to you."

"I just worry!" Connie calls after me. "You're at an impressionable age, and—"

I retreat to my room, slam the door. I blast *Rent* with no headphones and scroll through Tumblr. I'm furious at Connie, but I'm also still reeling from Melissa's weird brush-off.

It's hard to identify what makes someone a best friend. It's things like who you spend the weekend with and who you eat lunch with and who will always like your Instagram posts even though they're just food and selfies. It's who you talk to directly when you have a problem with them.

Your best friend doesn't ditch you for friends who are cooler and more convenient.

It's pretty clear that Melissa is no longer my best friend.

I seem to be losing those left and right this summer.

I spend the rest of the evening wallowing, but in the end, I don't act as melodramatic as I feel. I don't send Melissa any long angry messages or ignore her texts. I accept her offer to drive me to the mini tournament on

Saturday. Because what else am I going to do? Throw a fit? Act like a jerk? If I did that, Melissa might never bother to speak to me again. I'd rather have a non-best friend than no friend at all.

15

I don't know how to prepare for Saturday and a full day of quidditch matches. Karey reminds us to bring plenty of water. John sends a long team email about how the bracket will work, which I mostly skim. The internet tells me to chug liquids and eat carbohydrates on Friday night, which works out, since a plain baked potato is the only part of dinner I can eat.

Melissa picks me up in the morning. I'm too tired to decide how to address the smoothie incident (or really the Connie incident), so I don't.

The University of Houston sits squarely in the part of the city I never go, where the houses slouch and the gas station cashiers work inside bulletproof cages. It makes me very aware of being from the suburbs, and I feel like I should probably spend more of my time researching issues of socioeconomic privilege because it's definitely not my strong suit. Between the unfamiliar setting, the snaking roads that dead-end at the bayou, and the construction, we get lost about eight times heading over (which is at least three more times than normal).

"This would be much easier with Karey here to navigate," Melissa mentions for the hundredth time.

"Or Chris," I say just to be mean.

We finally spot hoops set up in an area we thought was undeveloped land. The teams clump, distinguishable by T-shirt color. I spot League City first, wearing the same green shirts they wore at our game. Alex waves and I wave back, watching his team lace up their cleats and stretch. I count three knee braces, one funky wrist/thumb Velcro contraption, and one pair of chasers helping a third wrap her right shoulder with athletic tape. I never see this much protective gear at practice. Seeing all the damage control makes me wonder how the original injuries were sustained.

"There you are!" Karey bounds over to us, beaming.

"Late forever," Melissa says. She doesn't blame me this time, which is worse than the usual teasing.

"Much better late than never." Karey shrugs and claps

us both on the shoulder. "You can drop your stuff there." She points to the area behind the farthest set of hoops, where our teammates huddle around John, looking almost uniform in black shirts. "Everyone will watch it."

League City has started warming up on one of the two pitches, sharing the field with the University of Houston group in red school jerseys and T-shirts. A pink-tank-top-wearing team shares a box of doughnuts over a picnic blanket and looks entirely unconcerned with warming up, while a group in light blue shirts high-kicks their way around the sidelines.

"Get your cleats on," Karey says when we reach our teammates, tugging Melissa's ponytail. "We're playing the first game in like ten minutes, and I'll give you one guess who we're playing first."

"Katy Quidditch?" Melissa asks. "We hate Katy Quidditch," she stage-whispers to me.

"Oh," I say, trying not to care that I couldn't guess. "Right. Why do we hate Katy Quidditch again?" Katy is a suburb far enough outside of Houston that it has its own Greyhound bus stop, but that doesn't seem like a reason to dislike their team.

"We don't *hate* Katy Quidditch," Karey starts to correct us as the huddle opens to make room for her, but as soon as she mentions the team name several people hiss, Erin rolls her eyes and flicks her bangs, and Carlos scowls.

"Katy Quidditch headhunted us," John explains, making room for me on his end of the circle when Melissa fills in the space next to Karey. "They formed last year and stole a bunch of our good players, right before the Midsummer tournament."

"The tournament went poorly," Chris adds, talking to the sky, since apparently eye contact with me is too buddy-buddy.

"And Katy Quidditch won the whole thing." Lindsay sighs.

"We hate Katy Quidditch," Melissa repeats with a nod.

I shrug. Maybe the players who left to join the Katy team had a good excuse for what they did. Maybe Katy was more conveniently located. Maybe Katy was really badass and shaved its head and wore shirts with ripped sleeves, and the players just got sick of hanging out with boring old Houston, who spent most of its time doing laundry and not talking on the internet.

"All right, y'all, put down the pitchforks." Karey flaps her hands until everyone gets quiet. "It's just summer quidditch."

"So you don't care at all whether we lose to the *other* Chris? And Cassie and Rex?" Chris asks.

"Wait, Rex defected?" Aaron asks. "I thought he retired. Screw him."

"Come on," Karey sighs. "You know that no team can

steal anyone who didn't already want to go. Good riddance, right?"

"She's just saying that because they tried to headhunt her," Lindsay whispers.

Karey is totally and annoyingly right, as usual. Good riddance to people who don't want to be on your team.

"But to answer your question," Karey continues, nodding at Chris. "No, I definitely do not want to lose to those jerks. I want to prove that we are the superior team with the superior Chris." Karey offers a hand for Chris to high-five. "So let's get warmed up and show them what we've got! John, are you done with the strategy meeting?"

"Our strategy," John says, looking around the circle and pausing to wiggle his eyebrows at me, "is to *crush them*." He smiles at Karey. "Yeah, I'm done."

I don't usually like to warm up (because it involves running), but right now my feet tap against the damp grass, fired up by some combination of friendship frustration, team spirit, and John's eyebrows.

"Looking good," Karey calls as we run a simple offense and defense drill. "It's two minutes until game time. Let's go, Team Johnny Cash!"

"Johnny Cash?" I wonder aloud as I wait in a nonlinear clump of beaters who still need to run the drill.

"If we had to be a *country* singer," Elizabeth moans, "couldn't we at least be Lil Nas X?"

"It's because of the black shirts," John explains.

"Besides," Lindsay adds, "ridiculous temporary team names are half the fun of summer quidditch."

Karey calls us to the center of the pitch after everyone's gotten a chance to practice. A girl in a striped black-and-white shirt and miniskirt—head ref—is chatting with the opposing team on their side of the pitch. I stare down Katy Quidditch, a team in gray T-shirts ranging from super light to that's-going-to-get-confusing-next-to-our-black-jerseys dark.

"Their name is Team Fifty Shades," Elizabeth says, staring in the same direction I am. "In case they weren't gross enough already."

I nod and make a barf face at both the team and the reference. Maybe I'm imagining it, but I think the corners of Elizabeth's mouth twitch up.

"Give your team another minute," the head ref calls to Karey. "There's an equipment issue."

"I should have known," Karey jokes back. "It wouldn't be a quidditch tournament if everything were on time." On the other pitch, the ref hasn't yet called Brooms Up for the League City match, either.

Elizabeth picks up a bludger, and we toss it back and forth, not trying too hard to hit each other, just keeping our arms loose while we wait. Carlos calls Jackson, Melissa, and Roshni over to work on quaffle passes.

"Pow!" John pegs me in the side with a second bludger and has the audacity to add his own sound effect. "Heads up!"

Ass.

"Why are you such a Slytherin?" Aaron asks after John knocks his baseball cap off his head with a face-beat.

"You know I didn't read those books, Levine." John shrugs.

"Wait, really?" I let Elizabeth's beat hit me because I'm busy staring at John. I guess I never thought I had to ask if a team full of quidditch players had ever read Harry Potter. "You haven't . . . But then what are you doing here?"

"I joined quidditch to tackle nerds," John says, like it should be obvious. Elizabeth scoffs, and Aaron wraps John into a retaliation tackle, which he escapes with a spin and a cocky grin. Then he looks over his shoulder at me. "Um, no, actually, I got into it because I used to do football and baseball in high school, and at some point it got really not fun. My little brother is just getting into that middle school sports culture, and it's just . . . the guys are gross sometimes, and the schedules are stressful. It reminds me how glad I am to be out of it."

I spent a lot of my high school career feeling totally baffled by (and, I'll admit, vaguely superior to) jocks. I'm only just starting to get that athletics might actually be fun. I definitely never thought about sports being a source of stress or having their own cultures with their own problems to solve, but it's probably the sort of thing S.P.I.F. deals with. "That's actually interesting," I say, and then I hope I don't sound rude.

John shrugs. "I thought I wasn't going to play anymore in college, but then I heard about this and it seemed like, I don't know, a chance to remember that sports are about hanging out and having fun with your team."

"Oh wow, I misspoke," Aaron says, clapping John on the shoulder. "You're a total Hufflepuff after all."

He pokes the bludger out of John's hands, and they chase it across the grass and wrestle for possession until Lindsay pulls John aside to whisper while watching the Katy team drills.

I hold my ball against my hip and examine the team on the other side of the field, too. Katy Quidditch—Team Fifty Shades—looks as big as League City, but with fewer injuries. It's intimidating to play against total strangers when I've gotten so used to playing against my friends.

"Hey, you." John pulls me into a growing beater huddle. "Listen up."

You?

"So we were just saying." John nods at Lindsay. "Since we have some time, and some of you are new, we should actually talk strategy. So that guy there, Chris—"

"Other Chris," I say.

"Other Chris," John corrects himself. "He's a beater. He trains his beaters well. Their team has a handful of good players—mostly stolen from us—who can chase and keep, but their strategy relies heavily on beaters. They play very aggressive, even the girls"—Lindsay frowns, but John doesn't pause to let her interrupt—"so do not let them scare you. We absolutely need to hang on to our balls. If we can keep bludger control, this game will be ours."

We nod. My intestines tap-dance around my torso, and I remember the impact of Alex's tackle in League City. So this team is super aggressive. Whatever. I can handle that.

I'm dangerous.

WE'RE ABOUT FIFTEEN MINUTES BEHIND SCHEDULE WHEN the head ref announces that we're ready to start and calls the Katy captain and Karey to midfield. Karey gives the tall blond boy a thin smile that he returns with a smirk.

"The other Chris," Chris whispers, his shoulders hunched like a cat facing down a vacuum cleaner. I look over my shoulder, but there's no one else in whisper range, which means he must've been talking to me.

I snort in appreciation. "Definitely the generic-brand knockoff." Chris almost smiles back before jogging to line up as a starter.

He passes Melissa, who looks like she wants to say

something to him but doesn't. Instead she comes to stand with me, Jackson, and the rest of the new players clumped near the pile of water bottles and extra headbands that forms our bench. The veteran subs, who have a better idea of what's going on, are more spread out and less intently focused on the field.

"This is going to be fine, right?" Roshni asks.

"It's going to be great," Melissa replies, a little too quickly.

"It's going to be terrifying," Jackson says. "Did you see how hard they were throwing during their *warm-up*? I hope none of those bludgers hit me."

I decide not to tell him about their super-aggressive beating strategy. I'm also feeling a little anxious about getting hit or hurt. Too late to back out now, though. The players are kneeling on the field; the ref has all the balls lined up at midpitch. The game is starting.

From the second the ref calls "Brooms up," things go poorly for us. John loses his race to the bludger and gets beat by Other Chris. A Fifty Shades chaser with a buzz cut and sports goggles grabs the quaffle and plows through our defense. He runs straight through Karey's tackle, fools our Chris with a fake shot, and sends the quaffle sailing through the tall middle hoop. The head ref blows a single blast on her whistle to acknowledge their goal. It's been maybe five seconds.

On the sidelines, we deflate. Our defense tries to recover, but another minute passes with two more goals for Team Fifty Shades.

Karey calls subs a minute later, but John refuses to come off the pitch, shaking his head and holding up one finger.

"Emotional," Karey mutters breathlessly between swigs of water. "We don't need him worn-out this early." But she presses her lips together and shrugs when John stops a score with a well-timed beat, and she doesn't call him out again.

The gray team keeps making fast breaks, and I cringe to see Melissa and Jackson throw themselves in front of Goggles Chaser one after the other, trying to slow him down before he can make a shot. Erin and John shut down plays here and there, but too often the gray team slips past them like smoke. I shade my eyes to read the small dry-erase scoreboard across the field: 0–50.

"Time?" Karey hollers at the girl on the sideline who's holding the whiteboard.

She glances at the stopwatch around her neck. "Seven minutes."

I cringe. The snitch joins the game at the eighteen-minute mark, and games usually last twenty to thirty minutes. It is early for us to be so far behind.

Melissa drops a pass right behind the gray team's hoops, missing a perfect opportunity to score.

"Yates!" John yells as he runs back to the hoops after

a beat. "Get the good players back in here already!"

Melissa must hear him. Her head drops, and she sprints back for defense. Karey's shoulders tense, and she slams her water bottle into the ground.

Good plays or not, John is kind of a huge ass.

The tap dancing in my stomach becomes clog stomping as Erin wipes sweaty bangs off her forehead and waves one finger in my direction. One more play, and then I'm supposed to sub in for her.

Oh boy.

"Freaking. Balls," Jackson gasps, dropping his broom on the sideline next to me and pulling his *Game of Thrones* T-shirt away from his chest to fan himself. "How am I supposed to worry about scoring when I have all these stupid balls hitting me in the face?"

"Feeling okay?" I ask.

"Yeah, the bludgers don't even hurt as bad as I thought," he says. "There are just way too many of them."

Erin runs to me, tags my hand. I gulp as I jog onto the field, bludger slippery in my sweaty hands. I take up Erin's post a few feet in front of the hoops.

"You!" John yells at me.

Seriously, what's with the *you*? I guess now's not the moment to ask, because John is running up to me still shouting instructions.

"We're changing"—he pushes sopping brown curls

out of his eyes and gasps—"tactics. Forget defense. We're attacking"—gasp—"Other Chris. When I say." He pauses while Carlos subs out, letting our Chris back in as keeper. "Ready?" I don't have time to answer. "Now!"

I sprint. I explode forward on legs that know how to run now. My nerves and butterflies push me forward, anxiety potential turning kinetic. The chaotic field becomes a pointless distraction; I know the attack-the-beater drill. I can do this.

Other Chris spots me, spreads his legs in a crouch. I want to knock the smirk off his face. He takes one step back, widening his stance further, one arm cocked to throw his bludger.

But he won't do it. He doesn't want to waste a ball on me, not with Karey and Roshni charging the goals. He wants me to throw first so he can catch or dodge or block. He wants me unarmed and out of his way.

So I do what he wants. I throw my ball, which he blocks easily, and then follow it to crash my shoulder into his abdomen before the slight smirk fades from his face. My tackle catches him off guard, which is the only reason it gets even a sliver of traction, and within seconds my feet slide out from under me as Other Chris digs his cleats into the ground and raises his ball to hit me.

That's when John appears with my recovered bludger and beats him in the back of the head.

Other Chris growls, his beating partner turns toward us, and Karey sinks a goal straight through the shortest hoop. John and I scramble to pick up the dropped balls and sprint back to our side of the pitch, bludgers raised in triumph.

WE STILL LOSE, BUT WE LOSE LESS BADLY THAN WE COULD have.

The handshake line is a subdued affair, with none of the hugs or jokes we shared with League City, just lots of grim sweaty faces and clipped "Good game"s. I'm not sure what our opponents look so glum about until Karey pulls us into a huddle back by our bags.

"Hey, y'all," she says, her voice quieter than I've ever heard it. "I am so proud of that comeback. I don't care what the scoreboard says—we were only thirty points down! If we'd pulled the snitch and made it to overtime . . ." I avoid looking at Aaron, who was seeking when we lost. "That just shows how much stronger we are this year. Did you see how frustrated they were? They expected an easy blowout. They didn't want to have to work hard to beat us." Karey throws her arms around Melissa on her left and Lindsay on her right. The rest of us lean in, hands on each other's backs. My sweaty arm sticks to John's damp shirt and Elizabeth's braid, which drips from when she poured her water bottle over her head.

"We have about an hour and a half until our next game," Karey continues, "so meet back here at eleven fifteen to warm up. I'm going to go watch the MILFs take down the Plastics."

Our huddle breaks down as people scatter toward the bathrooms, toward the other teams to greet friends, or toward the pitches to watch one of the two games starting now. John squeezes my arm and then heads for the restrooms. Erin puts Aaron's hat back on as they share a tube of sunscreen. Melissa follows Karey toward the sidelines of the other pitch without looking back at me, and I freeze for a second, not totally sure whether to follow her or not.

"Hey, Ellen." Elizabeth crouches next to her bag and digs out a Tupperware container. "Want any grapes? I'm going to watch the game."

"Thanks," I say, pulling one green grape off the bunch and popping it into my mouth. "Thanks a lot." It's too much gratitude for a piece of fruit, and nowhere near enough for the offer of company. I smile at Elizabeth's shrug and follow her toward the nearest pitch.

We end up sitting next to Karey and Melissa along with most of the team, but I'm still glad that Elizabeth is becoming my beater buddy. Aaron and Erin scootch closer to us, too, talking beater plays and fighting over a snack pack of pretzels.

Now that I'm sitting still, I am more aware of the sun

beating down on every inch of exposed skin, light heating my black cotton shirt into an oven.

"Hey." Melissa leans over Karey and Lindsay to wave at me. "Where'd you go?"

"You were killing it today," Karey says, offering a high five. "You and John kept bludger control for that whole streak of points." Only because John instructed me to stand practically on top of our hoops and not move, but I take the compliment with a smile. "Oh, and remind me to introduce you to some of the people who play for UT during the normal season."

"I want to meet A&M players!" Melissa squeaks. "You'll introduce me, right?" She leans back so I can't see her and draws Karey and Lindsay into a discussion of A&M quidditch, which doesn't make me mad at all, because I am surrounded by beater friends and completely focused on watching the game in front of us.

"Oh," I say after a second. "I get it. MILFs. Because they're cougars." The UH summer team wears red school shirts, most of which display their cougar mascot's paw prints.

Elizabeth nods. "Yep, 'cause that joke isn't overdone."

The MILFs face off against the Plastics, the team with the pink bro tanks. I practice watching the beaters, trying not to get distracted by the rest of the game. If I concentrate hard enough, I don't even notice Melissa a few feet away, laughing loudly at something Karey said.

"Ellen!" A pair of arms engulfs me from behind, and I turn to see Alex-from-League-City's sweaty face hovering over my shoulder. "Nice to see you! How'd y'all's game go?" He settles onto the ground behind me and gulps from a bottle of blue Gatorade. Other green-shirted players whose faces I vaguely recognize sit down with him. Karey turns to hug the League City captain.

"We lost." I shrug, twisting to face him. "But not badly."

"We were in snitch range," Elizabeth adds, and a League City player whistles while Alex nods.

"Nice. I thought y'all would crash and burn for sure." He leans up behind me and rests his head on my shoulder. "You're coming to the post-tournament after-party, right?"

"Um, after-party?" I reach up to pat his hair, probably an awkward way to return his friendly affection, but oh well. The shiny combed-back waves crunch under my hand. Sweat drips down his face and onto my T-shirt.

"Yeah, Lisa and Alissa are hosting in their dorm. It's going to be fun!"

I don't know those people. I don't know most of the people at this tournament. But Karey nods excitedly. "Yeah, you should stay." She looks from me to Melissa. "You aren't rushing back to anything, are you?"

"Um . . ." I got a break on my chore list for today, but that doesn't mean that Connie won't expect me home to help with some random project in the evening. "I'm not sure . . ." I didn't know how long the games would last, so I don't exactly have a time I need to be home, but I'm supposed to keep Dad and Connie updated about where I am.

"No," Melissa interrupts, "I'm staying."

"Awesome." Karey's smile splits her face.

I shrug, dislodging Alex's head from my shoulder. "I guess I'm staying, then. That's my ride."

"Yay!" Alex chugs more of his Gatorade. "Okay, I'm going to pee. See you on pitch, my lovelies!" He kisses the air next to my ear. "We're going to destroy you!" He skips away, grinning.

Our game against League City (Team Viridian City for this tournament) is closer than last time, and it stresses me out. This time Aaron does manage to tie the game with a snitch grab, sending us into overtime, with a second Brooms Up lineup that's even more hectic than the usual kind and a second chance to catch the (extremely buff) snitch. We even have a ten-point lead when the Viridian City seeker does an involuntary front flip past the snitch and emerges with a handful of snitch sock. It's not a win, but it's not an embarrassment.

I'd like to win a game, though. Just to see what it feels like.

"Hurry up and grab water," Karey yells after the handshakes. "We're scheduled almost back-to-back this time, so we start warming up in fifteen minutes!"

I empty my water bottle for the second time and follow Elizabeth to the water fountain in the student center, stopping in the doorway to enjoy the blast of cold air-conditioning. "How many games are we playing today?" Our last game went on for more than half an hour thanks to overtime. One of the pitches is getting more and more behind schedule because their snitch refuses to be caught, dragging games out longer than the average twenty minutes. Even though I'm not playing nearly as many minutes as John or Lindsay, I'm getting exhausted just thinking about too many more rounds.

Elizabeth squints hard at the water fountain. "Um, at least four? Or five? It depends on how much we win. So, you know, not that many if we don't change our luck."

I nod, fill up my bottle, and soak up the air-conditioning for a few more seconds before heading back into the heat of the now midday sun. I shield my eyes as we make our way to our team huddle.

"Sunscreen," Karey reminds everyone. "If I need it, so do you. There's extra here if you didn't come prepared."

John squirts white lotion into his palm and then holds the bottle out to me. "Hey, you. Need any?"

I hold out my hand. "You know I have a name, right?"

I'm more amused than annoyed, but more unsettled than anything. Why do I care what John calls me? Is it just because he's cute and we played well together? Or is Melissa getting into my head? And if he really likes me like she says, why doesn't he just act nice?

John just shrugs and squeezes way too much sunscreen into my hand. "Shit, sorry. You can share that with Larsen."

Great. He knows Melissa's name.

I let Melissa scoop up half my puddle of sunscreen and then rub my face, neck, and arms while John and Karey give us a pep talk. Blah blah, we've been playing so well today, this team is young, we should make sure to have fun, but keep playing like we want it more than anything, but be good sports. My left calf cramps, so I touch my toes while they talk.

At least four more games to go. *You can handle that, legs.*

". . . Ellen at beater and Roshni at chaser." I glance up when Karey says my name.

"Sorry, what?"

"I want you to get practice starting."

I bite my lip. I've never done a real official Brooms Up at a tournament. "Uh, sure, I guess I can do that." I sip water to soothe my dry throat. Me starting? I'm not at all sure about this decision, but I take a deep breath and step onto the pitch. I just want to carry my weight in this game.

I get set up on the starting line with John as my partner, the only one on the field who's a normal starter. I'm not totally sure what Karey's thinking—Carlos is an experienced (if second-string) keeper who plays solid offense and defense, but Roshni, Jackson, Melissa, and I are all staring at each other like so many deer at a headlight convention. I kneel, sweaty hand clutching my broom, waiting for the ref to start the game.

Brooms Up is fast and disorienting. Carlos scores before I can finish losing the scuffle with a wiry dark-haired beater who laughs like he's having the best day of his life as he snatches the ball from my hands and beats me—*THWACK*—straight in the face.

My eyes water as I wobble toward our side of the pitch. I slap the hoops and turn toward midfield. Face-beating beater is going down.

It doesn't take many plays for me to realize why Karey let me start. Our team has no trouble breaking through their defense, even with both bludgers focused on keeping our chasers back. The wiry beater comes up to distract John when we're on defense, but for all the openings he creates, his chasers never make it in to score. The pep talk makes sense now that I know how to decode it. This team is terrible, and there's no way we're going to lose, but don't let that make us cocky, and don't be assholes about it.

The only one struggling at all is me. Face-beating beater

can't carry his whole team, but he is perfectly capable of ruining my beater game.

"Come on," John teases, recovering his bludger after another easy save. "We should have bludger control by now. Get in their faces!"

I want to say that I've been *trying*, but I use the breath to sprint past him instead, catching up with Carlos and then jogging a few feet in front of him to protect him from bludger attacks. My legs burn and my face drips and I might need to sub out soon, before I really lose my wind.

Face-beater approaches, flicks his eyes toward me, and then turns back to Carlos with an unconcerned smirk that says, *This wimpy beater isn't going to do anything to stop me*. He throws his ball hard, aiming over my head at Carlos.

But instead, I throw both hands up, legs crossed around my broom, and snatch the ball out of the air.

Carlos charges past the now useless defense and scores while I dash for the safety of our hoops. I've never caught someone's ball before, and the bubbling of triumph plus the fear of a revenge tackle gives me extra speed as I laugh my way back down the pitch. I look back at the opposing beaters, who both gave up chasing me around midpitch. The girl scowls and bites her lip, grinding her bludger against her hip—classic signs of "Dang it, how did you do that?" But the guy grins, and when he shakes his dark hair out of his eyes, he laughs. He even gives me a thumbs-up, looking so genuinely entertained by his mistake that I revise my previous assumption about his smirk.

So I'm feeling pretty good about myself when I sub out.

Karey and John pat me on the back, and Lindsay congratulates me. Our sidelines are full of chatter and cheers instead of the strained silence of our last game. The resulting wave of team love is so intense that when Melissa subs off the pitch and squats in the grass to drink, I take a knee beside her.

"Nice goal," I say. Melissa flashes a thumbs-up and keeps drinking. "I like this whole 'winning' thing. We should try it more often."

Melissa snorts, chokes on her water, coughs. "What an idea," she gasps.

"So this after-party . . ." I say as the one player with any muscle on the blue team scores their first goal.

"Oh yeah . . ." Melissa shrugs. "You don't mind, right? It sounds like it's going to be fun. And, hey, that boy Alex wanted you to come!" She wiggles her eyebrows at me.

This time it's me who almost chokes on my laughter. "Not even close, dude. He's, like, extremely gay."

"Oh." Melissa laughs. "I missed that."

"So you have zero gaydar, is what you're saying?"

"I don't know!" Melissa protests. "Gaydar is a flawed concept anyway. And he seemed to get attached to you super quick."

"As shocking as it is that I can make friends . . ."

"Okay, fine." Melissa leans close and lowers her voice. "What about John, then?"

"Why are you so obsessed with John?" I whisper back.

"Why is John so obsessed with you?"

I clap my hand over Melissa's mouth, and she giggles.

"Shut up," I scold. "Look, if anything happens with any quidditch boys, I will tell you immediately, okay? You don't have to keep asking."

"Oh." Melissa shrugs. "I mean, I guess. You wouldn't, like, *have to*."

"What?" I blink at her. "Of course I would."

"No," Melissa says, shrugging again. "I wouldn't expect you to report the second you started seeing anyone. I mean, we're not in middle school anymore. It's not, like, some huge deal."

"Uh, okay." Something angry and bitter rises in the back of my throat, but I push it down. I turn back to the pitch. Erin takes out two chasers in quick succession, leaving the ball carrier stranded without a pass option. Chris tackles the ball carrier, a tiny kid who doesn't have enough weight to stand up to the hit. The ball carrier's legs tangle as he tries to step free, and he crashes to the ground.

Chris gets up, quaffle in hand, already running. The kid stays down.

The ref's whistle blasts cut across the whole field, and

people watching the other pitch turn to see what's happening. Two tournament volunteers with first aid kits jog to the downed kid. The rest of the players stand frozen, waiting for more information or a command from the ref. Chris squishes the quaffle and glances between our bench and the hurt player with his eyes wide, in serious need of some moral support. I give him a thumbs-up.

The kid gets up pretty quickly, and the medics give him a hand as he limps to the sidelines, grimacing in what could be pain or just embarrassment. The ref calls no foul. On her whistle, play resumes.

"Scary," I say, craning my neck to see the kid getting high fives and back pats from his teammates. "Chris looks freaked."

Melissa shrugs. "It's fine. It wasn't even a hard hit."

I hate her for shrugging. I hate her for thinking everything is fine when it clearly isn't. I hate that she doesn't care about Chris, doesn't care about me.

We win the quidditch game. It doesn't feel as good as I thought it would.

Halfway down the handshake line, some touchy-feely player switches from handshakes to hugs, starting a chain reaction in the people behind them. I find myself pressed into sweaty stranger chests while carefully stiff arms swipe my back. "Good game, good game, good game . . ." I keep my eyes on the headbands to avoid the disappointed faces of our opponents. Chaser, chaser, keeper, seeker. Beater. Face-beating beater.

"Ugh." I laugh. "Good game."

"You too!" He pauses for a second, just enough to disrupt the flow of the line, just enough for his bushy eyebrows to disappear into his dark hair and his smile to light up his face. "You're scary!"

And then I'm leaning into his sweaty chest, and our carefully stiff arms pat each other's backs. Because of the height difference, he has to hunch forward, so I end up with my face pressed into his shoulder. Not for long. A second, less.

One thing about this playing-sports thing—you start learning to trust your body. You develop faith that it knows things you don't, like how to fall without impaling yourself on a PVC pipe between your legs, or how to dodge a beat, or how to catch a ball before you even know it's coming toward you. You let it make decisions you don't have time to make.

I haven't had time to develop an opinion about the face-beating boy. I barely have time to register his compliment. But somehow, somewhere, a decision happens.

We let go. We step past each other. I say, "Good game" to the next face.

And glance over my shoulder. Face-beating beater boy looks back at me and grins.

"Who was that one beater?" I ask Elizabeth, who seems like a safely disinterested party, when the line ends and everyone mills around waiting for Karey's instructions. "McAllister?" That's the name printed on the back of his T-shirt above something that is definitely not a normal jersey number. "He was good."

"Yeah, I don't think he plays for them normally. I think he's from Austin or San Antonio or something." She shrugs, squints. "The jersey definitely isn't his, because I know the girl he borrowed it from. I forget. I've seen him around, but he doesn't live in Houston."

I nod, trying not to be disappointed. In town for the weekend and wearing some girl's shirt sounds pretty unavailable; the tiny new-crush tendrils wilt behind my ribs.

"I miss back when we could do silly numbers like that," Elizabeth says, nodding to his jersey. "One guy used to have the TARDIS, and I used to do the infinity sign. Now we can only use those for unofficial games."

"Yeah, what is that anyway? It sort of looks like the feminist sign but . . ."

Elizabeth slowly lifts her goggles, face serious. "Ellen, are you kidding me?"

"What?"

"You don't know the love symbol?"

I shrug, face blank.

"Prince!" she says. "The artist formerly known as? 'Purple Rain'? 'Raspberry Beret'? Do you only listen to musicals?"

Kind of, yeah, but I nod and say, "Oooh, of course, yes," and let Elizabeth shake her head in relief while I watch the beater incorrectly known as Prince disappear into a team huddle.

"Okay, good. I was about to say we couldn't be friends anymore."

Yeah, yeah, grumbles the voice of self-pity in my head, *get in line*.

16

"So," Alex says, finding me on the couch pushed into the corner of the living room/dance floor of the after-party apartment. "How did you enjoy your first quidditch tournament?"

"Fun," I shout over the crooning falsetto pop song blasting out of the laptop speakers. "Congrats to your team, by the way."

Alex plops onto the couch, followed by his chaser friends whose names I really should remember. "Thanks. I wish we could've taken down Fifty Shades for y'all in the finals, but"—he grabs the tiny plastic silver medal hanging around his neck—"still not too shabby. How did Johnny Cash end up doing?"

I struggle to remember. "Maybe fifth? There were seven teams, right? Maybe fourth. We won a couple at the end." I consider leaning closer to Alex so I don't have to yell so loud to be heard, but a full day of sprints and tackles has turned my limbs into mush and my spine into cooked spaghetti. I stay where I am, head propped up with a pillow and aching legs curled under me.

"That's not bad." Alex nods, but his fingers curl proudly around his medal. Over-competitive.

"Plus, y'all could have easily won the game with us," the dark-haired chaser girl adds. "It just took you a few games to hit your groove."

"Maybe. Thanks." My head starts to throb along with the bass, so I make a (frankly Herculean) reach for my red Solo cup of water and drain it. In the middle of the room, Aaron and Erin dance close enough that the brim of his hat brushes her bangs, ignoring Chris and Roshni and Carlos and the rest of the people dancing. Chris keeps looking around, but he doesn't ask anyone to dance, even though I see him eyeing and hovering near one of the girls from the Plastics. Other Chris and a few of his teammates, gold plastic medals displayed (obnoxiously) around their necks, crowd around the beer pong table (modified to include mini quidditch hoops) in the hall with a lot of the older-looking Plastics.

I texted Dad and Connie that we were eating dinner,

which isn't a total lie, since we did stop by Subway on our way over. But even as lenient as they've been about my grounding, I'm pretty sure a college-kid party would be considered off-limits. Which is weird considering that in less than two months I'll be a college kid. I wonder if it will be like this.

Elizabeth was sitting with me until someone started a game of Cards Against Humanity in one of the bedrooms. Every few minutes, bursts of laughter emerge from the open doorway to my left and voices shout words and phrases that Tumblr would not find politically correct. Melissa and Karey and Lindsay went straight to the kitchen when we arrived here from the field, and I haven't seen them come out yet.

Not that I'm looking for Melissa. Not that I want her to come join me. Not that I'm expecting anything from her.

I haven't seen the Prince beater, either. Not that I'm looking for him.

"Don't you want to dance?" Alex asks, his face breaking into a smile as a new song starts. "Nobody can pass up Taylor!"

I shake my head and relax further into the couch cushions. "Go ahead. I'm dead."

I like sitting where I am, letting the music drown out thought and feeling while my body recovers from the trauma of the day. I like listening to the card game get out of hand

and overhearing two UH players discussing favorite fantasy books whose authors are less of a dumpster fire than JKR. I like having teammates pause by the couch to check in on me, having strangers say hi and compliment my team, discuss certain plays. I know that technically this situation should be scary—my first real party, my first party with alcohol, a huge group of new people to meet and feel awkward around. But I'm too tired to be nervous, warm and comfortable and slightly dehydrated on the couch, and none of it scares me.

Alex collapses back on the couch when his song ends. He entertains me with stories about his quidditch injuries and all the teams he currently holds a vendetta against. He pulls people in to sit with us, using his extrovert powers to introduce me to two players from UT, one here with League City and one who works full-time in Houston and played with the Plastics, the mercenary team formed from all the teamless players who wanted to come to the tournament.

"The good news," Layla, the Plastic, tells me, "is that there's a *lot* of quidditch at UT." She leans close enough that I can smell the tang on her breath. "The bad news is you have to be good if you want to make the travel team."

I nod. "I'm not sure I really have what it takes . . . I mean, I've only been playing for a little while . . ."

"Whatever," the second girl says, "you seem competent,

and they're losing a bunch of seniors. You should definitely try out. And if you don't make it this year, there's the JV or the community team. You'll still get to see all these losers at the local tournaments."

I smile. It's only a tiny anchor point, knowing that I can play quidditch in college, that I might keep going to tournaments and seeing Alex, Elizabeth, Karey, and Lindsay. But it's something. In the giant mental black hole that is my future after this summer, it's one possible point of light.

My phone buzzes.

Where are you? On your way home?

It's getting close to nine thirty, and I told Connie I would almost certainly be home before ten.

I respond: Almost. Waiting on Melissa.

You should really be heading back already, Connie texts back.

Uh-oh.

Extracting myself from the now crowded couch, I find people crammed just as tightly in the tiny kitchen. Melissa and Lindsay perch on the counter among empty and half-empty liquor bottles and overturned Solo cups. Karey stands over an open cooler full of ice and a smaller one full of Capri Sun and mini Gatorade bottles. The group scattered in chairs or leaning against the stovetop and refrigerator looks so clean-cut and buff that they must be the A&M players.

I wish I didn't have to invade Melissa's group to get home.

"Hey." I wave my hand. "Melissa?"

Someone taps Melissa's shoulder, points at me.

What? Her eyebrows shoot up, and I imagine her internal sigh.

I need to go, I convey through pointing, eyebrow raises, and mouthing the words. I hold up my phone. *Connie is pissed.*

Melissa shakes her head, looks at the ceiling. *You are ruining everything.*

"Hey." John appears behind me, his voice loud and close to my ear. "Everything all right?"

"Fine." I try to make my word snap, but its bite gets lost in the noise. "My parents . . ."

John snorts. "What, you have a curfew? How old do they think you are?"

"Yes," I growl. "It's annoying, okay? But I need—" Melissa very slowly and reluctantly hops off the counter. She pauses for a handful of chips, holds the bag up to me like she thinks she can stall me with snacks. "Ugh!"

"I can drive you," John offers.

"What?" My brain catches up with my mouth. "Oh, wait, yes! Please! That would be so—" My brain catches up with itself. *Nice.* John being nice, trying to help me out.

Melissa thinks he likes me.

He probably does like me.

"I mean, you really don't have to," I backpedal. Is it safe to ride with John? I hate that I have to do this mental calculation, but I do it anyway. John says jerky things sometimes, but he's not creepy. He's occasionally funny, and he's a decent trainer when he's not being a jerk. Maybe he gets away with too much because of his charm. And his generic but undeniable white-boy jock attractiveness.

"Okay," he says. "I'm leaving anyway, so it's no problem. Up to you."

"Well . . . if you don't mind . . ." I bite my lip. My gut says this will be fine. And besides, I tell myself as final proof, Karey seems to trust him. "That would be awesome, thanks."

John shrugs, runs a hand through his floppy curls. "Anything for . . . a teammate. Let me just grab my keys." He has to pass me to get back down the hall, and as he does, he bumps his shoulder against mine and grins.

I grin back. He totally likes me.

I turn back to Melissa, whose attention has turned back to the group. She laughs and then glances toward me, holding one finger in the air and flashing guilty puppy dog eyes. *Give me one minute?*

I shake my head and point at John's back as it disappears down the hall. I wave her back to her seat on the counter.

Melissa's right eyebrow arches up her forehead.

What, her face asks, *is going on with that?*

Nothing's going on with that, but I don't see how Melissa thinks it's any of her business with the way she's acting. So I make damn sure that my facial expression remains neutral. This isn't middle school, after all. *Wouldn't you like to know?*

And it's the same pettiness that drives me to smile broadly when John reappears with his keys, to make sure my hand brushes his bicep as we step around each other and out the front door. The bicep feels as nice as it looks, but even better is the double-eyebrow-raising surprise on Melissa's face as I close the door behind us.

The apartment complex parking lot smells like warm dirt and cigarettes, and cicadas scratch out a steady beat in the bushes.

"Sorry," John says as we walk past rows of cars under corrugated tin roofs. "Parking wasn't great, so it's kind of a walk."

I stop to stare up at Orion, the only constellation I've ever been able to find, hanging bright overhead. Then I have to break into a run to catch up with John. "That's fine," I say, "I don't mind." My chest bubbles with satisfaction at the image of Melissa's shocked face. I'm going to make it home on time, no thanks to my supposed best friend, but I bet Connie would look just as shocked if she knew her curfew was responsible for my riding home in the car with a boy who likes me. I stifle a giggle.

John looks back at me. "Huh? Did you say something?"

The giggle escapes. "Nothing."

"You," he says after a second, "are kind of a weird kid."

I shrug and push my tired legs to catch up with him. "You are kind of a jerk."

His mouth drops open in surprise, and I laugh out loud. I think all the sun and dehydration and quidditch has rendered me slap-happy. Or tackle-happy, I guess. I don't feel like my normal self. I feel like someone who could surprise everyone.

"Um, here it is," John says right as we reach the green dumpsters lined up along the tall wooden fence at the back of the complex. "I know, it's sort of . . ."

"Mom-van," I finish for him. The tan-brown minivan has a huge scrape down the passenger side and a dented back bumper. "I like it."

I climb into the passenger seat and strap my seat belt on, wincing when it digs into a bruise I didn't know I had. *Probably just rammed too hard into Other Chris when I tackled him*, I think with a tiny grin, investigating the ache.

John hasn't started the car. I look at him and find him looking—intently—at me. Me and my chest investigation.

"Oh," he says, snapping out of whatever trance my

sports-bra-clad boobs put him in. "Uh, do you— Is there music you like? What, uh, what station?"

"Whatever you like is fine." I feel like I'm going to burst out laughing again.

Stop being weird, my brain tells me. *Stop staring at John's face, and stop laughing. It's just a ride home, which you needed. Just be normal and get home on time.*

Am I staring at John's face? I guess I am. But it's dark in the car, and he probably can't see me. I'm not *staring* staring, just looking at the way his hair curls around his ears and watching the light of the parking lot reflect off his nose. I don't like him. But he likes me.

I shut down a blooming giggle fit with a huge yawn.

"Quidditch," John says, starting the car and flipping the radio on to the same classic rock station my dad jams to when Connie's not around. "That shit will wear you out."

I nod as we pull onto the street. "I need to work out more."

"Yeah," John says, and then laughs when I scoff. "What? You said it. We all need more conditioning. It's a team problem."

I give him my address, and we drive in silence, John humming and tapping his fingers against the steering wheel while guitar solos slip from the van's stereo. But he looks at me still, checks me like a mirror every few seconds.

I know, because I'm looking, too.

I wonder what Melissa thinks we're doing. I look

forward—evilly, gleefully—to letting her wonder, not telling her that nothing happened. Maybe when she asks I'll say, *Why do you care so much? It's not like it's a big deal. What are we, middle schoolers sharing secrets?*

Not that there will be any secret to tell, of course. I don't like John. I mean, he has cute hair, and nice biceps, and he's not a bad guy once you get to know him, I think. But he's an ass.

We drive in silence except for the guitar solos and the hum of the road. My head droops and presses against the window as we sail down the freeway with Orion following us, starry belt blinking above the trees.

Dad taught me how to find Orion. He taught me other constellations, too, but I never have any luck with those. Too much light pollution, probably. I almost say something about stargazing with my dad, but I'm afraid John will laugh at me. He laughs at me a lot. That's why I don't like him. I smile out the window and keep Orion to myself.

We're pulling onto my street, and John wakes me up to ask which house.

"Thanks," I say, yawning. It's only 9:57. I'm not even late. "Thanks so much for the ride. You super saved me." I stretch until I feel more awake. My arms and legs protest.

"Yeah, no problem . . ." John shrugs, runs a hand through his hair. "Well, good night . . . you." Before I can react, he laughs and holds up his hand. "Sorry, sorry. But, dude, do you know what's really annoying?"

"You not knowing my name?"

"No, your last name is annoying. I can't be like, 'No problem, Lopez-Rourke.' 'Good night, Lopez-Rourke.' What is that? It sounds ridiculous."

"I mean,"—I unfasten my seat belt—"there is a simple solution. You could just call me Ellen."

"Nah, that's not cool." John scratches his head. "You should just drop the Lopez. 'Hey, Rourke.' 'See you around, Rourke.' See? Perfect."

I scowl. Hyphenated names are not perfect. Hyphenated names confuse teachers who want to seat you alphabetically and standardized tests that only let you bubble letters. Hyphenated names get mixed up in computer systems and on learner's permits. I do not need to be told what's wrong with my last name.

"I'm not going to—" I sigh. "I have enough of an identity crisis about being Latina without literally erasing it from my name."

John cocks his head to one side. "Why do you have an identity crisis?"

Do I really want to get into this? I sigh again, but John looks like a curious puppy, so I make an effort to explain. "It's just, like, my dad is white Irish American and my mom was Mexican but not from Mexico, but she and my grandparents all died when I was not that old, so I'm missing out on some of the family experiences and, like, cultural touch points, but then my stepmom is *from* Mexico, like, got her US citizenship when I was twelve, and so sometimes it feels like that gives me more, I don't know, Mexican points, but other times it just feels like it highlights how not Mexican I am." Wow, I really got into this. "And, like, it's Texas, so there are lots of people who are Mexican and Mexican American and bicultural, and it feels like everyone is comparing experiences, and sometimes it just feels like I don't know if I really fit in, which I *know* is totally a white Latinx thing to complain about because, like, I have all these white passing privileges and citizenship privileges and language privileges so what am I even complaining about?" My words tumble out faster and faster and John's eyebrows climb higher and higher until I finally cut myself off with a deep breath. "So, uh, yeah. That's the identity crisis. In a nutshell. Or whatever."

John nods slowly. "Wow, okay. But aren't you just making it complicated? You seem like you're basically white, you know?"

Well, what the hell does that mean?

John senses danger. "Uh, just because you don't really act like . . ." My eyebrows shoot up. "Because you're just really . . . you know what I mean."

Absolutely not. My heart is pounding and I am not

going to let him get away with that bullshit. "I know that you just heard me explain in great detail why my identity is complicated and personal and then you tried to flatten it down for your own convenience and explain it back to me. I know that I regret telling you any of this because you don't know or care anything about me and you're just using it as another excuse to be . . . to be . . ."

"An ass," John says. "Sorry, I'm sorry. Really. I didn't mean to invoke the rage. I'm just being an ass."

I take a breath, but I don't feel done yet. I feel breathless and antsy, and John's apology set me off balance because I was ready to keep yelling at him but now he's looking at me like yelling is the last thing on his mind. And it's a nice look and a nice face and it's close to mine, which might be responsible for at least half of the adrenaline rushing through my brain, but the other half is indignation, and why does such a nice face have to belong to such an obnoxious person? I swallow. "Yeah, you're being an ass. Why do you *do* that? Like, you're a cool dude most of the time, is it really that hard to not be an—?"

Ass.

But I don't get to say that.

Because my mouth is covered.

By John's mouth.

And John's hands catch and hold my hands, which I guess I was flailing, but now they're not flailing because they are being held by John's hands, which are warm, and his mouth is warm, and his breath is warm on my face.

The warmth is nice, like stepping out of an over-air-conditioned building into the summer heat. I lean forward a little bit, tilt my head a little bit, and it gets even nicer. But like the summer heat, it soon turns sticky and cloying and I want to go back inside.

I freeze, and after a second John pulls away.

"So," he says, his mouth quirked into a smile. "You're Mexican."

I blink. I stare at his smile. "I mean, I'm also Irish."

He kisses me again, and the heat wraps around me again, heavy and humid and not entirely unpleasant. I move my hand to John's shoulder and brush against his curls, so much softer than Alex's gelled hair. And I know I was yelling at him a second ago, but I get temporarily lost in those curls.

And it's not until after I've typed his number into my phone and waved goodbye and knocked on the front door and retreated into the shower that I even notice that there's a *problem* stuck in the pit of my stomach. And it's not until I get the good night text from John that I remember what the *problem* is.

Which is that I'm still pissed at John, and I still don't like him.

Oops.

I creep downstairs after my shower, hair damp and stomach growling. The house is quiet, all the lights dark. I expected more interrogation, or at least interaction.

The glow of the streetlights outside the kitchen window guides me to the refrigerator. I require food. Lots. Now.

I use the same spoon to cram mouthfuls of chocolate Rice Dream and peanut butter, sprinkling trail mix on top of each. My stomach swells, but my brain demands more.

I should research vegan sports nutrition. Beans? Protein shakes? Shit-tons of vitamins?

I reach for my phone, tucked into the tiny back pocket of my purple-striped pajama shorts, but stop before actually touching it. John's number is in that phone. John's text will still be displayed on the screen, unopened. Instead of my phone, I reach for more Rice Dream.

I kissed John.

I mean, technically John kissed me, right? This was definitely all his doing. Well, except that I kissed him back. And put my hand in his hair. And I think I maybe bit his lip a tiny bit.

I grip my spoon tightly to keep my hand away from my phone. I don't need Melissa's advice. I don't need to tell her anything. Wasn't that the whole point?

Clearly, this revenge plan is working out great for me.

I can't text Melissa, and I can't text John. I shake my head, spraying drops of shower water across the table. Why did I kiss him? Is he going to want to make this into something? Is he going to want to kiss me again?

Do I want to kiss him again?

It shouldn't be a hard question. Kisses, especially first kisses, are litmus tests, right? You either get the swell of a symphony orchestra or sad trombone sound effects. Fireworks or the slow fizzle of a dud. Not some confusing no-man's-land in between.

I would kiss John again. I liked kissing John. But in order to kiss him, I would have to talk to him, and that feels unbearable right now. Which could just be nerves. Or embarrassment.

Oh man, I thought John was good at making me feel stupid *before* this . . .

My stomach is full and my brain is empty and my legs ache. I put away my food, rinse my spoon and bowl.

In desperation, I text Xiumiao. I don't know where we stand, really; I don't know if she wants to hear from me, but I feel like I'll explode if I don't tell someone. I'm pissed at her for making everything weird and ignoring texts and talking to her new roommate more than me. Why did both of my friends decide to dump me just when I needed them most?

I kissed a bro from the quidditch team and it was medium. I am taking questions and comments this is an open forum please discuss.

I text her on my way upstairs, and I wait for a response, but none appears.

I settle on my bed, finally opening John's text just so the notification will go away. If the evidence is gone, then it's almost like it never happened. I could almost believe it never happened, except that when I lie in bed and close my eyes, I can still feel the press of John's lips and his hair between my fingers.

Shit.

This is going to be a problem.

• • •

When I wake up the next morning, I have another text from John. hey lopez-rourke . . . what are u up to this week? wanna hang?

I shove my phone under my pillow and leave it there while I brush my teeth and get dressed. Stupid phone. Stupid John. Stupid John's stupid mouth.

Why hasn't Melissa texted? Why hasn't Xiumiao answered?

I dawdle in the bathroom, flossing my teeth and inspecting the blackheads on my nose to avoid going back to my phone or, worse, downstairs. Isn't it bad enough that my (barely existent) social life is falling apart? Do I really have to deal with Connie's chore list as well?

As soon as the thought crosses my mind, so does the solution to my problem. I hop on my bed and answer John's text: Funny story: I'm actually grounded forever. Like, literally until I go to college. But I get out for quidditch things.

Hitting send is like dropping one of the twenty-pound medicine balls Karey brought for conditioning practice last week—I feel much lighter and a tiny bit sweatier. My excuse was one hundred percent truth, so I definitely don't have to feel guilty about it.

I head downstairs to see what my list looks like today. My phone buzzes on my way to the kitchen.

damn, girl, what did u do to deserve all that? (and can u do it to me?) ☺

I have a thousand uncomfortable feelings and zero idea how to express them. Ha. I wait a minute, then add, Unfortunately, I'll have to see you on Wednesday.

Can't wait ☺

I'm not sure what's worse—that John keeps sending winky faces or that my stomach jerks excitedly at the sight of each one. *Calm down, internal organs. I don't even like him, remember?* I definitely don't want to kiss him again. Or pet his hair. Or trace the muscles of his arms.

Stupid hormones.

Nice? Or not nice? I don't know, I need more information to properly react. I met up with another girl who's going to be in my dorm next year. She seems like a talker.

That's what Xiumiao finally texts me.

Like, really? Just immediately on to her new college friends? She can't even work up an entire text's worth of interest in the most dramatic make-out session I've ever experienced?

I know Xiumiao isn't super into the hetero gossip, or any gossip, really. There's a reason I usually take this sort of talk to Melissa. But you might think my oldest friend would at least be able to register my confusion (there was barely any punctuation in that text!) and muster up a smidge of concern.

I feel like I keep banging my head against the same walls. Xiumiao said she wanted space from Melissa, but the way she's acting makes it pretty obvious that she wants space from me, too.

I don't answer her message.

On Wednesday, Melissa and I share our first communication of the week in the form of a text message conversation.

She asks: Should I pick you up?

I answer: Yeah, thanks.

Connie has me back in the garage, and so far I've purged most of my and Yasmín's baby stuff, about half the holiday decorations, and an embarrassing amount of outgrown roller skates, pogo sticks, and scooters. Today I sort through one of Dad's many toolboxes, trying to figure out what's useful and what's broken or pointless clutter.

Well, except I'm also spending more than half my time on my phone, looking at pictures from the mini tournament. It's fun to realize that some of the people I was playing with are actually names I know from the S.P.I.F. boards. I should make an effort to meet them next time. I want to be friends with those people in real life.

I also—and I am not super proud of this—look up Prince songs. Not because of the cute beater boy *necessarily*, just because, you know, I'm curious. And it's something to talk to Elizabeth about. Anyway the music is chill and makes the time pass quicker, and I'm extremely jealous of his vocal range. Also there's enough space in the garage now for dancing, which most of the songs basically demand, so that's a bonus.

Melissa texts, omw, a little before practice, not even bothering to spell out the words "on my way," which is a new low. I'm waiting at the front door when she pulls into the driveway.

"You're early," she gasps when I slide into the passenger's seat. "That's twice now. Did hell freeze over?" I just smile and nod. Melissa doesn't take the hint. "Dude, what's up? I've been . . . I feel like I fell into a black hole and warped through the whole week. What's going on?"

"Oh, you know." I shrug. "Lots of nothing. Confined to the house and all." *I kissed John. I kissed John. I kissed John.* I'm surprised she can't read the words scrawled on my forehead. *I went home with John because you ditched me, and we kissed, and you never even asked about it, so I'm not telling you. Also, we're in a fight.*

Melissa nods, waits for more. When the silence gets awkward, I pretend to check my phone.

"That's it?" she asks. "No evil Connie hijinks? No updates from the angry vegan feminists? No news at all?"

I shrug. "Nah." The effort of sounding breezy starts sweat trickling under my arms. I want her to stop asking questions so I can stop feeling guilty for lying. "What's up with you?"

"Oh, um, where do I start? Um, I sort of had something I wanted to . . . I don't know, so this weekend was kind of craz—ack, I mean, it was incredibly busy, and I know I was sort of crappy at the after-party. I am sorry about that, but it's just . . ."

"Whatever." I don't want to hear Melissa's half-hearted excuses. "Don't worry about it."

"Yeah, no, but what happened was—crap!"

I flinch as Melissa runs a red light.

"It's fine," she says before I can complain. "It was way too late to stop. Nobody was coming the other way. It was fine. Shut up."

"I didn't say anything." I turn back to my phone and whistle to prove my innocence.

"Oh my goodness, shut up!" Melissa groans.

We laugh, and it's almost enough to break me, make me put my phone down and tell Melissa exactly what's happening, how many times John has texted me and how much I've stressed over the wording and punctuation of each response.

"So I was going to tell you . . ." Melissa says, at the same time that I blurt, "Oh, so guess what?"

We laugh again. I am not great at fighting with Melissa.

But before I can spill, we pull up to the park. People are already milling around the tree, and Melissa returns

Karey's wave while almost causing a traffic accident with her parallel parking.

"Um, you were saying?" I ask. But Melissa's already yanking the keys out and slamming the door behind her.

"Quidditch!" she shouts, pumping a fist into the air and striding toward the half-set-up hoops, and anything I was going to say or hear seems totally forgotten.

Footsteps pound behind us. I turn around, and my stomach trips over itself. John jogs up to me, huge grin spread across his face.

It's his grin's fault that I can't stop looking at his mouth. *Cut it out, mouth. Cut it out, grin.*

"Hey. Hi, Ellen." He does not stop grinning. I do not stop glaring at his grin, and at his use of my name. It's not a very angry glare, though. For some reason, I just can't work up any real venom.

This is all his fault.

"So just so you know," John says, "you're going to need to start mapping out some escape routes, because this whole 'grounded' thing isn't working for me."

I don't have an answer to this. Blood rushes hot in my face and stomach. Melissa looks from me to John, from John to me. She raises one eyebrow in a perfect arch.

"I . . . uh . . ."

John's grin turns into a lopsided smirk. "Yeah, I tend to have that effect on women."

Both of Melissa's eyebrows climb up her forehead. She says nothing, but her face transmits her thoughts loud and clear:

When exactly did this *happen?*

I refuse to feel guilty. I refuse to feel stupid. A giggle comes out of my mouth, a high-pitched and uncontrollable response to the awkwardness. John's smile gets wider and his chest puffs out, like the laugh is an award I gave just to him.

"Ellen," Melissa says, "I left my sunscreen in the car. Walk with me?" *Get over here right now and explain yourself.*

"I applied already," I say as breezily as I can manage. What can I say? I'm petty.

John starts toward the pitch, and I match his steps. Part of me is so pleased to leave Melissa behind me, her mouth hanging open, but only the part that doesn't feel nauseous.

Melissa catches up fast, makes a beeline for Karey without looking at me. John nudges my shoulder and smiles a smile of pure ignorance, no idea of the tension he's caused.

Karey gives us two speeches about the Midsummer Flight's Dream tournament a couple weeks from now. The first speech is a pep talk, which I take with a heavy dose of salt. (Are we really the best team? Do we really want this more than anyone else?) The second speech is logistics, most of which I ignore. Karey's found willing

Austin players to give us floor space to sleep, and she needs a headcount by Monday. She tells us to finalize our plans, take our vacation days, reserve our seats in cars.

John stands nearby while Karey talks. He's a little bit behind me, and he keeps moving closer until I can feel heat and electricity in the inch between his side and mine. He props an elbow up on my shoulder, leaning his head on his hand, and I try to pretend like this is a normal thing, normal physical contact between teammates, happening in a normal context that includes zero make-outs.

Across the huddle, Melissa's eyes bore holes into me.

"LET ME GIVE YOU A RIDE HOME?" JOHN ASKS AT THE end of practice.

I keep examining my skinned knee, pouring water to wash away the clotted blood and dirt and grass stains. Head down, I spot Melissa's bright orange cleats just a few steps away. One of them taps the grass as the leg attached to it jiggles up and down. I move my eyes up just enough to assess the crossed arms.

I do not want to be trapped in a car with Melissa right now.

"Sure," I say to John, "a ride would be awesome." I wipe water off my knee and take John's outstretched hand. He pulls me up. I like that he pulls me up. I like that he offers rides.

I look for Melissa, but she's already turned her back on me, talking to Roshni with way more hand waving than is necessary. Fine. I know she heard us.

I follow John to his car, even though I see Chris and Elizabeth and Lindsay watching, squinting, working out the significance. I can't tell if their watching bugs me. I can't tell if I should have said no.

"What happened to your van?" I ask, ducking into the inconspicuous and undented silver car.

"Mom's using it to cart the soccer team around," John says. "Little brother," he adds when I look confused.

"Oh, so it really is a mom-van."

"Sometimes." John turns on the radio.

"I have a little sister," I say, and feel stupid immediately after saying it. I sound like I'm at show-and-tell, desperate for the class to find me interesting.

"Nice." John smirks. "Is she cute?"

My eagerness evaporates in a grimace. "She's ten." John looks slightly embarrassed, but not enough to wipe the smirk away entirely.

Why does half of what comes out of his mouth make me not want to talk to him? Why do I keep talking to him anyway? I turn to look out the window. John fiddles with the radio station until louder guitar chords fill up the empty space between us.

He stops the car at the corner of my block.

"It's the yellow one," I say, pointing, "with the azaleas."

John laughs. "I know, doofus." He puts the car in park.

"Hey," I say, but then John reaches to push strands of hair behind my ear. His fingers trail down my neck. Oh.

"Sorry," he says. He doesn't say what for.

The sun hovers below the tree line, but the sky is light and the streetlights haven't even come on yet. The difference between making out in a car in the dark and making out in a car where any random neighbor could see me feels stark and expansive, but John doesn't seem to recognize the distinction. He leans over the cup holders.

"I have to go," I say. John leans in to kiss me anyway, which I don't like on principle. I've been kind of wanting to try kissing him again, but now I pull away (though not quite fast enough to avoid a peck). "I—really, I do have to go. Um, thanks."

I mean for the ride, but John beams like I meant something else. "My pleasure, Lopez-Rourke," he says. "I'll see you on Sunday."

"Uh, yeah. Bye." I unhook my seat belt, open the door, stand on the sidewalk.

"Hey," John says. "You're going to the Austin tournament, right?"

"Uh, I guess?"

"Perfect," he says. "Don't forget your sleeping bag."

He has a little smirk that makes me very aware that in

less than two weeks we'll both be spending the night in a random dorm room in a random city. I guess that's one way to get more privacy for kissing.

I duck my head to avoid his smirk. "See you later."

I have to walk for eight hundred years before I get to my front door, and then I have to wait seven hundred more years for Connie to let me in. Every time I look back, John is smirking. It makes my stomach lurch and the muscles above my knees ache. It makes me feel stupid.

18

What the hell? **Melissa's text demands. It's followed** two seconds later by a second message: What the actual hell, Ellen?

I shove the phone back into my pocket. Normally Connie will at least pretend to be annoyed by phones at the dinner table, but tonight she has her own phone on the table. She texts with slow, clumsy fury, fingers flexed to keep her nails from hitting the screen.

The salad wilts in the middle of the table while Yasmín taps her fingers against her empty plate.

"Your father," Connie says, scowling at her phone, "is on his way."

Dad's been promising to make it home for dinner all week, so I understand Connie's frustration. It's 7:13. Dinner was supposed to be at seven, already later than usual to give me time to get back from quidditch.

Yasmín drums her plate. Connie jumps out of her seat and starts wiping the already clean countertop. I tap my pocket, wriggle my phone free, twirl it in my hands, and finally open Melissa's messages.

What? I type. I hesitate before hitting send, but Melissa probably already saw me typing anyway. Past the point of no return.

Even that *Phantom of the Opera* reference can't calm me down, though, especially when the three dots appear to show Melissa typing. They go on . . . and on . . . and on . . .

"Mom," Yasmín says. Connie drops her rag. "Um, we could just start eating the salad. Dad will be here in a minute, right?"

My little sister is too cute for her own good. Connie glances at her phone, but she doesn't hesitate to load Yasmín's plate with greens. She even remembered to keep the ranch dressing on the side today. I fill my own plate.

Family dinner isn't as consistent for us as it is for the Larsens. I'm just as likely to eat peanut butter in my room as at the table, and Connie will usually give Yasmín food whenever she asks, totally wrecking any normal eating schedule. But some days, maybe a few times a week, we'll all sit down and eat whatever we were going to eat at the same time. Nothing scheduled. Not officially planned. Not a big deal.

Until Dad started missing it.

My phone buzzes.

You know perfectly well what, Melissa's text reads. Are you dating John now? Were you going to say anything? Are you trying to prove a point?

I'm trying to decide how to respond when the front door slams open. Dad drops his briefcase in the doorway and walks into the kitchen, phone in hand.

"Okay," he snaps, "I'm here."

Even though it's an *I* statement, he sounds like he's looking for a fight.

Connie sniffs. She sits down and gestures for Dad to take his seat. The chair scrapes horribly against the kitchen tile.

"Bless us, oh Lord," Yasmín says while Dad adds a tiny helping of salad to his plate. We all bow our heads while she finishes the prayer.

"Amen," Connie and Dad say. I let go of my phone to twitch my fingers toward my forehead, chest, and shoulders.

Sometimes I can't wait for Yasmín to get a little older, just so I can ask her if she does this kind of thing on purpose. I can see Dad's shoulders relax and a smile creep into Connie's eyes as Yasmín raises her head and unfolds her hands. Is she so clever that she knows exactly how to dispel the tension in the room? Or is she just being herself?

"Well," Dad says. "Family dinner. This is nice." He takes a bite of salad. "And this," he says between bites, "is delicious."

Connie doesn't smile or anything, but she doesn't sniff.

My phone buzzes again.

???

Damn. I try to remember Melissa's questions, try to think of some answer to give her.

"Ellen . . ." I drag my eyes away from the screen at the sound of a sniff. Connie looks down her nose at my phone.

"But . . ."

"Ellen," Dad says, "let's put the phone down for a few minutes. Not at dinner; you know that."

Um, sure, right. Nobody cares that Connie has been on her phone since I sat down, or that Dad couldn't even be bothered to get here. But my phone? Ruining dinner.

"How have you been?" Dad asks me, his head tilted and his face unnatural, trying to engage me, trying to force me to interact. It's a fake question.

I give a fake answer. "Fine." My phone buzzes again. I fill my mouth with iceberg lettuce.

Dad tries again. "How are Melissa and Xiumiao doing?"

His face is still stiff, his gaze too direct. Anything to communicate that now—right now—he gives a fuck.

"I don't know," I say with a fake-patient smile. "I can't read my texts."

Connie clicks her tongue. Dad's eyebrows twitch into a tiny frown before settling back into interested-parent face.

He turns to Yasmín. "How's math going, kiddo?"

"Good," Yasmín answers, explaining how she got the highest score in her class on the most recent test.

"That's great, mija," Connie says. She and Dad glance at each other, and their smiles don't look forced.

"Mrs. Sorgalla said we're going to start multiplying fractions next week, and then it will be our last week, and then I just have swim lessons and writing camp, and then summer will be over." Yasmín only sounds the tiniest bit wistful.

"Good, good." Dad nods. Face relaxed now, he accepts the platter of chicken Connie passes to him and slides two grilled and seasoned chunks of meat to sit next to his salad. "Keep up the good work."

I know this is horrible, but sometimes I almost wish Yasmín were my half sister, Dad's biological kid, instead of my stepsister. Because if Connie and I had the only stepkid/stepparent relationship in the house, I wouldn't have to compare it to anything. I could watch Dad love

Yasmín as much as I do, as much as everyone does, and it wouldn't feel so unfair that Connie and I don't have the same bond.

"Ellen, how's your quidditch going?" Dad asks once the chicken's circled the table and I've retrieved my vegan burrito from the microwave.

"Oh." I hesitate, but Dad half ignores me as he digs into his chicken, no fake sincerity in his eyes. A real question, and it makes me want to give him a real answer. I swallow my last bite of salad. "Quidditch is going really well, actually."

"You were late on Sunday," Connie says.

"I wasn't!" I protest too quickly and too loudly. "I told you, we were eating dinner."

"I just mean it went later than usual." Connie shrugs.

"It was a tournament. We had a lot of games to play." I breathe and will my face not to flush with the memory of my ride home. "We played all day, and the games kept running late. The tournament directors weren't very organized. They're from UH." I can tell I've given too many details. Despite my best efforts, my cheeks start to heat up.

"Tournament?" Dad asks. "Do you have other teams to play?"

"What? Yes, of course." Dad's question jars me so much that I forget to keep blushing. "We have— I think there were six or eight. From all around: Katy and League City and everything." My voice gets a little squeaky when I'm defensive, but come on. *Do you have other teams to play?* How did he not know about the League City scrimmage? How did he totally miss that I was going to a tournament?

Dad chews his chicken. "Huh. How many quidditch players are there?"

"Do you mean in the greater Houston area or, like, worldwide?"

Dad's laugh is a single grenade of sound exploding across the table: "Ha!"

"Not joking, actually," I mumble, but Dad doesn't hear.

"They do all know they can't really fly, right?" he teases.

I have no answer besides a suppressed eye roll and sigh. I get it. The sport is based off a fantasy novel. Clearly all the players must be living in a fantasy world. I wonder if Dad's ever heard the theory that soccer was invented by kicking around a skull.

"They don't fly. They run with brooms or little sticks."

I can't tell whether it's me or Connie who's more surprised when Yasmín speaks up. We both stare while Dad smiles and asks, "What, between their legs?"

Yasmín nods. "And the snitch is a person," she says. "And the seeker has to catch his tail."

"Their tail," I correct her, but it comes out sounding like a question.

"And people tackle each other so they fall down."

"Wow." Dad nods. "Why haven't I gotten a good look at this sport before now?"

He says it casually, but the question stings.

"We should go watch the big summer tournament coming up in Austin," Yasmín says. "You're going, right, Ellen?"

I blink at my little sister. Sometimes I still catch myself looking down at knee level for her, or reaching to help her open her juice boxes. "How do you know so much about it?"

Yasmín's whole body rolls in a shrug. "I looked it up."

I guess I shouldn't be surprised that she knows how to use the internet, but I still am, and more than that, I'm surprised that she bothered looking up quidditch.

"Oh," I say. "Yeah. Did you watch any of the YouTube videos? There are some full matches—" Yasmín's already nodding. "Okay, that's cool. And the tutorial videos, is that how you—?" Yasmín nods again and glances at the ceiling in the world's most polite eye roll. "Wow. Okay. That's awesome. I didn't know you'd done all that."

Yasmín shrugs. "You made it sound cool."

I snort to cover up the sudden lump in my throat. "Cool. Thanks."

Dad watches our exchange with a bemused smile. "Austin, huh?" he asks. "Were you going to let us know?"

"Yeah, sorry. It's coming up the weekend after next,

but I hadn't really gotten around to planning it yet."

He shrugs. "I might be able to get the weekend off, if you don't mind having us tag along. I mean, it seems like I have a lot to learn."

Yasmín beams. Dad beams. I even manage a quick grin, but my phone vibrates in my pocket, souring the moment. Still, all three of us turn to Connie with the same hopeful question.

Connie sucks in her breath.

"It seems like short notice," she says.

"Oh, but we can afford to be a little spontaneous," Dad says. Smiling, but I don't miss the tightness around his eyes or how his fingers tap the edge of his glass.

"Can we?" Connie snaps. "You're not struggling to find the time?"

Shit.

"Connie," Dad says, in the voice he usually uses to say "Ellen."

Connie jumps out of her chair and storms to the empty sink. She stares at it for a few seconds before stalking back to the table and grabbing all the dishes that aren't held down—serving spoons, my water glass, her own plate. Everything slams into the sink, and the kitchen fills with the clattering silence of Connie's anger.

Yasmín stares at her lap, her whole body curled in on itself. All her efforts to make peace, and we end up here.

Dad pushes up his glasses and runs a hand through his thinning hair.

I pull out my phone.

First message: Is this a joke? Are you trying to get back at me or something?

Second message: Whatever.

Third message: Btw, I can't give you a ride to the tournament, so don't count on that.

Fourth message: Fuck you.

I've been mad at Melissa for a while now, but that still hurts. I turn my phone off, telling myself she doesn't mean it, that she'll apologize in a second. This is not how I imagined my revenge working out. I glance up at Dad. Now would be a great time for him to decide to drive up to Austin, conveniently offering me a ride.

But first, Dad needs to apologize for his lateness.

We all wait. I don't actually mind the tension that much—I'm just relieved not to be at the center of it for once. But I know Yasmín's slow chewing covers her anxiety.

Dad picks up his fork and digs back into his plate. It's a bold move, the kind of aggressively fake nonchalance I would expect from me, not him. Dad doesn't pout. He explains. He smooths. He apologizes.

Right now, he *should* apologize.

Connie runs out of dishes. She hovers in front of the sink, looking lost.

I don't know if it's her or Yasmín I'm trying to save when I break the long silence. "A trip would be good so Yasmín can learn about the game. She might want to start playing, for exercise and college app padding. Unique activities are good, right?"

I'm not thinking hard about what I'm saying, so I'm not prepared when Connie spins like a horror movie villain, blasting me with the full force of her rage.

"What are you talking about?" she barks. "She's not going to play *quidditch*." Aunt Petunia herself couldn't inject the wizard sport's name with more contempt. "She's not going to join some weirdo clique of misfits and— Why are you always trying to drag her into your world of *freaks*?"

If I'm the starship *Enterprise*, the crew of the bridge are all stumbling to one side and grabbing their chairs, and Scotty's voice is warning, *She's hit bad, Captain. Shields at thirty percent.*

"Haven't you caused enough problems?" Connie walks right up to my chair, and she looks tall now hovering over my plate, and her face twists with spite. "Can you just grow up already?"

"Okay." Dad stands up. "That's enough."

The United Front crumbles in front of my eyes, which should be cause for celebration, but there's nothing good in the cold way Dad and Connie stare each other down. How long have I wanted Dad to stand up for me? Shouldn't it feel better?

To everyone's surprise, Yasmín leaves first. She runs out of the room and slams her bedroom door. I follow her example, not sure what else to do. This is all kind of unprecedented.

In my room I slip in my headphones and crank the volume on the *Spring Awakening* soundtrack to drown out the yelling downstairs.

I hope Yasmín has louder music than I do.

Connie and Dad stay mad overnight. Dad leaves for work before I wake up, but I can still feel the tension in the way Connie stomps around the house and regards her intermittently chiming phone like some animal just peed on it. Melissa hasn't texted me since last night, and I keep waiting for an apology that doesn't come.

Yasmín takes the day off of camp, claiming a headache. She tiptoes around the house like a timid barometer of Connie's anger, distracting me from my dishes-and-laundry routine. She eats three bowls of ice cream before noon, so I finally give her a peanut butter sandwich.

"You're okay, right?" I ask her while she mopes on the couch with Connie's iPad, getting in the way of my clean clothes piles. "You're not letting this bother you?" I tilt the iPad back so she'll look at me. "They're going to be fine. You'll see, in a couple weeks we're all going to be watching quidditch together and everything's going to be fine."

Yasmín blinks at me, her eyes puffy and moist. "You don't know."

"I do, actually," I tell her, "because my dad is awesome and your mom . . . is also awesome, and they love each other."

"Hmph."

"What?" I drop my handful of socks and perch on the couch next to Yasmín. I nudge her shoulder and try to poke her pouting lip into a smile.

Yasmín shoves her hands under her knees and kicks her legs against the couch. "You don't even like Mom. You don't even care if they get divorced like Samantha's parents and if Dad moves to Kentucky like Samantha's dad." She scowls fiercely.

"Whoa, whoa . . . You're mad at me?"

She buries her head in the iPad.

"Look," I sigh, "your friend Samantha sounds like she has a big mouth, okay? Connie and Dad are not getting divorced. It's one fight."

"It's not one," Yasmín says stubbornly.

"Right." I twist my hands around each other, remembering the college money fight, the Christmas break fight. "Well, still, occasional fights are normal. Even big ones. It doesn't mean they can't—"

"They fight all the time," Yasmín cuts me off. "Every time you fight with Mom they fight. And Dad stays at work. Samantha said her dad did that before her parents got divorced."

My hands drop to my lap. "When do they fight?" *Surely we can't be talking about the same United Front*, I want to say, but the sarcasm sticks in my throat. *It's not my fault*, I want to say, but I can't say anything.

"At night, all the time. I can hear them from my room. They fight about you. Not yelling. Quiet fighting. Mad fighting."

Yasmín hops to her feet. She stomps toward her room, iPad tucked under her arm.

"Hey, wait . . ." I stare at her ponytail, stunned. "Wait."

Her bedroom door slams.

Connie's heels tap into the living room. "What?" she snaps. "What's going on?" Her bun is a mess.

"Nothing." I retreat to my room. I barricade myself under my blanket, where I can't hear any more accusations. I hold my phone against my burning chest and pretend that at any second I'll text Melissa, or I'll go downstairs and talk to Yasmín, convince her to forgive me or to admit that there's nothing to forgive. Maybe I'll even call Dad and tell him to come home already and fix this.

I don't do any of those things, obviously. I read Tumblr. I fume. I do what I always do: nothing.

• • •

A WEEK PASSES WITH THE SAME COLD WAR ATMOSPHERE. Xiumiao texts to let me know that her parents aren't hosting Fourth of July this year. (Too busy with college prep, she says, and plus I didn't really want to do it. I couldn't really avoid inviting her, and that would undo everything. You know.) So the holiday tiptoes by our house with barely a whiff of grill smoke while I surf the internet and dream of the smell of Mrs. Li's barbecue brisket and Mr. Li's lecture about who invented fireworks in the first place.

At least I have the quidditch trip coming up. Erin and Aaron spam the team group chat with hype memes all week, and at Sunday and Wednesday practices we spend half the time learning new plays to use at the tournament. John gives me rides to and from practice, which is weird because I don't know what it means but good because Melissa and I seem to be officially ignoring each other. Good thing we play different positions or things would get awkward on the pitch. I remember Erin's and Elizabeth's warnings about team breakups.

It's Wednesday night when a knock on my door makes me jump.

"Um, yeah? Hello?" I wasn't asleep exactly, but I still sit up feeling disoriented, eyes blurry from staring at my phone.

Connie swings the door open and steps inside. She doesn't hang near the doorway like Dad when he just has something quick to say, and she doesn't sit on the side of the bed like Dad when he's gearing up for a long talk. She marches right into the center of my room, sweeps her gaze around my bookshelves and the pile of dirty laundry at the foot of my bed.

"What are you doing in bed?" she asks.

"I finished the list."

Connie shrugs, like asking the question took up all the concern she could muster. "You need to babysit Yasmín this weekend."

"What?"

"Greg and I are going to spend the weekend in Galveston," Connie says. "We'll be close if you have any emergencies, but we need time away from everything." Her eyes dart around my room without meeting mine. "Just a mini vacation. A break. We need it."

"I have quidditch. I'm going to Austin."

In an instant, Connie's face snaps from "vulnerable human being" back to "angry authority figure."

"You're going to Austin?" she asks, an approximation of a smile stretching her lips but leaving the corners of her eyes dead.

"Yes," I say, "for the tournament. We talked about it at—" At the disastrous dinner that started her and Dad fighting.

"I don't remember you ever *asking* us for permission to leave the city," Connie says. "With a bunch of strangers? I'm sure you can see why that's not something Greg and I would get very excited about, even if you weren't grounded."

Which you are, her smirk adds.

"But quidditch things . . ." I try to think how Melissa would handle this, but instead I just whine, "Dad said I could go."

Connie sucks in her breath, and for a second I think I've made a good argument. But then she lets the breath out in a call that travels the house. "Greg! Will you come up here a minute, please?"

"I think we need to reevaluate your deal," Connie says as Dad's footsteps approach, "now that I've heard how dangerous the game is. I don't know if we want you getting tackled by college boys."

Dad appears behind her, a hand going to her shoulder and a nervous smile on his face. "How can I help you ladies?"

"Connie isn't letting me go to the tournament this weekend," I say quickly, before she can spin it herself. "Please tell her you already said I could go."

In the long silence that follows, a sick frozen feeling climbs up my chest.

"Ellen," Dad says, "Connie and I were both hoping that you could put your fun on hold to watch your sister this weekend. We've been very accommodating, but you are supposed to be on punishment, and an out-of-town trip is asking a lot."

"But you said . . ."

"I said I was interested, but then things changed. I'm sorry that you thought we had a binding contract, but . . ." He throws up his hands. "We're all trying to make this work. We're not on opposite sides." He returns his hand to Connie's shoulder. "And I would appreciate it if you stopped trying to make us out to be."

I guess that's the end of the short-lived "Dad actually stands up for Ellen" phase. I guess he's reached the same conclusion Yasmín did: that I'm the reason for all the conflict in the family.

"Okay, Ellen?" Dad asks. I nod. He nods back, then pats Connie's shoulder and retreats back downstairs. I watch him go through blurry eyes.

Connie doesn't leave. She walks farther into my room, shakes her head, and starts straightening the line of choir trophies and my lone YMCA basketball participation award. "You should clean off these shelves sooner rather than later," she says. "We might not start work on my studio for a while, but I'm sure you'll be busy once you move out."

When I don't answer, she spins in a slow circle, sucks her breath in between her teeth, and then, finally, leaves.

Fuck.

The covers twine hot around me. I kick them to the floor and stalk to my desk, pulling out my phone as I collapse into the spinning chair.

There's a Facebook post waiting for me in the Summer Quidditch group.

> **Karey Yates**
>
> Wednesday at 8:34 PM
>
> Hi everyone! Y'all did great at filling out the initial tournament interest survey, but I need a clear and FINAL headcount on who's actually coming and how you're all getting there. So this is the official reminder for those of you who are bad at deadlines: we need to finalize our plans yesterday, so let me know if you're in and what you need in terms of carpool, housing for the weekend, and equipment (I'm picking up a whole pack of sports socks if you don't have red ones). Hope to see all of y'all there!

I stare at the message.

Actually, Karey, I should be typing, *I really hate to do this because I so wanted to go . . .*

Actually, Karey, my parents hate me, so . . .

My thumbs refuse to move across the tiny keyboard.

Nope, can't go, I should type. Rip the Band-Aid off.

It should be simple now that Melissa wants nothing to do with me. The whole point was to hang out with her, to make sure we didn't miss best friend moments and all that.

A long string of comments stretches under Karey's message.

Lindsay Trouble Young
Don't forget sunscreen!

Elizabeth Lomas Ramirez
And chug water. Also, after-party info?

Erin Barone
☺

Aaron Levine
😃😃😃

Erin Barone
😃x10000

Aaron Levine
😛

Jackson Hu
Do we need any special equipment? Like padding or mouth guards? Or helmets???

Karey Yates
No helmets! Grab a mouth guard if you can; I'll

pick up extras. Also bring cash for food and to pay drivers for gas. Message me if you need a team scholarship.

Elizabeth Lomas Ramirez
Are we going to sleep slumber-party-style on dorm room floors, or will we have beds?

John Bauman
Don't count on beds . . . unless you find a UT player to share ☺

Karey Yates
Yeah, most likely slumber-party-style. But hey, all part of the bonding fun!

Erin Barone
😃😃😃

I drop my phone on the desk and shove my chair back to crash into the bed frame. I don't want to see everyone's excitement.

As my anger fades, my chest has room to fill with something else, something cold and dark instead of burning. I'm disappointed. I want to play quidditch this weekend.

Sometimes when I have a hard time with something, the struggle makes me not want to do it anymore. Quidditch is just the opposite. Sometimes groups of people make me so nervous I want to sink into the ground. Quidditch players don't make me feel that way. Sometimes—lots of times—I feel weird and out of place and dorky and scared and powerless. But on the quidditch pitch, I feel like I could be strong.

I want to go to the tournament. I have my heart set on it. I just didn't realize it until now.

When Connie left over Christmas, she proved that Dad needed her. I thought she was punishing both of us, but that was never it. She showed him that he had a choice: her or me. And now he's chosen.

I think of how hard I've tried, all summer, to show Dad that I'm part of the family. All pointless.

The rules I've followed, the words I've swallowed, every forced smile and fake apology and scoop of shared Rice Dream feels extra pathetic now that it's clear how little difference it made.

I don't want to try anymore. I want to rip away from this whole mess. I finally see the appeal of getting space. And I sure as hell don't want to sit at home all weekend babysitting for a family that doesn't need me.

The idea doesn't start as a plan, but it blossoms into a rough one pretty quickly.

19

First, I stalk my chat contacts until I see Xiumiao come online. I'm frustrated that I have to do this, that I can't count on my friend to answer me without scheming to make myself extremely hard to ignore. Xiumiao hasn't even acknowledged that she dumped me right along with Melissa, and I just let her keep sending memes like everything is fine, and I'm done with it. Maybe I won't get closure, but I can at least ask for something I need right now.

Ellen: Hi, can you answer this please?

Xiumiao: I know this isn't exactly news but I'm obsessed with Hamilton.

It's an answer. Not great textual communication etiquette, but I'll take it.

Ellen: I need a favor
Xiumiao: Whatever you say, sir
Xiumiao: Jefferson will pay for this behavior
Ellen: Not a musical-quoting favor. An actual one.

My thumb hovers over the phone keyboard. I could leave it at that, but I can't stand to let Xiumiao ghost me without at least telling her that I noticed.

Ellen: I know you've made it clear that you're done being friends with me or whatever, but honestly I will never bother you again if you do this for me.

I wait for twelve long minutes before getting a response.

Xiumiao: What are you talking about?

Xiumiao: Why would I not want to be friends?

Xiumiao: Have you been secretly mad all summer because I didn't want to hang out with Melissa?

Well. That I was not expecting.

Ellen: I wasn't secretly mad. You wanted to be done with high school so you can start college with your new college friends and never look back. And you barely answered my texts.

Xiumiao: Have you met me? I'm terrible at responding.

Ellen: Well, that's shitty.

Xiumiao: Okay, it's shitty. I thought you understood that I needed a break from her.

Xiumiao: From Melissa. Whom I'm over.

Ellen: I'm not Melissa.

Xiumiao: No, but you would have been talking about her all the time. You know you would.

Ellen: I mean, I could have tried if you gave me a chance. I did try.

Xiumiao: You were literally spending all your free time with her this summer. I saw you for like five minutes at Tea Corner and you brought her up in the first sentence. And it seemed just as shitty to be like "Do not speak her name in my presence." Or make you choose who to hang out with or whatever. It was my problem. I didn't want to make it your problem.

Xiumiao: Plus it was pretty clear who you'd choose if it came down to it so . . .

Ellen: ???

Xiumiao: I didn't say I didn't want to see you this summer, Ellen. I said I didn't want to see Melissa, and your immediate reaction was "Oh, so I guess we can't hang out." So that's what happened.

I try to remember if this is true.

Xiumiao: I know you and Melissa are better friends. But we're older friends, and I thought you'd get that I just needed a short break from it all. I didn't expect you to get all worried. And then . . . yeah, I got kind of excited about college and I didn't check in that much. You were grounded and I was busy and . . . Okay. I'm sorry. Just because I warned you that I was going to avoid you doesn't make it any less shitty that I avoided you. And if we're going to live in different cities soon, I should try harder with texting.

Xiumiao: Do you want me to give you constant updates that we're friends?

Xiumiao: We're friends.

Xiumiao: You know I'll do whatever you need. I'm, like, here for you.

Xiumiao: Or whatever.

Xiumiao doesn't do polite greetings, "make you feel better" apologies, or sentimentality. She also doesn't make empty promises.

I try to find the right way to express my relief, to tell her that it means a lot to hear her say that and that I value her friendship, too. Instead I just end up typing Thanks.

Xiumiao: So what's the favor?

It takes a little bit of backstory, but I fill her in on the plan.

> **Xiumiao:** So . . . a babysitting gig but you can't pay me and you can't guarantee I won't be implicated.
>
> **Ellen:** When you put it like that, I sound like an asshole.
>
> **Xiumiao:** You are an asshole. But . . . I was an asshole all summer. Plus your little sister is cool.
>
> **Ellen:** I will honestly love you forever.
>
> **Xiumiao:** You spelled "owe" wrong.

I shower her with a rainbow of heart emojis just to make her uncomfortable. And also maybe because I love her and I'm glad to have her back.

I talk to Yasmín before we finalize the plan.

"I want to ask you something," I start, in the doorway of her room. I'm trying to look casual, so Connie doesn't suspect me. "A favor. A big one."

Yasmín looks up from her vocabulary workbook, tugs the lacy edge of her sleeve thoughtfully, then pops out of her desk chair and pulls me into the room, closing the door behind me.

"You're going to Austin," she whispers. "Right? You're going to get in big trouble."

"I know . . ." I shrug. "Do you mind?"

Yasmín looks at me, tugging her sleeves over her thumbs. "Why do you want to go?"

The directness of the question freaks me out a little. "I don't know," I tell her. "All my friends are going, I guess. And it sounds like fun. And I get in trouble anyway. I just decided it wasn't worth it to miss this."

Yasmín frowns. "My friend went to horse camp this week, but I had to do writing class."

"Sorry," I say. I look around my little sister's room, from the slightly crooked but neatly tucked pink bedspread to the wall of ribbons and certificates. "Maybe next year you can do horse camp instead."

"Mom would get mad," Yasmín says, her face reproachful.

"You know it's not my fault," I blurt. "When they fight? You know that, right?"

Yasmín shrugs, twisting the edges of her sleeves.

"And"—I look at the achievement ribbons and the piles of summer homework—"it's not your responsibility to keep them from fighting, either."

Yasmín's hands drop to her side, her mouth pinches shut, and she doesn't meet my eyes. "I guess."

"I mean it. I know you're a good peacekeeper, and it's nice, but . . . you get to demand horse camp. They can figure out how to deal with it."

I wait for so long that I suspect I've upset her, but finally

Yasmín mutters, "Horse camp probably isn't that great anyway."

"Okay." I nod. Of course Yasmín doesn't want to defy Connie. "Forget I said anything." Why am I trying to turn my sweet baby sister into some rebel, anyway? Why am I trying to turn myself into one?

"Are you going to ask Xiumiao to babysit?" Yasmín asks. "Will you tell her to order pizza?"

A grin spreads across my face. "I'm sure I can make that one of the conditions."

Yasmín nods. "Text me the scores. And make sure your team wins."

I nod. I tell myself that Xiumiao has babysat Yasmín plenty of times, and Connie and Dad trust her, and I'm definitely not doing anything capital-"B" Bad to my little sister by letting her have a fun day with a semi-responsible teen. I give Yasmín a thumbs-up as I leave her room.

I'm going to be in *so much* trouble when they find out.

After that's settled, I text Karey. I'm officially in, if you've got a ride and a room for me.

She texts back, Absolutely! Get pumped!

My phone shakes in my hands and sweat trickles down my armpits as I imagine the look on Dad's face when he finds out. I delete the last two texts from our chat history. I crawl back into bed and pull the covers over my head and wonder if I'm really doing this. And then, annoyed with myself, I send one last text, a shout of false bravado.

So pumped! Can't wait!

OVER THE NEXT WEEK, I COME SO CLOSE TO CHICKENING out.

It's one thing to impulsively declare I'm done seeking my parents' approval. It's another to actually deliberately sneak away from home for a weekend, especially once the tension in the house has mostly calmed down. I could probably skate through the rest of the summer on this thin ice, and instead I'm planning to torpedo it.

When not immersed in active denial, I type and delete apologies and excuses to Karey, explanations of how Something Very Important came up and I just can't get out of it. But I don't send them.

Karey puts our schedule up online Thursday night. On Friday I wake up to a text from John that, in addition to wishing me good morning and linking me a YouTube video of trick basketball shots, lets me know that he'll be at my house at six a.m. Saturday to pick me up.

Actually . . . I type, my parents are leaving town tonight, and I have to watch my sister. Sorry . . .

I still don't hit send.

The garage offers a convenient distraction, and I plunge

in immediately after breakfast. I'm getting into the mildewed underbelly of storage now, with the boxes of long-outgrown clothes and plastic bags that never quite made it to Goodwill and—finally—the hints of Mom. Her junk mail falls out from between the pages of a romance novel with a waterlogged back cover. I tuck the special credit card offer into my pocket instead of the growing pile of trash.

I need to pack. If I'm really going to, I don't know, run away from home for the weekend, then I need to pack my quidditch things. Or if I'm *not* going to sneak out of the house and spend a parentally forbidden weekend in Austin, then I should probably text my ride not to show up here tomorrow morning.

Instead of doing either of those things, I reach for the next box.

This one's plastic—opaque white plastic turning yellow with age and gray with dust. Prying off the lid catapults grit into my face, and I cough and rub my eyes and . . . smell floral perfume.

I don't recognize the shirts folded and rolled into tight tubes at the top of the box, but their size means they're not mine, and their soft bright colors mean they're not Dad's, and the fact that they're packed away instead of already donated means they're not Connie's. I unroll a purple blouse. Mom's blouse. It's shaped funny, the shoulders bulky and the collar oddly oversized. Out of style. Not even old enough to be retro, though I'm not really the kind of adventurous dresser who could pull off the retro look even if it was. The blouse is useless. Probably all of them are. They should go in the trash bag or the Goodwill bag.

They should. But they don't.

"Ellen? Are you making progress? I'm just about finished packing, so if you need anythi— Oh."

Connie sees me. She sees the box and the unrolled blouse. She stops in the doorway. "Oh."

Part of me wants to wave the blouse to shoo Connie away like an oversized fly. Part of me wants to hide it behind my back. I don't want her looking at this, at me. I want this moment to be mine.

"I was just going to . . ." I say, and then I don't know how to finish the sentence.

"Of course," Connie says, and then she hovers for a few more seconds before walking closer.

Shoo. I think she's being nice—I know she's being nice. But I don't want it.

She stands next to me, both of us staring at the box. I can't toss out the clothes with Connie watching. I can't.

"Do you . . . do you think any of them would fit me?"

Connie's eyebrows shoot up in alarm, either because of the musty old clothes or the sentimentality.

"I'm sure this isn't easy," she says. "If you want, you

can go inside and take a break. We can wait for Greg, or I can deal with them if you don't mind. I have a friend who—"

"No!" I drop the blouse into the pile so I can hug the box to my chest. Letting Connie throw away the clothes is a hundred times worse than throwing them away myself.

"I wouldn't be . . ." Connie stutters. "I didn't mean to—to interfere, but you seem upset, and—"

"I am not upset."

Tears well in my eyes, surprising me as much as Connie. I don't cry about my mom, not for as long as I can remember. She's more black hole than memory. I've always had Dad. I wonder about her, of course, and play the "what if?" game, and I collect Dad's stories and memories to store with what I remember from my grandparents. But I don't cry.

Why am I crying?

"Here," Connie says, one hand landing on my shoulder and the other gripping the box. "I'm sorry about this, Ellen, really, I am. Why don't you go inside and—"

"Stop!" I yank the box away from Connie's prying fingers, and the whole thing topples off my lap and spills rolled-up clothes and purses and shoes all over the cracked cement. "Damn it! What are you— Can you just—" I try to stop, try to breathe, try to wring out my eyes with the heels of my palms. "I'm sorry. Obviously it's not you. Can you just give me a minute?"

Connie is already backing away, hands up. "Of course. Of course. I'm sorry. Do you . . . ? I'll make lunch." She disappears as fast as her heels can take her.

"Thanks," I say. *Shoo, fly, don't bother me.*

I try hard not to sniff, but I end up sniffing. I start picking up the clothes, wondering if I should just trash them now that they're covered in dried leaves and bug corpses and dust. I reach for a strappy sandal with worn-down soles. The heel strap hangs at an odd angle, fake leather cracked. Useless, no question. I drop it into the trash bag.

I look for something else easy, moving aside a gray sweater and digging into a pile of stretchy leggings. And that's when I feel it.

Spiky, rough plastic. I tug a long shoelace and unearth the shoe, a white soccer cleat stained with green and brown streaks down the sides. Broken in, but not worn-out. I dig through the overturned pile and fish out the second cleat, run my hand over the stitching, trace the spiked pattern of the soles. I pull up the tongues and read the size: US 5 UK 3 EU 35.

That should fit.

Cold tears still hang in my eyelashes, but now laughter bubbles up in my chest. Am I PMS-ing? Is this some kind of cosmic sign? After all these years, my mom finally makes contact from the other side in order to . . . encourage me to play quidditch? I wrap the shoes in the ugly purple blouse and walk inside, straight past Connie and the peanut butter and banana sandwich she's set out on the table. I get to my room and sit on the floor with my back against the door to prevent any sneaky fake-knocking tricks. I kick off my flip-flops, pull my hair off my neck to enjoy the breeze of my fan.

I stick my right foot in the cleat. I lace it up. Perfect.

I dig my backpack out of my closet and search through my dresser for black T-shirts. I have a lot of packing to do before morning.

Dad is only too happy to let me invite Xiumiao to spend the night. I would almost think he feels guilty. Besides, Yasmín got in on it, saying how she missed Xiumiao. My little sister turned out to be an excellent co-conspirator. Which isn't proof that she doesn't hate me, necessarily.

She will be fine. She said she would. She'll be fine, and so will I.

"Is this officially the new hoodie?" I ask Xiumiao when she turns up in the same gray-and-blue one she was wearing at Tea Corner. "I like it."

"Oh, thanks, yeah." She tugs the straps of her backpack.

"Thanks for coming," I say quickly, and then we stand in the front hallway staring at the floor until Dad saves us by poking his head out.

"Xiumiao! I was wondering when I'd see you." He dumps his packed duffel bag by the door, just about ready to leave.

"Hi, Greg. I was wondering when you'd free Ellen."

Dad just smiles. He's not only used to Xiumiao; he's half the reason she's like this. He was totally amused and encouraging when *she* hit her teen attitude phase. "The girls couldn't convince you to come out to the park?"

Xiumiao shakes her head.

"Well, I'm glad you're here to keep Ellen and Yasmín company," Dad says.

"Yeah." Xiumiao shrugs. "Seemed like a good way to end my babysitting career."

"Huh?" Dad tilts his head while my eyes bug out of my head in panic.

"You know, before college starts." She smirks at me.

I drag her upstairs before she can give me any more heart attacks.

Six a.m. is just cool enough to turn the normal humid air into clammy fog soup that soaks into my lungs as I stand ankle-deep on the Freemans' dewy lawn, wishing for a sidewalk. My Converse sneakers are already soaked, and I fear for my socks if John doesn't get here soon.

A car door slams behind me, and I spin around, but it's

just the neighbor on the far corner, the one who works as a teacher and commutes an hour every day to summer school. At the sound of an engine I spin back to the road, but it's just some anonymous sports car revving in the distance. I don't know why I'm so amped up. Connie and Dad are already in Galveston. But I'm about to jump out of my skin at every noise.

I don't know what I'm doing. I know that there are clothes in my backpack, and toothpaste. I know, distantly, that this is an overnight trip. But I have no idea what it means to drive to another city without my parents or a school-appointed chaperone. I've never spent the night anywhere but Melissa's or Xiumiao's houses, or my grandparents', maybe once at Aunt Mal's apartment with Dad. Where are we sleeping? I should have asked more questions. I should have thought this through more.

The sky gets brighter and I get more nervous. 6:02. I'm not late, but John is. I could text him, if I didn't have a rule of not texting him whenever possible. I don't even know why, exactly; I just feel weird about it. I'm afraid texting him will mean something. So I've let conversations die, and I've let Karey arrange our ride situation. And now, instead of texting, I wait.

Nine annoying minutes later, the sun breaks over the trees, the first prickling hint of summer heat washing over me. Like a mirage, the van appears around the corner, swinging around and pulling to a stop in front of me, big and mom-like and clunky and practically glowing in the light.

"Orange!" I laugh as John rolls down the passenger-side window. "It's orange." The van is not tan or brown, like I assumed in the moonlight. It's bright citrus, construction-work orange.

I pull open the door, toss my backpack into the space under the seat, and climb in, still laughing. John sticks his tongue out at me, and I'm distracted enough by the ridiculous car and the sight of his quirked grin that I don't notice who's sitting in the back seat of the van. At least, not until she speaks.

"Yep, it's orange," Melissa says, her voice cold. "Can we get going now before we get chased down by an angry stepmother? We're already late."

What is she doing here? Why isn't she taking her own car? Wasn't that the whole point of rescinding her offer to drive me?

"Chased down?" Karey asks in the seat next to her. "Who's getting chased down?"

Crap. I turn in my seat to lock eyes with Melissa. *Don't.* Of course Melissa would know immediately why I'm practically dying of nerves. *Please don't.*

"We were supposed to be on the highway ten minutes ago," Melissa says. "Chop chop!" She whacks Karey's shoulder with each word, effectively distracting her out of concerned team captain mode.

I wait until Melissa looks at me. *Thanks.*

She turns to stare out the back window while my house disappears around the corner. She doesn't smile.

But at least we're on the road.

"On a scale from 'one' to 'pass an empty bottle,' how badly does everyone need to pee?" John asks once we hit the freeway. "Also, now's the time for music requests if you have them."

"Hmm?" I'm checking my phone for the millionth time, expecting a frantic call at any second. "I don't know. Nothing. Whatever."

"Everyone should really have peed before we left," Karey says. "Since I specifically mentioned that in my itinerary."

"Can I connect my phone to your speakers?" Melissa asks before Karey can get too exasperated. "I have the *Rocky Horror* soundtrack."

"Um . . ." John says. I don't think my disappointment can get any greater until he adds, "Isn't that the freaky movie with the cross-dressing?"

"You say that like it's a bad thing." Karey shrugs.

"Uh, yeah. Sorry. This car is a strictly showtune-free zone."

I try so hard not to look at John that I accidentally look back, straight into Melissa's judging eyes. *Your boyfriend is bad*, her stare says, *and you should feel bad*.

To which I can only glare back, *He's* not *my boyfriend!* I'm sure there must be some examples of good people who don't like musicals. I just can't think of any right now.

"So," I change the subject, "did we have so many drivers that we didn't need Melissa?"

Melissa snorts, and Karey starts inspecting her cupholder.

"I thought your car died," John says into the rearview mirror.

Melissa pulls headphones out of her pocket and shoves one into her ears. "It did."

She taps her phone screen and then tilts it toward Karey, who smiles and accepts the other earbud.

A hundred bucks says it's *Rocky Horror*.

What am I getting myself into?

20

The road saves me. I just really like riding in cars, feeling the sway of the seat and watching the flat green expanse of Texas scroll by and nodding off with my head rattling against the window.

I wake up when we hit our first Austin stoplight. The corrugated tin roofs, cow-dotted fields, and pecan-selling general stores have disappeared, replaced by the snarl of gray freeway ramps.

I spy the pitches first, probably because I'm staring idly out the window instead of trying to help navigate. The trios of hoops have become a familiar sight, and they bring a familiar jolt of excitement that turns immediately sour and settles in the pit of my stomach, the same about-to-hurl sensation I get before choir concerts and finals. I swallow. Silly to have performance anxiety when nobody really expects me to perform.

I mean, it could also be the looming threat of being caught by Connie and Dad, but I've decided to shove that as far to the back of my mind as possible.

Karey groans in pleasure as she stretches her legs and steps out of the van. John rolls his shoulders and beams at me, and even Melissa smiles in my general direction. I stretch my arms over my head and try not to wish for another half hour of traffic. Just the nerves.

A lot of yawning people in cleats and headbands swarm past us, toting balls and brooms and bags of all sizes. I follow Karey to a table under a plastic awning, where a volunteer chatters into a cell phone while checking us off a registration list.

"Last name?" she asks me.

"Uh . . ." It's too early for this. "Lopez-Rourke?"

"Huh?"

"It should be under L-O-P . . ."

"David Lopez?"

"Uh, no, it's actually hyphenated."

"Huh?"

"Try R-O-U-R . . ."

The girl shoves the list and pen into my hand. "Sorry,

can you just . . ." She grabs the sleeve of another volunteer and pulls them into her phone conversation.

I find myself (as "Lopez, Rourke Ellen") and check the space with a sigh. Scanning the list shows the names of my teammates and League City players, along with some names I know from Facebook only. Merrick (whose last name is not really TheGreat) from S.P.I.F. is reffing, and Nico (whose last name really does start with an "X" and is too long for me to read at a glance) is apparently here somewhere. The prospect of meeting new people amps up my nervous stomach, in a sort of good way.

Erin's car arrives, and I join the huddle around a tree near the parking lot. I dub it Replacement Tree and drop my bag between the roots. The Katy team warms up a few yards away, and Alex stretches with his League City teammates one pitch over. I recognize some of Karey's A&M friends and UT players from the last tournament, but there are still so many new faces.

"Okay, folks, time to get pumped," Karey orders. "Let's take a couple of laps and then start stretches. We play San Antonio as soon as the refs are ready. Game faces!"

Elizabeth yawns and lifts her goggles to rub her face. Erin and Aaron cross their eyes at each other. Jackson wobbles on his right foot while trying to tie the laces of his left cleat. Lindsay and John bicker about potential starting lineups. Nobody starts running.

"Y'all," Karey sighs. "I said game faces. Come on, we've got to kill this first game—set the tone of the day." Her voice turns extra Southern and extra loud. "Who's ready to kick some ass?"

Sleepy and reluctant, we start running.

We don't exactly kick ass. Our game against San Antonio is short and close, but we scrape a win thanks to a desperate, beautiful snitch grab by John that brings the game to an end before San Antonio has time to run up their lead. For five solid seconds as we rush the field, I actually *want* to kiss him.

With so many beater subs and such a short game, I didn't even make it onto the pitch. I shake hands with the San Antonio team, relieved but restless.

"Y'all are superstars," Karey gasps at us, sweat soaking her tank top. Chris shakes his head, definitely beating himself up for missing a couple of crucial shots. I pat his shoulder, and he leans an elbow on my head in response.

"Beaters, we'll aim for quicker subs next time." Karey looks pointedly at John and Lindsay, who are not great at remembering to take breaks when the score is close. "Next game is against Austin. Meet back here at eleven thirty to warm up."

I follow Elizabeth to watch a game between League City

and College Station. Someone from San Antonio passes a tube of sunscreen down the sidelines. It's fry-an-egg-on-the-top-of-my-head hot, but I'm happy surrounded by other sweaty quidditch players, cheering for Alex as he rips a bludger out of the hands of the other team's weak link.

"He's my role model," Elizabeth deadpans as Alex beats a charging keeper in the face from point-blank range.

My laugh turns into a yelp as someone pokes me, hard, in the side.

"What the hell?" I spin around and turn my best death glare on—oh. John.

"Hey, you," he says. "You ran off before you could tell me how great I am."

"I said you were great," I protest, and then immediately wish I hadn't.

John's smile is positively smug. "Maybe I just wanted to hear it again."

"Maybe we should be strategizing," Elizabeth interrupts John's preening. "Did you catch the end of the Austin/San Marcos game? I think our next game might be one of our hardest—their beaters are going to kill us if we don't have a plan."

John argues, because of course he does. He and Elizabeth discuss the relative strengths and weaknesses of our opponents while I shift to let the sun bake a slightly different plane of my face.

Melissa sits on the opposite side of the pitch—not that I'm looking. She pours water on her head and flicks drops at Karey to distract our captain from her intense study of the gameplay. Only a very petty person would be annoyed by Melissa's apparent happiness. I guess I'm petty.

We have every advantage over the Austin team, in theory. They had a much shorter break between games than we did, for one, and the majority of their team lost sleep for days prepping the tournament. We even win the coin toss and get to choose the side of the field that puts us with less sun in our eyes.

And yet . . .

Austin scores on a Brooms Up fast break before our line can get on defense. Lindsay takes a tackle wrong and subs out with a sore ankle, putting everyone on edge and messing up our beater pairings. By the time I go in, we're down thirty points.

With no ball, I'm on mosquito duty, trying to get a ball back and annoy the other team. One bright side: my cleats bite deep into the grass, planting each step secure and solid. I wonder if my mom felt like this on the soccer field.

For a few possessions I buzz around the other team's hoops, swatting a ball here and there. Chris and Karey make some impressive passes, but they can't bring the quaffle in close enough to score.

So the next time I approach the tall opposing beater, I drop into a crouch and tackle him.

My cleats work like magic. Instead of sliding to my knees, I stay upright through the tackle, pushing into the grass as my arm gropes toward the crook of my enemy's elbow. I even get a hand on the bludger before the team's second beater swoops in to take me out. As I disentangle myself, I hear Karey's triumphant whoop and the joyful whistle blast—goal!

We pick up momentum, but the score still hovers near a tie, and the thin plastic of someone's empty water bottle (future landfill waste) crackles as I twist it between my hands on the sideline. Next to me, Elizabeth's lips move silently as her eyes track the snitch. I watch her because I can't watch the pitch for more than a few seconds. Lindsay calls for a sub, and I look up just in time to see Austin's seeker wrap her fist around the snitch and rise into the air.

The refs huddle around the snitch. John's lips move, his scowling face red and wild and standing too close to their circle. The *tweee-eee-eee* of the whistle follows the sweeping of the head ref's arms as she signals the end of the game. The Austin team erupts in cheers.

I clap a hand over my mouth to stop a tirade of language that could get me red-carded. Elizabeth kicks another empty bottle with a growl. John tries to speak to the ref—not a good sign—but Karey grabs his arm.

"Line up," she calls to us. "Come on, y'all, we'll talk after this." She lets us form our line in the middle of the pitch before towing John to the end of it, whispering quietly to him.

"At least it was close," Lindsay says, her face bright red, lips tight as we approach Austin's lineup.

"So close," Chris groans. "We could've had it."

"Good game, good game, good game."

The tall Austin keeper leads the line, his expression so pleased and surprised that it's hard to keep hating him.

"Good game," I tell him, shaking his hand and then the hand of the blonde chaser behind him. The girl I distracted gives me a smile and a shoulder pat, and I nod back. "Good game, good game, good game . . ." Like it always does, the molten pain of losing starts to cool and crust as I meet face after smiling face. It's a good tradition. It's a good community. It's a good game.

21

Karey gives a pep talk, but I tune it out, already over the loss. We put up a good fight, we'll get them next time, etc. I slide to the ground and dig my phone out of my backpack to check on Yasmín. Sure enough, I have a text waiting.

Xiumiao is fun. Are you winning your games?

Some of them, I text back. Text if you need anything.

John plops down next to me, angry energy still radiating off him. "Such bullshit," he mutters like it's a complete sentence.

"What is?"

"Huh?" He frowns at me.

"What's bullshit?"

"The refs." He throws his hands up. "The call. No way was that a clean catch."

"I mean, it was probably fine . . ." I say, even though I know it will make John's eyebrows scrunch. "Whatever. I don't know; I wasn't looking."

"Well, take my word for it," John grunts, "it was bullshit."

"It just seems like the refs probably had a better angle than you did. Anyway, it's just a game." John's face tightens, and he hops to his feet, mumbling about water as he storms away. Guilt and relief mix in the pit of my stomach.

I glance at Elizabeth, who's eyeing me, and roll my eyes.

She snorts. "You doing okay?"

"Yeah. I'm not upset about the call. He just doesn't like to lose."

"I meant about other stuff. You and Melissa seem . . . off." With her goggles around her neck, Elizabeth's eyes look almost soft.

"Oh." I shrug. "I mean, it's fine. You know . . ."

Elizabeth's stare rips right through my non-answer.

"I just— I didn't tell her about John," I finally say.

"Oh, okay." Elizabeth shrugs. "I mean . . . I was wondering, too . . ."

I groan. "I don't exactly know what to say! Was I supposed to give a *formal announcement* that we kissed, like, one and a half times and I'm not sure where it's going?"

I'm hoping to make Elizabeth laugh and drop it, but she doesn't. "Hey, it's totally up to you. It just seems like saying something would still be less awkward than making everyone guess. But I can't really blame you—this team has a thing for drama and secrets."

I smirk. "You mean like Aaron/Erin?"

Elizabeth nods solemnly. "And this is only your first year here. Those two are impossible. But I meant—"

"Karey's on her way over here." John rejoins us with a half-empty water bottle pressed to his (very pouty) lips. "Y'all should get ready to warm up," he says. "We've got one last game, and it's our easy game, so we really have to crush this one." He hesitates, sighs, and then kicks his toe into the ground next to my knee. "No more careless mistakes like in the last game."

Elizabeth snorts, but I accept John's vague half admission that the last game wasn't entirely decided by incompetent refs as a win. I chug some more water, tighten my ponytail, and let John drag me to my feet. One more game, which will tell us whether we get to play for first place in the bracket tomorrow or whether we just get consolation matches. Everyone cares, but I've been in the sun all day and my legs are getting sore. An easy game sounds good right about now.

• • •

Luckily, it is easy. The Galveston team is too small, too new, and too used to playing beach quidditch. I feel very badass overpowering and stealing balls out of the hands of their newbie beaters. This must be what Alex feels like playing against me, I realize, and the thought makes me want to get good.

We line up in triumph, sure now that we'll get a shot at the bracket tomorrow. The Galveston team (with no wins yet today) won't get a chance to play for first place, but they don't seem too broken up about it. Their redheaded, pigtailed, bearded seeker runs down the line with one hand up, screaming, "Quidditch!" and whooping with each high five.

I collapse happy next to my bag and accept a handful of grapes from Elizabeth's Tupperware. The sun isn't quite setting, but it's definitely shining with less malice than it was two hours ago. I roll back onto the dry grass and close my eyes, tired limbs relaxing.

Someone nudges my cleat.

I look up at a storm cloud the shape of Melissa's face. "Car's leaving," she says. She nibbles the nail of her pinky and furrows her brow, but I'm too out of the loop to figure out if she's upset at me or something else.

Standing highlights every ache and bruise and scratch up and down my body. Elizabeth offers me a wave and a grimace as I slip on my tennis shoes and shove my cleats into my drawstring bag. "See you at the party," she says, her eyes twinkling over her straight face. "Whee."

I gulp and try to smile. I wanted to party with my teammates, after all. That was part of the plan.

Wheeeeee.

22

Our stop for dinner takes longer than anticipated, which is definitely my fault, but totally worth it. I can't be happy pulling into a McDonald's or a Subway when Austin has so many vegan options! Melissa sighs when I suggest driving farther to check out a food truck park, but she isn't exactly complaining about her gargantuan organic mint-chocolate milkshake.

I get to live here. In not very many months, I can eat chickpea salad to my heart's content. Hard to believe.

It's easy to find the apartment where we're sleeping because of the clear directions our hosts provided, the chalk arrows scrawled on the complex paths, and the pounding bass not quite drowning out the chatter of every quidditch player in the state. Yep. Our hosts are also hosting the after-party.

Everyone has been busy while our car tracked down dinner—not only is the party in full swing, but I also see an awful lot of wet hair and clean clothes. Judging by the crowd, I'm guessing I won't be squeezing in a shower tonight.

Which I wouldn't mind that much, except that as I step into the living room/dance floor area, the face-beating beater from the mini tournament—Prince Jersey—walks straight through my personal space, ducking his head apologetically as he pushes through the crowd. Argh, cute boys who can probably smell me.

"Ellennnnnnn!" Alex attacks me with hugs as I stumble through the door after Melissa, grimy and sore and lugging my sports bag as well as my overstuffed backpack.

"Hey." I step past a gaggle of A&M blondes and around a kiddie pool full of ice and cans. "Where, um, do you know where I can put . . . ?"

"How did y'all do?" Alex shouts over me. With his arm around my shoulder, I lose my place in the duckling-like line of teammates following Karey toward what I hope are bedrooms (or extra bathrooms).

"We did fine. We made it to bracket play tomorrow." I push away the cup Alex offers me. "No, thanks."

"Water," Alex says too loudly in my ear. "I'm playing tomorrow, too, so I had to cut myself off. Are you going to dance with us?"

People jostle my bags and elbows, and I spy Melissa's ponytail disappearing down a hallway. "In a minute," I yell, extricating myself from Alex's affection. "Be right back."

I squeeze past a couple with matching undercuts making out against a wall and find my teammates dumping stuff in a small dark room. Our hosts (typical college kids) have squeezed two beds into a room only meant to hold one. Extra pillows, blankets, and a few towels clutter what little floor space there is, all speckled with dust bunnies and suspicious stains. I'm grateful for the sleeping bag I packed.

Elizabeth nods at me. "Slumber party," she intones, clapping her hands together slowly. "Tee. Hee. Hee." She slumps in slow motion to the floor and fakes a snore.

"Restroom?" I ask. Lindsay gestures. I dump my backpack but keep my drawstring bag so I can sneakily apply some deodorant. I barely get into the hallway when I crash into a string of drunk guys and then Melissa.

"Oof," Melissa says, which isn't really a word, but I count it as initiating conversation anyway.

"Oof yourself."

Melissa looks at me like I've just crawled out of a heap

of unrecycled landfill waste. While she glares, I pick up on the red shiny ring around her eyes.

"Whoa, are you okay?"

Melissa tries to shove past me to reach the bathroom door.

"Hey!" I shove back, just a little bit, just to prove that she can't blow me off so easily.

Melissa wheels.

"What?" she demands. "What, Ellen? What do you want? What are you even doing here?"

I've seen Melissa snap before—at her mom, at her brother, at several different boyfriends-of-the-week. I've seen her eyes flash like this, seen her lips curl and heard the sharp bite of her voice. I've just never had all of it pointed at me.

Has she been this mad all day? I thought things were getting sort of friendlier by the end of the car ride. Where is this malice coming from?

"I'm trying," I say, already feeling angry tears constrict my throat, "not to let you and my parents ruin my entire summer, thanks. I'm here because—and I know this will come as a surprise to you, since you haven't talked to me all month, but—I really, really like quidditch!"

Some intoxicated person cheers and claps me on the back, utterly misreading the tone of my declaration. "Quidditch!" they yell in response.

"I didn't ruin your life," Melissa hisses (even though that's not what I said), "and frankly, neither did Connie. You're perfectly talented at doing that yourself."

"What is this?" I ask. "Is this because I didn't tell you about John? *I'm sorry* I didn't tell you about John! You're the one who said it didn't matter. You didn't care."

"*I* asked questions. *I* tried to talk." One last unsteady person crashes into us on their way to the bathroom. Melissa throws up her hands. "I can't right now; can you please just—" She turns to the bedroom door, stalks inside, and slams it behind her.

Great. That's my freaking bedroom, too. I don't want to continue this fight in front of the whole team, or out here with drunk people. And Melissa doesn't seem to want to continue it at all.

I walk back toward the main room and kitchen (the dance floor and bar, currently). I'm sort of looking for a second bathroom. I'm sort of keeping an eye out for water and snacks. I'm planning to snag a spot on a couch and ride out this party the same way I survived the last one: listening to music and maybe letting Alex convince me to dance. Paying even less attention to Melissa than she pays to me.

But then I see John waving at me from the center of the mass of bouncing and swaying bodies. He smiles and sloshes brown liquid out of his red Solo cup. I know he wants me to join him—and dance with him, and probably make out with him—on the dance floor. I'm not entirely opposed to that idea. It could be fun, a good and desperately needed distraction. But I also know that if I go over there, John won't ask me what's wrong. He won't notice anything off, won't see beyond the excitement or the dim lights or the sheen of sweaty bodies.

At some point I'll have to figure out how to make John stop trying to kiss me and I'll have to confront Melissa, but right now I wave and point to the kitchen, and then let a very tall and very wide keeper step in front of me while I escape out the front door. I didn't come all the way to Austin to be yelled at and not seen.

23

Outside is dark and muggy, full of bugs, and still loud.

The door keeps opening and closing, creating waves of music and noise that rise and fall like the pounding of my head. People stumble past me, usually laughing, often supported by heroic sober friends holding car keys. I swat a mosquito and scratch my knee, leaning against the window and letting the bass shake my shoulders.

"Hey." A very tall stranger with a green topknot and a keeper headband still around their forehead smiles. "Do you need a ride or anything, Houston? You good?"

"I'm okay, thanks. Just crowded in there."

I accept a high five. "I feel you," my new friend says. "Have a good night. Good luck tomorrow."

"You too," I say, even though I don't know what team the keeper plays for. It just feels nice to be supported and supportive. I wave, swat another mosquito, and consider returning to the party.

An image of Melissa's scowling face stops me. *What are you even doing here?*

"Hey!" A girl from the Clear Lake team waves at me while I try to remember her name. "Good night!"

"Night." I smile. "Good luck tomorrow."

The smile stays after the girl disappears. None of the quidditch people question my belonging or demand explanations. Quidkids don't make me feel invisible or unwelcome.

I swivel to press my aching head to the glass behind me. Dehydrated, probably. Should chug more water.

Melissa doesn't belong here any more than I do. I should march back in there and tell her . . .

The door opens, and the person who steps out derails my momentary self-possession. The boy with the Prince jersey. He blinks against the darkness, takes a step out the door, turns to walk the opposite way down the sidewalk.

"Hey," I say.

I startle him. I startle myself, too, to be honest. He recovers first.

"Hey," he says through an ear-to-ear grin. "You scared me."

"Sorry." I laugh, tilting my face so that my flushing cheeks cool on the window. "That's, uh, what you said last time. That I was scary."

"And I stand by it. My team will have to play you tomorrow, right?" I shrug because I don't know the schedule and I'm not totally sure which team he's on. "Suddenly I feel better about having to miss the second day of games to go to work."

"Oh no, that's crap," I say. His turn to shrug. "Besides, if anything, I think our last game proved that you can hold your own against me."

His laugh is as big as his smile. "So is this where the cool kids loiter?" he asks.

I snort. "I think it's where the socially anxious people hide."

"Huh. I'm surprised there's not a longer line, in that case."

I laugh, he grins, someone honks in the parking lot, and I prepare for the cute boy to turn away, as cute boys always do, and move on with his cute-boy life while I catch my breath.

Instead, he joins me in front of the window.

"How'd your team do today?" he asks. "Y'all have a lot of great players."

My legs are sore and my emotions are exhausted and talking about quidditch is easy, especially with this boy who has a pretty face and a glowing smile. At some point I slip into a crouch on the cement, and he follows my lead, and soon we relax below the window with our feet tucked under us.

"I'm so mad I couldn't get off work," he sighs, "but at least I got to play today."

"I guess skipping isn't an option?" I ask, having never been employed. "Or calling in sick?"

He laughs. "Quidditch is great and all, but paychecks are necessary. Why, did you risk your livelihood to be at this tournament?"

I try my best casual laugh, but it's not convincing.

"Wait, you didn't, did you?" he asks. "I feel like Karey would not condone that."

"No, no livelihood endangered." I hold up my hands. "Just . . . I slightly maybe snuck out of my house and broke my grounding to get here. But it was an unfair grounding anyway. How do you know Karey?"

"Just a year of tournaments, plus some mutual friends at A&M. She's great. Should I let you change the subject, or can I ask about the grounding?"

I laugh because it's an awkward question, and it's an awkward topic, and I'm an awkward person.

"It's, uh, I mean, you can ask, it's just a silly story. And a long one."

The boy turns his high-watt smile on full blast.

"Well . . . so I pissed off my stepmom at the beginning of the summer by going to my first-ever quidditch practice . . ."

Behind us, the party gets louder, and in front of us, the stars get brighter.

". . . and then, like, we got into some fight about feminism or something, and then my little sister acted like it was my fault . . ."

"Ugh, who even argues with feminism? Like, do you want to be the villain in a docudrama fifty years from now? My parents pull that crap all the time . . ."

". . . and she was so freaking rude about Karey, who's, like, the sweetest person in the world, obviously."

"Obviously."

"Obviously!"

There is something undefinably cozy about finding someone who likes the same things you like and hates the same things you hate. Our conversation meanders comfortably, which makes me feel better about what is becoming a pretty long rant about my dysfunctional family.

"Such trash! I have this econ professor who's the same way. Sorry, background tangent, but he's probably the richest, whitest, straight-cis-est old dude in the history of rich white straight-cis old dudes. And—speaking with all the privilege of a straight-cis white-ish Greek dude—he's completely insufferable. Like, okay, we get it, capitalism has worked really well for you, specifically . . ."

My head spins from the noise and the dehydration and the laughter.

"They never listen!"

"They don't listen, and they refuse to learn."

"And she's just so— She hates me, and I don't know why. I'm never good enough."

"Can I offer some advice?"

I meet his suddenly serious eyes.

"I mean, maybe it's terrible advice considering I don't actually know your stepmom or your complete situation or even you, really. But, uh, when you have toxic people in your life, even in your family . . . just speaking from personal experience, sometimes it's better to just ignore them."

"Talk to the hand, Connie." I smirk.

"I know, I know, it sounds silly. But I mean it. Don't measure yourself by their standard. Don't wear yourself out for their approval. Don't let their voice be the voice in your head. Just . . . let it go."

"That . . ." That's remarkably similar to what I was trying to do when I planned this trip, isn't it? I wanted to not care what anybody thinks of me. But it's already not working. I can't imagine not caring about Connie's jabs, her sharp breaths, her fiery glares. I can't imagine not seeing myself through her eyes, not expecting everyone to look at me and find the same flaws. And if ignoring Connie seems difficult, Dad is impossible. "I don't know if I can."

Two staggering figures interrupt by bursting out of the party, the smaller one clinging to the door for support and the larger one clinging to the smaller.

"I love you so much; I'm so sorry," someone slurs, and someone else makes comforting shushing noises, and before I have any time to react, the larger, drunker shape doubles over a foot in front of me and pukes a thin stream of watery sludge that smells disconcertingly like citrus.

I bolt up and back, crashing my shoulder into the windowsill as vomit spritzes my ankles.

The puke-spewer groans, and the companion—one of the girls I played against today, though I can't remember which team—offers a sheepish apology. "He had a lot of lemon drops . . ." She shrugs, and then pats the boy's shoulder. "But we're going to get you a PB&J and some water, okay?"

I nod, tensed like an upright mummy with my lips sewn shut in disgust. Once they leave, I stare down at my Converse in horror.

"Andrew McPherson." The cute boy shakes his head and grimaces at his own tennis shoes, which seem to have taken even more damage. "Not my favorite Andrew. You okay?"

I nod. I know I have to go inside and wash up, but that means facing more drunk people, a long bathroom line, Melissa, John . . .

I start laughing. I can't stop. "This is my life," I say. "This is my big rebellious adventure. Every remaining scrap of respect or goodwill my parents might've had for me, thrown away for this."

The boy slides his body across the window, and for a second I think he's going to sit, but instead he slides sideways until his shoulder bumps mine. "Hey," he says. Then he doesn't say anything else until I get curious and raise my head to meet his shining black eyes. "You're okay," he says, smiling that unbounded smile. "It's okay. Do you want to use my room to wash off? It's just a floor up."

Here is the thing about cute college boys inviting you to their room: you are supposed to consider your answer very carefully.

However, here is the thing about someone else's vomit drying on your legs: your priorities shift.

So without letting my brain get caught up in the quicksand of cute-boy analysis, I say, truthfully, "That sounds amazing. Thank you."

I think this might be his biggest smile yet.

24

The whiteboard taped to the front of the door has a note addressed to Andrew and Phil, which serves as a reminder that I do not know Prince Jersey's name. Did he introduce himself while I was busy looking at his face? I definitely told him my name . . . I think.

I watch him fiddle with the key. Andrew? Phil?

"It's pretty much all college kids in this complex, huh?" I ask, nodding at the whiteboard. "I was wondering how we were getting away with such a loud party."

"I don't know." Andrew or Phil jostles the doorknob. "It seems like it is, more or less." He finally gets the door open and beams. "There's a big community of Deaf people, too, because Texas School for the Deaf is nearby, and I hear their parties are even louder. My friend keeps promising he'll get his neighbors to invite me to one someday. Here we go, sorry. The lock hates me, apparently."

I follow him inside and crash when he stops in the dark doorway. The door swings shut behind me, and I feel Andrew or Phil's chest move as he mutters, "Ah, damn it."

By the time his scrambling hand hits the light switch, every one of my internal filaments glows bright and hot because, well, dark room and cute boy and close quarters. I'm sure that the overhead light is revealing bright red cheeks, so I quickly scoot past Andrew or Phil and enter the apartment living room.

It looks a lot like the party apartment, only mirror-imaged and less crowded. Couch, coffee table, lots of papers and textbooks. Dirty dishes, snacks.

"Uh, sorry," he says. "I thought other people would be here, but . . . you can use the bathroom right there, and I'll just be over here." He points me toward one door and then heads toward another with a handwritten notebook-paper sign declaring *Stay out of my room, Phil!*

Andrew, then. Thank God for college boys' obsession with marking their territory.

Andrew enters his room, and I catch a peek at more sleeping bags and an unmade bed. Then I enter the closet-sized bathroom and scrub my ankles down with hand soap and toilet paper, running my shoes and socks under the tap until they smell more like Tropical Island Fresh than Lemon Drop Barf.

"Hey . . ." I stick my head out the door, not quite confident enough to say Andrew's name. "Do you, sorry, but do you have any towels?"

Probably-Andrew walks into the bathroom barefoot and glances around. "Sorry, I don't know if . . . will you be grossed out if I offer you this?" He holds out the dirty T-shirt in his hands. "I used it already, but . . ."

"Yeah, whatever, that's fine." Priorities.

I drag my feet against the shirt until they're more or less dry. The motion reminds me how much my legs ache. I sling my bag back over my shoulder and carry my wet tennis shoes and socks back to the living room. Andrew follows and watches me collapse onto the fuzzy blue couch.

He approaches, his smile twisting up on one side as he scratches his shaggy hair. "You're welcome to hang out for a bit, if you want. It's quieter here. But also, definitely I'll walk you back if—"

"Yeah, I'm not standing back up anytime soon," I interrupt. "Everything hurts."

It's more than half true, but my stomach still flops over itself when Andrew plops onto the other end of the (small) couch, his arms and legs splayed out so that his knee almost brushes mine. I breathe deep and let my body sag the extra half inch to the right.

Andrew's smile gets bigger, but then he shifts a tiny bit, pulling his leg away.

Boo. Come back here, leg.

"So tell me about, uh, your . . . stuff," I say, like the brilliant seductress I am not. Andrew blinks at me, his smile inexplicably undaunted.

"My stuff?"

"Like, your, I don't know, classes. Or your life goals. Or your fandoms."

He laughs. "Well, Harry Potter minus everything JKR's said since book seven, obviously."

"Obviously."

"Are fandoms a good way to get to know someone?" he asks. My cheeks probably flush again, but he stares straight into my eyes with that sincere smile. Not mocking. Curious.

I don't feel like being sincere back. "I gave you the option of life goals. You have no one but yourself to blame."

The comment earns another laugh. I like Andrew's laugh and his smile and the way his eyes hold mine, interested.

"You first."

I blink. The ceiling fan spins lazily above us, the glare of its lights hurting my eyes. "Life goals . . ." I shrug, and my shoulders protest. "Dismantle white supremacy and the patriarchy. Save the planet from environmental destruction. Maybe . . ." I almost bite my sentence in half out of habit, but what do I have to hide right now? Chances are I'll never talk to Andrew again, right? "Maybe become a lawyer."

Dad used to tell everyone we met that I was so stubborn I was bound to follow in his footsteps. By the time I was eight or so, I was dead set on growing up to be anything but a lawyer—which I would scream, loudly, at every opportunity. So Dad dropped it, and we've never talked about it again, even though I'm not eight anymore. He thinks Melissa would be a great lawyer, though.

"Lawyer?" Andrew asks, smiling. I brace myself for an insulting joke, but he just says, "Not a politician? It seems more in line with the other goals."

Huh. "Honestly, I've never thought about it. Most politicians are horrible."

Andrew's smile tilts. "I did a year as a poli-sci major," he says, and then laughs when I wince. "But don't worry; I'm history/philosophy now, and I'm becoming vaguely anarchist, so no offense taken."

"Oh really?"

"Yeah, or like some socialist-anarchist hybrid. You know, capitalism is violence and all that." He shrugs, rolls his eyes, and shakes his head like he's joking, which is how I know that he's telling me something close to his heart.

"My parents just love the new leftist ideals, of course. Make for great dinner conversations over the breaks."

"Yeah, I know the feeling." We grin; Andrew shrugs again. Our legs press together.

"You know," he says, "I never know if I'm an introvert or an extrovert until I go to a party, and then it becomes very obvious."

I laugh because I, too, am immensely relieved to be away from the blare and the crowd, and also because our skin is touching and his dark eyes glint above the submerged treasure of a weird, smiley, introverted semi-anarchist brain. I want to get to know this brain, and maybe also the body it inhabits.

"And here I thought you were enjoying my company," I say, almost stumbling over the bordering-on-flirty words. "But it turns out it's just the lack of company you like, huh? I see how it—"

"That." Andrew holds up a finger to interrupt me. "Is not." He points the finger at my face and leans forward. "What I said."

He moves his outstretched hand closer, like he's going to tap my nose, but before he can reach, I snap my teeth (gently) and catch his finger between them.

Which, for the record, I've done to Dad, Yasmín, Melissa, and probably lots of other people lots of other times. And it's always been silly.

It is not silly right now. Abort, abort, this is way beyond the flirting border. I jerk my head back, but I can't avoid Andrew's finger brushing against my lips.

Which, yikes.

Good yikes. Quivery, melty yikes. Andrew's smile turns catlike, and I watch him blink in slow motion high-def while my torso tilts forward like it's run by wires and magnets totally independent of my brain, and then—

Andrew turns his body away, laughs nervously, and wrings his hands.

"Aren't you, like, in high school?"

"No!" I yelp, sparking with two very different kinds of frustration. One is the old kneejerk annoyance from years of living with a baby face and the constant exclamation that "You *can't possibly* be in fifth grade/a middle schooler/an upperclassman." The second frustration is new and immediate, and I don't enjoy it any more than the first. "I just graduated," I admit. "I'm not *in* high school." *And why haven't you kissed me yet?* I don't add.

"Right, yeah." Andrew shifts and smiles, running his hands through his hair, and I stifle a growl because I want to do that! "Sorry," he says. "It's just . . . we're not really supposed to hit on freshmen when they're young and vulnerable, you know?"

I could punch him in his stupid thoughtful face.

"I'm sure that is a great rule to keep freshmen safe from

creepers and focused on their studies," I huff, "but are you insinuating that I am vulnerable? Because as a kickass beater, I find that very annoying."

I am absurdly into Andrew's smiles. I want to decode every muscle twitch and eyebrow tilt until I know exactly which thoughts he's broadcasting. I want to know what he's thinking now, but I'm too impatient to ask.

"And anyway," I continue, "if a freshman or pre-freshman were hitting on you, and if you, I don't know, were at all interested in her—or him, or them—and if y'all had, you know, at least talked about some salient life philosophies so you knew you didn't hate each other and in fact might actually get along super well, especially if you're as open to learning about environmental issues as I am about anarchist ones—uh, I mean, as they are, about, umm . . ."

Oh, stop my mouth. Seriously. Please.

"Besides," I rant like the runaway train I am, "you're not, like, a senior, are you?"

"Sophomore," he says. "I'll be starting sophomore year."

"Right, so a one-year difference? That's nothing. Totally socially appropriate. And very legal. But I guess that isn't as strong of an argument for you, is it?"

"Lawful is no guarantee of moral," he says, but I think his smile means that he's listening.

"So . . . in conclusion . . ." I laugh at my own ridiculousness and am relieved that Andrew laughs with me. "Those are, like, at least two or three reasons why we can totally make out now. Um, if you want to, I mean. Do . . . do you want to?"

Andrew doesn't need to move much to put our faces inches apart. I guess I moved closer while ranting, or he did, or something.

"Yes," he whispers, sucking me into his dark eyes. "Yes, please."

Fucking finally.

25

My first kiss: dry and scratchy and exciting.

John kisses: warm and sticky and fun.

This kiss: cool water pouring down my throat, and also a lot of giggling.

"I haven't showered," I warn Andrew as his lips brush my neck. "I probably smell."

We're in the middle of the couch, upright, but my body melts into his and my hips and legs whine to move from their twisted position. Which would put me either in his lap or horizontal, so I leave them where they are.

He pauses. "Do I smell?" He breathes into me, sending goose bumps down my arms and up my legs.

He smells like sunscreen and grass and bug spray and some tangy boy deodorant and, yes, sweat. Eyes closed, I bury my nose in his soft curls and inhale loudly. "No."

Andrew returns to my neck, softly grazing the spot on my jaw where his bludger hit weeks ago.

"I'm pretty sure . . ." I lose focus halfway through my sentence because I require more mouth kisses, but after a minute I try again. "I'm pretty sure I have grass in my . . . everywhere."

A pause.

"Do you want me to check?" Andrew's fingers find the line of skin between my shirt and my shorts, and linger.

I wrap my arms around his back (how does he have so much back?). I spread my fingers and squeeze to hold him very, very still as I consider the question. Not with all my quivering melty body parts, but with my brain. Assuming I still have one in here somewhere.

"No sex," I say, and then because I am ridiculous I add, "No sex for me today, thanks."

Andrew laughs and starts to pull away, but I lock my fingers to keep him in place until he relaxes against me, breathing into my chest. For a few seconds I can feel his heart beating.

"Maybe just . . . more of this?" I ask.

Andrew's kiss has more weight behind it this time, and I use it as an excuse to sink back toward the armrest, drawing my bare feet up onto the cushions and pulling Andrew down with me until we're slotted together sideways across the cushions.

"As much as you want," he says, slipping a hand into my hair to scratch my scalp. I shiver, my grin as wide as his.

It turns out I want a lot, exploring the vast wilderness between kiss and sex. I'm deep in that wilderness, striking out in the inhabited but uncharted frontier, panning for gold with small shaking motions until all the bits of sand and silt and fractured frivolous pieces fall away.

I sparkle in the light, and the flash is blinding.

Andrew sits up and I stay flat, catching my breath with my limbs still buzzing and my lips aching like muscles after conditioning practice. He maneuvers my feet into his lap and runs his fingers across the soles, which normally would be tempting fate, but I guess I've moved beyond ticklish.

Eventually I extract myself from our couch heap and head toward the restroom, leaving Andrew with a smile on his face and his head leaned into the cushions. I stumble on my overturned bag and my phone, which lies on the floor where it must've landed after falling out of my pocket.

The second I close my hand around it, the world

reappears, intruding into my sleepy bubble of ignorant bliss to remind me that there are words for what I just did.

One-night stand. Random hookup.

Other, less kind descriptors pop into my head, words for the people who do this. Words that I would never use because they're totally antifeminist. Words that shouldn't echo in my sex-positive brain but still somehow do. My stomach lurches, and I shove my phone into my pocket without glancing at the screen. I trudge to the bathroom.

After I pee and wash my hands, I stare into the bathroom mirror for a few extra seconds, trying to examine my face like an objective outside observer. Is that a sunburn or a blush on that person's cheeks? Is her hair hanging stringy around her face because of a long healthy day of physical activity or because of her nocturnal physical activities? Does she look different now than she did an hour ago? And is that a smile sneaking in at the corner of her lips?

I suspect that if I really were looking at a stranger, I would be glad that she was enjoying her life. If it were Melissa (prefight), I'd give her a high five. But when she's me . . . it feels weird. I don't know how I feel.

Andrew's curled into the couch, eyes closed, the fingers of one hand twitching in what I imagine is a dream about face-beats. But it's all imaginary. I have no idea what he might dream.

I need to talk to Melissa.

I find a pad of Post-its next to the laptop on the desk in Andrew's room. After a minute of hesitation, I leave my note:

> *Ellen Lopez-Rourke. I was going to leave a number, but honestly just find me on the interwebs.*
>
> *(Also thanks.)*
>
> *(Also sorry.)*
>
> *(Also your room is kind of a mess.)*
>
> *(Also fuck the patriarchy.)*
>
> *(Okay, I'm done now.)*

I leave the note on the keyboard of the silver laptop. I can't think of a safer place to guarantee he will find it, fast.

I slip my feet into my wet Converse and grab my bag off the floor, shoving a spilled sock back into its open mouth, and then I sneak out the door. I follow the noise back down to the party, toward the only person I want to tell about this night. Toward a conversation I need to have, gossip too exciting and confusing not to dissect. Toward the high fives I can't give myself. Toward an end to this pointless fight. Toward Melissa.

Music still blares, but the party is winding down. 12:06 a.m. isn't exactly the end of the night, but most people have early games to play. I scan the kiddie pool of melting ice water, the dance floor area, and the quidditch beer pong table. I spot a sleepy-looking Alex swaying to the music on one of the couches, a few familiar faces chatting in small groups, but none of my teammates. I check down the hall. The door to our temporary team housing is closed, and no light peeks into the dark hallway from under the crack. Is everyone asleep already?

Actually, Melissa is almost definitely asleep. Crap.

I reach for the doorknob to ease the door open, but

before I can get my hand on it, the bathroom door swings open. A familiar startled squeak, and I glimpse a shoulder and a ponytail before the door slams shut.

"Melissa?" I move toward the bathroom, excited to catch her out of bed. "Are you in there?"

"What?" Melissa calls from the other side of the door. "You—you surprised me."

"Look, I know earlier I . . . Can you come out, please? I have a *thing* to tell you."

In the long pause, I relive Melissa's angry texts, the week of cold shoulders, how angry she was at the end of the tournament. Maybe it's not realistic to think that we can just drop all of that, but I do. I know she recognizes the urgency in the word "thing," so I know she'll open the door.

And a second later, she does.

"I was going to bed," she mumbles, slipping into the hall and standing, arms crossed, with her back against the door.

"I know, but . . ." I'm too excited to start properly. "But gossip."

I expect excitement, or maybe another few seconds of stubborn pouting. I don't expect Melissa to widen her eyes and swallow, raising a hand to nibble her nails.

"Fine," she says, and she stalks toward the front room. "But fifteen minutes, and then I'm going to sleep."

I scramble after her, past the winding-down party, past our weary hosts gathering red Solo cups, and out the front door onto the sidewalk.

"Watch out." I steer Melissa away from the drying lemon-scented puddle, and we lean against the wall a few feet down. "So . . ."

How long has it been since I was sitting here (well, a few feet to the left, closer to the throw-up) with Andrew? An hour? Two? Less? Where do I start telling this story that I still barely believe?

"So what?" Melissa's arms are still crossed, her shoulders hunched. "You heard about Erin and Aaron?"

"Wait, what?" If the comment was meant to derail me, it works. "Did they finally get together?"

Melissa huffs, tilting her head up to examine the night sky. "Sometimes you're so oblivious it's painful. They're in a huge fight."

Her harshness puts me back on track. "Okay, listen, I'm *sorry*. I'm sorry I didn't tell you what was going on with me," I sigh. "I was being a baby, plus Connie kept picking fights when you were texting me, and honestly I didn't want to talk about it anyway because, well, I don't know, I guess because I didn't really care about him, you know? But now—"

"Just because you don't talk about someone doesn't mean you don't care," Melissa snaps.

"I mean, it basically does, though." I smile, thinking about Andrew's smile and how badly I want to describe every detail of that smile to someone: the dot under his bottom lip, the crinkles around his eyes, the—

"I made out with someone," I say while still daydreaming. "Like, hardcore make-outs. A guy from the Austin team. And he seems super cool, and I might be super into him. Or, like, I don't know, maybe not, right? Maybe it was just a meaningless one-night stand and I'll never see him again, and I guess that's fine, but I just needed to tell someone. Because, I don't know, it was really fun and weird. And fun. So yeah."

I thought I would feel calmer after confessing. Instead, my cheeks flush and my chest flutters as Melissa blinks at me.

"You . . . what?"

"I met a guy. And we sort of . . . hooked up."

Melissa blinks several more times, her shoulders and crossed arms dropping but her eyebrows furrowing. "You," she says, "are going to need to be a lot more specific with your terms here, dude. Because a second ago it was 'made out' and now it's 'one-night stand' and 'hooked up.' What exactly happened?" She doesn't pause long enough for me to answer. "I mean, isn't this kind of a big deal for you? Unless . . . how far did you get with John? Wait, what about John? Weren't y'all dating earlier today? I thought y'all were dating."

"No, of course not." But my hands ball at my sides. In all the excitement, I sort of . . . completely forgot John existed. Or at least I forgot that he might have feelings about me kissing someone else. Crap. I might be a slightly terrible person.

Melissa throws up her hands. "How am I supposed to know? You haven't told me anything, and apparently it's hard to keep up."

"I already explained: I didn't tell you about John because he doesn't matter." Harsh, but, I'm finally realizing, true.

"That isn't what that means!" Melissa snarls. "Stop saying that like it's a thing."

"But it is a thing—I'm telling you, because as soon as I met this guy I realized that I'm way more excited about him, and if you're excited then you want to talk about it with your best friend, and that's why I wanted to tell you—"

"Oh my God, Ellen, *shut up*."

I shut up. My pink cheeks turn dark red. The butterflies in my stomach drop dead. Someone slams a car door in the parking lot, and I flinch.

"You can do whatever you want." Melissa waves her arms and rolls her eyes. Her ponytail bobs, strands that were already ruffled flying free to brush her cheeks. "You can date your way through the whole quidditch community—oh, sorry, not 'date.'" Her sharp laugh hurts.

“But don’t turn around and lecture me about relationships—or friendships, for that matter. Seriously, who are you to tell me anything about anything?”

She stomps back into the apartment as my vision melts into a warm liquid blur.

I sit, curl my knees to my chest, and let the tears spill down my cheeks. Silent. Still. Not even shaking. I’m not angry. I’m nothing.

The feeling that finally breaks through is something like guilt. I did something wrong by kissing a stranger; Melissa didn’t say it outright, but the idea was there. It was there when I first looked in the mirror, when I tried to ignore it. It’s here, crashing down around me, because I pathetically wanted Melissa to make it go away. To tell me I didn’t.

Melissa, who’s never kissed anyone until at least a month of consideration and trial runs. What else would she have to say to me, who can’t stop kissing guys I’m not dating?

John . . . I need to talk to him, and it is not going to be fun.

I need to go back inside, go to sleep. I have quidditch games to play tomorrow. But I don’t want to move. I want the humid night air to dissolve me into vapor so none of my problems can find me.

I hear footsteps approaching. I close my eyes in case another tirade is coming.

"It's fine," I whisper. "Just go to bed. You were right."

But it isn't Melissa who sits down next to me. It's Karey.

What is Karey doing awake? Her itinerary was very specific about the importance of a good night's rest.

"I think I owe you a couple of apologies," she says while I try to subtly wipe my face. "But I can't give them to you right now. Anyway, more importantly, are you okay?"

I scrub tears off my knee. "I'll be fine," I tell my captain. "I should go to bed so I'll be rested for the games tomorrow." I try to stand up.

Karey puts her hand on my shoulder, then snatches it away and runs it over her head. "Ellen, I don't care about the games. I'm trying to— I'm worried about whatever happened with you."

I flinch. "Nothing happened with me."

Karey sighs. "Do I need to go kick this boy's ass? That's what I'm asking. I will, Ellen. I will kick the shit out of him."

"No, you don't . . . Melissa told you?" I don't understand Karey's threats. I don't understand what she's doing here at all.

"I'm here if you want to talk," Karey says, and I finally notice the anxiety in her eyes, the way she searches my face. "And there are options for reporting, if you want—not just the police, but wherever he goes to school, or the quidditch officials have a policy in place."

"It wasn't . . . I didn't get, like, *harassed*." My voice squeaks, my chest curls more firmly around my knees. "I'm fine; I'm definitely fine. I mean, I'm embarrassed because I . . . but it wasn't anything bad. I just met a cute guy and we made out. Or hooked up. Or something. But not in a scary way. In a good way."

Karey lets out a long breath. "Okay. If it turns out that's not the case, please, please know that you can talk to me whenever you feel comfortable."

"I promise, it's fine," I say.

"You're sitting on the ground sobbing," Karey points out. "And you smell like vodka. I feel like maybe someone deserves an ass-kicking."

"It's been a long night."

Karey smiles. I search the sky for constellations. Someone flips off the music inside, and cicadas and night birds quickly fill up the momentary silence.

"You know . . ." Karey shrugs and shifts so that her legs stretch out against the cement. "You can talk to me about Melissa, too. I make no promises about kicking her ass, but . . ."

I laugh. "I was being stupid. She's mad at me, but I wanted to pretend like everything was normal. I wanted her to . . . I don't know, give me a high five or something. Which wasn't going to happen. You don't get high fives for being promiscuous at a quidditch party."

"I mean . . ." Karey trails off, and I stop staring at the sky to look at her. She holds out her palm.

I ruin the slap of our hands with a snotty sniffle. "Thanks."

"You know," Karey says, "it might not seem like it, but she just wants to talk to you."

I snort through my snot. Sure, Melissa is just dying to talk to me. That's why she avoided me for weeks, acted so weird, kept grilling me about John without listening to—

The light switch flips. I blink at Karey.

"She has a secret." I knew that. I remember thinking that a long time ago, right after she broke up with Chris. I thought she was hiding something, a new crush maybe. At some point I got too involved in my own feelings and I forgot. I thought it was all about me, Melissa wanting to ditch me like Xiumiao did—like Xiumiao didn't, actually.

God, I do have an abandonment complex.

Karey's poker face is good, but it doesn't matter. I stand up, something between a laugh and a growl bubbling up in my throat.

I rush inside, ignoring the scattered figures sleeping on the couches and armchairs. The apartment feels implausibly silent and my damp shoes squish loudly against the floor, but I can't slow down as I rush to see Melissa stepping out of the bathroom, her face red and her fists balled.

She sees me, and she scowls, and now that I can see the

hurt behind her anger I can't believe I ever thought she didn't care.

"Melissa, I—"

She faces me, the scene so similar to what happened just a few minutes ago, but . . . changed. The bathroom door hangs open, and as soon as I notice how little attention Melissa pays it, I also realize how intent she was on keeping me away from it before. Because she didn't want me to go in, because there was something in there she didn't want me to see. Or—I think of my own recent party activities—there was some*one* in there.

More light switches, a whole wall of them, connected to a whole bank of fluorescent lights that flicker, sputter, and blink on full-blast as I connect dot after dot after dot.

"What?" Melissa demands.

I open my mouth to release my question, but instead the truth creeps out.

"You have something to tell me about Karey."

In the silence that follows, a buzzing noise convinces me that the cicadas followed me inside. And then I notice that the buzzing is coming from my pocket. And then I pull out my ringing phone and see that Dad is calling.

Melissa and I stare at each other, identical stupid expressions on our faces. Because we're both caught.

27

“It’s my dad,” I say, even though Melissa probably already read the caller ID.

She grimaces. “I knew you didn’t have permission.”

I answer the phone. I hold it a few inches from my face, shying away like it might explode.

“Hello?”

“Ellen? Everything okay?”

I stare at the unfamiliar hallway, the bathroom door, Melissa’s wide eyes. I can’t think of a single way to answer his question.

“Connie got worried when you didn’t answer her texts. Are you asleep? How is everything holding up?”

"Is the kitchen clean?" Connie's distant voice asks.

Melissa watches my mouth drop open and stay there. She twirls her hands around each other frantically: *Say something!*

"Um," I start off promisingly, "yeah . . . Yeah, Yasmín went to bed, like, a couple hours ago." *Not a lie*, I think even as my face starts to flush. I have Xiumiao's text to prove it. "How was your day?"

"We were worried," Dad says. "Connie hasn't been able to fall asleep."

"Sorry, I think my phone was on silent. Yasmín wanted to watch *Moana*." True, I just didn't happen to be there to watch it with her.

"Great." Dad's voice relaxes. "Well, we'll let you get back to bed. Keep a closer eye on your phone please." He talks about the beach for a minute while I hyperventilate and Melissa offers unhelpful panic faces. I only tune back in to hear, "So we'll see you in the morning, probably, or around lunchtime at the latest."

"Wait, tomorrow?" I wince at the squeak in my voice. *Chill, vocal cords.* "I thought you were staying another night, taking off Monday . . ."

Melissa's eyes widen, and her mouth twists comically. My face feels frozen in place.

"Well, we missed our girls. We can all have a family day on Monday. We have . . . some apologies to make."

A distant rational part of my brain realizes that this is my last chance to confess, that lying right now will only postpone disaster. But instinct beats logic.

"Okay, yeah. Sounds good. I'll see you then."

Straight-up lie.

"Love you, Jelly," Dad says, and I slam my finger into the end-call button so I can pretend I didn't hear him.

Melissa stares at me staring at my phone for a few seconds. "There's a moment you know . . ." she sings softly, "you're fucked."

I snort. Check the time. Weigh my options.

If I really don't want to get caught, I could try to find a way home. Megabuses run overnight sometimes, or I could catch an early one and hope I make it back before Dad and Connie. I'd have to ask Xiumiao for a ride from the bus stop, but she'd probably do it. I could text her right now and start looking up schedules . . .

But that's not why I came on this trip in the first place. And that's not what I want to focus on right now.

"I think I'm going to head to bed," Melissa says, at the same time that I say, "So as we were saying . . ."

"You're not going to . . . ?" Melissa gestures at my phone.

"I have roughly twelve hours before I'm even more grounded than I am now. I probably won't have a phone this time tomorrow, and we definitely won't be hanging out, catching up on gossip." My breath comes out shaky, but my eyes stay dry and focused on Melissa. "So."

"So," she repeats.

"Got any gossip to share?"

Melissa snorts. "I told you everything I know about Erin/Aaron already."

"You can't fool me this time," I say. "I will pester you all night if I have to, but that's going to make both of us quidditch zombies tomorrow, and I know you don't want that." Melissa snorts again. "Seriously. I'm listening. I want to know."

"Okay," she whispers. "Well, for starters, I almost broke up with Karey earlier tonight because I'm an insecure ball of jealousy who can't handle the fact that my girlfriend has exes in the quidditch community."

"Oh . . ." That didn't come out exactly like I was expecting. "Oh."

"Yeah, I'm a mess." Melissa laughs and rolls her (watering) eyes. "You're actually lucky that you missed the defining-the-relationship stage. All the frustrated confused angst. And when Chris figured it out, he didn't talk to Karey for a week."

Chris figured it out. Figured it out, threw a fit, and reached acceptance, all while I pouted. My stomach aches with how much I want to go back in time and be a better friend. Melissa has always been my supportive friend, the one who makes me feel like I'm okay. I hate that I missed my chance to be that for her.

"I'm sorry. I was so oblivious. I thought you were avoiding me to, like, make cooler friends. I thought we were growing apart or whatever, so I pouted. I'm the worst."

"I . . ." Melissa shrugs. "I was going to tell . . ."

"Yeah, but I should've made it easier. Or, you know, asked in a non-heteronormative way. Or not fallen for the 'gals being pals' assumption. Xiumiao would be ashamed of me." I'm ashamed of me.

"I was actually being the worst, though," Melissa says quickly. "I'd never had jealousy issues before! I didn't know how to deal with them! And I was afraid Karey liked you, so . . ."

"Oh, wow, what? I mean, definitely not. Also I wouldn't do that to you, even if Karey *is* seriously a catch!"

I'm a notoriously terrible hugger, but Melissa is not. She pulls me in with a shuddery breath. At first I feel off balance and stiff, but after a second I settle. We stand there for a minute, supporting each other.

"Oh, man," I whisper into the space behind Melissa's head. "Xiumiao . . ." *is going to be so pissed,* I don't say, because still not cool to reveal people's crushes even if they're over them. ". . . is going to want to hear about this at some point." I hope my voice sounds casual, or that Melissa is too distracted to notice if it doesn't.

"Ughhhhh," Melissa groans, dropping her face onto my shoulder with what has to be a painful thud. "I know, I know. I'm putting it off because I don't want to hurt her feelings. But honestly, just because I'm not straight doesn't mean I'm going to find every girl attractive. It doesn't work like that, and I know it's frustrating for her, but I can't help it. I'm sorry, okay?" Even muffled by my shoulder, her voice squeaks in my ear.

Huh.

"You knew?"

Melissa laughs. "She wasn't exactly the sneakiest, and neither were you. And you know, it's not hard to tell when someone likes you." She sighs. "I could tell she was pulling away, and I get why, but it was also so crappy. It would have been really nice to be able to talk to her."

"I'm sorry," I say again. "You should've been able to talk to me."

Melissa nods, but then snorts. "I mean, it might be for the best that you didn't have to try to hide it from Xiumiao."

"Damn. All this time, I thought I was capable of keeping a secret."

"I'm sorry," she says, sniffling a little. "But you're awful." We both laugh, and Melissa finally breaks the hug. "We probably should go to bed."

"Wait! I have so many questions."

She snorts. "Sure, now you have questions."

"Come on," I plead. "Lightning round?"

She nods once, which is all the agreement I need to jump in with the most pressing question: "So y'all are definitely officially something?"

"Dating." Melissa squares her shoulders as she says it. "Definitely officially dating."

"And so *you* are definitely officially . . . ?"

". . . something," she says, her posture dipping into a shrug. "Something not straight. I'm not positive, but, like, probably bi? Or is pan better? I need to investigate."

"I mean, I guess this shouldn't be a surprise considering how many female celebrities you're in love with."

"Yeah, that was a definite tip-off, but I didn't fully really realize it, either. Heteronormativity is a hell of a drug."

I nod because this is lightning round, and as much as I want to chat about Melissa's evolving sense of identity, there is one important topic to address.

"So on a scale from zero to sex . . . ?"

Melissa doesn't blush as easily as I do, but she turns bright red now. "Tell me about you and this stranger you hooked up with," she counters.

Stalemate. "Fine, talk tomorrow."

We giggle, but then Melissa says, "We'd better do it before we get back, though."

"Yeah, because once I'm home Connie's going to turn me into vegan hamburger meat . . ."

While Melissa argues that human flesh is definitely not vegan, we head the rest of the way down the hall to our team bedroom.

"Can I get in without trampling anyone?" I ask before I open the door.

"I think so." Melissa shrugs, glancing over her shoulder. "Step lightly just in case. I'm actually going to go get Karey; I think she's still outside . . ."

I can't believe I missed the way her mouth smiles around Karey's name. I can't believe I misinterpreted the duckling-like attachment. I should have recognized those weeks of bright laughter and soft looks—I've seen enough of them, just usually directed at Melissa instead of coming from her.

"You really like her, huh?" I ask, but it's not much of a question.

Melissa shrugs. "I mean . . . yeah . . ." When I giggle, she covers her face with her hands. "Shut up. Whatever. It's weird and desperate and I should probably stop. Quit laughing!"

I roll my eyes at her stinking cuteness. "Okay. Go get Karey. But I'll be waiting up for you." I point my finger at Melissa with my best mom face. "So no more funny business in the bathroom."

She wraps her arms around her chest and blushes. "We weren't—we were just talking about the exes and our—it wasn't like we were—" Her protests turn into an indignant squeak as I stick my tongue out and slip into the bedroom. I hear a huff from the other side of the door, then footsteps down the hall.

After my eyes adjust, I pick my way through the dark room and unroll my sleeping bag between Elizabeth and Erin, lying with my head on my backpack.

Then I see the glow of a phone screen across the room, and a second later my phone buzzes. Chris texts, Hi everyone's asleep do you have any toothpaste I can borrow?

I laugh, wave my lit phone at him, dig my toothpaste out of my backpack, and hand it off to the tall shape creeping through the dark, half lit by his phone. "Thanks," Chris whispers. "It's bad enough we can't really shower." He squeezes past me and out the door.

I lie down again, hesitate, then pull my phone out and send a response to his text. I talked to Melissa.

He types for a long time but doesn't send anything.

I mean I talked to her about Karey. I know they're a thing.

He texts back a thumbs-up. I was hoping she'd tell you soon. Sorry I didn't give you a heads-up.

Well, now we're even, right?

Nooo, I'm sorry I was pissy before. I just didn't like getting dumped. Hot take, I know.

I send a laughing cat face, because I'm awkward.

After a minute, Chris texts, Thanks for the toothpaste, buddy.

I try to laugh quietly, but Elizabeth rolls over and grumbles something unintelligible.

I'd better get to sleep, I text quickly. You too. We need our quidditch prodigy tomorrow.

I shove my phone into a pocket of my backpack and lie back down. In spite of needing rest for tomorrow, I don't feel calm enough to close my eyes.

Melissa and Karey.

I'm thinking, mostly, about the first boy Melissa kissed. Not Martin, the first boy she dated circa seventh grade. Andreas. The quiet ninth-grade new kid with dreamy black eyes. Everything was normal for the first two weeks of their relationship—our middle school version of normal, which meant constant giggly speculation about what the boys we liked were thinking and feeling. And then two weeks in, Melissa went silent. For a whole lunch period she refused to mention Andreas. I thought maybe they had broken up.

It only took me until dismissal that day to guess the truth. I was more persistent back then. Melissa had kissed Andreas—a real kiss on the mouth. And when I asked why she didn't just tell me, she couldn't give me a good reason.

"I don't know. I thought you'd think it was weird."

I was sad then because why didn't Melissa trust me?

I'm sad now because why didn't I trust Melissa? I thought she abandoned me, but I was the one who got scared and got mad and got petty. I wish she had talked to me from the beginning, but I can't blame her for needing time, for wanting me to figure it out. She needed me to be patient, and instead I was the one who disconnected.

I roll to find a softer patch of carpet. Elizabeth murmurs in her sleep. My hair smells like grass, and my bag smells like sweat (okay, maybe the other way around), and an ache starts up in my right shoulder.

Melissa is dating Karey.

Dad and Connie are going to catch me.

And I hooked up with a cute stranger.

The last is easier and more fun to focus on (especially since I decide to conveniently forget that John exists for at least a few more hours), so I pull my sleeping bag over my head and blink against the brightness of my phone screen as I conduct some super sneaky Facebook stalking.

I nod off before I can figure out much, my cheek pressed against my lumpy bag and my arms shooting with pins and needles as it falls asleep with me. I dream lemon vodka and Tropical Island soap and cool water.

28

Three different phone alarms blare, chime, and rattle their way into my sleeping bag cocoon, and orange light seeps through my stubborn eyelids. Karey starts her morning pep talk at full volume with maximum pep levels while I stagger upright and follow a grumpy and red-eyed Erin into the bathroom. We share a mirror as I brush my teeth and she applies eyeliner, and then I end up piled into her car, heading to the fields. I work on keeping my eyes open and remembering that quidditch is fun.

"Heads up," Melissa says, walking toward me in the parking lot. I tear my mostly vacant gaze away from the groups of volunteers lugging hoop pieces into the dewy grass.

"Morning," I say, and accept the peanut butter breakfast bar Melissa offers (perks of not being in a fight anymore). I even try to listen to what she says next, except that my pocket starts to vibrate, distracting me. My sleepy-numb fingers turn scared-numb, and I fumble to pull out my phone. Dad. I guess they didn't wait until lunchtime.

"Hello?" Fuck.

Dad's long breath crackles in my ear. "Really, Ellen?"

"I . . ." At some point before I left, I convinced myself that my sneaking away for the weekend was, in fact, an act of maturity and self-determination rather than a really shitty thing to do. But even if I still believed that, I wouldn't know how to begin to explain. "Uh . . . yeah. Sorry."

"Well," he says, "at least you answered."

The voice is all wrong. Not the forced calm and reasonable of a lecture, not the annoyed disappointment of a scolding, not even the icy sarcasm that slips out when he actually gets mad. This dead monotone doesn't even sound like Dad.

I wait for him to continue, but he doesn't.

"I'm sorry," I repeat. "I didn't . . ." But there's nothing to say to make this better. Melissa taps my arm, and I shake her off. "Um, I'll be home soon. Well, today. Kind of late this evening, probably . . ."

Only a slight grunt lets me know the line isn't dead.

"But I'll let you know when we're on the road and

when we'll be back." I'm spiraling. "And I'll do double chores for the rest of the summer. And, oh, if you try to get hold of me and I don't answer, it's just because I'm playing, but I'll call back as soon as I can . . ."

"I have to talk to your sister," Dad says without any indication that I've spoken.

"She's fine. I know she's fine. Xiumiao's really responsible and CPR-certified and—"

Dad gives a short "Bye" to prove he's not hanging up on me, then hangs up on me.

Fuck. My throat tightens, which is ridiculous because I knew I wasn't going to get away with this. The point was not to get away with this.

The point was to get out on my own terms, to prove that I want as little to do with them as they do with me. Which is a great idea, except that the second I heard Dad's voice, I realized how untrue it was. If I was trying to prove that I don't need his approval, I think I accidentally did the opposite.

A hand grabs my elbow, and I turn to unload some of my panic on Melissa, but it's not her glaring at me, chest puffed out. It's John.

"What's up?" he asks the way you might ask "Et tu?"

"Hi. Nothing. I don't know. I'm actually kind of"—I shove my phone in my pocket and shake my arm free—"not having a great morning."

"Hungover?" he shoots, and before I can do more than raise my eyebrows, he launches the real attack: "Where did you disappear to last night?"

I take a second to process the fact that life is not cutting me any breaks this morning. I knew I would need to talk to John at some point, just like I knew I would have to face Dad's anger, but I didn't think it would have to be right now, while I'm sorting out eighty more important emotions.

"I didn't disappear." I shrug, looking around to find Melissa hovering far enough away to look innocent but close enough for me to see her twitch her shoulders up, like, *I* tried *to warn you*.

"You weren't at the party or in the room," John says. "You didn't get back until after midnight."

"Yep. So?"

"So?" John holds his palms up, and for a second the confusion in his eyes almost tugs at my conscience, but then he swipes back his hair and steps right into my personal bubble, his face too close to mine, his breath hot, eyes steely. "So do you have anything you maybe want to explain to me?"

My face flushes, and sweat wets my armpits. Melissa's behind me in a flash, and I feel the sting of curious eyes as the rest of the team starts to notice the showdown.

"Chill," Melissa advises John. "Y'all can talk after the game."

"Why do we have to 'talk'?" His voice spikes. "Why doesn't she just tell me what the fuck is going on with us?"

I know what I could say if I wanted to de-escalate the situation. The Dad script, the hedging, the *I* statements combined with half-truths. But what's the point? Maybe it's just because I'm less afraid of John's disapproval than Dad's, but I no longer have any desire to delay the inevitable.

"You want to know what's going on? Nothing. Nothing is going on with us, because there is no 'us,' which you would know if you ever stopped flirting long enough to have an actual conversation."

The warmth climbing up my neck is equal parts guilt and rage, fear and frustration. I can tell by the way that the team turns their backs and stares at the ground that everyone heard. My face probably matches John's bright cherry tomato ears.

My pleading eyes find Melissa's, and she suddenly realizes that she needs my company to go top off her (still mostly full) water bottle. I walk with her to the water fountain, legs shaky, sweat trickling into my sports bra. Stupid John. Stupid everything.

The water fountain gives us enough space not to be overheard, but not enough to block the anger radiating off John as he paces around the meetup tree. Melissa fills her bottle in silence, but once the lid's back on, hers comes off.

"Well?"

"What?"

"You just dumped John—really emphatically, I might add—over a one-night-stand." She wiggles her eyebrows. "Now I know the details must be juicy, and I want all of them."

"I didn't dump him! We weren't a thing! I don't even like him!" I steal her water and gulp down a guilty swallow. I was too harsh. I know I was. It isn't John's fault that I'm in huge trouble with my family.

"You say this like I'm supposed to know it." Melissa shrugs. "All anyone knew until today is that he said y'all were dating."

"He did?" My guilt sparks back into annoyance. He shouldn't have done that when we never even defined the relationship!

"Well . . . he implied it heavily, at least."

"Oh my God . . ." I look over to where John now huddles with Aaron and Chris, shoulders hunched and fists balled. "Everyone's going to hate me."

"Nah," Melissa says, but her shrug doesn't stop my pounding heart.

"I have to go tell them . . ." I have to explain. My teammates, my friends, have to know that I didn't break any promises. At least, I didn't mean to.

"Show me the guy from last night," Melissa says. I

know she's trying to distract me, but it works, at least a little. I pull out my phone, still glancing toward the growing team huddle.

"How much time until our first game?" I ask.

"They're running late getting the pitches set up. We have time. Let me see."

On Facebook, I type "Andrew Burns" (a name I learned last night) into the search box. I wait. "Huh." I hit refresh. "I think the service here is crappy. He was showing up earlier."

Melissa looks over my shoulder. "But . . ." She points at the string of search results—Andrew after Andrew, all loaded and ready to stalk. "He's not that one?"

"No, his profile was a quidditch team picture," I say, sliding my finger down the screen.

"You didn't get the name wrong, did you?"

"He was the first on the list last night. We have mutual friends, so it should—"

"Did you . . ." Melissa cuts me off but doesn't finish her sentence. I have to look up to see the pained twist of her mouth and the way her hands clench.

"What?"

"Well, did you, um . . ." Melissa breathes like she's defusing a bomb. "Did you send him a friend request?"

"Yes," I answer quickly. Then my brain catches up with Melissa's implication. "No . . ." I hit refresh again. "No, no way. That doesn't even make sense . . . You think he blocked me?" The list of wrong Andrews stares back at me. "Why would he . . ." I stop, because the squeak in my throat is embarrassing, ridiculous.

Melissa produces her phone (from inside her shirt, of all places). She taps the screen, then taps it again, then gets distracted responding to a message while I age into a wizened grandmother with dust for bones.

"Well?"

She tilts the screen toward me. A square photo of tiny quidditch players next to the name. Top of the list, just like he was when I first looked him up.

"Damn. Damn it."

He blocked me. Not even rejected my request, which would have been bad enough. Blocked. As in, I want to erase you from my social media experience forever. As in, get lost.

"Do you want me to beat him up?" Melissa asks, putting her arm around me. "I can totally get Karey to help. He's asking to get beaten up."

"I wish you two would stop offering that." I try to laugh. "It's whatever, really. It's fine."

Didn't he say he wanted to get to know me better? Didn't he at least mention being friends? I'm sure we talked about future quidditch tournaments—wasn't the implication that we would see each other again?

Okay. Clearly I imagined everything. I am probably not the first person in the world to get seduced by a guy who seems genuinely interested but is really only . . . fuck. Warmth drips down my face, and I taste salt. Fuck.

"Porta potty," Melissa says, grabbing my arm and steering me to the line of blue plastic. I managed to avoid using these slightly icky accommodations yesterday, choosing to hold it until we left the fields for lunch break, but now my best friend squashes both of us inside the first one and yanks the door shut. "It's okay," she says, patting my arms with a worried look in her eye. "You're okay."

I'm laughing. Snot-dropping, tear-spraying laughter bubbles up in me, demanding to be released to echo off the acoustic nightmare of sticky hot plastic around us.

"What?" Melissa asks, her upper lip curled to protect her nostrils from the chemical-fruit stench.

"I'm just." I laugh. "I'm just really lucky."

"Slash sarcasm." Melissa frowns.

"No, no. I mean"—I take a shaky breath and gag—"yeah, this is a shitty morning. But so what? You're here. And you're talking to me."

Very carefully, making sure her arms don't touch our surroundings, Melissa gives me a hug.

"And, like, this is a blessing in disguise, really. Imagine how crappy it would be to get all involved with a boy just in time to lose all phone and computer privileges forever.

And, like, now I'll have a legitimate excuse to avoid John for the rest of the summer. Really, all my problems are working themselves out."

The porta potty stinks and my eyes sting and I'm angry and humiliated and anxious, but what's any of that when you have your best friend to soak up your snot and hang on for as long as you need?

We emerge from the porta potty (to a couple obnoxious wolf whistles) when Karey texts us that it's time to warm up. Melissa lies that nobody can tell I've been crying as we jog to join the stretch circle, too behind to stop for cleats or water. Everyone counts quietly, and Elizabeth shifts to make room for me to join in the hamstring stretch. She raises an eyebrow and shrugs in what I'm hoping is a show of sympathy.

I don't look at John, but my peripheral vision is good enough to catch his death glares. He huffs between stretches, catches my shoulder as he sprints past me during laps, and refuses to acknowledge me as a teammate when we start drills. It doesn't take long for Karey to—oh so casually—pull us both aside.

"Do we have a problem?" she asks, eyes turned to the other side of the pitch, where the San Antonio team tosses a quaffle around a circle of chasers. "We need everyone's head to be in the game if we don't want to get eliminated."

"No," I say, mortified, at the same time John says, "That depends."

I want to crawl under a rock and die. Or maybe I want John to crawl under a rock and die. Or maybe both—as long as they're different rocks.

"On what?" Karey's gaze holds John's now, and even though I can guess what he wants to say, I'm still shocked that he actually says it to her stony face.

He points a finger at me. "Is she playing?"

Karey grows at least three inches taller as she squares herself to face John. "Like I said, we need every player to win this."

"Do we really, though?" John scoffs, and I flinch even though of course I've always known what John thinks of my playing.

"Look," Karey says, and I feel her bracing herself for a fight, see her chest expand and her fists clench and her jaw tighten. And I appreciate it, and I get it, but it also doesn't seem fair for the whole team to risk upsetting their best starting beater for a mediocre sub.

"Actually, it's fine. I don't really need to . . . You can just . . ."

"Ellen, don't—" Karey says, and I mutter, "No, really, it's not—" and then someone fast and small shoves past me and reaches up to sock John in the shoulder.

"Don't be a fucking jerk," Erin says while John steps away, eyes wide.

"Hang on." Karey puts her arm up between them, but Erin's eyeliner-edged glare packs enough venom to send John back another step.

Erin doesn't pay Karey any attention. "You're literally the biggest baby. Grow up. You're not the only one with drama." She glances toward Aaron, who stares guiltily at the ground just a few feet away.

John opens his mouth. He looks around. Nobody's running drills anymore; instead, we face a loose semicircle of judgmental faces. Not that I blame my teammates—my life is a high-quality shit show right now, and I'd probably be entertained if I weren't the one drowning in the muck.

"I think you're forgetting who cheated on who," John mutters, his ears glowing red.

"I think you're forgetting that I don't give a shit," Erin snaps back. "You're on a team. Suck it up and play the game."

Chris is nodding, and Elizabeth is, too, and Melissa coughs something that sounds like "Jackass." Even Karey lowers her arms, crosses them over her chest, and pivots to stand with Erin between John and me: a living wall of support. John looks around, runs a hand through his hair, opens his mouth. His eyes dart around the pitch, never landing on me.

"I didn't cheat on you," I say. "You never asked if I wanted to be . . . a thing with you. So you didn't know that I didn't. I wish I could have found a way to tell you that was . . . nicer, and more timely. I really am having a bad morning, and I shouldn't have taken it out on you. But, like, seriously, people don't become your property just because you kiss them." I know that extremely well now that I've been blocked by my one-night stand. "So that's no fun, and I guess I'm sorry *for* you." I glance at Karey, who nods. "But I'm not sorry."

"Whatever," he says finally. "Whatever. I have to . . . Whatever."

He walks off the pitch. Past our bags, stopping to grab his without breaking stride. Into the parking lot.

"He's not going to . . ." Elizabeth says, as we all watch him do exactly what she's denying.

He gets in his van, starts the engine. Karey takes a few steps toward him, but he doesn't even glance back at us as he pulls out of the lot and speeds away from the park.

"Wow," Erin says, breaking our tense silence.

"Glad I didn't leave my inhaler in there," Karey spits. "How am I supposed to get everyone home now?"

"He fucked up," Melissa mutters. Erin nods.

But my blank brain floods with one loud and clear message: this is my fault.

Karey checks her watch.

"Back to drills, y'all. We have to play now; logistics can come later." She touches my shoulder and walks me toward the bags.

"I'm sorry. I'm really sorry."

"Don't be," Karey says. "It happens. All the time. Usually people handle it better." She takes a breath and then lets it go, hesitating. "I, um, I've seen my fair share of quidditch drama and love triangles." She raises an eyebrow, and I laugh along with her. "It's actually how I got into the sport," she adds. "Chasing my ex-girlfriend. God, that was not a good look. But it got me onto the team, and I fell in love with it, and she never threw a fit about playing with me, because that's not how it works."

"But it wasn't . . . *I* fucked up." In so many ways all summer, but especially with John.

Karey tilts her head at me. "Okay, sure, but you're not responsible for his emotions—that's on him. Next time be upfront or whatever. Text him an apology if you feel like it."

"But . . ."

"I don't know what you want me to say. You fucked up, but you're our fuck-up."

"You're a really good captain," I whisper. "And I'm really happy for you and Melissa."

Karey beams. "Thanks—hopefully I don't ruin it by being myself. Now, are you going to be okay? Ready to kick some beater butt?"

"Please." The prospect of pushing my sore muscles and tired brain past exhaustion has never sounded so appealing.

"That's the spirit. Forget boys; make tackles." Karey claps my shoulder and strides back to the pitch. I sit by my bag, fighting a yawn, more tears, and the urge to replay the whole scene in my head just to torture myself. Instead I reach into my bag for my cleats.

I don't need to check my phone right now. I don't need to imagine what John thinks of me, what Andrew thinks of me, what Dad and Connie think of me. Later I can feel terrible for all my bad decisions and all the bad will I've gathered in the past hour. Right now I need to focus on this game. I need to put on my cleats and finish this warm-up.

. . . I need to find my other cleat.

I empty the bag on the ground. An extra headband, old chapstick, my wallet, and a lot of dried mud falls out along with my left cleat. Only my left cleat. I shake the empty bag.

I check my big backpack, but there's no reason for it to be there, and it isn't. My heart pounds. I didn't *really* think the cleats were a blessing from beyond the grave, so I don't *really* think that this is proof that even my dead mom is disappointed in me. But maybe a little.

The voice in my head sounds suspiciously like Connie when it hisses that this is exactly what I deserve.

"Not your day, huh?" Karey asks when I tell her. Elizabeth scowls sympathetically, and Lindsay gives me such a kind hug that I can't help worrying that she's secretly judging me like I'm judging myself. The cleat must have fallen out in Andrew's room, when my bag spilled. What kind of mess was I last night?

Karey asks around, but my feet are small and people aren't exactly falling over themselves to lend expensive equipment to an irresponsible out-of-towner. Plus, we have to start our game.

"You'll still play," Karey assures me. "We're too low on players to leave you out."

Which is also my fault. I nod, even though the idea of playing in tennis shoes—now that I know what I'm missing—frustrates me.

Lindsay and Erin take starting positions with the chasers, and I sit on the sidelines and try not to let my thoughts spiral. I refuse to check my phone to see if Dad's called back. I remind myself that I'm excited for the team, for the game.

That is the whole reason I came to this tournament.

The game goes well, but I play badly. After some painful misses and a failed race to the third bludger that ends with my feet slipping out from under me, Lindsay quietly calls me off and doesn't sub me back in.

"You okay?" Chris asks, hands behind his head as he

catches his breath after subbing out. "That was . . . a lot."

I look up (way up) at him. I can't believe he knew about Karey and Melissa for weeks and just . . . played on the team like normal. Didn't even make enough waves for me to notice. According to Karey, that's the normal way to behave, but it still seems awfully mature for the team youngling. "You're a good egg," I tell him.

"Uh, thanks?" he says. "I didn't do anything. But I can if you want someone to beat up John."

"Will people stop offering to beat people up for me?" I groan. "New rule: if I want someone beaten up, kicked, or otherwise physically harmed, I will do it myself!"

From somewhere behind me, where the spectators sit, I hear Alex cheer. "That's the spirit, Ellen! Kill them!"

"The downside of bracket play," Karey warns us after we win, "is that scheduling is more complicated, so we'll have a while before our next game. Stay hydrated and grab snacks if you need them. We're still in this!"

Everyone grins, proud that we didn't get eliminated. I want to be proud, too, but I'm mostly exhausted, hot, and anxious.

The tree near our bags offers almost enough shade to lie in, so I stretch out with my face relatively cool and my toes scorching. With my bag as a pillow and a beater headband over my eyes, I take the opportunity to cry some more.

I don't fall asleep, exactly, but my moping becomes gradually less conscious until someone kicks my sunbaked shoes. I startle, wiping sweat and drool and snot as I sit up and blink at a stranger with a highlight-streaked ponytail.

"Hey, are you Ellen?" The girl looks bored, or maybe angry, but I have no idea what I've done to offend her.

"Um, yeah?"

She tosses a white plastic grocery bag into my lap. "Apparently you lost this."

"Ah!" I feel the shape—and the spikes—through the bag. My cleat. "Thank you! Where did you find it?"

"Hard to get your stuff back if you don't even bother with a 'Thank you for a funky time,' huh?" She rolls her eyes.

I blink back at her. Why does this magical cleat-deliverer make no sense?

"I'm supposed to say"—she sighs and squints at the sky—"that he had a lot of fun last night, and that he totally gets if you don't want to see him again, but that wasn't what he wanted, necessarily, and you ran off before he could tell you that. And that if you ever want to talk, his number's on the Post-it." She gestures at the bag. "And he would've come himself, but he had to get back to San Antonio for work. Lucky me."

I blink at the plastic bag, brain working slow. "But . . . I left a note. I friend-requested . . . San Antonio?" I untwist the knot and read the note stuck to my missing cleat. I look up into the mildly annoyed face, my brain spinning in confusion. "Who the heck is Nico?"

The messenger turns with a hair flip and an eye roll. The back of her jersey says McAllister.

"Um, wait," I say. "Are y'all . . . Are you mad at me?" It's an extremely awkward way to ask my question, and it earns a grimace from McAllister, but she turns back to me.

"I'm protective of my *friends*, especially when it seems like someone is treating them like crap. He was confused and sad and very annoying this morning." I start to protest again, and her face softens. "Look, you're good, it's all okay. Just maybe text him and clear up whatever you need to clear up."

I need to clear up so many things. I reread the note, pull out my phone, and start putting the pieces together.

"NICO WHOSE-LAST-NAME-I-STILL-DON'T-KNOW," I SAY, holding my phone out for Melissa to inspect the profile. "Also known as Nico X from the feminist Facebook page, also known as the guy I kissed and stuff last night, also known as the guest staying in Andrew's apartment yesterday, also known as *not* Andrew."

"Also known as cute." Melissa nods in appreciation. It's

almost time to warm up for our game, but I dragged her away from Karey's side to gossip with me in the shade of the tree. She inspects the note. "And thoughtful in the face of a delicate situation." She nods again. "Approved on all counts." She hands the phone back. "So are you going to text him?"

"Oh . . ." I glance down at my phone. "I already did? Should I not have?"

Melissa laughs. "So I guess I don't need to ask if he was a good kisser?"

I would answer, but my phone buzzes and my stomach somersaults and Melissa laughs louder.

Text from Nico: (1) That's hilarious, but sorry you thought I rejected you! (2) I *told* McAllister to be nice even if you didn't want to see me again . . . but I'm really glad that isn't the case. (3) Gotta work—I'll text you later if that's okay. (4) Good luck with the tournament!

I text back a smiley emoji while smiley emojis explode across my face. It's a small win, in the midst of everything, but I'll take it. Until the second Dad pries my phone out of my hands, I'm going to enjoy this.

"And to answer your question," I tell Melissa, putting my phone back in my bag, "fantastic."

29

Between my cleats and Nico's (Not Andrew's) text, it's easy to fly at Brooms Up. The bracket has us facing the Louisiana team, who must've partied too hard last night, because they lag behind us in speed and goals from the start. I help Lindsay regain bludger control and then let Elizabeth sub in as I jog to my water. The sharp stab of each breath and the buzz of tired muscles feel familiar by now, but still consume my attention until Melissa taps my shoulder, her sweaty face grim.

"Is that . . . ?"

I follow her nod to the parking lot, bracing myself to see John even as I irrationally hope to see Nico (Not Andrew. Nico).

Instead, I recognize a pair of heeled sandals stepping out of a familiar car, manicured hand pulling a smaller fidgety hand out of the back seat. Connie, Yasmín . . . and Dad. Standing a few feet ahead of both of them, he must've been the one Melissa saw first. He shields his eyes and surveys the two pitches, the tent of volunteers and bracket coordinators, the players and spectators gathered in sweaty groups. I don't know if he finds me. I can't see what expression he makes.

With zero idea whether I'm violating some obscure clause of the rulebook, I jog away from the field. My family does not disappear like a mirage or a stress-induced hallucination. They see me before I get close enough to speak, and only Yasmín returns my hesitant wave.

"Hi." I stop a few feet from Dad, brush loose strands of hair away from my face, cross my arms. "What are y'all . . . What's up?"

Dad and Connie turn, inexplicably, to Yasmín.

She shrugs. "I wanted to see the tournament."

"She insisted," Dad says quietly, stepping closer to me. "Wouldn't let it go."

We lock eyes for a long second, his forehead wrinkled, mouth opening and then closing, and I can almost feel the questions he's going to ask, the rant bubbling up in his brain, before he shakes his head, rubs the back of his neck. "So here we are," he says to the asphalt.

I nod like I understand, but I don't. Why would Yasmín

care? Why are Connie and Dad smiling fake smiles instead of unleashing serious punishment?

Yasmín tugs Connie's arm. "Ellen has to finish her game," she says.

My stepmom sighs. Everything about her face screams that she doesn't want to be here, but here she is. For Yasmín. And for Yasmín, I guess, she's not going to interrupt my tournament. "Isn't there anywhere to sit?"

"So those were the quarterfinals," I babble after the game ends, back to standing awkwardly with my disapproving family. "So now we move on to the semifinals."

This is my first tournament, and I'm no expert, but it sounds pretty impressive to me. I wish Dad or Connie would look even slightly impressed. They didn't see much of the game, focusing more on finding the bathrooms and buying food from the concession stand set up on the other end of the park.

"How many more games?" Connie doesn't sound impressed, either.

"Until they lose," Yasmín pipes up. "Right?"

"Right, except they let the losers of the semis play for third, so I think it's two more games either way." I point to the wall-sized whiteboard that contains the full schedule. "See? Next we're on pitch two playing College Station, and then they'll update the results of that game . . ."

Dad's poker face doesn't break, but he eyes the white-board closely. "This is all pretty elaborate, isn't it? I mean, for . . ."

I shouldn't mind his hesitation or the confusion in his eyes. I should be glad he's here at all and that he hasn't dragged me home yet. So I take a breath and ignore his almost hidden smirk.

"For a Harry Potter game?" Connie's smirk does not hide, and Dad's mouth twitches more firmly upward at her words.

I round on her so fast my ponytail lashes against my cheek. I know it's unfair to blame her for saying what Dad was hinting at, but I can't stop myself. "Not that you have any context," I snap, "but I put a lot of time and work into quidditch, and so does everyone else here. And it's not a game. It's a sport."

Dad's eyes widen and Connie's flash, and our volatile truce almost detonates into a full-blown public disturbance, but then Yasmín catches my eye over her shaved ice and shakes her head.

She came here to watch quidditch, to watch me, not to watch another scene.

"Sorry," I say. "I just . . . Sorry."

Connie huffs. Yasmín sighs. The stiff and formal peace settles back over us. Except . . .

Dad is staring at me. Or at the ground in front of me. Or . . .

"Those are cleats," he says. "Where did you— Why are you wearing cleats?"

I swallow. "I found them," I say. "I need them. To play."

"Okay," Dad says. "Of course. I didn't know you wanted a pair. I didn't . . . They fit?"

There are so many questions hidden in that one. "Yeah, they fit."

He blinks fast. "Good, good. I'm sure she'd want— She'd be happy to see you getting into it. Into a sport."

He coughs, and I stare at the sky while goose bumps crawl up my arms and threaten to release a flood of irrational tears. I don't want to have emotions when I'm trying to be a jock!

A middle-aged woman with a burnt orange T-shirt and a fancy camera interrupts our teary moment, walking up and introducing herself as Austin's team mom-slash-photographer. I use her friendly chattiness to cover my retreat.

Karey calls the beginning of warm-up when I reach her, and I'm happy to dive into the routine even though I'm physically and mentally exhausted. The whole team moves like the grass is knee-deep Jell-O, even our stretch counts sluggish. Karey tries to pump us up, but her "y'all"s drawl more than usual, and a tiny sigh escapes her when she says, "Whatever happens, we've done an awesome job this weekend, and y'all should be proud of yourselves. College Station is tough, even in the summer when I don't live there."

So basically it's no surprise when we get our asses handed to us.

Dad, Yasmín, and Connie come find me after the game. Connie's eyes stubbornly scan the field where Katy Quidditch is presumably trampling San Antonio on the way to the finals.

"Well," Dad says, raising his hand and then hesitating and glancing at Connie before clapping my shoulder lightly. "Good effort. You were all really . . . running hard. It looks complicated."

I don't contain my eye roll as much as I turn it into an inspection of the cloudless blue sky.

"Is that girl okay?" he asks. I glance at Lindsay, who rolled her already sore ankle during the snitch game and now sits surrounded by first aid volunteers.

"I think so."

"You have one more game, right?" Yasmín asks. "For third?"

Connie tugs the neck of her blouse to fan herself. I sense her restlessness, her impatience, and I feel myself rising to the unspoken challenge. But then Dad shifts, checks his watch. "Do you have to stay for it?" he asks.

I deflate. "I guess we can—"

The thwack of running footsteps interrupts our

departure as Melissa crashes into me from behind in an enthusiastic hug.

"Did you see?" she asks, breath hot on my neck. "Katy lost! We're playing them for third—we can beat them!"

I spin to see the San Antonio team celebrating. "Wait, really? I thought there was no way . . ."

"Yeah, big upset." Melissa bounces in place. "And now Katy is exhausted and cranky, and we have a shot at redemption and sweet, sweet revenge!" She raises a fist in the air, then drops it with a giggle. "Hi, Mr. and Mrs. Rourke. Yasmín. Having fun?"

"Melissa," Dad says, face and voice chilly. "I guess you had a hand in this great escape?"

Melissa shrinks a little. I don't think she's used to disappointing my parents.

"She had nothing to do with it," I say quickly. "Nobody did. Well, Xiumiao did. But I asked her to do it. And Melissa didn't even know. It was all me." And I'm not sorry I came.

Dad raises his eyebrows while Connie hisses a long breath. "Okay then. Sorry for jumping to conclusions."

Melissa shakes her head. "No, you're right; I definitely would have gone along with it if I'd known," she says. "Sometimes drastic rules call for drastic measures." She holds both Dad's and Connie's scandalized gazes. "Brooms Up in a few minutes," she tells me, giving my shoulder a squeeze.

Dad turns to Connie, then to me, but I don't give him a chance to say we're leaving. "I want to finish the tournament with my team." The words come out breathy and rushed, but at least they come out. "I know I broke the grounding deal, and I get that there will be consequences, but this is important to me."

Connie rolls her eyes up to the sky but stays quiet. Dad stares hard at me, head tilted, and then nods.

"Dude," Melissa whispers as we scamper back to our team. "I've never seen your dad look scary before."

"I know, and why is Connie so quiet? I just want her to scream at me already."

"Maybe your new punishment is going to be psychological torture," she speculates as we reach the tree.

"Psychologically torturing who?" Karey asks, pausing her conversation with Lindsay when we plop down in the vague half circle of people and bags.

"Ellen's parents came to get her, since she technically snuck out to come here," Melissa says, shrugging when I shoot her a *What the hell?* look. "What? You already got caught."

Karey blinks, looks from me to my family and back. She points an accusing finger first at me, then at Melissa.

"Someone should've told me that," she says darkly. Then she turns to Lindsay. "So you were saying that you might want to captain next year, please? Handling the hijinks of all of these hooligans is stressing me out."

I stick out my tongue while Aaron and Erin groan and Chris glances at Melissa and then quickly away, but Melissa shoots Karey a raised-eyebrow smirk. The captain hasn't exactly steered clear of drama herself.

"You're staying for the game, though?" Karey asks me, and when I nod she relaxes. "Good. I'm worried about beaters."

"Seriously," Lindsay tries to protest, "I can play."

"*You* can sit down and follow the medic's instructions," Karey scolds.

"We can always send in chasers as beaters," Elizabeth suggests, "just so we can catch our breath."

Chris raises his hand, but Carlos drags it down. "You're *my* sub," he protests.

"I volunteer as tribute," Jackson pipes up. "I'm not much use for anything else anyway."

"Not with that attitude." Lindsay holds out a hand for Jackson to hoist her up, then hobbles with one hand on his shoulder. "Let's get some warm-up drills going, then, so we can see what we're working with."

"I have some tiger balm in my bag if you want it," Jackson offers as they make their way slowly to the pitch.

We start throwing balls at each other while Lindsay works with Jackson ("I can't throw a ball at an injured girl!" he protests as she beans him in the side with her bludger).

After about five minutes she calls us into a strategy circle.

"You two"—she waves a hand at Erin and Aaron—"can I count on you to start together?"

They make eye contact for maybe the first time all day. Erin shrugs, Aaron pulls a couple of faces, and then they turn back to Lindsay and nod.

"Good. Sub as soon as you need a rest. Jackson, stay back and stick to close-range beats. Ellen and Elizabeth, y'all can play up or back depending on your partner, yeah? Sound good?" We all nod. Elizabeth tightens her goggles and glares at the Katy team. On the pitch, the head ref gathers her assistants and calls for team captains.

"Ellen"—Lindsay reaches for my elbow—"give me a hand back?" She points at the pile of bags, and I help her hobble toward it. "I'm counting on you this game," she tells me as we walk. "You got this."

I shrug as best I can with her arm on my shoulder.

"You do," she insists. "With John and me gone, Katy's going to expect an easy beater game. They're going to underestimate you because . . . you know."

"Because I'm small and lack muscles," I laugh.

"Because they don't know you," Lindsay corrects me. "You are a total badass who will never let a ball go without a fight. Who shuts down ridiculous boys with poise and who—apparently—runs away from home to play quidditch. You're tough."

I stare at the ground, not sure what to do with Lindsay's words. "Thanks."

Tough. Badass. I don't know how accurate it is, but it's better than "nice" and "quiet." And even if it feels like a gift right now, maybe it's something to work on, to live up to.

"Perfect," Lindsay says as I drop her back down against the tree. "Melissa's rumor says you might not get to come to practice after this, but it's been great playing with you. Hope to do it more next summer. You're cool, Ellen."

I turn several shades of red and manage to mutter, "You too." I clear my throat. "I, uh . . . I'm really glad I got to, um, meet and play with—and you're, like, my beater role model, so . . ."

"Okay, okay, get out there before Brooms Up." Lindsay shoos me back to the pitch with a smile.

"Yeah. Yep. Hope your ankle feels better." I jog toward Karey.

"Kick ass," Lindsay calls behind me. "If we're going to win, we have to stay on top of the beater game."

WE DO STAY MOSTLY ON TOP OF THE BEATER GAME, AT least for the first two minutes; it's the chaser game where we start to fall 30–10. Aaron and Erin sub out for me and Jackson, who gives me a wide-eyed nod and whispers, "I don't really know what I'm doing."

"Just . . ." I shrug. I barely know how to move around the pitch strategically, and I've had months of practice. "Maybe stay by the hoops. Don't let them score." It's a bare-bones plan, but it's the best we have, and I want to make it work. I take a deep breath, and Jackson takes one along with me. I want to win.

With Jackson playing close defense, I move up the field to play more offensively, painting a nice target on my back for the opposing beaters. I'm so busy fighting with them, losing and regaining bludger possession and trying to make it easier for my chasers to score, that it takes me a minute to realize that Katy isn't scoring. That they haven't scored, in fact, since I left Jackson in front on the hoops. Where he still stands—I discover as I spin around—his feet planted and throwing arm cocked with the wicked grin of someone who knows just how intimidating he looks.

Like Lindsay predicted, the Katy beaters focus on me. They have no idea that Jackson probably wouldn't survive a one-on-one duel, much less a two-on-one attack. As long as they keep going after the apparently easy prey, he's safe. And in the meantime, he's kicking ass at defense.

"You're doing it," I gasp at him while I run to tag my hoops. "You're stopping them."

"I control the balls now," he mumbles back. His bludger sails straight into the face of the redheaded keeper with a vicious thump. "I am the ball master."

It's amazing to see. And it's amazing to recognize the rush of pride that I feel when I see it. It's bigger and better and less self-conscious than being happy with my own performance. That's my teammate, this is my team, and this is how we fly.

WHEN AARON PULLS THE SNITCH, OUR SIDELINE BURSTS into excited squeals that Karey has to shush until the refs confirm. The three-whistle blast sounds, and her "Hold on!" turns into a "Hell yeah!" as we all rush in for a dogpile on top of our very smooshed seeker.

We don't try very hard to contain smug smiles as we line up to shake hands with Katy. Of course, Other Chris ruins it by being totally gracious and congratulating Karey on her coaching, even proposing a joint practice and scrimmage session before summer ends. Which would be awesome if I thought I'd be allowed out of the house for it.

"Third place, third place," Melissa singsongs happily, hands on Karey's shoulders in a two-woman conga line back to the tree. "We are the best—and by best I mean third best, which is still pretty good!"

I want to continue jumping and high-fiving, listening to Jackson gush about how much better it is to beat other people, watching the final match that started almost the second ours ended (because the tournament is already running late enough). But Connie inches closer and closer to me with a polite smile etched across her face, her head nodding toward the parking lot.

"I think I have to go." I sigh. Aaron and Erin have their heads together debating some minor play and don't respond, but Elizabeth gives me a solemn nod as I retreat to Connie.

"Bye, Ellen!" Melissa calls, running to wrap me in a final hug. "Don't worry," she whispers, "you'll be fine. Just, like, text me if they take your phone away."

"How would I even . . . ?" I let it go. "You and Karey have a ride home?"

Melissa nods. "We'll be squished, but we won't be breaking any laws."

Most of the team has found seats along the sidelines to watch the finals alongside League City and Katy players. Jackson helps Lindsay limp to join them.

"Text me who wins?" I ask, watching a San Antonio chaser score on College Station. I don't want to leave.

"Of course."

"Ready?" Connie asks when my dragging steps bring me close enough. I nod and follow her toward the glare of the sun setting over the parking lot. Tiny noisy insects bat against my face, and Yasmín ducks a june bug with a squeak. A whistle blows behind us, and I try not to wonder which team scored.

"So," I say as my eerily quiet family climbs into the car,

"sorry you had to drive all the way up here. Well, you didn't have to, but, um, sorry."

Yasmín's enormous yawn is the only response I get. She's fast asleep before we get on the freeway, and she stays curled up with her head in the middle seat even when we stop for gas and gas station dinner. Dad stops at a place with a Subway, one of the only fast-food restaurants where I can eat, without even needing a reminder. He barely looks at me the whole time we're inside, though. This distant niceness, first at the tournament and now on the road, freaks me out. I thought we were all silently agreeing not to fight in public, but now I don't know how to read his mood at all. Something big must be coming—my stunt basically demands it—but the suspense is killing me.

My phone buzzes an hour or so into the trip. John.

I get what u said.

But I'm still mad.

But I'll c u at practice.

If Karey lets me stay on the team.

Sorry for being a dick.

I really want to put off responding, but instead I text, I'm sorry, too. See you when I see you.

Sooner than I expect, the dark shapes of trees and black sky give way to a purple-orange glow that dims the stars. Not a sunrise, but a city-rise as we approach Houston's light pollution. I shift my legs, finding new aches to add to my list of minor pains: sunburned neck, scraped knee, shin bruises, and sore right shoulder.

The meandering roads of our neighborhood make me dizzy after hours of straight freeway. I lurch forward when the car stops, just as Yasmín opens her eyes and blinks out the window. Dad opens her door and collects her in his arms while I drag my bags over my shoulder and hobble up the path to the front door. Nearly halfway up the stairs, already dreaming of my hot shower, a long inhaled breath stops me in my tracks.

"Ellen," Connie sighs behind me. "Can you come to the kitchen, please? Your father and I want to talk to you."

Of course I knew this had to be coming. But exhaustion and sore muscles spit out an answer that Yasmín would shake her head at. "Now? We can't do this in the morning?"

"Drop the indignation," Connie responds. "What you did . . ."

Okay, that's fair. "I'm sorry," I say, hanging over the banister. "But Xiumiao was here the whole time. You know she's a good babysitter. I wouldn't leave Yasmín if I didn't know she was safe."

"It doesn't matter," Connie snaps. "We need to know what's happening in our own house. We need to know where our kids are and who they're with."

"She was right here with Xiumiao," I repeat, starting back up the stairs.

"I wasn't just talking about Yasmín!" Connie shouts.

It surprises me enough that I stop climbing the stairs.

"If you don't realize what you put us through . . ." Connie shakes her head and climbs up a few steps after me. "Greg was . . . we *worry* about you. You can't do that."

"I—I'm sorry," I say, and I actually mean it. I knew they'd be angry, but I didn't think beyond that. I'm going to be in college soon anyway, so they'll have to get used to the idea of not knowing where I am. Besides . . . "I was just giving y'all what you wanted!"

Dad opens Yasmín's door, holds a finger to his lips. I remember what she said about overhearing fights from her room.

"Garage?" I suggest. Dad nods, and Connie hurries down the stairs to check in on Yasmín.

"We'll be there in a minute," Dad says before closing the door behind him, closing me out of the family. They might have been worried about me, but nothing's changed.

Three more weeks until we're all free. Three weeks until I'm gone.

That's all they want.

30

I flick the garage lights and blink at the glare. I stare at the concrete floor, visible and navigable now except for the staggered towers of plastic boxes, labeled and stacked along the far wall, and a scattered handful of flat cardboard boxes deemed in good enough shape to move out with. There's still a smattering of trash piles and donation boxes, but this place is more or less ready for remodeling. The one thing I didn't fuck up this summer.

I take a seat on one of the plastic boxes and stare at the water-stained ceiling. Things aren't really that bad, despite the deep pit of dread in my stomach. I'm proud of my team. I'm happy for Melissa and Karey. I made up with both my best friends. I'm excited about Nico. Shouldn't all of that be enough to outweigh whatever the United Front is about to throw at me?

What are they going to throw at me? And what's taking them so long to come out here and get it over with?

The door opens. I guess I'll find out.

"Ellen." Connie comes into the garage alone. "Greg and I thought it might be better if we talk to you separately." The way her mouth twists, it seems more like Dad's idea than hers.

I rise to my feet, gelatinous muscles and all. Connie takes a few steps toward me, and I hurry to meet her at the door. "Here." I offer the phone to her. "It's getting confiscated, right?"

Connie stares at my hand for several seconds, then accepts the phone and holds it between her palms. My fingers twitch to snatch it back, to pursue my phone like a lost bludger and wrap Connie in a tackle until she lets it go.

She walks past me, dusts off the box I was sitting on, and perches on its edge with a grimace. With nowhere else to sit, I sink to the floor several feet in front of her, knees to my chest.

"I came to apologize," Connie says. With her face aimed down, her stiff words thunk to the floor. "I'm sorry."

I didn't see that coming, and I'm afraid that anything I say will change her mind.

"Greg thinks . . ." She stops. "Greg and I talked this weekend." With a pained smile, she shoves my phone back into my hands. "He helped me see that in the past year I've been . . . harsh. Hard on you. I'm sorry."

My fingers close around warm plastic, and I stare, mouth open.

"It doesn't mean there won't be consequences for going to Austin," she says quickly. "But we wanted to make sure we did this."

I still can't think of a safe response.

"It's just that"—she frowns, staring at her feet as she adjusts her skirt—"you always seemed so big. When I met you, you were so tall and serious, and I didn't have any sense of kids past my five-year-old students. And Yasmín was so tiny, and she needed me, and it seemed like you could take care of yourself."

I cradle the phone, afraid to breathe and break the spell.

Connie gives a real sigh, letting all her breath out instead of gathering it in. "You were only eight years old. Younger than Yasmín is now."

I remember thinking Connie was so tall, so full of energy and ideas that she made Dad excited, too.

"Your father is always going to see you as little. You're always going to come first, no matter how big you get."

Since when? I want to ask, but I stay quiet.

"So I have to be the adult, and you get to be the kid."

Connie pops to her feet and paces the perimeter of the garage, grabbing the broom from the corner and dragging it along beside her while I watch from the middle of the floor. "I'm sorry I forget that sometimes."

She sounds mostly sincere, except for the tiny barb of accusation. That I'm immature, hard to deal with. The implication hurts a little, but there was more than one apology, too, and besides, her approval isn't how I measure my life.

"You all did seem so young today," Connie says, "playing your game—your sport. When I was your age . . ." She shakes her head like she's trying to dislodge a fly. "Things were different, or I was different. I guess it's just hard for me to relax when I know how quickly teenagers can get into trouble."

"I'm not getting into *trouble*," I groan. But my face flushes as I think about following Nico up to his room. I would like to be able to talk to Connie about stuff like that. I wish she would tell me what being a teenager was like for her.

"Maybe it would be easier if you were." She sighs. "I don't understand what you're doing. On your phone worrying about politics and pollution all the time—it's not normal."

"Why not?" I ask. "Why is it not *normal* to care about the world? It's important. Things are bad, and you know the world isn't just going to fix itself if we don't—"

Connie's shaking her head already. "You want to fight to . . . change all the laws and all of society? You want to tell *me* the world is unfair, unsafe? I know that. That's why I'm trying to keep you from . . . I'm trying to raise you to be . . . you're going to get mad if I say 'normal,' but you know what I mean."

I stare at my stepmom, mouth slightly open. I've never heard her talk like this, vulnerable, agreeing that the world is every bit as messed up as I say.

"You can't fight the world," she says. "You just have to survive it."

She knows. She sees that the world is a mess—of course she does, how could she not? But she wants to hide, and hide us, from it.

It's infuriating. It's kind of understandable. It's not who I want to be.

"My job is to keep my kids safe."

Her kids. Plural. Something prickles behind my eyes, and it's only half frustration. "I just don't think we're ever going to be safe if we don't stand up for things that matter."

"Okay," she says. "Okay." Her voice is confused and resigned, and I recognize it. She hears me the way I hear her. She doesn't think I'm right, but she doesn't need to prove me wrong.

She spins slowly, like she doesn't know where she is,

leans the broom against the wall. "It's looking good in here," she says. "We're almost ready to start putting in new sheetrock and flooring, and you still haven't looked at any of the plans for your new room."

"My room?"

Connie blinks at me like I'm very clueless. "You keep avoiding me when I try to talk to you about it, so I followed my instincts mostly, but there's plenty of time to change things."

It dawns on me that I'm very clueless. "That's what we're turning the garage into. A room for me." Because my room is becoming Connie's studio. This makes a lot of sense actually.

Connie raises her eyebrows but politely doesn't ask how I got through the whole summer without realizing this. "I have the plans whenever you want to look at them."

"Thanks," I say.

She shrugs. "It will be a bit more independent," she says. "And we can rent it out short-term when you're not here, to earn back some of the expense."

"Right, of course." I knew that part.

Connie stares down at the pile of dust and leaves she's gathered. She sucks her breath in, and I think she's going to launch back into some kind of argument, but she doesn't. "This floor is filthy, and I'm exhausted." She walks out of the garage without looking back.

I stand up and walk to the broom she left, thinking I'll sweep. Not to prove anything, just because it needs to be done. I can't figure out whether Connie's more mad at me now or less, whether I'm surprised by her kindness or annoyed at her stubbornness. But the garage is going to be my space sometime in the near future. That's cool to know.

I've barely gotten Connie's pile into the dustpan when the door opens again and Dad knocks on the garage wall.

"What's going on?" he asks.

I shrug, nod at the broom.

"Did you have a good talk with Connie?" he asks. His voice stays light and even, but his smile stretches too tightly across his face.

"I guess." I shrug again. "She sort of apologized? It was weird." Dad laughs softly. "Am I still in trouble?" I feel like I should be in trouble.

Dad leaves the doorway, takes the broom out of my hand, glances around the empty room. I gesture to the boxes, and he follows, sitting gingerly next to me. "The apology was overdue," he says. "And I'm here to offer one, too. We haven't . . . we've let our own problems take over."

"You and Connie?" I ask.

Dad sighs, a big long one that makes the lid of the box creak and dip lower. "Since I started the new job," he says, and I nod.

"You disappeared."

"It seemed like a smart move," Dad says, "with college tuition looming. But . . . well, your stepmom and I haven't been seeing eye-to-eye, and I know a lot of that has been coming down on you. You became—we *made* you the . . ."

"Battleground."

"It wasn't fair," Dad says. "I thought if we could work it out without showing . . . I thought it was important to present a united front."

I snort. "The United Front sucks."

"Well." Dad hides a smile. "Maybe."

He clears his throat, and I watch his hands twist around each other. I can tell our talk isn't finished, but this whole day has been so strange that I can't even guess where Dad's going next.

"I've left Connie to play Bad Cop too often this year. It's hard on her and on you, and it's part of the reason Christmas got so out of hand. It's something I want to correct."

I shift on my box seat. I didn't think Connie was playing Bad Cop. I thought she just was one.

"But I've also noticed," Dad continues, "that you're more willing to fight with Connie and not with me. Why is that?"

My throat tightens. "I don't know what you're talking about."

Dad raises an eyebrow. My mind flashes through moments: Dad laughing about feminism, Dad scolding me or lecturing me, Dad making fun of quidditch. I yell at Connie for doing the same things, but when it's Dad, I always end up letting it slide.

"I don't know," I repeat. "Everything just turns into a fight with her. She hates me."

"Hmm," Dad rumbles. He rubs his palms on the knees of his jeans, and the silence grows heavy.

"She already hates me," I amend, the words squeaking out of me, even though I'm starting to realize they're not true. "She already hates me, and I don't want you to hate me, too."

"Hey," Dad says, and even though his tone suggests that he probably already noticed the batch of tears welling up in my eyes, I still refuse to look up, because then he'll know for sure. "Ellen, you know that's not . . ."

"I didn't mean to make her leave," I say, the words rushing out of me. "I didn't do it on purpose. I'm trying to fix it."

"That's absolutely not what I meant!" Dad says. "That's not on you."

"No, but I was fighting with her all the time—I'm trying not to anymore, it just—"

"Stop." Dad puts a hand on my shoulder. "You didn't make Connie do anything."

I gulp the words that try to spill out, burning and guilty and sorry.

"Ellen?" Dad asks. "Do you hear me?"

I can't find my voice.

We sit in silence.

"You caught me by surprise," Dad says, "becoming a teenager. A teenage girl, no less. I'm not . . ."

He struggles for words, but the worst is already out, and it's surprising how much it *hurts* to hear "girl" in that tone, directed at me like a weapon. I don't even know if I'm hurt because of the careless misogyny or because it doesn't fit me or both. I can't tell which way Dad's letting me down, and I don't know what I could have done to avoid letting him down.

"I'm sorry," I say, the words barely reaching my own ears. I don't feel like a teenager at all. I feel like I'm nine years old, crying because Yasmín is so little and cute and Aunt Mal pays more attention to her than me.

"Don't be!" Dad says, putting one hand on my shoulder and looking alarmed. "Ellen, I didn't mean for you to take that as something *you* did wrong. That's . . . that's me failing my job."

I sniff, shrug Dad's hand off to wipe my nose on my sleeve, and I might as well be throwing a six-year-old tantrum as I whine, "You don't want me here. Everything will be better when I leave."

"Ellen . . ."

"Why did you even come get me?"

Dad shushes me and pats my hair as my words melt

into snot and tears. I'm four years old, and I'm losing my family, and nothing will ever be safe or secure again.

Except, just like when I was four, and six, and nine, Dad's arms wrap tightly around me until my breathing evens out. The sound of his voice echoes through his chest.

"Ellen. Listen to me. I don't want you to leave. I'm terrified for you to leave."

"What?" I cough, spraying tears and snot.

"I'm not handling this well," Dad mutters. "I'm making a mess—"

I sniff, reaching to wipe my nose, and Dad pulls one hand away to fluff his hair nervously.

"You're so excited for me to go," I whisper.

"I'm trying to be excited, for your sake." Dad laughs. "College is supposed to be— College is an important time. I'm trying to . . . and you think I'm trying to rush you out, when really I'm fighting every instinct I have to grab you and keep you here forever. And I—Ellen, this is important." He waits until I meet his eyes. "You're my kid. I will always come get you."

We're both crying now. I remember what Connie said, about me coming first. I didn't believe her, but I guess I kind of get it. Dad didn't follow her when she ran away.

"It's hard. It's hard to watch your kid grow up, to know

exactly how to let go and when," Dad says. "It's hard to do the right thing, and I've been taking the easy way out, letting you and Connie fight battles that should have been mine. I'm sorry. I'm so sorry."

I shift on my box, pulling away just enough to balance myself without leaning on Dad. We sit in silence. Our silence.

"I'm sorry I ran away from home," I say.

"Yeah, that wasn't great, kiddo. Good thing you're already grounded."

I snort. "Am I, though? You're not great at enforcing a grounding."

"Hey, watch it," Dad warns. "Don't bite the hand that's letting you play quidditch."

"So can I keep going to quidditch?"

"I really don't have it in me to stop you from playing a sport. Much less a sport with cleats."

I nod, looking at the box to my left, where I packed the nicest of mom's old clothes. Just in case my style ever changes. "Thanks."

"Are you going to be okay?" I ask. There are so many parts to that question. "With work and . . . tuition . . . and Connie . . ."

"I'm going to look into my options at work," Dad says. "Connie's been talking to the neighbors about her new business. And we're going to look into, you know, counseling. She's not . . . we're not going to let our issues hurt you girls anymore."

"Yasmín thinks you're getting divorced," I say, because it doesn't sound so silly anymore.

"That's what we're trying to avoid," Dad says, so quietly I decide to ignore it. We sit for a minute in silence, and I try to process everything we said and didn't say.

Then I take a breath. "Um, Dad? In the spirit of not just yelling at Connie . . . it's sexist to act like teenage girls are some unknowable force of nature. Teenage girls are amazing." The last sentence comes out so fiercely I surprise myself, the truth of it bubbling hot behind my eyes. The world—my world specifically—is a better place because of the love and loyalty and passion of girls. I don't fully know how I identify—I have all the time in the world to figure that out—but it doesn't change the fact that girls are rad and my dad—and I—need to know it.

Dad nods slowly. "Of course. I'm sorry. I . . . didn't mean it like that."

"And, um, also you spent a lot of time this summer telling me I should hide my anger to make other people happy, which isn't cool. And you and Connie should really make sure that you're not putting pressure on Yasmín to make peace all the time. And you shouldn't let Connie do all the housework alone." The words are tumbling out, and I take a breath to stop them.

"There's my Ellen," Dad says with a little smile. "I need you to tell me when I mess up, not just Connie. How else can I improve?"

I let my breath out, relaxing into silence. This isn't my only chance to talk. We'll have more conversations.

Another minute passes, marked only by the dip of my eyelids.

Dad yawns. "Get some sleep, Jelly," he says. "And if you can, try to cut your poor parents some slack. We don't know what we're doing."

I nod and sniff, and even though I want to hold him accountable, I'm too tired to ask *But shouldn't you?*

I TRY TO REPLAY DAD'S WORDS AFTER I FOLLOW HIM upstairs and finally get into bed. I try to understand everything he said, everything he meant, what's different now. But the deeper I burrow under the covers, the less the sentences and syllables make any kind of sense. *It's not the talk that matters*, I think sleepily, *it's the talking*. Like Karey and Erin standing next to me, folding their arms. Like Xiumiao covering for me and Yasmín driving to me. Like Melissa.

They make the future less scary.

EPILOGUE

Halfway through the last week of September, I finally wake up and reach automatically to the left instead of the right to turn off my phone alarm. I navigate the maze of dorm furniture—matching light wood, blocky and hard to budge—and make it to the bathroom without crashing into anything. The walls of my room don't look so bare since my roommate, Laiba, and I spent last weekend decorating with discount Christmas lights and filled-in coloring book pages, plus I've started a wall of club pamphlets and flyers to help me keep track. As I stumble into the quad with half a granola bar hanging out of my mouth, I catch myself wishing I could stay home instead of dragging myself to a ten a.m. history class.

Home.

• • •

YOU'LL BE IN HOUSTON FOR THANKSGIVING, RIGHT? XIUMIAO ASKS in the first of several texts I read after class. And we can hang out? Please tell me we can hang out. You owe me, remember?

I type my response while dodging a group of long-boarders in burnt-orange tank tops and a line of students stretching from a corner food truck that smells distinctly un-vegan. We can hang out. Why?

I just keep thinking about how I have to go home and be in the closet again after half a semester of being The Gayest™, and it sounds like hell.

I see the problem, but I can't help typing: I mean . . . do you have to?

Yes. The reply pops up immediately.

Okay.

Xiumiao spends a couple minutes typing and then sends, Are you suddenly going to go home and tell your dad about your gender questions? Or that his ignorance of his own privilege means he's tacitly upholding the patriarchy and white supremacy? Or are you going to say, "Thanks for tuition" and eat your white people food?

I fumble for my ID to enter the dorm as I consider. I am trying to be more honest with Dad, but . . .

Yeah, okay, fair. We'll hang out a bunch. You can help me paint the new room.

Thanks. Tell Melissa hi this weekend. And good luck.

• • •

In the afternoon, I procrastinate my sociology work by looking over Chris's college essay. UT is his first choice, and he seems to think that current students possess magical admissions knowledge when actually I can barely remember filling out the applications. His essay is good, though, a funny but thoughtful narrative about what he learned from playing quidditch. I'm pretty sure he's going to be fine.

I get distracted for a few hours with food and S.P.I.F. discussions, and then I have an interest meeting for a campus environmental club I'm thinking of joining, so pretty soon it's late afternoon and I'm agonizing in front of my laptop.

"Just send it," Laiba advises, standing over my shoulder eating (my) peanut butter with a spoon and watching me stress about submitting my sociology blog post. "You worry too much. Also you have to finish, because isn't your friend staying here tonight?"

I click, sending my 650 words about the devaluation of low-wage work in American society into the harsh light of our half-hearted class message board.

"You didn't sleep for three days finishing your self-portrait," I remind her.

Laiba grimaces, her eyes still shadowed from that stunt. "Yeah, but art students are supposed to be malnourished and overcaffeinated wrecks. It's part of our aesthetic.

You are supposed to be the chill liberal arts slacker."

I'm still deciding whether Laiba's jabs about my (as-yet-undeclared) major are friendly or annoying, so I stick out my tongue and steal back the peanut butter. We settle at our desks on opposite sides of the (small) room and plug in our headphones.

My phone buzzes, and I read Melissa's text with a grin.

So the bus is definitely delayed, she writes, but just aim to be here to pick me up at the normal time, and it should be perfect. Get it? Because you are always late.

Melissa hops off the bus with her new asymmetrical bob, dressed head to toe (actually clip-on bow to ruffled socks) in A&M maroon, which I guess is her idea of a joke, since her school is my school's rival. She politely oohs and aahs as I walk her around campus, though, and claps when she sees the new *Little Shop of Horrors* poster hanging in its place of honor over my bed.

"You're a lot taller than you look on Ellen's phone," Laiba notes with a wry smile and a wave.

She has a point. After more than a month, it's weird to have Melissa actually standing here in the middle of my college life. She doesn't quite fit in the room, or in my head. Weird.

"Thanks for letting me stay," Melissa says for probably

the third time, eyes betraying the awkwardness behind her smile.

"No problem." Laiba shrugs. "I've resigned myself to Ellen's popularity. If you weren't here it would be Nico." She pulls the half smile that might mean she's kidding or might mean her passive-aggressive jab is deadly serious.

"Oh really?" Melissa's eyes sparkle, and she finally drops her overstuffed backpack on the ground and hops up onto my bed. "Ellen, you are supposed to keep me updated!"

"It's not a big deal," I say, shaking my head while Laiba nods vehemently. "Really! I am still figuring out how to find my classes. I'm not trying to date anyone right now."

"Sure." Laiba rolls her eyes and leans in to fake-whisper in Melissa's ear, "I had to enforce a 'No Nico after Midnight' rule just to make sure I got any sleep."

"Oh my God, you make it sound like we're— " I flush and make a mental note to spend more time in Nico's room or any of the dorm common areas. "We just talk."

"Yeah, you talk forever," Laiba complains cheerfully. "Other people get 'sexiled'; I get 'that issue is philosophically complex'-iled."

Melissa raises an eyebrow at me, and I blush less at Laiba's pun than at Melissa's (correct) assumption that Nico and I aren't quite strictly philosophical.

Teasing me breaks the ice, and Melissa and Laiba make

small talk for a while. Part of me listens, but mostly I soak in Melissa's presence. I reacclimate to the cadence of her voice, noticing the slight perky A&M Aggie twang she's picked up already. I adjust to her moving and talking in real time, with no lagging or pixelated screen limiting our communication, and notice how her wardrobe has shifted to include shoulder-baring tank tops. When Laiba launches into a rant about her painting style being misunderstood, Melissa shoots me a look that I only take a few seconds to decipher: *I see what you meant about the temperamental artist thing.*

"So you're here to hang out for the weekend?" Laiba asks. "Go to Sixth Street? Hit up some clubs? I think there's a public TGIF party tomorrow night."

"We'll have to miss it." Melissa shrugs. "We've got the tournament starting Saturday morning. But I came a little early so we could do some partying tonight." She winks at me, because we know that by "partying" she means Disney sing-alongs.

"Tournament?" Laiba asks.

"Yeah, for quidditch," I explain. "We're totally going to wreck A&M."

"You wish," Melissa mutters.

"Quidditch?" Laiba tilts her head. "That Harry Potter fan club you and Nico do? There are tournaments for that?"

Melissa and I exchange a quick eye roll, but my mood is too good to take offense.

"Yeah, it's a sport. You know, all the early-morning runs with Alice and Gabby? We're all on the team. It's sort of intense; we tackle and stuff."

"That . . . sounds awesome." Laiba flicks hair away from her face. "Can I watch you play?"

"Totally! Come out this weekend." Melissa beams at me. *I approve of your new roommate.* "You should try playing, too."

"I mean . . . maybe?" Laiba shrugs and laughs. "I'm not exactly a joiner, or a team player, or an athlete . . ." In spite of her words, I see the gleam in her eye, the spark of dork peeping through her hipster art exterior. "I mean, I used to be super into the movies. I wanted to cast spells and fly around; I did some"—her voice drops to an even lower mumble—"fan art. I'll have to check it out at least, for sure."

I know my huge smile matches Melissa's. *One of us, one of us.*

"Quidditch," Laiba says quietly, "how cool."

I nod because I won't be able to find the right words to explain the magic of the sport and the community, but I'm so ready to show it to her.

"But wait." My roommate glances between me and Melissa, a crease forming across her forehead. "Just one question."

Melissa smirks. Like me, she's heard the question a million times by now.

"If it's quidditch . . ."

I'm laughing because I know what comes next.

"How do you fly?"

ACKNOWLEDGMENTS

As often as quidditch players are asked, "How do you fly?" writers are asked, "How do you publish a book?" The short answer to both questions is: I don't. I am extremely grateful to be part of a team with so much talent and depth, working tirelessly so that this story (and so many others) get to fly.

MVP award goes to my agent, Patricia Nelson, for always backing me up and believing in the heart of the book. Also thanks to Victoria Marini for the assist on this one.

Major high fives to my editor, Kelsey Murphy, brilliant captain of the Philomel team. Thanks to Cheryl Eissing, Kristin Boyle, and everyone else whose skills brought out the best in this story, and to Ali Mac for the beautiful cover illustrations.

Nearly six years (and several lifetimes of world news ago), a version of this story was my thesis project at The New School, so I have to thank my cohort, professors, and mentor Sarah Ketchersid for reading those earlier, much worse drafts and helping me find my way. Thanks to Dhonielle and Sona for giving me a literary family and career while I took my time making better drafts.

And thanks to all my beta readers throughout the years.

There isn't enough space in the book for a(nother) love letter to the quidditch community, but I owe so much to so many quidkids around the world. Rice Quidditch crew, thanks for the training, the cheers, and the passion. Badassilisks, thanks for taking in a displaced existential-crisis-on-a-broom and giving me a home. Quidditch México, gracias por aceptarme como especialista de hidratación e incluirme en sus aventuras internacionales. Houston Cosmos, I love y'all to infinity and beyond.

To the real-life quidditch feminists, and everyone dedicated to having the hard conversations about the sport and the fandom, thank you so much for caring enough to hold us to a higher standard. Unending love for every queer, trans, and questioning athlete and every athlete of color trying to navigate systems of oppression while mounted on a broom.

Sometimes I take a break from beating faces and I sit down and write words, and I couldn't do that without the support of my writing community. Thanks once again to Laura Silverman, Amanda Joy, Kiki Chatzopoulou, and Meghan Drummond. (I did it, y'all, I made the quidditch book a thing!) Thanks to my Houston author friends for helping me find the actual time and space to write (looking at you Cory), to Las Musas for all the apoyo and chisme, to all my conference buddies and social media friends.

Thanks especially to readers, librarians, booksellers, bloggers, and teachers who cheered me on through the Love Sugar Magic series and continue to support my foray into YA.

Claire, Merric, Devon, thanks for the musical singalongs and friendship bonding moments. Ariel, I'm glad you're my person and I hope we keep doing quidditch things until we're eighty.

Apologies (and thanks always) to my parents, Frank and Rita, for writing about teen angst instead of happy families this time. Poop to Michael and Gabriel. Thanks to all my family members who are still showing up for and putting up with me, even when I name antagonists after them, which they totally don't deserve.

Finally, and most importantly, thanks to everyone who sees part of themself in the book. I hope you enjoy.

ABOUT QUIDDITCH

Quidditch is a full-contact, mixed-gender sport played by over 9,000 people in nearly 40 countries! The sport was founded in 2005 at Middlebury College in Vermont by Xander Manshel and Alex Benepe. Looking for a variation on their normal Sunday activities, they gathered friends and laid the foundation for a game that has grown in leaps and bounds to become a widely respected, physically intense sport that gives athletes of all gender identities and backgrounds opportunities to compete together.

Quidditch has a unique mix of elements from rugby, dodgeball, and tag. A quidditch team is made up of seven athletes who play with brooms between their legs at all times. While the game can appear chaotic to the casual observer, once familiar with the basic rules, quidditch is an exciting sport to watch and even more exciting to play. To learn more about the rules referenced in this book, go to US Quidditch's website at https://www.usquidditch.org/about/rules/.

Quidditch has always been a mixed-gender sport. Every edition of the rulebook states that "the gender that a player identifies as is considered to be that player's gender."

GET INVOLVED

There are lots of ways to get involved with quidditch! To find a team in your area, start by going to the International Quidditch Association's website at https://www.iqasport.com/teams. They have a directory of all the leagues around the world, and the leagues have listings of teams in their respective countries on their websites. If you're looking to start a team in your area, US Quidditch has resources on their website at https://www.usquidditch.org/get-involved/start-a-team. If you're interested in attending events, volunteering, or just learning more about the sport, check out https://www.usquidditch.org/ for more information.